THE OPIUM PRINCE

THE OPIUM PRINCE

JASMINE AIMAQ

SOHO
CRIME

Published by
Soho Press, Inc.
227 W 17th Street
New York, NY 10011

Library of Congress Cataloging-in-Publication Data

Aimaq, Jasmine,
The opium prince / Jasmine Aimaq

ISBN 978-1-64129-311-2
eISBN 978-1-64129-159-0

1. Opium trade—Fiction. 2. Afghanistan—Fiction. I. Title
PS3601.I43 O65 2020 813'.6—dc23 2020015485

Interior design by Janine Agro

Printed in the United States of America

10 9 8 7 6 5 4 3 2 1

In memory of my father, Fazl Ahmad Aimaq

THE OPIUM PRINCE

PROLOGUE

THE GIRL LIES CRUMPLED AND STILL IN THE ROAD, LIKE A THING THROWN AWAY. IT CANNOT BE that I am the one who has done this to her. Just a moment ago, she ran across the road, lively, smiling, and quick. Beside me, my wife is screaming. I cannot move, but I do, my hands heavy as I take them from the steering wheel and step into the desolate road. My legs protest, but I walk. I fall to my knees and take the girl's hand. A small whimper. She is alive.

"Please, don't move. You're going to be all right." My voice breaks, sounding alien, each word between a quiver and a sob. The girl's limbs are tangled, her head tilted at an impossible angle. A bruise blackens her neck. Her red dress grows darker, blood blooming through the cotton, which rises in the breeze and settles back onto her body a shroud.

The endless desert, the Afghan sun, the silent sky. They watch. The road is the only thing in motion. The asphalt ripples in the heat, as if ready to open up and engulf us, making the sands of Kabul Province our tomb. I stroke her hair as her pain threads its way into me. Into places I didn't know existed. I let out a sob, but it sounds far away.

As she tries to sit up, blood spills from her brow, streaming down her face and throat. Her bare feet are wrapped in a film of dust and sand. I try to steady myself, but my hand slips in something greasy and slick, a rainbow of engine oil and blood. The asphalt buckles again.

"Where are your people?" I say. "Tell me. I'll find help." I squeeze her fingers gently, afraid to break another thing.

Her lips barely move when she asks, "Am I dying?"

"No. You're going to be all right," I lie.

She starts to speak. "Don't talk anymore," I beg, fearing the words will end her, take the last energy that could keep her alive. Where are her parents? Sewn on her dress are little round mirrors, and I see a hundred fractured close-ups of my face.

She struggles again to raise her head and say something. I cradle her in my slippery hand. In the car, the music plays on. Beethoven's chords shred the air into shards. Rebecca is crying, fumbling at the buttons and dials in vain, plucking at the cassette that won't stop.

With shocking force, the girl grasps my arm and hisses, "I'm only ten. Maybe nine. It's not fair." She tries to point to something. "My doll," she says. Her eyes close.

"No. Stay awake, please. Please try. I'll find help." I say these words, but I understand for the first time what it means to be helpless. I hear what will be her last breath, air drawn in sharply as she dies. I watch her face for a single sign, wondering if maybe I believe in miracles after all. I swear to a god I don't believe in that I will be faithful if he shows his power now, just this once. I will never ask for anything else.

I wish I could say that I didn't see her at all. That she whipped into view from nowhere, an apparition out of the desert. But it isn't true. I saw her, but only as a blur of color trailed by a playful tangle of long, dark hair. The music stops at last. Then Rebecca is there, bending over the sunbaked road. She has something in her hand: a yellow-haired doll with a mirror-dotted dress. Sweat and tears trickle from my face, salting my lips. I gather the child in my arms and hold her close, rocking her back and forth. Her form is so small, bones hollow like a bird's. Still, her weight nearly breaks me. I must find her people. I rise, afraid I might drop her.

Rebecca insists she will go with me, her tears flecking the girl's feet, and I am a mere echo when I respond, *No. Please, wait in the car and lock the doors*. I have never been so alone, the gates in my mind clicking shut, walls closing in until everything is crushed but my unbreakable guilt. I look up. No clouds, no birds, no god. Only sun, hitting the desert like acid rain.

I walk in the middle of the road, counting my steps, turning the rhythm into a two-note lullaby. One-two. Three-four. In 108 steps I reach the steep incline in the road. I climb, knowing what I will find on the other side.

At the top of the hill, the desert stretches below me. There they are. I see hundreds, maybe thousands, of Kochi nomads in reds, greens, blues, and every tone of beige and gray. This is what infinity looks like. An undulating mass of men, women, children, animals, and tents against a wall of sky. I see rifles slung across men's backs, the glint of steely blades at their hips. *Fearless*, was how my father described them. *Fearless and proud*.

I have few memories of my mother, Dorothy, but one stabs into me now. I used to run to greet the nomad caravans when they came into town because I wanted to play with the children. My father told me they lived off the land and fought for what was theirs, that even their youngest were brave as lions, and I longed for adventures with six-year-old nomads in the desert. My American mother would stop me, my hand in her iron grip until my fingers hurt as she told me about their thousand-year-old laws, by which even unintentional sins could be capital crimes.

I try to forget her words as I start down the sloping highway. I cross the line where asphalt gives way to sand. It takes me eighteen steps to be noticed and thirty to reach the first goatskin tents. It must have taken the girl less than four running steps from the side of the road to the middle of it. I try to banish the image of that blur. But a child's voice whispers, *Look at me*, from the deepest recesses of my mind.

Kochis of every age assemble to take in the curious sight of us. For years, they will talk about the stranger who walked among them wearing city clothes and carrying a dead girl. I meet the gaze of an old man, his face a study in shadow, strands of gray escaping from his turban.

"Telaya," the man says, pointing to the girl. Then he asks, "What happened?"

I cannot say, "I found her like this. Someone must have hit her." There is no phantom killer; there is only me. I tell him she was running so fast that I didn't have time to stop. He watches me in silence.

The crowd hovers, a ring of strangers coiling and uncoiling like a cobra. Staring at the corpse, people ask questions I don't answer. Others are quiet. I want them all to disappear. The accident and the girl's death are a private disaster between her and me, made profane by prying eyes and whispered speech.

"Go that way," says the old man.

He points to more tents, more sheep, and more people in bold colors lit brighter by the implacable sun. As I walk, people abandon their tasks to join the silent congregation forming behind me. I pass two men brushing strips of shorn wool. Sitting cross-legged on a rug speckled with sand, girls who would be children in America but are women here sew tea leaves into pouches. As I pass, the sounds of life and work stop, and I feel as if the silence will make me deaf or blind or mute, destroy one of my senses to match the loss of some other indescribable thing the moment the girl died. A few feet away, several tents are wide open. They are brimming with artifacts, jewels, carpets, and mirror-dotted clothes. These are things the nomads will sell as they trek from village to village on their way to Kabul, Ghazni, Jalalabad. But today, I am the wanderer and the nomads are the ones who are still.

A woman sitting on the sand points a bony finger, not looking up from her lap. Two women polishing copper plates notice as I make my way toward them. One of them begins to rise, then sees what is in my arms and falls back to her knees with a stifled cry. Leaning against a younger woman, Telaya's mother sobs, terror and sorrow melding together on her face. I am not a parent, though only a few months ago, I thought I would be. When I see her fear, I think I know. I want to embrace her. I hear myself utter worthless apologies, dwarfed by the enormity of her pain and of what I have done.

"Baseer!" Telaya's mother cries out.

I turn around. The girl's father is only a few feet behind me, staring. His hands start to shake. His eyes widen. "Telaya?" He takes her in his arms, and all I had planned to say is replaced by all I do not. I am a fraud, the quixotic wizard behind the curtain who can't make anything right. I hear Baseer's fractured breath, a whispered word to his dead child. On his face, I see that same fear. Telaya's mother is crying freely now.

Then the crowd ebbs, parting for three tall men with silver beards. Word has spread to the elders, who have left their work, their tea, their wives, and come here to deliberate my crime. I meet their gaze as they approach, hoping Rebecca is still inside the car and will drive off without me if she must.

I hear one of the elders say, "Go find Taj."

There is some commotion as young boys spin this way and that, nodding and shouting, "Where's Taj Maleki? Get Taj!"

A man with thick sideburns cuts through the now-silent crowd. He reaches me and stops. One finger gleams with gold, an onyx adorns the front of his turban, and his *piran tomban* tunic and trousers are finer than the other men's, made of silk. A revolver sits in his holster, a Colt with a delicate pattern engraved on its grip. I stand before this strange man whose eyes are bereft of light, as if even the sun conceded defeat long ago.

"Who are you?" Taj asks in Farsi. I am relieved I speak the language, and that no one here could guess that I spoke more English than Farsi as a child.

"Daniel Abdullah Sajadi."

The man takes a step forward, but his face betrays nothing. The Kochis will not recognize the name Sajadi like people in the city do. Maybe this man knows who I am, maybe not. He watches me silently.

"Did you not see her?" His voice is as flat as his gaze.

"She ran straight into the road."

"And now she is dead."

"I'm sorry."

Taj nods. "Who do you work for?" he says. From his dialect, I hear that he isn't a Kochi. He's from the city.

"The American government."

A thousand eyes are on me. The only two people not looking at me are Telaya's parents, who are standing behind Taj.

It seems indecent to watch a mother and father in their grief. I stare instead at the horizon. An outsider would not know that this arid land is a great fraud of nature. Just behind these deserts are acres of vibrant opium poppies with emerald-green leaves, thriving under the sun. The great Yassaman field, with its rich bounty of flowers, is not far. Nature has surrounded these fields with the most fallow land on earth, giving the poppies better camouflage than it has given me. It is these flowers that I have dreamed of killing since I was a boy, not the children who help harvest them, the descendants of those who followed my father into war against the British empire.

These thoughts speed through my head, but her voice slices through all of them. *Look at me*, says the dead girl. The desert has flung me at the feet of its dwellers. I am that most vulnerable of creatures: a man out of context.

I can almost smell the poppies on the wind. They seem so trivial now, when just hours ago, they weighed more than anything else in my life. I fought for months at the office to convince my colleagues to begin the Reform with Fever Valley's largest field.

Taj looks at Telaya's corpse. Paper-white bone protrudes from her arm. Something glimmers in the sun: a shard of glass, lodged above her eyebrow, nearly invisible in the curve of her hair. I feel a throbbing pain above my own eye.

Baseer sobs, his words tumbling over each other in despair. "God, why have you done this to us? I have no other daughters." His wife squeezes his hand.

"He killed her," Baseer says to Taj, pointing at me as if sentencing me to join his daughter in death. Between cries, he whispers, "She was the only thing of value in my life."

The crowd is still silent, watching them. Taj places a hand on Baseer's shoulder and says, "What a terrible day for you."

His words are compassionate, but I wonder if the others can tell that the man is not. He is probably one of the callous merchants from the city who trick nomads into parting with their wares for less than they are worth, who travel with them for days at a time, choosing the best rugs and jewels and bartering them for a little food, money, perhaps medicine. Kochis are sophisticated tradesmen, too sharp to fall for such tricks, and yet there are exceptions. Some earn enough to become members of the country's sliver of a middle class, but Taj Maleki must be one of the tricksters taking advantage of those who do not with his expensive clothes and his cheap sympathy.

He goes on. "Your loss is a great one. She can never be replaced." He assures the parents that they must not worry. There will be restitution. The word is an escalating sequence of four notes, the final syllable a battle cry. When he moves, his gun gleams in a familiar way I cannot place. The Colt is an ordinary weapon—my father taught me to fire one when I was six—but there is something else about it that is familiar. The memory is there, but I cannot connect past and present.

The girl's mother trembles, her face contorted as she spears me with her gaze. I take a step back, walking into the person behind me. I turn around and tell the young man I'm sorry. He stares at me, unmoving. All around me, I see menace painted on men's faces. Their knives and guns fill my vision; I fight back the stories I grew up with.

"Where were you traveling to?" Taj says.

"Herat."

"From Kabul?"

"Yes."

"Of course."

"I'm so sorry." A voice inside me says I should not have come into the desert among these men. I know I don't want to die here. But there is another kind of knowing, one that rests deep in my bones like fossils in shale. My father used to tell me, *The rich world has rules and regulations. The poor world has rituals and traditions. These worlds weigh the same.*

Taj raises his hand and stops me before returning to the elders. They whisper things I am not meant to hear, shaking their heads as they speak, gesturing in turn to the road and the desert and the tents. "Yes," one of the elders says loudly. "That's fine."

Taj shakes his hand and stalks toward me, grasping my arm without stopping. He jerks his chin toward the road. "We are going to the police."

I am ashamed at my relief. I want to get away from here, even if this man is the only way out. As we pass the girl's parents, Taj gestures toward the road and they fall in step with us. Baseer is still holding the corpse, but I feel the child's weight as if she is back in my arms. I know that she will always be in my arms.

The trek back to the car feels shorter than the walk into the desert. Soon, we will be at the police station, where I will again have to confess. They will know who I am. It may save me. But Taj is watching me like the wind watches the leaves, knowing it may toss them as it likes, loosen them from trees at will.

Rebecca's arms are wrapped around her, her hair whipping in the breeze, face pale and eyes swollen. Today is our anniversary, but it seems small now, too. I had hoped to see her as she used to be, to find even a trace of joy. Instead, I have added to her grief from three months ago.

She has moved the car to the edge of the road. She sees no one but me, her clouded eyes searching my face. I can scarcely glance at her, much less meet her gaze. I am crushed by the weight of Telaya's death and further by the weight of my wife's love because at this moment, I do not deserve it.

No words are exchanged, no introductions made. The girl's parents wedge into the backseat with Taj, Telaya slumped across their laps. I see Taj gently pry the shard of glass from her face and I feel that stabbing pain above my eye again. Taj asks if I know the station north of here. I do.

I dig my hands into the scalding leather of the steering wheel. It comforts me, one pain making another recede. The radio, now warped with indentations, is mercifully silent. On the floor are ordinary tools I usually keep in the trunk.

"I had to make it stop," Rebecca whispers.

But I'm not staring at the tools. Under her seat is a mop of yellow wool. The tousled locks of the broken doll. The car is spangled with pastel rainbows cast by the mirrors on Telaya's dress. It must have been the finest one she owned. The mirrors on the doll's are making rainbows, too, smaller ones that dance across Rebecca's ankles. I turn the key and the engine comes alive. High above us, a bird of prey soars into view, shuddering against the burning blue dome.

1

ON THAT SCALDING AUGUST DAY, SERGEANT NAJIB SAT BEHIND HIS DESK, POLISHING THE barrel of his gun. He liked being a sergeant, despite the fool of a constable they had given him and the discomfort of his starchy uniform in the heat. Outside, there was nothing but a two-lane highway and the beige, boundless desert dotted with the occasional grungy bush or approaching mass of a nomad migration. Najib was proud to be king of this solitary mud box perched on the Kabul-Kandahar highway. From his station, he proudly served the young republic, proving that it was a serious entity. So serious that there were outposts of law and order even in places where the only real laws were those of nature, and the only real orders those of a warlord. Najib had loyally served the king, too, before the coup that had sent him packing four years ago.

Slipping the gun into his holster as noisily as he could, Najib stroked the cover of his well-thumbed Koran, then cast a glance at his young underling. Najib liked to think that the boy was a dedicated servant. It was an accepted fact that Kochi nomads were up to all sorts of trickery, and soon he would catch one of them in the act of something expressly forbidden, like passing off tin as silver or riding mules loaded with the remains of harvested poppies in the hope of starting their own field.

The grumble of a car interrupted his daydreams about glorious arrests and impending promotions. The constable shuffled out of his seat, turning to him for a cue. Najib might have walked to the station's only window, a cutout in the wall split by three vertical bars, but he would see no car from there. What imbecile had placed the single lookout point facing the desert instead of the road? He stalked out of the station, the younger man on his heels. A sand-colored Mercedes was slowing down by the station. It dipped onto the shoulder of the road, kicking up dust before coming to a stop. Najib's eyes fell on the hazy veil of blood on the grille, the red-streaked hood, the spider-webbed windshield. Inside the car was the strangest mix of folk. A stunning yellow-haired woman caught his eye first, then an urban type at the wheel and a cluster of Kochis in the back. It occurred to him that these might be the outlaws he had been waiting for.

He hooked his thumb into his holster and stood still. He would let them come to him. The driver stepped out. Above the man's right eye was a swollen, bloody gash. His shirt was stained, too. The blonde woman emerged, moving with a determination that reminded Najib of one of his wives. The last time this many people had turned up at once was when some hoodlums had organized a pack-beast race and a luckless camel had tried to outrun a big rig instead of the other animals, an unanticipated yet exciting twist that ended with the parched beast collapsing in a heap on the highway, making the asphalt look like it had grown a hump, and the terrified driver swerving off the road, his eighteen-wheeler belly-up like a giant bug. Luckily, there had been no deaths. Except a woman who had worn a *chaderi*, a blue burka, whose name no one knew and whose age no one could guess because they made sure she remained covered as she died.

◆ ◆ ◆

Daniel had passed the solitary police outpost before, paying it little mind as he drove toward the fields of Fever Valley. As he stepped out of his car, the breeze rising from the desert was like a whisper from the poppies to the north. The policeman studied him with narrowed eyes, his hands behind his back. An airplane glided over them, leaving a feathery wake in the sky. The officer tilted his head and spoke.

"Salaam, *saheb*. You have some business for the police?"

"There's been an accident."

The officer nodded at the Mercedes and called him sir again. "I see, *saheb*. Why are there Kochis in your car?"

"A girl was run over. I brought her here."

"Alive?"

Daniel shook his head.

"Are you the one who killed her?"

A psychedelically painted eighteen-wheeler downshifted as it passed, curious heads poking out of paneless windows, a dozen men sitting tailor-style on the tarp-covered cargo. It lumbered up the highway amid puffs of diesel. Daniel closed his eyes. A series of images surfaced in his mind like sepia photos in darkroom chemicals. He was driving. *You never think of how it is for me*, Rebecca had said. An accusation. She was wrong, he told her. She cried. *Sometimes I wish we hadn't come here*. He tightened his grip on the wheel. More accusations. All the while, that wretched sonata played on. He fumbled in the glove compartment, looking for a tape. A stupid Neil Diamond tape, which would lighten the mood because she thought he was corny and it would make her laugh. He looked away from the road, only for an instant. He had wanted to make her laugh, and instead he'd made her scream. A thin scream, not more than a single note, yet so vast it could not be contained by the car, slamming against the windows and breaking right through the glass.

"Daniel." Rebecca sounded far away, and when he opened his eyes, he found that he had wandered into the road, where he stood wrapped in the lingering vapors of the vanished truck's exhaust.

"Come inside," the sergeant said.

Daniel shook his head. "We can't leave the girl in the car."

The man shrugged and went inside. Taj and Baseer lifted Telaya's body out, her toes dragging against the metal door-frame. Her dress bunched up around her knees, and Taj covered them back up as if they betrayed a lack of modesty. Daniel watched through the haze of the brightly lit day, his eyes falling on the child's mangled arm.

Many years ago, in the back of his father's car, Daniel saw a Kochi boy running along the edge of the desert, flashing a brilliant smile as he waved. Daniel waved back, mesmerized by the boy's bare feet, the way they kicked up no dust and seemed never to land at all. A rabid dog was running toward the boy, and Daniel tried to warn him, banging on the window and pointing. But the boy only kept on, chasing the car and laughing, until the dog was upon him, and at the very last second, the boy hopped to the side and produced a blade, lodging it in the animal's neck.

Daniel begged the chauffeur to stop, but his father forbade it, warning him that Kochis did not make good playmates. Later, he asked his father if everybody's feet were made the same, and Sayed answered, *Their feet yes, their heads no.* That night, Daniel dreamed of heads that floated up from bodies and small, battered heels that split open to reveal pockets of shattered glass. As he walked now, he felt that shattered glass push up through his feet and move through his body.

Something in the car drew his eye. A mirror had come loose

from Telaya's dress, gleaming in the empty backseat. It was small and solitary, sending the sun's rays back to the sky as if to say, *No, I have no more use for your light*. Daniel picked up the mirror and put it in his pocket. He wanted something of hers to remain with him.

The group filed into the station, Daniel the last to enter. Flies descended on the dead girl, nesting in her blood-matted hair, her ears, her drying wounds. Her mother waved them away, but they returned as if attached by springs.

Sergeant Najib introduced himself curtly and presented his constable as Mir. The younger man twisted his mouth into a smile that suggested both surprise and apprehension. Taj was asked to surrender his gun, which he did without quarrel. The Kochis sank to the floor against a wall, Telaya across their laps, the mother smoothing the child's dress, polishing its mirrors with her tears and a finger. The sounds of her grief played awkwardly in concert with the one-note drone of the flies and the hiss of the damaged fan doing its best from a corner. Daniel felt a quiver of nausea. The station was powered by a diesel generator that gave off a noxious odor, which blended with that of the remains of fried food peeking out from wax paper in an overflowing bin. Afraid he would buckle, Daniel leaned against a wall. Beside him was a three-legged table where a chess match stood abandoned, marble pieces darkened by a veil of dust. Najib offered Rebecca the only chair besides his own. The rusty metal screeched as he dragged it to where she stood. She lowered herself carefully and mouthed a thank-you. Daniel watched her, wishing he could wrap her in his arms and tell her that everything would be okay.

On the wall near Mir's stool hung a calendar made for Westerners and Western-minded locals. Miss August reigned over the station with a sultry eye and an outstretched hand.

Daniel recognized her as someone who had once modeled jewels made from the gemstones in his father's mines. Daniel still called those mines his father's, even though they were his now. His father had made the mines famous, raised armies of villagers and nomads throughout the country, and used his fortune to pay for weapons of war: bribes and the most modern guns in the world. Anything to help expel the English and keep the Russians at bay. Sayed Sajadi had outshone the king's own armies with his troops of Kochis. Now one of their children had died at Daniel's hands. Najib asked for his name. When he replied, the sergeant lowered his pen. "Related?"

Daniel nodded, and the sergeant's body relaxed. With a broad smile, he insisted on shaking Daniel's hand before asking Mir to bring Coca-Colas for everyone.

"We're going to drink Cokes now?" Rebecca held her arms out, palms open as if the answer to her question might trickle down from the ceiling. "Shouldn't we take this girl to a hospital?"

Najib scoffed. "For what? She's obviously dead."

"So they can make a record. Write down the cause of death."

When Najib indicated that no such thing was needed, Rebecca breathed out slowly. Daniel could hear an emotion in her exhale, though it was unclear what kind. He would tell her later that no record could be made about people who never officially existed in the first place. In America, his friends sometimes used the phrase "becoming a statistic" like it was something to be avoided. They complained about the government turning them into a number. What a luxury that would have been for Telaya, to find her name on a ledger. To be a statistic.

The now-unctuous sergeant asked excited questions about

Daniel's father and other things that had nothing to do with the accident, which he seemed to have forgotten for a moment. Then he returned to the subject, checking off boxes and filling in blanks. "What is your job?"

"My husband works for USADE," Rebecca said. "He's the director here."

"The United States Against the Drug Economy?" It was not Najib who had spoken, but Taj. With a thin smile, he added, "And what do you do there, exactly?"

"*I* ask the questions," Najib said. A sheen of sweat was visible above his lip, and Daniel heard the tremor in his voice. Mir stood in a corner, jerking his head toward whoever spoke.

"What do you do there, exactly?" Taj repeated.

"We help farmers stop growing poppies and teach them how to plant other things. Like food."

"Does that work?" Najib said.

Daniel told him four fields had already been reformed. He did not say that only a few small-scale growers had agreed to the change, nor that of the seven important fields of Fever Valley, just one would be reformed—and by force—in the hope that the great opium khans, invisible like gods, would capitulate. He did not say that a farmer had approached his agency with a message from these poppy overlords, quietly offering money in return for being left alone. USADE had, under Daniel's direction, refused the bribe.

"And you are the director? You are young for such a post," the sergeant said. "I suppose a man like you rises quickly through the ranks."

Daniel had no intention of explaining how he had come into the position he'd only held for seven months. He had even managed to avoid explaining it to his staff.

Najib asked how fast Daniel had been driving, where he'd

been heading, and where the accident happened. He sounded bored. With every answer, Daniel replayed another part of the accident in his mind, wondering what would have changed if he'd looked up just a moment sooner. Or if they had left Kabul a few minutes earlier. Or if he hadn't forgotten the suitcase and gone back to the house.

"Enough!" Taj said as if hearing his thoughts. He pointed to Baseer, who was weeping softly. "Look at the state my friend is in!"

"I'm not sure she knew what a car was," Daniel said. Sometimes, Kochi children didn't. They would watch from the side of the road, laughing, dropping whatever they held, and run dangerously toward the giant metal animals. Baseer shook his head, eyeing Daniel with contempt.

"She knew what a car was," Taj said. He was the only thing in motion in the room except for the blades of the fan and Najib's fast-moving fingers.

Daniel fought the nausea that twisted in his gut. It came not only from the stench of diesel and stale smoke, but from the crash and from Taj and his gun and a memory he was still struggling to conjure.

Through the window bars, long afternoon shadows leaned into the room. The day was slowly cooling, but Daniel only grew warmer, as if his body absorbed each degree the dead girl lost, her corpse growing rigid and cold as he burned. He slid down the wall to the floor, looking here and there, anywhere but at her. Above him, Miss August sparkled with empty promises of magic flight. He drew the back of his hand across his brow. Only when he saw the smudge on his cuff did he realize there was a cut above his eye. The insignificance of the injury struck him as obscene.

Najib tore the wrapper off a packet of Winstons, tapping the bottom and sliding out a cigarette. When Daniel had been in college, Winston had sponsored *The Flintstones*. On the rare days Rebecca took a break from the piano and before she'd sworn off substances that dulled her senses, they'd spent afternoons smoking cigarettes and weed in her apartment and giggling at the Stone Age family.

"She is an unregistered person, so the compensation to the parents will be low." The sergeant spoke as if the words left a bad taste in his mouth, not because he objected to Telaya being described as unregistered, but because he objected to her being described as a person. He wrote something on the form, taking his time before bringing it to Daniel with a pen.

The page was sparse, a few vacant rectangles with captions in Farsi and English, and in bold print across the top Daniel read the English version: CONFESSION OF PERSONS MAKING ACCIDENTS BY ANIMAL OR AUTO. Underneath was the option to check off WITH DEAD or WITHOUT DEAD. At the bottom was a space for the sergeant's comments. Najib had described the event in Farsi, and closed with his version in English: *With car, Daniel Sajadi killed the girl. Moneys are 10,000 afghanis.*

So that was it. Telaya's parents were due just over one hundred dollars. Daniel's gaze dissolved into the word that spelled his deed: *killed*. He felt the sharpness of the *k*, one of its arms angling diagonally toward the sky, the other downward toward hell. *K* for kid, Kochi, Kabul, and Keystone Cop. Between the two *l*'s, he saw the road.

The Kochis couldn't write, so it fell to Daniel to provide details about the victim. What was Telaya's last name? Her family had none. Her age? She had said ten, or maybe nine. Her parents weren't sure either.

"Where do we send the money?" Rebecca said, her voice quiet and hoarse.

"You pay before you go," Najib replied, tightening his

lips as if suppressing a chuckle before adding, "Kochis do not keep postal boxes, madam."

She fetched her handbag from the car and gave Baseer a clip of bills. There had been more than ten thousand afghanis in the wallet, and Daniel wondered if she had offered it all, too embarrassed to count. He hoped she had. Baseer studied the money like it posed a problem to which he had no solution. It occurred to Daniel that if the Kochis could not read or write, maybe they could not count, either. Baseer passed the money to Taj, who leafed through the bills, counting out loud as he went. He nodded. Telaya's parents thanked Taj for his kindness, tears trickling down their faces. Safeguarding the bills in his holster, Taj gathered Telaya in his arms, leading the parents to the door.

"You can't bury the girl near my station." Sergeant Najib waved dismissively at the corpse. "Take her back where she belongs."

Daniel wished he could bury her on a gentle green hill. Instead, her time on earth would end with terse last rites in a desert with no shade and no name, an unmarked grave no one would visit, and kin who would return incidentally, if at all. In the world of cities, buildings, and streets, people's memories of those they loved were framed by places and times. When no place was different from any other, only deserts and fields that looked alike, and there was no measure of time other than sunup and sundown, what frame preserved the dimming faces of the dead? Nomads did not have photos to remember them by, nor a home to return to and say, *This is where she walked, this is where she played*. But Daniel would always know exactly where she'd died, and he thought the burden of honoring her memory would fall partly on him, her killer.

Outside, Mir was walking back to the station with a bucket of water in his hand. A wet rag was flung over his arm as pink droplets vanished into the earth. The blood was gone from the car. Baseer and his wife climbed in the back. Taj loaded the girl onto their laps.

Rebecca stood by the car, bracing herself for a second ride in a confined space with a corpse, grieving parents, and a man whose flat eyes she'd avoided all afternoon. The bills bulged awkwardly in Taj's holster, drawing Daniel's attention again to the gun. It was familiar, like a song that Daniel knew the words to when all that mattered was its name.

"Do you know what happens next, Daniel Sajadi?" Taj said.

Daniel heard an echo in his mind, something from long ago. *What do you see?*

It was a line from a game he used to play after his mother walked out. He would sit behind his father's desk after Sayed had gone to bed and pick an object: a jewel, a glove, or a comb. He made himself guess if it belonged to his mother or to the woman his father was married to now. With a flashlight and magnifying glass, he would examine the piece, turn it over, weigh it in his palm like he'd seen antique dealers do. Then he would render his verdict, declaring if the object was "Mother" or "Other." He would make it his mission to find out without asking his father, checking instead with the housekeeper. When he was right, it was like remembering something he wasn't sure he had ever really known, a haze of memory hardening into fact.

Taj had retrieved his gun and began polishing it with a handkerchief.

What do you see?

And now Daniel saw. The flower carved into the Colt was a poppy. The corpse and the accident and the station receded, and the flowers grew until they filled his vision. Daniel wondered why he had not seen it before. It was the second time today his sight had failed him. Taj Maleki was an opium khan.

2

DANIEL RUBBED HIS ACHING BROW AND OPENED THE WOUND, BLOOD DRIPPING ONTO HIS lashes. Offering his handkerchief, Taj said, "You must return to the camp with me and the parents." He could have been issuing an invitation to lunch.

"Then why did you bring me to the police?" Daniel said, wondering what kind of trick the man was playing. He refused the handkerchief, blotting the blood with his sleeve. "There's nothing more I can do. I'm not going anywhere with you."

"Honor requires it, *saheb*. You know this." Taj lowered his head and his voice. "I assure you, you will not die."

Daniel understood why some locals called the great opium khans Manticores, after the mythical creature with the body of a lion and rows of razor-sharp teeth like a shark's. The Manticore's dragon tail was filled with poison, and when it attacked a man, it left no part of him behind.

Rebecca stood by the car door, which she held open, watching Daniel. In her eyes, he could see it. She wanted to leave not only the station but the road, the desert, probably the country.

"They know where you work," Taj said.

Daniel wondered if the Kochi tribe would send men after him to extract revenge months or even years from now. Rebecca. What if they avenged the girl by harming Rebecca?

"I'm not afraid of them," he told Taj.

Taj smiled, revealing a hairline crack in one of his incisors, a single flaw in an even row of teeth. "A man who says he is not afraid is afraid. So why not come now, while I am here to protect you?"

From the station, an Indian chanteuse whined out a song that Daniel had heard a thousand times. Sergeant Najib sat in a chair visible through the open door, uninterested in his lingering Kochi guests.

"I hope you understand my point, Daniel Sajadi," Taj said. He ran his sleeve over the gun one last time before returning the weapon to its holster.

Rebecca approached them with quick steps. "Let's go," she whispered.

Taj drifted back into the station, the end of his turban floating in the wind. Once alone, Daniel and Rebecca argued. When she learned that he planned to return to the desert, she swayed as if the things holding her together were escaping. He held her by the shoulders. He didn't say that he had no choice. He only told her he would be safe.

And he believed it. An opium khan would not kill an American official. This was not Burma or Colombia, with their turf wars and drug killings. There was no such violence here. The khans were not cartels, but a scattering of powerful and mysterious men who ruled more because people needed them than because people feared them, though no one wanted to cross a Manticore. Nor would Taj allow the elders to execute Daniel. What then would have been the point of bringing him to the station? All they would want were ceremonial apologies, perhaps more money. Daniel's confidence slowly returned. He would manage. He was the son of Sayed Sajadi.

Rebecca's eyes were red, and her breath was faint and

light. She was watching Taj, who stepped back inside the station and asked Sergeant Najib a question they could not hear.

"We need to leave," she insisted, pulling Daniel toward the car. Her hair had come loose from its ponytail, golden strands clinging to her brow. Daniel took her hand and promised he would return quickly. That it was just a formality. Tradition.

"You're crazy," she said. "Don't do this."

"Madam," Taj called out. "I'm sure the young constable would be honored to escort you to a hotel of your choice in Ghazni."

She crossed her arms tightly and lowered her head, her lips trembling.

"But it is the closest city," Taj said, as if her resistance were due to apprehension about geography.

The rumble of an engine was followed by the appearance of Mir, who had brought a car around from behind the station—a Moskvitch, the Soviet answer to Datsun. It had three hubcaps and a bent fender.

"He's harmless," Daniel told Rebecca. It was true. There had been men like Mir in Sayed's every warehouse and factory.

"If you think that's the guy I'm afraid of, you've had a different day than me."

Taj held the back door of the Moskvitch open, but she took the passenger seat and slammed down the lock, shutting out Taj, her husband, and the day itself. Daniel told Mir to drive to the Ariana Hotel in Ghazni, whispering the directions, aware of Taj lurking. The young constable steered Rebecca onto the highway.

The drive back to the Kochi camp was aggressively silent, like the aftermath of an explosion. Daniel resisted the urge to turn over the wheel to Taj. He would have let anybody drive the car, if only he could avoid passing the place where it happened. He could control the car, he told himself. More difficult were his thoughts. Those childhood memories returned. Dorothy's stories of the violence of the Kochis. The paintings that hung in his father's offices and factories, depicting nomads heading into battle with zeal. His foot was rigid on the gas pedal, hands tight on the wheel.

Baseer and his wife had known all along what Taj was. Of that, Daniel was sure. In a month, the great opium harvest would begin, so, like the other khans, Taj was likely searching for workers in the nomads' sprawling camps. Daniel should have known the moment he'd seen the man, so out of place there with his onyx and silk. But Daniel had always assumed that Manticores sent their underlings to choose workers. Maybe the khans didn't trust anyone they hadn't seen with their own eyes. Maybe they wanted fear and love from those in the fields, and these sentiments were best engendered face-to-face.

A convoy of tanks rolled past them toward Kabul. The last one stood out, though Daniel could not say how. The tanks shrank in the rearview mirror, where Daniel also found Baseer's eyes. The old man's weathered features softened into a smile, a look of pity mixed with something inscrutable.

At the Kochi camp, Taj assisted the parents with the body, declining Daniel's help. The day was ending, the sun burnishing the silver-plated sky.

"Wait here," he said.

"For what?"

"Would you prefer to come and face the elders?"

"I don't understand."

"You don't have to."

Taj said goodbye to the parents and watched them cross the road. Daniel's pulse was unsteady. The Kochi couple was soon out of sight.

"What is this?" Daniel said. "You told me you were bringing me to stand trial with the elders."

Taj gestured to the driver's seat, but Daniel hesitated. He looked toward the Kochi camp, wondering if he could seek safety there, then realizing that he was trapped between two forces he knew little about. Somewhere deep inside, he had the answer, but all he could hear was Telaya's voice. *I'm faster than you*, she whispered. *Do you see me?*

The khan bowed slightly and waved his hand toward the car again.

"If you have something to tell me, you can call my office. Most of your colleagues have agreed to work with us," Daniel lied.

The khan laughed as if he'd just heard a long-anticipated punchline. "My colleagues! The small farmers you work with are not my colleagues." He said "small" the way people in Rebecca's Los Angeles neighborhood said "southern." He pointed to the car again, this time with the barrel of his gun, and it was like he had never laughed at all. "Drive," he said. "If you behave yourself, everyone lives."

I didn't get to live, the girl hissed. *The man who took my life should die, too.*

Daniel tightened his grip and engaged the gears too hard, heaving the car onto the road. The Kochi camp fled behind them, the desert stretched taut like a colorless canvas, and in the side mirror, Daniel could still see that small boy from long ago with his wild smile and flying feet and sunshine that caught his mirrored cap like a halo. He drove faster.

In Fever Valley, poppies bloomed red, purple, and white, a Technicolor maze inviting you to lose yourself. These were not the cheerful blossoms of California. To Daniel, these flowers signaled death. But for others, they signaled life. Since childhood, he had heard about the rhythm of the opium harvest. Every fall, the poor came to collect on the hopes of a year. Their wages were so small, they counted them in fractions. A destitute man could proudly call himself a farmer because he helped reap a field. In the spring, he would help sow seeds. His wives, his daughters and sons, everyone came with a small blade, same as last year, working alongside the professionals. The old uncle who never found a wife, who aged alone in something that looked like a town but had no name, he came, too, though he moved slower than the others. He might earn enough to buy a box of potatoes, a jug of oil, and save a little money to someday buy a goat of his own. Every summer, those who knew him asked, *Did you buy the goat? Not this year*, he replied. *Next year, inshallah.* God willing.

Daniel grew up on these stories, told to him by his father and Sherzai, the man who had become his guardian after Sayed died and the Iranian woman Sayed was married to decamped to Tehran with her relatives. Even today, Sherzai would tell Daniel stories about a time he recalled only vaguely. The days when there was no Fever Valley, just vast fields in the northeastern corners of the country and lesser-known plots hundreds of miles south of here in Helmand Province. Tucked away in the south were hidden swaths few people could find, beyond the flat deserts where only camel thorn grew.

He wondered how much Taj knew about Sayed Sajadi. He spoke like someone who wanted others to think he'd had an education, but something in his inflection, the way he seemed to strain to articulate longer words instead of swallowing the middle syllable, told Daniel that the khan had been born someone else. His name sounded impossible, too, chosen by a person who had come into the world without one.

That the Sajadis were rich was no secret. Schoolchildren learned about Sayed the war hero, but depending on the teacher's leanings, Sayed either became the republican who bravely challenged the king or the traitor who insulted the monarchy. He had gained followers after helping to drive out the English and eventually challenged the king's candidate for the governorship of Helmand, promising he would rid the province of the small but growing opium farms. Daniel was only eight when the royal army arrested his father. Sherzai explained that no king could abide a man who was more popular than he was.

Maybe Taj only planned to extort money, demanding cash in return for not broadcasting the accident within the better circles of Kabul. Drug lords understood money, never content with what they had, spending their lives like magpies hoarding shiny things. Daniel wondered if they also understood the shame that decent people felt when they harmed the less fortunate.

"Turn here," Taj said after more than an hour on the desolate road.

Daniel found himself on an unpaved path, surrounded by a night so black he never knew what was ahead. And yet he knew Taj was leading him to the Yassaman field. He had been here four times in six months. How different it was at night, empty of USADE's crews, who came and went each day with their notebooks, shovels, and bright, shining hopes. How much more alive it seemed in this darkness with the wind and the flowers in a whispered dialogue.

The car lurched along like a skiff on stormy waters. Daniel skirted a curve in the road, his headlights gilding over stunted trees dying of thirst on the margins of a great opium field, the well-watered poppies a cruel taunt.

"I know who you are," Daniel said at last.

"You know *what* I am. You do not know *who* I am."

"Why did you tell me we were going back to the elders?"

"I wanted to talk to you, man to man. I'm sorry if I frightened you."

"You didn't."

"Forgive me. It was presumptuous to think a man of your lineage should be frightened by anything a humble servant like me might come up with." Taj signaled for Daniel to stop in a clearing and follow him into the field, gesturing again with his gun. They passed the equipment that stood along the edge, the power plows that USADE had brought to the field. A cloud slipped away from the moon, and the Dannaco-Hastings logo was briefly visible on the machines, which looked like reconstructed dinosaurs in a museum. Daniel's crew had already begun digging channels that would bring water from the thin river nearby. Though they would not be used for several more weeks, Daniel had made sure tillers and cultivators were brought to the field, too, warning the khans of what was to come. Pressuring them to abandon these poppies, this life. Judging by the man beside him, Daniel had failed.

They walked into the night, crossing what should have been a stream but was a dry ditch. The poppies rose up before them, a fragile truce between beauty and poison. They rustled, protesting Daniel's clumsy advance, while Taj nipped forward with ease and purpose. A small breeze lifted, scattering lost petals and leaves. Along the eastern margin of the field were boulders and shrubs Daniel had never noticed before. The rest was familiar.

"Every year, I need more workers," Taj said. "The nomads are good. They're used to sleeping outside, and they'll take scraps of food as payment. They are not so different from animals."

Something violent bloomed in Daniel's mind, and it was the color of Telaya's dress. "There are animals that compare favorably to you," he said.

"I did once know a cat who displayed an enviable talent for strategic planning. And I'll admit to a fondness for llamas."

"Llamas?"

"They command a certain respect. It takes great insight and spirit to spit at human beings."

"They rarely spit at human beings. They spit to remind lower-ranking llamas of their place."

The khan stopped and faced him. "Is that so?"

Not far ahead, a flicker of white light danced above the poppies, the moon reflected in a window. It was the shack Daniel had entered a few months ago, hoping to find a place to leave his jacket and briefcase. He'd turned back around at the sight of rats gnawing on an old mattress. They were heading straight toward it now.

"How long have you had this field?" Daniel said.

"I don't know. I don't like time."

"That's understandable. Time isn't working in your favor. Your days here are numbered."

"Everybody's days are numbered."

"Some of us have more favorable numbers than others. You're up against men who are smarter than you, with much more money. This will become farmland."

"It's already farmland," Taj said.

Daniel wished this pointless tour would end. He had essentially been brought at gunpoint and couldn't decide if he was supposed to behave as if the gun was there or not. Part of him thought the khan meant to end his life, but he was strangely unafraid. It was as if the accident had snuffed out some capacity for perspective or feeling. Some events were so immense, they could drain someone of a lifetime of emotions.

"Make this disappear." Taj spoke as if reiterating something they had already agreed upon. The gun was still in his hand. "Leave my field."

"That's impossible."

"Did I not take you away from the elders when you begged for someone to save your life?"

"I didn't beg. And it's not the same thing."

"Indeed it isn't. Some would say the favor I'm asking for is small in comparison."

Daniel began to wonder if his faith in the region's safety was misplaced. He thought again about the war on drugs in other countries. USADE had lasted just four weeks in Burma, its director gunned down on an open road. The violence had to start at some point, before which people said, *Those things don't happen here.*

Daniel turned and walked toward the car.

"Not yet," the khan said. "Give me an answer."

Daniel kept walking. "I'm only one man."

"You're a Sajadi, and the director of your agency. They'll do what you say."

"You don't know what you're talking about. It's my government, not me, that's taking your field."

"Men like us don't have governments."

"Men like us?"

"Whenever a man has a government, then the government has the man. If you are wise, which of course you are, you will aim your loyalties elsewhere." Taj pointed to the shapes at the eastern edge of the field. "Look closely," he said. "Do you see?"

Daniel's eyes fell on the lumpy bundles beside the machines. They looked like large, grotesque weeds sprung from the earth without order or design. He walked toward them. One of them stirred. They were not weeds; they were human beings. Dozens, maybe more, with threadbare clothes and provisions bundled into sacks. A pageantry of want.

"Without an opium harvest, they will be paid nothing," Taj said. "Don't you care?"

"Your fake concern isn't any more convincing now than it was—"

"When you killed the girl?"

Daniel didn't reply. He looked at the poppy pickers. Seth and Iggy, USADE's best engineers, came to Yassaman two days a week, sometimes more, and had told him the channels were coming along, the crews working diligently. But there were other crews, too, the poppy workers, mainly villagers and Kochis, whom Daniel saw each time he came to observe. They worked from sunrise to sunset, serving the khans, whom no one ever saw. This year, the poppy workers kept to one edge of the field to avoid the machines and crews on the opposite side.

"Leave our land alone," Taj said. "It isn't yours. It belongs to the poppies and those who pick them."

"The people who want you out have more resources than you could dream of."

"You have no idea what I dream of. And I have a resource they cannot match."

"What would that be?"

"Hunger," Taj said. "It is the greatest resource of all, because it is infinite."

"It won't exist anymore once we're done here."

"Americans watch too many movies. You think people in poor places dream of fields of rice and wheat. But the poorest people don't dream about the means to an end. They dream about the end itself: enough money to live and something extra to give to their children. Your crops will never outearn the poppies."

On the gentle wind, the flowers whispered in agreement. Or maybe they were mocking the nearby land, visible from Yassaman. The Gulzar field was a naked, barren lot where a handful of poppies struggled to grow. Fever Valley sometimes reminded Daniel of New York, where Tiffany neighborhoods were divided from ghettos by mere blocks.

They stood at the threshold of the shack, its metal door ajar. The smell of old tea, sweat, and tobacco drifted into the night, but there was another smell, too, pungent and foul. Daniel heard a scraping sound. He turned toward the road, which he could barely see. "I'm going back to the car."

"No, you're not." The Manticore touched Daniel's shoulder and added matter-of-factly, "I'm not ready to leave. And you're my ride."

Daniel pulled away. He could not orient himself in the vast darkness. He tried to gauge where the car was, but they hadn't walked in a straight line.

"Do you know why this business will always exist?" Taj asked. "Even if the people in these fields stopped being hungry, I could count on a different hunger. The wealthy world's famine is its craving for drugs. There will never be enough." He vanished into the shack. "Come in. I want to show you something."

Daniel hesitated before following. Inside, the stench was immeasurably worse. Taj lit a candle on a paper plate heavy with hardened wax. Vomit was pooled on the floor beside a metal frame bed Daniel recognized. What he did not recognize was the person in the bed, covered with a blanket. Rodents had chewed holes in the thin fabric. They were lapping at the vomit now.

"This man is one of my new workers for the season. He has stolen poppy pods from me. My men said he was so heavily drugged when they caught him, he could barely speak."

"He overdosed?"

"He couldn't even wait a few weeks for the resin to perfect itself. He just tore at the pods."

Daniel was unable to look away.

"I said they should leave him here," Taj continued. "I had other matters to tend to. Your friends with their machines didn't seem to notice him collapse. Perhaps noticing is not part of their job."

The rats scattered as Daniel sank to his knees and removed the blanket, discovering that beneath was not a man, but a boy in the throes of adolescence, a thin stubble and a sprinkling of blemishes on his face. He was chained by his wrist to the bed. He tried to say something, but managed only a moan.

"He's alive," Daniel said.

"They usually just fall into a long sleep and never wake up. That must be a pleasant way to die. But this way isn't bad, either."

The crack of a gunshot blew apart the air. Daniel sprung to his feet and he thought he was shouting but could barely hear his own voice. He'd instinctively covered his ears, the room ringing with the aftermath of the shot. His movements were a series of reflexes. He seized Taj's shoulders, surprised at their slightness. He lost count of how many times he yelled the word no. He was shaking Taj as if trying to force loose a response. None came. Daniel let go and leaned against a wall, overcome by heat and the sense that he was unable to breathe. The boy's blood was on his skin and his clothes. Taj headed for the door, and Daniel followed. Outside, he shoved Taj hard from behind. The man stumbled but recovered, turning to face him, and dug the gun into his ribs.

"Don't do that," Taj said, cocking the barrel.

Daniel heard Telaya say, *Men who hurt little girls deserve to die.* He scrambled backward and lost his footing. The

Manticore grabbed his arm, breaking his fall. He returned the weapon to its holster and walked away, an ordinary man on an evening stroll. "You are not useful to me dead."

"Stop!"

"If I stop, how am I supposed to lead you to the car?"

The wind tickled the flowers. Daniel's breath, thoughts, and vision were trapped inside his thirst for righteous violence.

"You're not going to kill me," Taj continued. "You know how I know? A man like you doesn't kill two people in one day."

For a moment, Daniel's desire to harm the man became as blisteringly alive as he was, and he could not distinguish between his life and his desire to end Taj's. What purpose did this man serve? What did he bring to the world that was not better destroyed? Was killing a man like him not right and honorable?

Traces of reason returned. It was true; he wouldn't kill the man, and maybe Taj was right about why. Daniel was no murderer. But there was also the Reform. A man found dead in the Yassaman field, revealed to be an opium khan, might derail everything. Daniel imagined the State Department shutting down the project and maybe even the agency, the Reform set aside amid talk of rising violence in the drug trade. Mere rumors had wrecked initiatives bigger than this.

Taj pulled away and melded with the night. Alone, Daniel felt something in his body churn. He became violently sick. Again and again, every muscle and organ in his body wrenched involuntarily. Every heave was like reliving the moment of impact, those impossible seconds between his old life and what it was now. He fell onto his hands and knees, and eventually, it stopped.

The darkness was breathtaking. It was as if the universe

had simply switched off the lights above this place. Daniel slowly made his way back to the car, exploiting rare glimpses of moonlight. Taj was waiting in the passenger seat.

"Good, I was afraid you were lost. City people lack a sense of space. It has to do with perspective." Taj clicked the seat belt into place, flicked down the visor, and examined his wounds in the mirror, complaining about the blood on his *piran*. Daniel sat in the driver's seat doorframe, feet on the ground and back to the khan. He used his shirt to wipe his mouth and the blood from his skin. In his suitcase in the trunk, he'd found clean clothes.

"I had to kill the boy's brother a few months ago for the same reason," Taj said. "Now his mother has no children, unless you count the girls."

"Get out of my car."

"Really? All by myself here? It's not a safe area, as you can see."

"Get out." Daniel reached across Taj and shoved open the passenger door.

The opium khan glanced toward the shed in the field. "That's what happens to those who don't understand the rules."

"You might as well kill me, too, because I'm not driving you anywhere. I'm sure *you* would have no qualms about killing twice in one day."

"What makes you think it would only be twice? By the time we met, it was late in the day for a humble working man like me. Nevertheless, as you wish. I wouldn't want us getting off on the wrong foot." Taj climbed out of the car and raised his hand in farewell. "Until next time, Daniel Sajadi."

The tires whined as Daniel spun the car around. The air inside was dense with sweat, sour breath, and the copper-penny smell of blood. He wanted to leave this place far behind and return to the city, to Rebecca. To the normalcy of a room, a shower, and a bed. A bed that had not been the scene of a killing. Daniel looked in the rearview mirror and saw Taj standing alone in the clearing, flooded by the car's taillights. His robes floated on the gentle wind. As Daniel drove away, the khan called out a warning. "Watch your speed. That's how you ran over the girl in the first place."

I'm fast, Telaya said, clutching her doll. *I can do it.*

"No, you can't," Daniel said. "You should've stayed out of the road." He slammed his fist into the dash, and his hand and his head throbbed as the car lurched over the rugged roads that led from the poppies to what passed for civilization around here.

SNOWMAN

When the children come outside, it isn't to play, at least not with Boy. It's cold, but they have coats that are fat like sheep. Boy has a good coat, too, but it's his only one and Mother doesn't want him to get holes in it, so he doesn't wear it all the time. He hears her say it is the worst winter she can remember. He knows she is telling the gardener or the housekeeper or the lady of the house or the man who comes and goes in his big car. Sometimes those people come to the little tent in the garden to see Boy and Mother. She says thank you, God bless you for your kindness, when they give her a pair of shoes, toothpaste, soap, a towel. Warmer socks. The good oil that burns a little longer. The cook comes by in the evenings and gives them a pot of soup, naan, rice and meat, and chocolate. Boy likes the chocolate and dreams of it.

His mother tells him the story at night when he cannot sleep. He loves the story. She says that long before this house was built, she used to be very poor, begging from people on this street. This was before Boy existed. He nods when Mother says this, although he does not understand how there could have been such a time. Mother says she lived in the shadows of the big houses then, sleeping beside a tall hedge. On a cold night with quiet snow and a loud wind, a rich man came out of his house and gave her a tent, a mattress, and two blankets.

That tent changed her life, because she could light a fire and cook, even when it was raining or snowing. But mostly, it changed her life because it's where Boy was made. A man with a donkey cart used to come to the street every afternoon to sell vegetables to the rich. When the evening came and the light faded, he would stop at her tent and give her what he had left. Onions, lettuce heads, radishes. He told her he'd sold vegetables all over the country, moving from city to city, and told her about the red tulips of Jalalabad, the shimmering mosque in Herat, and the great statues in Bamyan. He had seen so much. One day, she invited him inside and he stayed late. He left her with a wondrous gift: the seed that would become Boy. Then the man stopped coming by, disappearing like a djinn, a magical spirit. When Mother tells this part of the story, she makes a whooshing sound and opens her arms toward the sky.

When the seed was big in her stomach, a wealthy family arrived on the street and wanted to build a home near the hedge. There was so much room, and so few houses. At first the builders left Mother alone, but after a while, they told her she would have to leave. They were going to pour the foundation for the house and sow seeds for grass. The wife, a beautiful lady with henna hair and a waist like a wasp, stopped them. Let her stay here, she said. And so the house was built around the tent, and the garden, trees, and walls all came up around Mother. When Boy was born, a special doctor came, and the house-dwellers brought candy and clothes. Mother kept some of the candy, although it had turned so hard you couldn't eat it anymore, and a lock of his baby hair, a single curl in a metal tin. She painted the lid with swirls of green and blue, using watercolors that the rich man's children had thrown away. She told Boy she envied the people in the house not for what they had, but for what they could give away. They are so generous, she said. She would really never know if she was generous, because she would never have anything she could give away.

The tent is near the rosebushes in the garden. In the spring and summer, Boy wakes up to the smell of flowers and goes to sleep to the smell of freshly cut grass. He lies on the ground at night and looks at a sky full of golden things. But now it is winter. Boy hates the winter.

The house-dwellers have two daughters, and they are in the garden tonight, wearing their sheeplike coats. They're throwing snowballs and chasing each other in circles around the man they made out of snow. Boy's mother pulls him into the tent and tightens his coat over his chest, and they warm themselves by the small fire. A pot of lentils is cooking on a rack.

The girls sneak up to the tent. Boy hears the crunch of their steps, their muffled giggles. All of a sudden, chunks of snow come through the opening, one after another. They land on the blankets, his coat, the flames. The fire dies.

Mother runs outside and shouts after the girls. Boy is five or six years old, old enough to start a new fire by himself. But the snow melts faster than he can remove it. Everything is wet. He leaves the tent and calls after Mother, who comes back crying, and he pulls her back inside. They curl up together. After she stops crying, she tells him to remember that he is lucky to be living in a garden with walls because many people do not have them at all, and Boy thinks of the people he sees living in tents in fields, people called Kochis, and he thinks they must be walking across the whole country looking for a big garden with walls. Yes, Boy is lucky.

3

REBECCA MUST HAVE HEARD DANIEL COME IN, BUT SHE DIDN'T TURN TO FACE HIM. SHE WAS watching the city, which was suspended by lamplight in the hotel window. The sight reminded Daniel of the windshield just before the crash. The way the glass warped the road just a little, making the asphalt ripple in the sun.

He had brought up their suitcase and lodged it in a corner. When he slipped his arms around his wife, it was like embracing a column of marble.

"It went fine," he responded to a question she hadn't asked.

She loosened his arms from her waist. "What happened?" she whispered, not turning toward him.

He told her he had met with the elders and been absolved, the fee accepted as compensation.

She turned and looked closely at him. "Why did you go? And why did it take so long?"

"I'm so sorry." Daniel stroked her hair. "How are you? Have you had anything to eat?"

She gestured dismissively to a tray full of untouched cakes and cold tea. "The owner sent this up." She asked again why he'd been gone so long.

"You know how these things are."

"Actually, I don't."

"It's over now."

Rebecca nodded slowly. On the other side of the door, a couple in the hallway prattled on about their lovely evening. The woman spoke with the inflection of a girl newly in love, her high heels languidly striking the tiles. This was how Daniel and Rebecca's anniversary should have been. Dinner on the town. Returning to the room light-headed from illicitly acquired wine, laughter, expectations.

"I came back as fast as I could," Daniel said. The couple's door clicked shut, their honeyed voices fading. Daniel sank to the bed and took off his shoes, arranging them by the nightstand. The softness of the mattress had a surreal quality to it, as if his body had expected to find only hard, inflexible things. The telephone was on the pillow, the receiver slightly off the cradle, its cord tangled. "Did you call someone?"

"Laila."

"What did you do that for?"

"Because she's my friend. And your friend. And I wanted to talk to her."

Daniel had known Laila all his life, and as a doctor she had helped Rebecca through that terrible time, so why shouldn't she know what had happened? Rebecca had needed to talk to someone. That he could understand, but it rattled him that anyone else should know what he had done. He asked Rebecca to tell no one else about the accident. When she asked why, he said, "It's nobody's business."

They held each other's gaze until her expression softened and she curled up beside him. She touched his face with the back of her hand, her wedding ring cold on his cheek.

"I canceled the hotel in Herat," she said.

He nodded.

"Daniel?"

"Yes?"

"Why did you change your clothes?"

He was prepared for this question. "I spilled something. Tea. They gave me tea."

"Tea." She inhaled sharply. Rising from the bed, she ambled about the room, alternating between nodding and shaking her head. "Tea," she repeated. "Sounds like a pleasant gathering."

She pushed open the window, the city's sounds invading the room. A frantic bicycle horn. A flock of sheep. The unmistakable laughter of teenagers, carefree yet somehow discernibly self-conscious. She inhaled deeply, then came back to the bed and sat beside him, extending her hand. "Daniel," she whispered, "talk to me."

He rose. "I need a shower."

She dropped her hand in her lap as he walked away.

In the bathroom, Daniel undressed and stepped into the blue-tiled stall. He raised his face to the water and pressed his fingers into his temples, desperate to quiet Telaya's voice.

Are you going to look up? she said.

He ignored her. But what sort of man did this make him? Was it not enough that he'd taken her life? Now he was trying to expel her from his head, silence her. A final act of annihilation. He turned the hot-water knob as far as it would go, and steam enveloped him. He thought of the dead Kochi boy in the shack, elegized only by the wind. A boy plucked from a crowd of thousands who could have died in a poppy field just as easily and invisibly as he could have grown old in one.

When the water went cold, he turned it off and stepped onto the bathroom's linoleum floor. His fingers were red and wrinkled. He stood naked before the clouded mirror. With the palm of his hand, he wiped away its condensation. Watching his hand move back and forth, he looked like he was waving to himself. He felt as if it were her. The dead girl was inside him, using his hand to wave to him in the mirror.

Hey, she said.

"Stop," he whispered.

Watch me run, she replied.

Behind him, small pools of water formed and unformed on the tiles of the shower stall. Every drop looked like one of the tiny mirrors gleaming in the backseat of his car. Daniel still remembered the time he had emptied himself of tears, although it seemed like a century since that summer day when his father had caught him eating a bowl of cherries before dinner and, instead of scolding him, crouched down and told him Dorothy had gone back to America. Before that day, he hadn't known that tears could turn from liquid to solid, building a wall around your heart so that you couldn't even cry. For a week, the wall stood rigid in his chest, until one night he fell headlong on the gravel, chasing a wild dog, and it broke apart. He began to cry. He was ashamed to have driven his mother away, ashamed to face the other children at school who still had a mom.

Standing before the mirror now, Daniel felt that wall come up again, hard inside his ribs. He fought Telaya's voice until she vanished and a calming narrative appeared in his defense: the accident was not his fault. But Daniel's conscience shot down each of his defenses like toys gliding by in a carnival game. He splashed cold water on his face.

In the bedroom, Rebecca was pulling a T-shirt over her head, the lace she'd brought with her forgotten. She loosened her hair from its rubber band and turned to him. She was just a shadow, backlit by the fading city.

"I don't know what you need," she said softly.

"We both need sleep." For three months he had longed for her, but she hadn't been ready. Not once had he tried to persuade her. He always said he understood, even when he no longer did. Last night, after packing for the trip and turning the lights out, she had returned to him. It had been tentative, but had felt like a milestone nonetheless, the end of a long winter. Now a different kind of cold was upon them.

Slipping into bed, Rebecca pulled the covers up to her neck and curled up tightly. Everything about her seemed completely closed. Daniel turned the room's only armchair to face the window. In the alley below, men played chess, drank tea from small glasses, and smoked from hookahs. Shopkeepers strolled over to each other, told stories, compared the day's earnings, traded a melon for a Sprite. Men and women appeared and disappeared in the windows of the homes dotting the hills. Daniel watched until they had all gone dark, flickering off like dying fireflies. He wasn't sure what time he went to bed. He slept fitfully, half-awake most of the night, consumed by a feeling that something wanted into his mind and something else wanted out.

Awake before the sun, he repacked their suitcase. Rebecca moved slowly, brushing her hair and twisting into yesterday's blouse and capris. She seemed to pass through several emotions, unable to choose one. Someone brought breakfast to the room, but they barely ate.

"Are you ready?" Daniel asked when Rebecca emerged dressed from the bathroom.

"In a minute."

He took their luggage down, checked out, and waited in the car. The starburst in the damaged windshield made everything look fractured: the sky and the road and the thick morning crowds, and Rebecca when she came out of the hotel. When they reached the highway, it seemed different. The asphalt was darker, the side ditches deeper. Daniel thought he saw shadows rising from them. Then came the moment he could not avoid: the sight of the Kochi camp in the distance. It felt like the nomads were moving toward Daniel instead of him toward them. Rebecca offered her hand, just as she had last night, but he pretended not to notice, afraid she would feel his tremor. She pressed her mouth into a thin line and turned to the window, wedging the hand under her leg.

"Are you all right?" he asked.

She shook her head as if Daniel had asked the wrong thing. He drove over the incline and reached the site of the crash. On the asphalt, the tire marks, splotches of sunbaked blood, and shards of glass were visible. *Out, damned spot!* cried Lady Macbeth in the schoolboy recesses of his mind. Another voice joined her.

I was only nine, Telaya said. *Maybe ten. It isn't fair.*

Suddenly, Rebecca wrapped her arms around her waist and released a whimper.

"What's wrong?" Daniel said, alarmed. Every time she winced like this, he remembered that terrible night when, curled up on the bathroom floor, she wept as he tried to clean the tiles, the towel only swirling blood over the marble floor. Sometimes Daniel thought he still saw a halo of pink hovering beneath him. Laila had talked about infections and scars and trying again.

"I'm fine."

"The medication's in your bag."

"It's not that bad."

"It's bad enough that you're crying."

"That's not why I'm crying." Rebecca struck the window with her fist in frustration. Daniel went silent.

"Do you still want to have the party on Saturday?" she asked an hour later as they neared Kabul. "For Peter."

Daniel had forgotten about Peter Whitbourn's visit. Until yesterday it had loomed over him, but the ghost of a dead child weighed more than the one of a past betrayal. "Sure," he said.

"He's staying with the Sutherlands. They're still friends from when Peter worked for Nixon."

Naturally, Professor Whitbourn would be staying with none other than the American ambassador.

"I don't care if we see him or not," she said.

Daniel had always thought Rebecca was a bad liar. They drove in silence. The smells of Kabul greeted them when they reached the city. It was the scent of naan baking in fiery holes in the ground, of fried meat in carts sold to hurried passersby for a coin or two. The stench of donkeys, urine, gasoline, and dust, but also the perfume of the acacia trees and roses people grew in walled-off gardens everywhere. Maiwand Boulevard was closed, barricades forcing cars into detours because a Russian envoy had passed through here and would do so again tonight. His visit was scheduled to last three days. The detour wasn't well marked, but Daniel knew his way through the city. At the last major intersection before home, on Darlaman Road, the traffic light blinked red, broken since February.

"When are they going to fix that?" he said.

"They're never going to fix that, Daniel." Rebecca sounded like she held him personally responsible for this and many other things.

Watching over their house and the unpaved road, the snowcapped mountains welcomed them back. Even after a short absence, the sight of the majestic range usually left Daniel inspired. Today he found it disquieting, with its strange angles and peaks. Born of the mighty Hindu Kush, the Asmani peaks leaned subtly to the west, so the effect was one of gathering motion, like a cluster of men on the verge of a run.

4

IMRAN HAD BEEN A STREETSWEEPER FOR EIGHT MONTHS. HE HAD LEARNED TO TELL TIME LAST year and measure things like days and weeks, so he was sure it was eight months. Sweeping was a spiritual act for Imran. Every forty strokes, he imagined he was sweeping something away, making room for something new. Forty strokes: forget about the girl who had left him for the fourth time in ten years. She was getting fat anyway, and hairy, like a big sheep with too much wool. Forty more strokes: stop wanting to kill the landlord who had thrown him out again. The son of a goat wasn't worth a prison term.

Dragging his broom along the pavement, Imran passed the national bank, Sajadi Enterprises, and the Ministry of Finance, with the fancy Khyber on the ground floor, a restaurant where Imran could never afford to eat. He made piles of cigarette stubs, candy wrappers, and greasy wax paper mixed with dust and leaves. There was more work than usual this morning. What chaos there had been yesterday—a man shot at 14:05, people shouting and waving flags. Men running around with one of only two ideologies: Communist or Muslim. Imran's parents were Bahai. Sometimes God was prone to excess. Why three religions? If He wanted to see men fight, He only had to make two. Imran swept carefully around the tanks that lined the street like the bums lined the sidewalks. Soldiers peered out of round windows. One stuck his tongue out.

Mr. Sajadi appeared earlier than usual and arrived by bus. Usually, he arrived in a Mercedes. He usually smiled, and Imran smiled back, though he kept his lips together because showing your teeth to a man like Mr. Sajadi would not do.

The gentleman looked different today. Dark circles made his eyes look small. He was hunched over like he was walking through a strong wind. He did not smile. Mr. Sajadi looked like a man who needed to sweep something away.

In the early morning light, Daniel's last name gleamed across the granite facade of the building that housed both Sajadi Gemstones and USADE. He had moved the agency office to his family's building for one simple reason: it had air conditioning. Daniel began every day with the vague sense of having performed a great swindle. He was never sure who the impostor was—whether he was the owner of a great company and scion of a local legend posing as a US official, or the other way around.

His steps echoed on the marble floor. In his mind, they faded into echoes of bare running feet that made no sound when they landed. Gracing the lobby walls were the paintings he'd remembered at the police station. One commemorated the last war against the English. Men of every age were following their young leader, Sayed Sajadi. They rode horses, their scabbards against the animals' flanks, guns angled across their chests. The warriors moved as one, creating a sense of wind-like speed as the eye traveled with the army from left to right. Daniel stepped into the elevator. When he pulled the iron grate over the sliding doors, it was like drawing drapes over blinds, creating the second layer of the solitude he craved.

He walked past the Sajadi office and remembered that Rebecca's earrings would finally be ready, after delays caused by his own insistence on the perfect lapis lazuli. The anniversary had passed, but the jewels should still be hers.

At USADE, the work rose in tidy piles across his desk like a skyline, mocking the city's contours outside. Mud houses climbed up the sides of mountains—Kabul had nowhere else to go. By the phone was a stack of messages, including several from Elias at the newspaper. Daniel spent the morning on mindless tasks—taking phone calls, asking his secretary to make appointments, signing invoices. Miss Soraya brewed tea between errands and brought him a tray. "You're back early from your trip," she said.

When she spoke, she showed deference by lowering her head. She didn't ask about the gash on his brow. She looked different today, as did everyone. Daniel's staff envied him for having the prettiest of the secretaries, but today, Miss Soraya's most striking asset was not her beauty but the fact that she was alive.

When she came around his desk to refill his cup, he slipped his hands into his pockets like a thief hiding evidence. He leafed through the newspapers on his desk. Elvis Presley had died—that was the biggest story, accompanied by a comparison of him and Ahmad Zahir, the Afghan Elvis. Further down, a Communist member of the government had penned an article. He spoke of workers' wages, the dangers of Islamism and the religious right, the sexual exploitation of children, equality of the sexes, and the need for land reform. The Communists weren't wrong about everything. They were right enough to hold appeal, and Daniel sometimes wished their ideas were not so closely tied to one of the most brutal regimes in human history. Wherever there were Communists, there was Russia. And Russia had always pursued conquest, invasion, infiltration, oppression. But now they could pretend they were doing these things in the service of a glorious sisterhood and brotherhood and a better tomorrow that never came.

Below that, there was a short article by Elias. It talked about the scourge of the poppy fields and the need to distribute that land to honest farmers rather than let them fall into the hands of foreign interests.

Foreign interests. Daniel wondered what his own interests were. When he heard the voice of a youngster, he thought his mind was playing tricks on him again. Miss Soraya came slinking through the door after a gentle knock, a letter in her hand and amusement on her face. "An urchin just came by and left this for you," she said. "He insisted I deliver it personally."

The envelope was addressed to Daniel, not USADE. Daniel strode to the window, pushing aside the sheers. A boy in ragged clothes was running from the building as fast as his feet could take him, threading through the cars and crowds.

Before returning to her desk, Miss Soraya said, "Sir, the others are wondering about a staff meeting."

When he paused, she added, "It's just that . . . well, there hasn't been one. In seven months. Since you got here."

"Who's asking for one?"

"Everyone. Mr. Epstein, Mr. Romano."

"I see."

When she lingered, he asked if there was anything else.

"Mr. Kauffman held meetings every week, sir."

"Mr. Kauffman is no longer directing this office." He regretted his tone as soon as the words escaped his mouth. "But you're right. Let's set one up soon."

She left him alone. Staff meetings. Hadn't they been the undoing of his predecessor? Too many opinions, too much compromise, and not enough work. If Philip Kauffman had stopped taking advice from everyone, he might have stayed in his position and been able to achieve more than he did. Under his tenure, only one poppy field had been reformed, and the results were disastrous. Irrigating the land without proper planning, they had only drawn the salt up to the surface and ruined the soil. Since Daniel's arrival, three plots of land had been reformed. It was true that they were small, their khans poor and willing to work with USADE. But the Yassaman field wasn't small, and it would be the fourth. Daniel had planned to take it over since he'd first read the file back in January. The true Reform would start there.

He was still holding the letter. He slid the letter opener along the crease. The churning feeling in his gut had returned. As he read, he could sense what each next word would be, as if the author's intention could travel faster than light.

To Daniel Abdullah Sajadi, my esteemed new friend and compatriot:

I trust that God is keeping you well, and that you have recovered from your recent injury. While I am saddened by that unfortunate day, I am grateful that God has chosen to place a man such as yourself in my path, and I believe you will agree that God's reasons are evident. I would not dare suggest that I, a simple son of the land, am in any way your equal. But I was humbled to find that I share with you a great love of country and an abiding sense of duty. And I was overjoyed to learn you worked for the American

*government, for I believe I understand your agency's
mission better than most.*

*I hope you forgive me for taking the liberty of
writing, but I must ask for your indulgence in a
request. I should like to present you with a proposal,
from one patriot to another.*

*I shall call upon you soon and hope this missive
prepares you for my visit, so that my appearance will
seem neither impudent nor sudden.*

*My humility prevents me from writing my name in
a letter that contains yours.*

Your faithful servant

Balling up the paper, Daniel controlled the tremor in
his hands. He was grateful when someone knocked. Iggy
Romano and Seth Epstein stood in the doorway, a huddle of
farmers behind them.

"Just back from a workshop at the university," Seth said.
He had a jacket on despite the heat, his hair carefully styled
to cover his encroaching baldness. It was difficult to imagine
him digging ditches in Kenya and Bangladesh, where he'd
overseen the construction of complex irrigation systems,
dams, and canals. Daniel could smell urine and hay and the
warm, earthy scent of an animal, and noticed a mass of fur
moving in the hallway.

"One of the trainees brings his mule everywhere," Iggy said.
"His last one was stolen, so he won't leave it outside." His
young face was shiny, and his belly swelled against his shirt.

"We're going to take these guys to lunch and get Miss Soraya's birthday present while we're at it. We still don't have your
share." Seth held out his hand, and Daniel retrieved his wallet.

"Did you read my memo?" Seth continued, again making
his case for more workshops and equipment.

What Seth and Iggy talked about would have bored most people. But Daniel admired them, because engineers understood that great civilizations were built on boring things like trenches and pipes. He gave them enough cash for a nice gift, apologizing for forgetting Miss Soraya's birthday.

"Kauffman never forgot things like that," Seth said, counting the bills. "I guess he was used to having staff, seeing as he'd been around a long time."

"I've got a lot on my desk right now," Daniel said, gesturing to the door. He was in no mood to be reminded that some people resented his arrival and blamed him for Kauffman's ousting. No one needed to tell him that an analyst did not become a regional director overnight at age thirty-one without connections.

The engineers left. Trying to concentrate on Seth's memo, which he found in the middle of a pile, Daniel couldn't stop his mind from drifting back to the letter. When the phone rang, he almost expected to hear Taj's voice, but Miss Soraya connected Laila, who had called to say Rebecca had been in bed at home all day. She just needed to rest, Laila explained.

"Is she okay? Did you figure out what was wrong? She was really in pain yesterday, even though she kept saying it wasn't bad. You know how she is."

"She's fine. She was almost five months in, Daniel. It's going to take some time."

Daniel could hear the bustle of the clinic in the background. A baby's cries escalated to screams. Before disconnecting, Laila added that she was looking forward to the party Saturday night.

He threw the khan's letter into the trash bin and was suddenly overwhelmed by fatigue, as if the sun had pierced his skin and shot a sleep serum into his veins. He pulled off his jacket. Something fell from the pocket. It was the mirror from the girl's dress, winking in the light. He held it in his palm and stared. Long ago, he'd asked his father why people sewed mirrors on their clothes. Sayed said, *Because sometimes they wonder if they are invisible, and this reminds them that they are not.* The telephone rang for the twentieth time.

"It's Leland." There were no pleasantries when Daniel's supervisor called him from Washington, DC. "I tried you at that goddamn hotel in Herat, but they said you weren't there. Now I find you here." Daniel could hear Leland Smythe puffing on a cigarillo. "Good news. It's going to be filmed."

"What's going to be filmed, sir?"

"It's Leland. How many times do I have to tell you?"

"What's going to be filmed, Leland?"

"What do you think? The whole Reform. From the time you pull those poppies out by the head to the moment the wheat grows in nice and tall. They'll try to put it on the air next year with Cronkite. We need to see a lot of happy locals. Is that clear?"

Daniel squeezed his eyes shut. "You're going to let them film the Reform?"

"You're welcome."

"I'm not sure the Ministry of Planning will be on board with that."

"They already are. It's going to be broadcast there, too, for whoever's got a TV, although I guess that's about the same number of people as a curling team in Cuba."

"Sir, if we needed to postpone the Reform, how would we go about that?"

After a prolonged silence, it seemed like a different man was on the phone. A measured, somber voice sliced through the receiver. "Was that supposed to be a joke?"

"It's just that—"

"Tell me I wasn't wrong when I convinced everybody you

knew what you were doing. A lot of them were pushing for smaller fields. Telling me you weren't ready. That you were too green, and that having a last name the locals could pronounce wasn't a qualification."

"I remember."

"Changing course is not an option."

Daniel apologized. "I was just thinking out loud."

"Well, don't. If you're thinking stupid, think silent. That's a basic rule of politics. Hell, it's a basic rule of life."

"Yes, sir."

"Whatever's going on over there, take care of it and see your project through. That's how it works. If you can't, pack your suitcase and stop wasting the government's time and dime. You've got Greenwood to help you."

"Who?"

"Dannaco-Hastings's new boy, Bob Greenwood. Christ, haven't you met him yet?"

Daniel had never heard of him.

"You've got a consultant coming your way," Smythe said, exasperated. "Dannaco insisted, after the whole bit with Kauffman. And all this filming means there's a lot at stake for them. Get to it. He's already there. How did you miss that in the report?"

"We don't need a consultant from Dannaco. They provide the equipment, that's it."

Another pause. "They need to know what's going on. They have a lot of money riding on this. Are you with me?" Smythe went on to say the new consultant would be easy to manage, since he lacked experience. He'd worked in Latin America in far lesser posts. "Besides, it's mostly about Agent Ruby for Dannaco. They don't care too much about the rest."

"Sir?"

Across the line, Daniel heard Leland chew. "This donut's

dry. Fuck it. Anyway, don't you read any of the stuff I keep telexing? I'm not writing these reports for my personal enjoyment."

Daniel retrieved the Yassaman file from his desk. Flipping through the pages, he found the telex. It was dated yesterday. "I'm just getting caught up, Mr. Smythe."

"It's Leland." He made a slurping sound. "Damn, this coffee's weak. But what else is new. Okay, catch up quick and let me know. Agent Ruby's a great thing. The committee likes it. Get those godforsaken poppies out, plant something else, and feed those folks. I'll tell you something, Daniel. A good piece of land is like a young woman: with the right touch, it can really be turned into something." Before abruptly ending the call, he added, "Follow your orders."

In the report, Agent Ruby was described in two pages authored by Robert Greenwood, whose photo was stapled at the top. Peering out was a frat boy with antiseptic eyes and a formaldehyde smile. Daniel read over the appraisal. It was typed on paper so bright, it was an affront to his mood. He had managed to silence the dead girl's voice, so she resorted to trickeries of sight. On one page, the word *Telex* blurred and became *Telaya*. The *p* in *prove* flipped itself, transforming the word into *drove*. *Danger* dropped its *d*, the word *anger* blooming in his vision instead.

Her game was not the only sinister thing in his files. It seemed everything had to do with Vietnam, and Agent Ruby was no exception. The war had given the DEA an idea for how to choke the growing supply of heroin coming into America, and the stakes were higher than ever because thousands of GIs had come home with more than missing limbs. Heroin had been cheap in Saigon, flowing through the city and soldiers' veins. Demand soon soared in Los Angeles, New York, and everywhere in between. In Mexico, growers stepped in to fill the void, quickly turning out what everyone called Mexican Mud, less pure than the China White of the Asian refineries. At first, Mexican Mud trickled into California. Then it poured.

Daniel had heard a lot about Mexican Mud, less because of his job and more because Rebecca's sister was mired in its murky depths, as addicted as any GI. No one had heard from Sandy in months, and the family worried night and day. Some absences made the heart grow fonder; others just made it break.

If the report was right, Sandy would soon run out of Mexican Mud. The effectiveness of Agent Orange in Vietnam had led the DEA to spray it over Mexico's poppies. The report described the operation in detail. Washington had declared a drug victory only days ago, after the Mexican fields were drenched with the defoliant. The heroin supply was about to fall dramatically. Demand might not, but the report left that out. Nor did it state that for farmers big and small in Fever Valley, for Manticores and hungry villagers and nomads, the existence of eight hundred thousand American heroin users looking for a fix was a gold mine.

Agent Orange was quickly making a bad name for itself. In Vietnam, the report said, children were being born with eyes missing and lungs that were too small. Young women developed rare cancers. Nothing would grow where Orange had been sprayed. Not soy, not beans, not even rice. Agent Ruby was Dannaco-Hastings's alternative. It had been tested in controlled environments but had yet to be used on a real field. The corporation promised its defoliant was safer, sparing human life and leaving the soil ready for new seeds within months.

This was the first time Daniel had read about Agent Ruby. On any other day, he would immediately have asked his staff to gather information, make calls, and set up appointments. Instead, he focused on the last few sentences of the report: *Kochis are cheap labor. Too cheap. Need farmers to hire local villagers, or land reform will fail.*

At least this was something the State Department had in common with both the Communists and the rising National Islamic Movement that had been quarreling for years. The Communists talked of settling the nomads in cities and towns, calling it a "civilizing mission." But everyone knew they wanted to register and settle them because they drove down wages, weakening the swelling working class, and because many would never belong to a state. The clerics didn't like them because they practiced religion the wrong way, Islam mixed with superstition. Daniel told his secretary to call the Ministry of Planning. "Ask Mr. Sherzai to come see me. Please tell him I'm sorry for the short notice, but it's urgent."

Twenty minutes later, Kabir Sherzai walked through the door. He'd been given an office in the Ministry of Finance nearby, specifically because it was convenient to USADE, and the agency now took up most of his time.

"*Agha*," Daniel said, addressing him with the honorific he'd used since childhood. They embraced, but Daniel let go more quickly than usual. Sherzai fell heavily into the chair across from Daniel, leaning his satchel and cane against the desk. His sleeves were too short and his trousers a little too long, accentuating his bad leg. Daniel felt the old man's eyes bore through him, and he was sure Sherzai knew about the accident, Telaya, about Taj, all the things Daniel didn't say.

"You're back early," Sherzai said.

"Something came up."

"You call me like this without explanation and expect me

to drop everything?" The Vice-Minister of Planning folded his arms over his ill-fitting belt. His caterpillar brows looked like they wanted to crawl off his face. He tucked his chin and narrowed his eyes, which betrayed his ancestry. They were his mother's eyes, the same Hazara eyes Daniel saw on the faces of housekeepers, gardeners, and cooks all over Kabul. His gaze made him look serious even when he wasn't, which was seldom.

"Even *you* need a good reason for this." He reached for Daniel's Marlboros, tapped out a cigarette, and snatched a solid-gold lighter from the desk. "I always forget how much this weighs," he said, turning the Davidoff over in his palm. His words were tinged with admiration. Long ago, someone had told Daniel that admiration was just a manifestation of resentment. It was hard to assign such a petty trait to Sherzai, but treating him as a colleague felt unnatural, too. To say Sherzai had raised Daniel wouldn't be entirely true, because Daniel had been fourteen when his father died. But Sherzai had been his guardian, and old patterns did not die easily.

"I wanted to know what you thought of this report, *agha*," Daniel said. "Who is Bob Greenwood, and why does he get to poison our fields?"

"This couldn't have waited?" Sherzai tapped the report. "It seems self-explanatory to me. We'll find out more about Greenwood on Saturday." Sherzai must have sensed Daniel's confusion, because he added, "At your party."

"Of course."

"You've invited Elias, too, yes? He's a good boy." On another day, it might have been funny to hear Sherzai refer to his Communist half-nephew as a "good boy," but laughing seemed indecent.

"Mr. Greenwood will be my personal guest," Sherzai continued.

"Does he have to be?"

"Do you want to call him yourself to rescind the invitation? Or do you want Smythe to tell him he can't come? He wants you to make the man feel welcome."

"Then I suppose I will."

"What's wrong with you today?"

"I just have a lot of work to do." Daniel was on his feet.

"Are you throwing me out, after summoning me here like a servant?" Sherzai rose as well, so they stood face-to-face with the desk between them. His face was a mask of creases, and Daniel felt, as he often did when Sherzai was before him, that he was shorter than the man, though he was taller by two inches. They had been enough like father and son to maintain affection and tension at once, but not enough to know what they really were to each other. The question always hung there, unasked.

"What's the matter with you, *batche'm*?"

"The trip didn't go as we planned." Daniel had spoken so quietly that Sherzai, who had just addressed him as a son, asked him to repeat himself.

"I keep thinking about Kauffman," Daniel said, louder.

"The old director?"

"They fired him because he did what everybody told him to, even when he knew they were wrong. I don't want to make the same mistake. That's all."

"That's what you're worried about? Kauffman did his best and was loyal to his government."

"Sometimes, laziness can look like loyalty. Being obedient can just mean you're a coward."

The vice-minister looked at the ceiling and opened his arms as if releasing a bushel of balloons. "No one would mistake you for a lazy coward. What has one day of vacation done to you?" He leaned in closer and studied Daniel's face. "Whatever hit you on the head has affected your mind."

Daniel remembered the gash, which had swollen overnight. "An accident in the tool shed."

"Given the state of your last woodworking project," Sherzai said gently, "I wasn't sure you were spending much time in the shed these days." He placed a hand on Daniel's shoulder. "What happened?"

"I think I wasn't paying attention, and I bumped into something." Daniel pulled away and dropped into his chair, the leather squishing under his body, wheels chattering along the floor. He pushed aside the thought of that last woodworking project, a half-finished crib meant as a surprise for Rebecca.

By the window stood a caddy stacked with bottles, most of them full. Sherzai limped to the makeshift bar, leaving behind his cane, which fell to the floor. His damaged leg rejected his attempts to walk faster. He poured whiskey, the neck of the bottle rattling against the edge of the glass. He steadied his hand and brought Daniel the drink, repeating his usual mantra. "Just medicinal. Never more than one. And never for fun."

The whiskey slowed Daniel's racing mind. Sherzai stood across from him again. "If they want to use this Agent Ruby"—he made a twirling gesture with his wrist—"you will have little say in the matter. And why be against it? Perhaps it will work." In his eyes was concern, perhaps even love, but Daniel could bear neither right now.

"Work for who?"

"Do you remember the Scale of Sages?"

It had been years since Daniel had thought of his father's illusory device. As a boy, Daniel would sit on his bed and mimic Sayed using the invisible scale, calibrating nonexistent pieces in his hands. He was in no mood for deciphering one of his father's many opaque notions, so he said, "Vaguely." He gestured to the piles on his desk. "I really should get back to all this."

Sherzai raised his eyebrows, which seemed closer than ever to managing their escape. "I am not finished," he said, and Daniel fell quiet. "Your father thought everyone was born with a sacred scale, a gift they didn't bother to use. If you had to choose between two principles, all you had to do was determine how much each one weighed." Sherzai made a scale with his hands. "The heavier one won out. Your father said it was easy, like riding a bicycle." Sherzai shook his head at the carpet. "But he was wrong. It's never easy."

"What happens when you put Agent Ruby on the Scale of Sages?" Daniel said.

"I hate the poppies, and that hatred outweighs my love of almost anything else. Let our friends at Dannaco bring their poison."

Over the years, after Daniel had gone to America and tried to put his childhood behind him, he'd sometimes wondered if those who criticized Sherzai had been right: maybe the vice-minister's war against the poppies was driven not by loyalty to his old friend Sayed, but by the desire to outshine him. But the people who whispered such things—neighbors, cousins, even classmates who thought everyone who looked like Sherzai had to be jealous—did not know the man. They did not know that Sherzai sat on the floor despite his aching body as he played with Daniel's electric train and told him his father would be back from prison before he knew it. They had never seen Sherzai wearing an apron, covered in flour and sweat, his sausage fingers doing their best with the sticky dough so he could make Daniel fresh naan when the cook left to tend to his sick brother. There were so many things they had never seen.

Daniel thought about the poison the government wanted to spray indiscriminately on the poppies, armed with studies and hopes and, most of all, the power that came from not caring too much what happened afterward. "There must be a better way to deal with the poppies," he said.

"Better ways don't matter when this is what Dannaco-Hastings wants. And the State Department. Mr. Smythe has made his decision."

"He's only one man."

"Some men's words weigh more than others."

Daniel had heard that phrase before, too. Sherzai had said it when the king's men came to arrest Sayed twenty years ago. Daniel had tried to free himself from Sherzai's grip, desperate to chase the car that was taking his father away. He'd insisted it was unfair, but Sherzai had reminded him that the king's words weighed more than fairness, more than anyone else's words.

"What do you think my father would have done about Agent Ruby?" Daniel asked.

"Your father would have done what was necessary to defeat an enemy."

As the silence between them grew, Sherzai gathered a sheath of bound papers from his satchel. "Since I'm here," he said, handing it to Daniel. "Read this, please."

"Where do I sign?"

"You should at least look at it. It's your company, after all."

"I didn't earn it."

"And yet it's yours." A quiet bitterness stained the vice-minister's words. Daniel had to stop himself from reminding Sherzai of the thing neither of them ever brought up. Sherzai had almost bankrupted the gemstone company after Sayed's death, righting the ship only by violating Sayed's wish that the firm conduct business only in local currencies and not take payment in pounds or dollars. To Sayed, the English were the enemy and the Americans their allies, Europe as a whole was too fickle to trust with its shifting alliances, and the Russians were worse than anyone with their false ideologies and true brutalities.

As Daniel signed his name where Sherzai indicated, he wondered if the anger he felt showed on his face. How could Sherzai make remarks about the Sajadis' wealth? If it wasn't for Daniel's father, Sherzai would have died at the age of three, the year he was struck by a nameless virus. The elder Sajadi brought in the best doctors from abroad to save little Sherzai, his gardener's son, because Sajadi's own child, Sayed, loved the boy despite a ten-year age gap and a much larger gap of a different kind. Sherzai was left with only a limp, which he cursed as a malediction and his family praised as a miracle. He had been lucky, but Daniel would never dare tell him so.

Perhaps he was being unfair. Sherzai's decision to finally let the gemstone company accept foreign currency had not only saved it, but brought its profits to new heights. There were no diamonds or fine rubies in the country, no stones that could make a nation wealthy, but there were enough semiprecious gems to make a few men rich. The only trouble was that being rich in afghanis was not like being rich in dollars. Not even close, as Daniel had found when he moved to Los Angeles for university, where he was suddenly nothing more than "comfortable" rather than rich. By his senior year, that had changed, thanks to Sherzai. Daniel had been lucky, too, but Sherzai never told him so.

Wedging the company report back in his satchel, the old man gripped his cane and stood. "I have work to do." He moved deftly, his walking stick like an extra limb that granted him a new physical power. "Take care of your wound." Sherzai gestured to his own brow. "You don't want it getting infected."

They shared polite goodbyes. Daniel closed the door. Slowly, the rhythms of the day began to feel normal. He could imagine a time when the accident would seem long past. Whatever Taj wanted, he would not get, and he would eventually recede into the background just like the opium trade. Rebecca would recover from this, too. She would recover from everything. She and Daniel would try again, and this time they would be luckier.

5

THE ROOM GREW SHADOWED AS THE AFTERNOON WORE ON, A RARE SUMMER STORM SWELLING outside. Thunder bellowed as lightning gilded the sky. Daniel looked out the window. Three stories below on the rain-polished pavement walked a blind man, arms outstretched, gait like a child's tentative shuffle. His wet clothes were pasted to his skin, his naked feet parting puddles as he struggled against the storm. Pedestrians hustled past each other and cars navigated the traffic circle at whatever speed the traffic allowed.

A businessman paced back and forth, glancing at his watch as a dark figure rippled into view, something billowing in the wind. It was a woman cloaked in a *chaderi*; she raised her head to look at the punishing sky through the mesh-covered eye panel. She drifted into the blind man's orbit. Walking into each other, they both lost their footing. The businessman helped the blind man to his feet but did nothing for the woman, checking his watch again as he crossed the street.

When Daniel took his briefcase and left the office, Miss Soraya and the others had already gone, the hallways dark besides the glare of fluorescent bulbs. A guard touched two fingers to his cap and wished him a good night. Outside, Daniel looked around, ready to help the woman, but she was no longer there. He set off toward home. It was a four-mile walk, but tonight he didn't mind, and he thought he would never again mind walking a long distance, nor did he mind the rain that lashed at his clothes and his face. He headed south toward the river.

The roads were thick with honking cars, their drivers frustrated by cyclists, imperious camels, flocks of sheep, and mules that refused to move. Tonight, all the cars seemed larger and louder than usual. A white Datsun honked, a long, plaintive sound, and the car filled Daniel's vision and the honking sound became the screech of brakes and it all dissolved in a burning smell that made him stop breathing until his instincts forced him to inhale. He passed small shops that sold everything from lentils and onions to Timex watches and American jeans.

He passed a billboard advertising a three-year-old movie, *The Godfather: Part II*, its arrival next week at the Ariana Cinema billed as a major event. Towering over the sidewalk, the poster was partly torn down the middle, the gash running the length of Al Pacino's considerable nose. On the edge of the sidewalk stood a man in an elegant suit. As Daniel walked by, the stranger turned and threw a convivial arm around him.

"What an honor," Taj said.

Daniel shrugged off his arm.

The opium khan recoiled in mock surprise. "Did you not like my letter?"

Daniel stepped into a puddle, splashing the cuffs of Taj's trousers and leather shoes and his own rain-soaked clothes. When he didn't respond, Taj continued. "We have much to talk about."

"I don't see it that way."

"You need glasses, then." Taj straightened his tie. "Which would explain why you didn't see me from your window. You came out terribly fast."

"I don't have time for this," Daniel said, recognizing Taj as the businessman on the sidewalk.

"I thought I might catch you at lunch, but my lookout boy told me you never came out.

The bloodlust Daniel had felt in the Yassaman field returned. He wanted to throw this man to the pavement and slam his head into it so hard he could hear the skull break and watch the blood matte his Brylcreemed hair. Watch the vain smirk turn into an incredulous gasp.

Before he could move, the khan took him under the arm. "Don't do anything stupid, Daniel Sajadi."

With his tidy sideburns and wire-rimmed glasses, which he likely did not need, he looked like any accountant renting space in Daniel's building. His aftershave smelled of cloves, and he was shorter than Daniel remembered, but just as thin.

"I'll try not to. As grateful as I am for the advice, I think I'll be okay."

Taj kept pace. "My poppies will be ready for harvesting soon."

"It's good of you to give me a heads-up. But I already knew that."

They passed a hookah lounge where four police officers were framed in the open window, sharing a water pipe. Tendrils of smoke escaped, the sweet fragrance drifting into the evening. "Those policemen might be interested in what you're up to," Daniel said.

"Indeed," Taj replied. "The efficiency of our law-enforcement stallions is such that I often find myself unable to sleep, trembling at the thought of their imminent arrival and the pioneering tactics they will use to subdue me." He gestured back toward the *Godfather* billboard. "When I say the poppies are ready, this is not some kind of mafia code for something else, like in your movies."

They had crossed the river and flanked the old part of the city with its labyrinthine streets and shops. They entered Shor Bazaar, where musicians sat in crooked stairwells, the sounds of the *tabla* and *rubab* rising in the air. They played only for each other, the passersby passing by. Daniel concentrated on his surroundings as if the sights and sounds could drown out the khan's presence. Three women with pageboy haircuts and skinny heels came clicking down the sidewalk, complaining about their salaries. A boy with a mule offered Daniel a half kilo of almonds and promised to throw in a bag of raisins. Against a crumbling wall sat the old man without arms Daniel often saw. Next to him was a boy, maybe nine years old, who helped fetch food and in return had a parent figure.

With Taj still beside him, Daniel didn't want to make the turn onto the road toward home, so he stopped at a pizza parlor that also made local specialties. He walked past a plastic table sheltered by a dripping umbrella, the name Cinzano printed along its scalloped edge. Although the restaurant complied with alcohol laws by trying to cover up liquor names with pictures of dishes from the menu, some of the pictures hung precariously, failing at their purpose.

The Pepsi sign in the window flickered on, the lights flashing red, white, and blue as they rippled. With Taj on his heels, Daniel considered turning back to the office, but that would be too close to fleeing.

"Invite me to dinner," said the opium khan. "You owe me."

Daniel sat at a small table with a red-and-white tablecloth, his briefcase awkwardly heavy. The opium khan sat opposite him and after a moment said, "The silent treatment? Very well. All the better that you should listen."

A waiter hurriedly lit a candle and placed it before them along with two glasses, which he splashed full of water. Daniel ordered lamb skewers to take home, just enough for

Rebecca. He wasn't hungry. He watched passersby in the street, acutely aware of Taj's warm breath and cologne.

"You've had two days to recuperate from your shock. I hope that you are thinking more clearly, as I am here to reiterate my request. It's a simple and reasonable one."

Daniel studied the open kitchen, where men in flour-dusted caps tossed dough in the air.

"I beseech you once more: Do not destroy the poppies in the Yassaman field. They are the fruit of my labor. Do you understand?" Taj smiled only with his lips. From his pocket, he produced a Milky Way, which he unwrapped carefully, tearing the foil cleanly along the seams. He picked up a knife from the table and shaved a slice from his chocolate bar.

Daniel pressed his feet into the floor, eyes locked on the blade. How did one talk to a man like this? His father would have known. He hoped his next words would convince the opium khan to leave him alone. "Let's say, for the sake of argument, that some parallel universe existed where I wanted to help you. I couldn't, because the fields are destroyed in order, and once that order is determined by Washington, it's carved in stone." Before today, the statement would have been a lie, but the call with Smythe made it true.

Taj closed his eyes and considered Daniel's comment. "Very well. Another approach then." Taj drank deeply from his glass until it was empty. "Mr. Sajadi, if you do not leave the Yassaman field alone, I will kill every Kochi that was to help with that harvest. Every man, every woman." He dabbed the corners of his lips with a napkin. He widened his eyes when he added, "Every child."

Daniel searched for some coded meaning in this declaration, something to make it less monstrous. He suddenly found himself wishing to see Telaya's face and hear her voice, as if her presence would give him courage and strength against the khan, but she did not appear. He leaned across the table, and it felt like he would never be able to lift his fingers off the sticky wax tablecloth. "What did you say?"

Taj repeated his threat, wiping his glasses with his sleeve. He shaved another slice from the chocolate bar. A dry, bitter fluid collected in Daniel's mouth. He was suddenly aware of the bad disco music bouncing off the walls. The waiter arrived with his order and the bill.

"Here," Taj said, pointing to his lip and offering Daniel a napkin. "You perspire easily." When Daniel did not react, the Manticore folded the napkin neatly and arranged it parallel to the table's edge.

In the seconds that followed, the past, present, and future crashed together in Daniel's thoughts. He chastised himself for the despair that he hoped did not show on his face, for wishing he could ask his father what to do, or *agha*, for wishing again to see the girl whose ghost threw him into another dimension where she ran free, where he'd held her hand and stopped her from running into the road. And yet he sounded composed when he said: "You would gain nothing from the death of all those people."

"You're right, which is not surprising, because you are in every way my superior. I gain nothing." Taj aimed a steady finger at Daniel. "But *you* lose a great deal. Because their lives are now in your hands." He pointed to the cardboard box the waiter had brought, a greasy stain spreading over its lid. "In any case, you must go, or your meat will get cold. Is this for your wife? Surely she deserves a finer meal."

Daniel felt his body clench when the man mentioned Rebecca.

"You appear to find my request unexpected," Taj continued. "You've left me no choice. If one cannot appeal to a man's honor, one must move on to his fear."

A trio of adolescents came in, ordering enough pizza for a large party. They leaned against the counter in their fringed denim jackets, their backs to the kitchen as they laughed at inside jokes.

"You don't know how the world works," Daniel said. "I can't stop the Yassaman field from being reformed."

"Which world? There is only your world and mine." Taj was on his feet. "I know you'll find a way to honor my request. I expect a confirmation of that tomorrow night. Come find me at the Zoroaster. You know the club, I assume?"

Daniel shook his head. "You'll never get what you want."

"I have a better chance than you, because at least I know what I want. And now, though you have been a charming dinner companion, I must take my leave." Taj walked away and vanished into the storm-cleansed air. He was nowhere in sight when Daniel resumed his walk home.

The rain had stopped. The restaurant bag felt slippery in his fingers, as did the handle of his briefcase. An aging voice rang out behind him. It was the man without arms, asking Daniel where he was going. He squatted beside the invalid and the orphan huddled next to him.

"I only asked where you were going, sir," the man said, eyes glistening with fear. "Don't hurt me."

The orphan placed a protective hand on his friend's leg, telling Daniel to leave him alone.

"I'm not going to hurt you, my friend. I'm just wondering: Why are you sitting here?" Daniel pointed south to the boulevard with more thickly populated sidewalks. "There's more food and money down that way."

The man said matter-of-factly, "I am full of broken glass. If I move, I'll be sliced up like a lamb from the inside. I have to be very careful."

"Take this," said Daniel, handing the bag to the child.

There was abundant food at home, and the cook would make something better.

"I'm not hungry," said the man without arms.

"You must be."

"I'm not. When my wife was alive, I had a home. We didn't have a home outside, but we had one inside." The man looked down at his concave stomach. "In here. You understand? Then my wife died and the home fell apart, and all the windows broke, and the pieces of glass stayed inside me. That's how it is."

Daniel gave the pair all the cash he had. As he walked away, the man said, "There is such worry on your face. I pray you find peace."

Find peace. Peace wasn't like a wallet, something you simply found when it was misplaced. Sometimes, it was just lost. As he reached the T-shaped intersection and turned right on Jada Maiwand, Daniel heard a chorus of angry voices rising. Looking ahead, he saw a dozen men assembling on the sidewalk. People were arguing about something. Their disparate cries coalesced into a single chant: "Death to Russia! Death to Communism! Islam is the true way!"

Men walked across the street or emerged from shops, joining the growing chorus. The police wouldn't be far behind. Women quickened their pace, pulling their headscarves tight and their children close. Those in *chaderi* glided by, padding along the walls like fleeing thieves. Daniel saw what had sparked the confrontation. An unmanned tank loomed at the curb near an alley, and while that was nothing remarkable, someone had tied a makeshift flag to its turret: a square of red fabric, the call to Russian sympathizers and Communists. Men with long beards scrambled up the tank, standing on its roof, broadcasting their contempt through cupped hands. One of them tore the banner off its pole and held it triumphantly in the air before throwing it to the pavement. His feet were bare, but his head was covered. Rebecca always described this as being "dressed upside down."

The chanting was accompanied by applause and shouting that was reaching a frenzied pitch. Daniel smelled gasoline. Flames rose inside a circle of cheering men. People knocked into him, rushing away from the turmoil. It was then that he saw her. Laila was striding down the boulevard, arms linked with women to her right and left. He sometimes saw her on his way home as she left the clinic for the day. But never like this. She was walking with a crowd defending that red flag, yelling against those who had set the fire. What was she doing? A man seized her elbow, barking something that Daniel could not hear. She snapped her arm back, her chin raised to his face. Sirens pierced the air. The melee grew with the fire, hordes quarreling on the sidewalks and spilling onto the street.

He dropped his briefcase and ran toward Laila. She didn't see him. She looked like she wouldn't see anything besides what she wanted to see. The sirens grew louder. Angry faces were disfigured by the strobing lights of police cars. It wasn't long before the crowd dissolved. Some fled the guns and batons, evaporating into the city's backstreets, while others crowded around the soldiers and cops, shouting.

Laila was not the only person Daniel recognized. Khaiyam, the cleric who had once been in charge of his admittedly pointless religious education, was with the first group. He had been at every protest, planned or otherwise, for as long as Daniel could remember. Protests were few, because neither the old king nor the new president allowed them. And Khaiyam had been part of that failed Islamic coup two years ago that no one seemed to care about. He'd survived the arrests and executions that followed and still managed to appear so often he was among the most famous clerics in the city, even though he was only a mullah, not an imam. The distinction didn't matter much here anyway. This wasn't like Iran, with its strict religious order and hierarchies.

Khaiyam had been kind to Daniel when Sayed was in prison. Even kinder after he died. Whatever strength Daniel had found in religion, he had found in those impossible months. He waved to him now, and Khaiyam waved back before being absorbed by the human mass. Daniel weaved through the crowd toward Laila but could not reach her. Her hair had slipped from its ponytail, and the scarf swung back and forth in her hand as she stalked up the boulevard.

Someone tugged at his clothes. It was the orphan. He was holding Daniel's briefcase, which made him look even smaller. "I kept it safe!" The boy's smile took up most of his moon face as he held it out for Daniel. A middle-aged man in a suit turned and scanned the boy lasciviously, but when he tried to talk to him, the boy spat in his face and decamped back toward the pizzeria. Daniel hoped his own child—the one he hoped would one day be born—would be as smart as that orphan.

He thought about the children of the Yassaman field, of an article in the day's paper about deepening inequality and the treatment of children. He could understand why people like Laila thought revolutionary communism was the only way. But they were wrong.

He turned left on Darlaman Road. The broken traffic light welcomed him from a hundred yards away with its glassy red wink. Eventually he entered that familiar section of smaller paths with no lights, leaving the chaos behind. He breathed deeply, grateful for the cool night air. As the sirens faded, so did the gasoline and flames, until the protest was nothing more than an echo. A cyclist rode past, clinking his bell, proud that he had one. They shared a small smile.

Almost home, he was relieved to feel the unpaved road, now muddy from rain, under his soles. Soon, he would hear Rebecca at the piano. Every evening she played arpeggios and scales for hours. Only afterward would she allow herself the pleasures of true melody. Rebecca had a simple goal: to spend more time at her piano each day than her office typewriter. On Mondays, Wednesdays, and Fridays, when she returned from her part-time job at the embassy, she sometimes played from dusk to dawn.

Daniel's house was at the end of the street, villas rising on either side, five in all. Beyond were hills, slopes of barren land. The street had no name, but some people called it Dollar Djinn Lane—djinns were mischievous, powerful spirits, and only supernatural beings could make people so rich even in dollars. It was easier to be a millionaire in the local currency, after all. A million afghanis was only about eleven thousand dollars. The residents of Dollar Djinn Lane were referred to as "American millionaires," though they were mainly locals, Daniel the only one with an American parent.

He had known most of his neighbors since he was a boy. Their parents still lived with them in their childhood homes, because their fathers were alive and their mothers hadn't left them. The Nesbars, who were bankers, lived diagonally across from Daniel and Rebecca, three generations under one roof. Daniel passed the lavish home of the Yusafzais, the heirs to a carpet empire. The elderly patriarchs would have known Sayed, but Sayed didn't have friends so much as followers, a role that didn't suit everyone. A few houses down lived a government official, a known Communist whose thirteen-year-old son, Keshmesh, had become buddies with Daniel.

Like on every night, lepers lined the walls around every

house on the block. Where their noses and fingertips should have been, there were red scabs and large open sores that loomed large in Daniel's vision, as if his sense of sight had grown sharper after its catastrophic failure on the road. The lepers looked at the flies on their ruined fingers the same way they looked at the world around them, like there was nothing they could do about it.

The line was longest at the Silver Skewer Shack, as everyone jokingly called the house of the city's premier restaurateurs, the Kherzadas, who dealt in everything from sidewalk snacks to white-tablecloth veal. Their lights were always on, as if they expected an emergency to strike at least one of their establishments every night.

At last, Daniel arrived home. A chorus of notes escaped through the open window. Rebecca had started her Beethoven. She'd begun practicing this piece a few weeks before the accident. Outside his walled property, the stench of urine overpowered the fragrance of the lilac trees, and through the courtyard gate, Rebecca's Ford gleamed under the moonlight. Its German companion was somewhere else, being repaired.

Ahmad, the housekeeper, appeared. He was carrying a cooler, and the cook behind him had a basket of naan that hid his face. They were enacting a nightly ritual, feeding the lepers. Ahmad greeted Daniel and held open the gate for him, but he didn't enter. An urchin suddenly emerged from the men along the wall. He was untouched by disease, all his limbs as they should be, a look of mischief on his face. He could have been a boy in any neighborhood, and Daniel wondered if he was Taj's lookout. The child broke into a run toward the hills. Daniel dropped his briefcase and followed, but when he turned the corner and peered into the emptiness beyond, the boy had vanished. The sonata from his house seemed to get louder and louder.

When Daniel headed into the hills, it was not because he wanted to find the boy. It was because he didn't want to stop. He walked quickly and then began to run through the dark, fallow land toward the horizon, aimless and unstoppable.

Telaya's eyes shone in the night. *I am faster than you.*

Daniel thought of the Yassaman boy rotting among the poppies. He wondered why the boy left him in peace, but the girl did not.

Look up, she said.

Telaya was in her mirrored red dress, holding her doll as she ran ahead of him through the desert.

Now.

Her voice was soft.

Please.

Why didn't she see that there was no cause to plead? He saw her. He always saw her. He saw nothing else—not the desert camp behind her or the sky above, not the tents or the road or her parents—because her face filled his vision. He could make out every detail of it: her unlined skin, her eyes marred by crimson blood vessels, her pupils like dark tunnels.

"Turn back," he told her. "Go home."

His voice was hoarse like an old man's. He fled into the wind-burnished night.

GOODBYE

Boy pushes off the blanket and gets up when it's still dark because it's too cold to sleep. He loosens the ties at the front of the tent and pops his head out to look at the sky. It's morning. Ice hangs from everything: the pointy black trees, the rich man's roof, the poles that hold up his tent. He feels the cold on his face and pulls his head back in.

Last night he tore a hole in his wool jacket, just under the left armpit. He was pretending he was a bird flapping its wings, to make Mother laugh, and he raised his arms too high. He decides he will surprise her by fixing the coat himself. She's still sleeping. As quietly as he can, he opens her box of sewing things. Boy sees well in the dark, so he's able to cut off a length of thread with his teeth and carefully push it through the needle's eye. Sitting cross-legged next to Mother, listening to her breathe, he smooths the coat across his lap, struggling to keep it still as he starts sewing. It takes longer than he thought it would, and he worries that he won't finish before she wakes up. He works faster, hurting himself with the needle and sucking on his fingers so the blood won't drip onto the shiny black coat. The stitches aren't pretty like when Mother sews, but she will still be proud of him.

She is still sleeping when he hears the rich family start their day. Like almost every morning, the girls come out of *the house fighting about something. In her high voice, the smaller one tells her older sister that she is a stupid donkey. The stupid donkey answers: You're so dumb and ugly, you must be adopted. Boy hears the sound of car doors slamming shut. Something is wrong when the driver tries to start the engine. He tries twice. Three times. Boy listens hard as the engine makes growling noises. The car doesn't start. Curiosity overtakes him, and he runs across the garden toward the house, where he stops and crouches low against a wall. He pretends to be playing with the spool of thread still in his hand, but he is looking toward the driveway out of the corner of his eye. They don't see him. They never do. The chauffeur gets out and pulls open the hood. Then he starts cursing in a way that sounds both angry and sad.*

Boy keeps his back close to the wall but shifts closer to the driveway. The back doors fly open, the sisters jump out and run to the driver's side as he pulls something out of the engine, shaking his head and saying woy woy woy. The younger girl balls her hands into fists and presses them into her eyes, and when she starts to scream, it is the most terrible sound Boy has ever heard. Her sister comes to her side and hugs her hard. The girls do not see the driver walk quickly toward the front door of the big house, holding in his arms a cat, its white fur matted with blood, its legs limp. The animal shakes so much that Boy wonders how the driver can hold on to it. The rich grown-ups from the house come out, everyone talking over each other, but the howls of the little girl are loudest of all.

Boy knows what death is. He has seen dead rats and donkeys and dogs when he and Mother go walking around to look for work. But he has never seen anything like this, a creature about to die. Not knowing what to do, he walks back to the tent and notices that he's forgotten to put on his shoes and that the snow is very cold under his feet. By now,

Mother will be awake, and he can show her the coat and tell her about how the car wouldn't start, and how the girl's cat must have climbed into the engine because it was a warm place to sleep on a cold night. He can still hear the girl's screams in his head even though it's quiet now. Back in the tent, Mother is still sleeping, lying on her side with the thick blanket pulled up high, covering her ears. He nudges her. She doesn't move. He strokes her hair. She is so still.

He calls out for her, pushes the blanket off, and pulls on her arm. She rolls onto her back, limp and heavy, her eyes open very wide and still. The spool of black thread still clutched in his hand, he screams, "Mother!" She doesn't answer. He screams again and again until he knows she will never wake up. Then he runs from the tent, his heart jumping into his throat, tears choking him. He almost falls as his feet sink into the snow, but he doesn't stop. He doesn't stop running until he is outside the garden, past the quiet street with the fancy houses, on the other side of the big road with all the honking cars. Boy knew about death, but he didn't really know before today.

6

IT WAS NEARLY DAWN WHEN DANIEL AWOKE, STRANDS OF LIGHT FRAYING THE SKY. HE WAS on the couch in his study, covered loosely with a blanket. Memories churned in his mind. Manticores, blackmail, and Kochi children who had died but knew how to live forever: by slipping into the minds of their killers.

Daniel got up, sure he was supposed to be somewhere. He remembered coming home when it was still dark and needing a drink. He wondered if Rebecca had woken up and found him missing. His body ached, his head thick from the whiskey. He decided to sleep it off in bed. As he crossed the study, he sensed movement behind him. He flicked on a sconce and turned to find Rebecca at his desk, spinning slowly in his chair, arms folded.

He squinted against the light. "What are you doing in here?"

She paused with her back to the room, then spun back to face him. "I could ask you the same thing," she said softly.

"I got home late from the office."

"Very late," she said, continuing to spin.

He apologized and added, "I kept working when I got home. I must have fallen asleep."

"So you clean your desk before you take a nap?" Rebecca swept her hand over the mahogany surface. "You put all your work away before moving to the sofa? There's not a single file or notebook here."

There was no right answer to this, so he said, "I didn't want to wake you."

She nodded. "You're always so considerate."

He asked her how long she had been in the study. No more than a few minutes, she assured him. "I put the blanket on you. You looked cold." She bit her nails. "What time did you come home?"

"I don't know, Becca."

Pushing her unpolished toes into the floor, she made the chair spin over and over. "Aren't you getting dizzy?" Daniel said, more sharply than he'd meant.

"Aren't you? This must make you disoriented, not knowing when you came home, not knowing when you went to sleep." She rose, pushing against the desk. She had on blue pajamas and a silk robe. Embroidered on the breast pocket was a butterfly.

"I'm tired." Daniel walked over to the desk and touched her hand, hoping it would bring the exchange to an end. It didn't. She removed her hand with a proprietary yank.

"I told you, I worked late. I'm sorry, Becca." He meant it. He was sorrier than he could ever explain to her. "Let's go upstairs."

"It's four in the morning," she said. She glanced at the window each time she heard a sound. The slap of a moth's wings against the glass. The distant hum of a car switching gears as it sped along the paved road, blocks away. Rebecca narrowed her eyes as if struggling to understand how everything outside could go on as normal.

"I'm going to make some tea," he said. On the way to the kitchen, he found his briefcase by the stairs. He heard the soft tread of her slippers behind him.

"Ahmad brought that in from the courtyard," she said.

In the kitchen he stood in front of the stove, watching the kettle. His limbs felt too heavy to make tea. Too heavy to do anything but stand. The cuckoo clock painstakingly ticked away the minutes. He moved to the refrigerator, opened the door, and simply stood there. Rebecca was behind him. She took his hand and stroked his fingers as if afraid they might break. "Daniel?"

"Yes."

She wrapped her arms around him tightly. "It wasn't your fault."

"Right," he said.

"Listen to me. Please. You couldn't have avoided her. It wasn't your fault." She turned him to face her. He nodded.

"Talk to me," she said.

"About what?"

She shook her head and made a sound of disbelief. "You think we can just take August seventeenth off the calendar, like it never happened?" she said. "Just leave it out, like the thirteenth floor of a building?"

"Becca, what do you want from me?"

Her voice broke and she fell into him. "Daniel," she said. "My God." The force of her sorrow brought out a strength in him, and he pulled her so close he was afraid they both might suffocate. She buried her face in his chest, and her tears felt like warm blood.

"I know," he said. "I know."

They stood like this for a while. The refrigerator door was still open, and he felt garishly framed in its rectangle of light. Then she pulled him to the kitchen bench. He leaned against its rigid back as she snuggled up against him, her face sticky with trails of dried tears. He kissed her on the forehead, holding her hand. She searched his face, waiting for words, but there was nothing more he could say. She climbed onto his lap, her fingers cool against his chest. She straddled him and grasped the back of the bench. Tilting her head back, she inhaled as if drinking something sweet from the air. Then she moved with resolve. Resolve was the right word, not passion. She had made a decision, not been overwhelmed by a feeling. He could tell the difference.

Her robe fell to the floor, and in her embrace he found a kind of peace, the crash, the ghost, all of it fading in the simplicity of her nakedness and her touch. He laid her across the table, which was hard and unyielding. Daniel whispered, "Let me move you," and lifted her. Not far, slouching against the pantry, was a large sack full of rock salt, the kind the grocer's boy brought on a mule along with enough onions for a month. Rebecca gasped in surprise as they fell softly against the canvas, the salt crunching beneath her body.

She laced her wrists around his neck. The night before their anniversary, there had been a single encounter, a cautious, almost virginal affair underneath blankets in the dark. Now a primitive version of her emerged. He lost himself in her. She had a way of making it seem like she was on top even when she wasn't. Rebecca didn't notice when a crystal of salt escaped from the canvas as she moved against it. Then another. And another. She never opened her eyes. Nor did she speak. She was only movement and breath. Salt streamed through the canvas now, forming crystalline trails.

Daniel wanted her to scream, not only to feel her pleasure, but because the terrible sounds were coming back. A body against a windshield. Brakes struggling against the laws of physics. His wife screaming a very different kind of scream, anguished and hoarse. The echo of a gunshot, the echo of a ghost.

When Rebecca came, it was like glass shattering. On the

wall, the cuckoo lurched out of its hovel. Five o'clock. They both laughed at the incongruity of their union and the clock's slapstick sound. Daniel's own laugh sounded strange to him, like something from another time. Rebecca cuddled against him and slept until the cuckoo made its clanking appearance again at six o'clock. She smiled, showing off those perfect California teeth, a result of the braces that served as a rite of passage for every suburban teen.

"How do you feel?" she asked.

It was the worst thing she could have said. Daniel felt like a patient being evaluated by a nurse who'd just administered a drug.

"Never mind me," he said. "How are you?"

She smiled again, shrugging into her bathrobe and tightening the belt. When she told him she wanted a shower, it sounded like she was asking for something, though Daniel didn't know what. He stayed alone until the cook, Firooz, came down to make breakfast. He said nothing about the salt, but later that morning, Daniel heard the Hoover running in the kitchen.

7

FRIDAY MORNING, HE WALKED TO THE BAKERY CLOSEST TO HIS HOUSE. THE AROMA OF FRESH naan filled the air. Crowds swarmed the counter. Poor men walked away with free naan and rich men tossed bagfuls of it into their cars. *Chaderi* wrapped it in towels and stacked it in baskets on their heads, while modern girls wedged it into shiny shoulder bags. Four men from three generations were at work in the bakery. Their movements were quick and practiced, matched by the rhythm and twang of a dusty radio blaring pop melodies, the guitar-like *rubab* mewling to a tinny beat. They worked on the floor, squatting by stone slabs, hair trapped in skullcaps.

"Sir, naan for you!" one of the bakers called out. With two spiky rods, he coaxed a sheet of naan from a smoldering hole in the floor and wrapped it in paper for Daniel, who dropped exact change in a copper bowl. Whatever you could pay was exact change. Rebecca was right: a sheet of naan looked like a snowshoe.

He went home, and the day ticked away slowly. Rebecca chose clothes, linens, and flowers for the next day's party. Daniel worked from his study. The office was closed. They ate lunch by the pool, their conversation shallow. As evening neared, he thought about the Zoroaster and Taj's request for "confirmation," as he'd presumptuously called it. He watched the sun set on the terrace, night tumbling over the city. He didn't go to the Zoroaster.

Rebecca was lying awake when he came to bed. She gave him her hand, and he took it. They slept. On Saturday morning, the servers for the evening arrived. They helped the housekeeper polish, prepare, and arrange. Rebecca grew cheerful as the day wore on, sorting through china and silver and fashioning napkins into boats. She shared jokes with the hired help and inquired about their families, asking about their children by name when she knew them. Daniel admired the white, fur-trimmed ensemble she'd chosen for tonight. She stood close to the full-length mirror, then took a few steps back to examine the effect from a distance. She experimented with hairstyles, tossing her hair behind her shoulders, gathering it in a ponytail, and finally settling on a loose, glamorous bun. In the early afternoon, she asked softly, "Do you think you'll shave for tonight?"

Daniel hadn't shaved since the accident—it had seemed indecent to concern himself with his appearance. When he looked in the mirror, he saw how unkempt he was after days of letting his beard grow. Under his eyes were purplish crescents. His shoulders were slumped. Rebecca stroked his arm. He straightened slowly and rubbed his face, then promised her he would shave.

The house was warmed by the heat from the cook's best recipes and the light of the summer sun. Daniel asked if he could help and took a tarnished silver vase off Ahmad's hands. He sat in an Adirondack chair by the pool, the sun quivering on the water, and began to polish, growing calmer as he worked. The transformation was remarkable. Like the gemstones from his childhood, silver revealed its beauty only after diligent work. Across the garden, Rebecca was gathering flowers beside Laila, who had come early to help. The doctor wore jeans and a blouse, holding up a garment bag with her evening dress in it. He watched their graceful forms move across the blue-white light of the day and caught snippets of his wife's laughter. Rebecca's laugh was one of the loveliest sounds he knew, a crystalline trill like the high notes of her piano. He hadn't heard the sound in months.

When he was finished polishing, he could see his reflection in the vase. He felt the sun lift a weight from him with its warmth. Only now was he starting to look forward to tonight. He had always liked big gatherings, ever since he'd watched his mother throw parties for businessmen and diplomats, the smell of liquor and cigars lingering for days. All would be well. He could manage Peter Whitbourn. The history professor had once been a close friend, and the only man who could beat Daniel in a fair game of chess.

Yes, everything would be fine. Taj Maleki's threat was a bluff. Massacres didn't happen here. Whatever Taj might be, he wasn't stupid. He wouldn't risk the punishment for mass murder, which was surely execution—if not by the blade of the law, then by the blades of the elders. When Telaya spoke, it was almost as if her voice was emanating from the silver.

He's been bluffing from the start, she said.

Daniel hugged Laila hello before going inside. Neither of them mentioned her presence at the impromptu demonstration earlier. He went upstairs to the master bathroom and steadied his hand as he picked up the razor. He began to shave, carefully, not because he was afraid he might cut himself, but because he was afraid it might provoke Telaya. He tried to think of other things. He remembered Peter trying to sport a beard for a while before finally acknowledging that he looked ridiculous, after much teasing from Daniel, who'd insisted he couldn't pull it off. Rebecca hadn't liked it either.

He stopped fighting against the question that had lurked

in his mind all day. What had brought back his wife's laugh? Daniel wanted to believe it was that they had made love. Another answer stared him in the face. The party was mere hours away, and Peter was set to appear after an eight-year intermission. If caring about his appearance had been indecent, jealousy was even more so. He lost control of the blade and slashed his right cheek. As he blotted the blood, feeling foolish, he saw blood blooming through a red dress, and she came back with a vengeance, a new cascade of grievances.

My parents didn't love me.

Sometimes, Daniel forgot that Telaya hadn't seen her tearful parents cradle her corpse. That for her, nothing more had happened after she closed her eyes on that scalding road. He was sure she was wrong. And what if she was wrong about Taj bluffing, too? Why was he listening to a ghost?

He did need advice from someone, though. He would go see his friend Ian, whose work at the Peace Corps belied his past. Ian had once been a policeman and could help Daniel make sense of Taj. And Daniel would give no further thought to Peter and Rebecca. Some things weighed more than others.

8

"GO," SAID REBECCA, WHEN HE ASKED IF HE COULD LEAVE THE PREPARATIONS TO HER FOR A while. "Laila's helping me."

He walked out into the impossibly bright day. The neighbor's boy, Keshmesh, was on his balcony, dancing around and playing air guitar. He wore large, clunky headphones plugged into a cassette player. The boy had turned thirteen in June and fancied himself a grown man, though his lanky limbs suggested the awkward stage had just begun. When he saw Daniel, he grinned and performed his best Pete Townshend. Daniel waved. Normally, he would have beckoned the boy down and they would have talked about rock bands. Today, he kept walking.

Less than a mile away, he reached Ian's street. He could hear someone revving an engine from the corner. Cars had once been the sound of camaraderie and leisure for Daniel, but now the engine was the sound of pain. He walked into the open garage, where Ian was working on a Chevy, hood up.

"Well, this is a surprise," Ian said, wiping his sooty hands with a rag. He wore an apron that looked like it had never been washed. They went inside and he removed it, revealing a soiled shirt and a silver bolo tie that clashed with his tidy haircut, middle-aged belly, and Brooklyn accent. On another day, Daniel would have made a joke. But today it felt cruel, though not toward Ian.

"I was just passing by."

"Not the weirdest thing you've ever done, Leinad."

Daniel was comforted to hear the nickname. Ian had turned *Daniel* backward because he said *Leinad* had a Celtic ring to it, and Celticization was an honor bestowed only on a friend. When Ian closed the door and shut out the day, it was like tumbling into a different world. Joan Baez played in the background. The house smelled of incense and potpourri.

Daniel followed Ian across the foyer and into the living room, which was laid with the same marble tile as the rest of the house. The color was so bad it was funny. Ian's wife, Pamela, called it "Matador Red." It was crimson with white and dark lines sinewing through each tile, so the floor looked like freshly butchered meat pounded flat and covered with a glaze. There was no carpet, so it was impossible not to be aware at all times of Pamela, who came and went in a fusillade of heels. Daniel heard her negotiate the stairs and wondered how she didn't fall and break her neck. She clapped when she saw him, showering him with pleasantries and scanning him head to toe. She wore frosted lipstick and a Formica smile. Her fingers ended in tangerine talons.

"I'm getting ready for tonight. My polish is drying," she said, waving her hands in the air. "I'll leave you gentlemen alone." With a flip of her studiously natural waves, she left. Ian had described her as one of the kindest, most loyal people he'd ever met, and Daniel wondered why she hid these qualities under an explosion of superficiality.

Ian closed the living room door and switched the music off. From the wet bar, he produced two glasses. "Howzabout we preload for tonight?"

He made cocktails, stirring the mixtures with long metallic

spoons. Each time his wife's stilettos came closer, growing louder and faster, the clinking of the spoons grew louder and faster, too, slowing when her footsteps faded. Marital synchronicity at its best. After much irregular mixing, Ian held the drinks triumphantly in the air. They were pink.

"Something we found in the recipe book from Harry's Bar, the joint in Paris that Bogie used to go to. Or Hemingway. One of those two." He shrugged.

They sat down in uncomfortable bucket chairs.

"You look like you need something strong," Ian said. "Or don't you? 'Cause I can drink both."

"Something strong sounds about right." Daniel took a sugared almond from a bowl and let it rest in his palm.

"You look like crap," Ian said. "You come by way of Bumfuck, Egypt?"

"Just didn't sleep too well."

They sipped in silence, Ian smoothing his new mustache between sips. Pamela's heels clicked from one wing of the house to the other. She was in the library now.

Soon, Daniel rattled the ice in his empty glass. "You got anything else?"

"Glad you asked."

Moments later they were drinking whiskey and toasting to Johnnie Walker, whom they thanked for always being there for them. "I got six bottles from the embassy last week," Ian said.

Two drinks later, when his limbs and mind had grown heavier, Daniel said, "Ian, have you ever been trapped?"

"You mean like in a building or something? Sure, back when I was on the force. Once."

"What did you do?"

"Radioed for backup. Only thing you can do."

Daniel asked what he would do if no backup came. If you

were really trapped, Ian explained, there was no way out if no one came to help you. "Unless you're Houdini or something." They sat in silence a minute before he said, "What gives, Leinad?"

"I've got a situation to figure out."

"At work?"

Daniel nodded. "I have to make a decision, and there's no way to know what's right. No matter what I do, it's probably going to end badly. Really badly."

"Got it. A rock and a hard place kind of thing."

"Yeah."

"Listen. When you think you're the only one who can deal with something big, that's when you really need to reach out."

Daniel didn't respond. He could feel Ian watching, waiting for him to say more. But he couldn't tell him the truth. He couldn't ask for advice about Taj, because then he would have to explain the rest. That he'd driven his car into a child because he was sick of listening to Beethoven. That he'd stood next to an opium khan while the man murdered a teenager. He could not say one thing without the rest, because these things had tangled together into a single mass.

So when Ian asked again, "What gives, my friend?" Daniel responded, "It sure is a beautiful day."

Ian nodded slowly. "That it is." Then, with a shake of his head, he changed the subject. "That Chevy back there? The owner thought it was beyond hope. It ain't."

"Does it run?"

"A little. But that's the easy part. Hard part's the sound. I'm useless with the radio. Good thing there's never anything on, unless you want to hear funeral announcements or propaganda or music that sounds like the theme song for a snake dancing its way out of your ass."

"How'd it go with the Volga?"

"Piece of crap, like everything the Russians make. Commies can't build shit. There's more of them in the city every day."

"Communists?"

"Volgas. But now that you mention it, Commies, too. Russians all over the place." Ian aimed the glowing tip of his Winston at Daniel. "The fan belt you replaced keeps slipping right back off like a hooker's bra." He laughed, pleased at his own joke, puffed up his cheeks, and exhaled. "You know my theory? Heartless dictatorships can't make cars. Rockets, yes. Cars, no."

"Why's that?"

"Because cars are about heart." Ian thumped his chest with his fist. "That's where they come from. In every man's heart, there's a little place for cars. The heart has . . . what, four chambers? One of those is a garage."

Daniel couldn't help but smile.

"That's only true for guys, mind you," Ian went on. "A girl's heart don't have no garage."

"Maybe it does."

"A garage is for cars, not unicorns and rainbows." Ian's belly rose and fell as he coughed out that Brooklyn chortle, but Daniel couldn't laugh, because buried in the fourth chamber of his heart was Telaya, the mirrors on her dress sparkling in the light like an explosion of crystals as she moved. "How's the Corps these days?" he asked.

Ian shook his head. "It's different, that's for sure. Pamela thinks it's cool."

With three Peace Corps volunteers freshly elected to Congress, the Corps was indeed front and center, but everyone knew "cool" mattered less to Ian than to the much younger Pam. He was the oldest person ever hired by the Corps, and he let everybody know it. "I can't complain," he added.

"Why would you? You used to be a policeman in a dangerous place. This must seem tame."

Ian set his drink down hard. "I'll tell you something: it's easier to face a thug with a gun than look a starving man in the eye." He picked up his glass and emptied it in two gulps. "I've offered you help a hundred times."

"Peace Corps help? You think that's any use against poppy growers?"

"As a matter of fact, I do."

"The government showers you with money and everybody talks about you guys, but my budget is so thin I can barely keep the office stocked with tea and no one knows who we are," Daniel said. "Seems a little upside down, that's all."

"Yeah, woe is me. Let's not forget, you and I are both here because of who we know. You didn't exactly fight your way to the top, my friend."

Daniel kept his answer down by drowning it in whiskey. It was bad enough having his staff question how he got his job. Whatever people said, he deserved his position in a way Ian did not. Having your socialite wife use her contacts to install you in the Peace Corps was not the same as earning a reference from a professor who had worked with the president of the United States, even if that president was Richard Nixon.

In the study, Pamela was still on the phone. She made a sound that could have been one of laughter, sadness, or shock. Ian shrugged. "Seeing as the phones don't work half the time, she goes in the study and picks up the receiver about ten times a day just to see if she can call somebody. It's like she lives her life just to talk to people who aren't here."

Daniel had little to say, because Rebecca rarely used the phone. She spoke to her parents on Sundays. Calls to friends were a monthly occurrence, if that. Instead, she wrote letters.

Daniel wondered how many of those letters had been written to Peter Whitbourn. He reached for a cigarette.

"If we're going to keep smoking, we have to go outside. Pammy can't stand the smell."

They stepped onto the terrace, flicking their ashes into a pot that housed an ailing palm. A cockroach watched them, perfectly still except for its antennae, which probed the air like a Russian listening device. Christmas lights still winked from the trellises because Pamela thought it might make the locals ask about American traditions.

Some traditions are ugly, Telaya said.

When Daniel ignored her, she threw an onslaught of questions at him the way children did when adults gave imperfect answers.

Do people love their daughters in America?

Parents love their kids everywhere.

You're not looking!

Leave me alone.

Are there nomads in New York?

Yes, but a different kind.

Do they move from place to place and sleep outside?

Yes, but unlike you, they don't choose to do so.

Children don't get choices.

Ian proposed a toast to the cockroach, which he admired for its ability to survive a nuclear war. The men drifted from topic to topic. They talked about the Chevy, the recent invasion of bees from Iran, the victory of the National League in the All-Star Game. They had listened to the game at Daniel's house at three o'clock in the morning, welcoming every American in the city, a few Englishmen, and a Japanese businessman no one recognized.

"How'd the radio work out? The one you put in the Mercedes last week."

"It broke. The tape player, too."

"On the trip?"

"Yes."

"You must've been glad. Becca was probably playing one of her hoity-toity tapes." Ian rose and took Daniel's glass from him. "You've had enough. Pace yourself for tonight."

They went back inside. Pamela had been in the living room; the coffee table was cleared now, revealing its design. At the center was a terra-cotta tile with a man-in-a-maze design, a stylized stick figure encircled by a labyrinth that started at his feet.

"I'll drive you back." Soon, Ian's Citroën was sputtering along the road. He switched on the radio and President Daoud's voice filled the car. He talked of drawing closer to America and Iran. While Daoud wasn't a Communist, his cabinet was full of Soviet-friendly types who'd backed his coup when he took power. People who cared enough to be paying attention could see he wasn't planning to give them as much power as they had hoped. At the same time, he'd pushed out religious men, arresting and executing Islamist clerics. Now he spoke of the future and of the inevitable, but he did not mention the most inevitable thing of all: that being left in the cold made devout men blaze hot as fire-breathing dragons.

9

GETTING DRESSED FOR THE EVENING, DANIEL LISTENED TO REBECCA TALK TO HIM FROM THE shower. She told him Sherzai had called and wouldn't be coming. His leg was especially bad today, as it often was after the rain. Daniel hoped *agha* would spend the day tucked into his *sandali*, which would keep him warm and ease his aches. A low table covered with a quilt and with a coal brazier underneath wasn't the most modern of methods, and Sherzai's table was old, but it was still the most effective heat remedy Daniel had seen. He also hoped Sherzai's absence meant Dannaco-Hastings's wunderkind wouldn't show up.

"Laila is changing in the guest room," Rebecca called out over the tumbling water. "You should see her dress! Very sexy."

Sexy was not a word Daniel associated with Laila. As a boy, he had wanted to love her in the way married adults loved each other, but *sexy* wasn't the right word, at least not when they'd been twelve years old and dreaming of lives as grown-ups who would make a difference. Rebecca knew Laila had been his first crush, but instead of causing jealousy, it seemed to bring the women together, as if they shared an understanding of what it meant to know Daniel and be known by him.

As Rebecca slipped into her blouse, fussing with the trim

on her transparent sleeves, Daniel opened his briefcase and retrieved a velvet box. There would be no better time to give her the earrings, and the longer he waited, the more awkward it would be. "I wanted to give you these the other day, but I didn't have them yet."

"The other day?"

"Our anniversary." Daniel studied her carefully, but if the word made Rebecca relive the crash, she managed to hide it. She looked down at the box and bent back the lid. The lapis lazuli was a rich blue, studded with flecks of gold. They reminded Daniel of the twilights Rebecca had loved when they had driven together to Nevada, Arizona, and Utah.

"How thoughtful," she said. "Thank you."

She looked unsurprised. Or maybe it was disappointment. When he asked if she liked them, she said they were beautiful and snapped the lid shut, placing the box on the dresser.

"You like lapis, don't you?"

"I said they're lovely." She pushed the box a bit farther away.

"I thought you could wear them tonight."

Her expression was clear now: it was disappointment. "Daniel, I know you like giving me jewelry, but have you ever noticed that I don't really wear any?"

"I'm sorry for giving you earrings," Daniel said calmly before turning and leaving.

In the hall, he almost walked into Laila, who materialized from the guest room. There was a long, inviting slit on the side of her dress. Her gait was different, and he noticed she was wearing heels. Her eyes were fringed with lashes that had to be fake, and her lips were red. Yes, it was true. Laila *was* sexy, and not just in the chess-club way of their adolescence.

It was six o'clock when the guests began to arrive. Daniel assumed Ambassador Jack Sutherland would bring Peter with him, since he was staying at his home, but instead the ambassador turned up with Greenwood, the Dannaco-Hastings consultant, who was dressed in khakis and a button-down shirt with a tie. Daniel was surprised he had come, but less surprised to learn that corporate priorities trumped old friendships: the Sutherlands had sent a car to collect Peter from the airport, and he had agreed to stay at the Khushal Hotel so they could accommodate Greenwood. Daniel could almost smell Agent Ruby on the young man, who stood in a wide stance and purposefully straightened his tie, which was adorned with a silver clip bearing the Harvard insignia. His class ring was the size of his knuckle. He turned back and craned his neck as he entered the house, looking back through the courtyard gates at the lepers, who had begun to form their nightly line.

"They won't bother you if you don't bother them," Daniel said.

"Ah." Greenwood nodded. "Kind of like bears."

In the parlor, gloved waiters came and went with trays, offering drinks and canapés.

Rebecca dropped a James Brown record on the turntable. The ambassador gave her a peck on the cheek. "How's my fastest typist tonight?"

She hugged him halfheartedly, like he was a toy she had outgrown, and when she walked away, she curled her fingers into her palms. Ian arrived with liquor on his breath and Pamela on his arm. She dispatched a series of quick, kissy hellos and began twirling to the music, her batik skirt a whimsy of colors, almost all of which matched some aspect of her makeup, nail polish, or jewels. She teetered on pink stilettos adorned with girlish silk flowers, part of a closetful of shoes that Rebecca had derisively nicknamed the "fuck-me collection." These were known as "Fuck me, I'm barely legal."

Laila stood with her hands on her hips, glaring openly at the million-carat diamond on Pamela's hand. "You could go ice-skating on that. Or feed a small country with it," she said.

"If you tell me which country, I'll send it to them." Pamela's cheeks grew red as she eyed the carpet. Then she looked up. "We're throwing a Labor Day barbecue this year. We're inviting some of the unemployed locals Ian knows through the Corps," she said, the words squeezing through a gridlocked smile.

She didn't seem to understand that people who spent their lives looking for work might not enjoy a day dedicated to celebrating labor. Daniel thought Pamela's gaffe would amuse Rebecca. He set off in search of her and found her near the door that divided the parlor from the foyer and the rest of the house, checking her watch and peering at the entryway.

"Shouldn't you be mingling?" he said.

"I have to powder my nose." She clacked her way through the foyer and disappeared into the guest bathroom.

Daniel didn't want to join the Sutherlands. They were glued to Greenwood, who stood with both hands in his pockets, rocking on his heels. Nor did he want to partake in Laila's increasingly animated dialogue with Pamela. Ian was mixing drinks at the wet bar. Rebecca returned, her nose looking exactly the same as before. On the stereo, James Brown managed to make an ordinary word sound obscene. There was still no sign of Peter Whitbourn.

There was, however, a sound that only Daniel seemed to hear. A car that came and went, idling in the street before crawling away. Cars were scarce on this unpaved cul-de-sac, and he knew what the neighbors' cars sounded like. This wasn't one of them.

"Peter's late," Rebecca said. She glanced at her watch and tapped its face.

She left behind a cloud of Chanel. It was one of only two perfumes he could identify, the other being Charlie, because Laila wore it. Rebecca asked a server for a glass of Chablis. Laila ordered the same. The house was filled with the aroma of saffron, cardamom, and rosewater mixed with hair spray and the women's clashing perfumes. Pamela spilled wine, her nails unable to negotiate stemware.

Outside, the engine growled. Daniel could no longer stand it, but by the time he reached the door, there was a knock. Elias and Peter had arrived at the same time. The journalist stood as far from Peter as he could while still claiming the same steps. They were facing each other as if poised for combat, their arsenals consisting of not guns but words, which could decimate the enemy in the hands of a skilled marksman.

Looking past them, Daniel could see the street through the courtyard gates. A sedan was in view, the Khushal Hotel logo stenciled on its side. With its missing taillight, it looked half-asleep as it inched away. It didn't sound like the prowling engine from before. Elias's Vespa was lodged safely inside the courtyard, leaning against the house.

The journalist stepped inside quickly, looking more relieved than happy to see Daniel. His jeans were torn at the knees, his shirt a tie-dye reminiscent of Pamela's skirt. He lifted a six-pack from a brown paper bag, casting a furtive look over his shoulder.

"We don't all know the American ambassador, but I have other sources." Elias winked. "Is Laila here?" When he learned that she was, Elias examined himself in the hallway mirror. He pulled his fingers through his hair, dusted his jeans, and strode off, politely greeting Rebecca, whom he crossed on the way to the parlor.

Alone with his wife and Peter, who was tonight's guest of

honor, Daniel extended his hand. Peter's grip was weaker than it used to be. Their hands remained clasped as Peter looked Daniel in the eye and wiped his shoes on the mat for longer than necessary. Rebecca greeted him with a smile that Daniel tried not to analyze. He was happy to see Peter, a man he had once called a friend, perhaps the closest he'd ever had.

Peter had aged in these eight years. Rebecca had once described him as "handsome in a pinched sort of way." The "pinched" was taking over. The professor had a lean build, brown eyes, sharp like a fox's, and an aristocrat's nose. But there were shadows under his eyes, and a few silver strands were scattered through thinning hair, though he was just thirty-nine. His shoulders were hunched from too much time leaning over papers, books, and solo meals.

"I have something for our hostess." Peter produced a cube from a bag he was holding and offered it to Rebecca. "I apologize for the ribbon. It didn't travel well." He fussed with the dejected bow, trying to coax life into its curls. "Open it."

It was a snow globe. Trapped under the dome, the Eiffel Tower was the backdrop for a tiny skater striking an Olympic pose.

Rebecca stroked the ornament like it was a precious work of art, the corners of her lips upturned sweetly and her cheekbones almost as pink as Pamela's shoes. "I left my collection at my parents' house."

Dancing in from the parlor, Pamela clapped her hands in delight before introducing herself. "Make it snow!" she said.

Rebecca shook the globe, sending silvery flakes into aimless shimmies. Only now did Daniel see that she was wearing the earrings. They swayed by her cheeks, softening the angular beauty of her jaw. Daniel wanted to thank her with a glance, but she avoided his gaze. From deep under the sands near a soulless highway, the dead girl said, *She doesn't see you. You're perfect for each other.*

In the parlor, Peter greeted each guest by turn. The hellos went on, Laila and Rebecca both mingling and darting back and forth between the kitchen and dining room, overseeing last-minute things. Daniel usually loved seeing his wife like this, radiant and lively, swaying through the room with a deceptive nonchalance. It was a stark contrast to Laila, who walked in self-consciously short steps, clutching at the slit of her dress. But tonight, something about both women was off.

The car returned, louder this time. It was approaching. Servants came and went with trays. Greenwood was on all fours, looking for his tie clip on the regal multicolored carpet, and Ian was on one knee, singing a tune from *Show Boat* to his wife. Meanwhile, Ambassador Sutherland smiled like someone used to feigning interest. Nearby, Elias was trying to keep Laila's attention. Would she be at the demonstration on Thursday, he asked. Maybe, she replied, distracted, although not by Ian's singing. Her eyes were on Peter. His eyebrows were raised as he listened to Greenwood, who was now back on his feet.

Daniel opened the windows, killing the ceiling fans in favor of the breeze. Outside, the failing day blazed Catholic red. Rebecca stopped the music by lifting the needle instead of pulling the off switch, and the screeching sound made the hairs on his arms stand on end. Half of their LPs skipped because of her. She loaded the cassette player with a tape of bluesy tunes.

The dinner gong sounded. Daniel led his wife and Laila from the parlor to the dining room and told them they were beautiful. Laila blushed and made too many self-deprecating jokes as she held on to his arm. Rebecca stroked his face and smiled quietly. He could see the outline of her shape under her white silk blouse and the floor-length skirt—no, not a skirt, but flowing slacks with sheer panels on the sides. She had painted her toes a frosted white. They matched the shimmies in Peter's snow globe.

On the table, crystal candlesticks glimmered next to vases overflowing with flowers from the yard. Daniel lit the candles as the guests stood behind their chairs, their features warmed by the flames and the dimly lit chandelier. They were waiting for Ian, who was using the restroom for the third time. Each place setting was marked with a name card. Daniel had forgotten to tell Rebecca about Bob Greenwood, so his had hurriedly been added. His name was scribbled in Laila's doctorly scrawl.

The servers brought in platters of rice piled high with lamb, chicken, and colorful sides. Peter smiled at Rebecca. Daniel wished he could leave.

Greenwood raised an eyebrow at his name card and turned a dinner plate over in his hands, examining its credentials. Peter stared longingly at his own seat. Signs of jet lag were etched on his face. Elias was watching Laila. Noticing, she firmly tied her scarf over her bare throat. Small talk rose and fell in little waves. Daniel thought of what his mother used to say: that some talk was so small it was easy to miss altogether. Ian returned, apologizing as he bolted forward with short steps, elbows high like a speed-walker's. Waiters uncorked bottles; wine splashed into glasses.

Before Daniel could welcome his guests and propose a toast, Greenwood said, "So Daniel, is it true that Professor Whitbourn got you your job?"

10

"HE WROTE A REFERENCE FOR ME. IT WAS VERY GOOD OF HIM."

Daniel did not say that Peter had owed him.

Back in college, it was Rebecca who had convinced Daniel to take a course with Peter. By his senior year, Dr. Whitbourn had become *Peter*. One night, over pints of Guinness at the Beerded Matron, Peter congratulated him on his engagement to Ms. Rebecca Menlow. As Peter and Daniel made progress on their goal of drinking immoderately, the alcohol loosened their inhibitions and tongues. The professor told Daniel he was tired of teaching. He had little respect for most of his students, even less for his colleagues. As for the school's administration, he was too civil to use any of the precise adjectives.

To Peter the whole world was, by and large, a personal insult. He found the glazed boredom in his students' eyes a direct affront. Ditto for their slouching torsos and unfortunate syntax. Those who were bright he disliked even more for the demands they made on his time. The dean had told Peter he had "great pedagogic talent," but that was an insult, too, an excuse to force him to expend energy on people destined to remain unsung.

After his fourth beer, Daniel confessed something as well. He wasn't sure how to handle girls. He had visited America with his father as a child, but living here was different. The idea of women in sequential or simultaneous romantic liaisons was alien. At parties, girls talked about sex like it was just another facet of life, joking about details, comparing notes. He knew there was nothing wrong with this, that it signaled a progress he believed in, but sometimes these principles were easier to praise in the abstract than to live. It was so hard to shake the rule he'd been raised with: that a woman should save herself for her one true love. As Daniel emptied his beer at the Matron, Peter listened, never taking his eyes off his own sweating bottle, refusing the day-old peanuts the bartender shoved into view. Finally, he said, "Daniel, every man has two selves caught in perpetual battle. You should ignore their fights, except for the epic ones. The Sonny-Liston-versus-Muhammad-Alis. Pay close attention to those. And don't choose sides ahead of time. Just let the best man win." When fighting with yourself, it wasn't always easy to tell who the best man was, but this seemed like something to drink to, so they did.

Less than a year after that, Rebecca revealed a secret of her own. Daniel knew Rebecca had been with men before him, but had never imagined there would be any more after him. After they'd graduated in 1968, she'd suddenly withdrawn, insisting she needed time and space. She'd spent that summer with friends in England and France, returning with promises of devotion and love. Daniel had taken her back without question.

Months later, he stared at her across the candlelit table in her beachfront studio, wondering when her speech would end. The candles flickered as she spoke. She insisted the "thing with Peter" had lasted only weeks, during the time she was away. Which meant that Peter had come to Europe to be with her. When she was finished, she sat with her head low. "Say something," she whispered.

Daniel fetched an almost empty bag of chips. The only ones left were broken and small. Faced with his silence, Rebecca tried to explain herself, her tone shifting between urgency, regret, and defiance.

Daniel prepared for a fight, but not with her. It was a death match between his two selves. He told her it was all right. He kissed her good night and walked out of the apartment, leaving her in her chair with her knees to her chest and her head in her hands. The screen door bounced shut behind him.

Stalking up Ocean Boulevard toward home, he passed the bluff where he'd asked Rebecca to marry him above the emerald-studded sea. He turned right on Montana Avenue. When he reached Wilshire, he picked up his pace, running past gas stations and convenience stores and homeless men who made comments about his speed or asked him for spare change. He had always wished he could fly, wanting to go faster, wondering why his feet wouldn't simply lift off the ground like the feet of a small Kochi boy alongside the road.

"Run, brother, run," said a man from his box for a bed. Daniel nearly fell over a shopping cart shoved into his path by another man who was cursing someone called Jane while waving a fist at the moon.

Once he was home, Daniel flipped through the phone book and looked for a place that would teach him to fly. He wanted to rise into the sky in a plane big enough just for one or maybe two, so he could watch the world from above when he couldn't bear to be in its midst.

Then he revisited a place he had not been in more than two years. When he'd first come to California in 1963, he'd been determined to free himself of old ideas that had no place in his modern life. But it wasn't as easy as throwing away the broken pieces of chips at the bottom of a bag. He decided to think of ideas as living things that belonged in one of two different houses: the good, modern ones lived in a sparkling high-rise, the old ones in a mud shack in Kandahar. When a belief he didn't like popped into his head, Daniel would seize it by its imaginary arm, toss it into the mud shack, and padlock the door. In the beginning, Daniel had to play this game almost every day.

The night of August 20, 1967, with Rebecca's confession about Peter reeling in his head, Daniel walked into his apartment, opened every window, and drank a warm beer while taking a cool shower, lay naked on his bed with his eyes closed, and let a storm flood the Kandahar shack, dissolving its walls and washing away everything inside until all that remained was a pile of sludge and a ruined lock he swore he would never need again.

11

SITTING AROUND THE TABLE WITH HIS GUESTS, DANIEL COULD SMELL THE MUDDY WATERS OF that old shack as it struggled to reconstitute itself. He tried not to think of yesterday's tryst in the kitchen, the shadow of another man tainting the memory. His efforts were in vain. Rebecca wrapped her hand around her glass, and he remembered her fingers like a shock along his spine. Her lips were pink yesterday morning, like now, but it had been the work of lust then, not lipstick.

Laila's voice pulled him back to the present. The others were silent, all eyes on him. "Daniel," she said loudly, as if he'd lost his hearing. "Can you please pass the salt?"

Ian reached across and plunked it down beside her. Daniel smiled and the guests stared as the waiters moved up and down the table like assembly-line drones. Ambassador Sutherland joined Rebecca in presenting the roster of Peter's achievements. "He was one of our best advisers at the Treasury Department," he said, describing Peter's role in the Nixon Shock, which had ended the convertibility of the dollar to gold.

The professor shrugged as if the compliments were too kind, but smiled in a way that suggested they weren't. "I didn't mind heading to Washington to do some real work. Getting my hands a little dirty."

"Very dirty," Elias said. "Working for a crook."

"History will be kinder to Mr. Nixon than you think."

"When is your conference?" Daniel asked, wishing he hadn't given in to Sherzai's pressure to invite Elias.

"Conference?"

"The one in Tehran."

Peter dabbed his lips with his napkin. "I'm not sure of the dates."

Ambassador Sutherland turned to him. "You didn't mention a conference."

"In any case, Kabul's a nice place to visit." Peter took a quick bite of food. "I haven't been here since I wrote my last book, which was about gold and the end of the Ottoman Empire."

"The *definitive* book about gold and the end of the Ottoman Empire," Rebecca added.

"There's a definitive book about that?" Greenwood laughed, the sound of a dolphin morphing into a mule.

"If anyone can make that topic seem cool, it's Peter," Rebecca said. "He has a way." When she spoke, Daniel pictured fragments of salt piercing through tightly woven fabric. Her sentence trailed off, and she laughed nervously, although her features fell and her shoulders slumped. If she regretted her words, then so be it. Daniel wasn't inclined to give her the forgiving look she sought when she glanced his way.

"They're making good progress here, don't you think?" Sutherland asked Peter, gesturing vaguely to the rest of the country.

Peter didn't respond, face more pinched than ever. As Sutherland filled the ensuing silence by explaining that this was his fourth assignment in the third world and how impressed he was with the locals, it was Elias who replied.

"I'm glad you're impressed," he told the ambassador. Then he turned to Peter. "Are you impressed with us, too?"

When there was no answer, he pushed on. "What's the matter, Professor? You afraid we won't be able to follow what you say?"

Rebecca's disdain was apparent on her face. Men like Elias were why she had first been drawn to Peter. In college, she had become disillusioned with the ideals of her generation, which were subsumed by salon socialism and the easy but unsustainable appeal of free love and drugs. What had begun as vision and optimism had brought leisure and narcissism; words like *peace* and *brother* were just fashionable argot, replacing the *cool cat* and *hopped-up* of the 1950s.

Daniel tried to thaw the tension by raising his glass in a toast and welcoming his guests. Nine men and women drank to friendship and health. Elias then dug his elbows into the table and made a steeple with his fingers. He was about to ask Peter something more when the professor finally answered Ambassador Sutherland's question about progress. "There was still a king last time I was here. The president is an improvement."

"Really?" Greenwood said. "Then you don't know about all the pinkos and reds he's surrounding himself with. Do you know what went on in the streets the other day?"

Peter blinked rapidly. "Of course I know." He made a sharp sniffling sound. "The Communists are an improvement."

Daniel wondered where this was coming from. Peter had worked for Nixon not because his career demanded it, but because he'd believed in the man, at least in the early days. Maybe he was saying things he didn't mean to prompt reactions that amused him, like a cat toying with a lesser animal. But not everyone seemed surprised.

Greenwood shook his head. "A lot of the professors at Harvard were pink. Or worse."

"And yet none of it rubbed off on you," Elias said. "Probably didn't even get close enough to the free-love chicks to let *them* rub off on you, either."

Greenwood chuckled uncomfortably, bouncing glances off the other men, none of whom gave him the reaction he wanted. When Sutherland displayed his diplomat's skills by declaring Daoud a leader America could work with, Greenwood said, "That depends."

"On what?" Elias must have spat the words, because Greenwood wiped at his left eye. Daniel remembered Taj saying something about llamas and fought back a smile.

"On whether he quits playing around with Commies and gets on board with destroying the poppies once and for all. They've got to go."

"The Commies or the poppies?" Daniel said.

"Both."

"I say long live the Commies," Elias said.

A heavy silence laid itself over the table. Daniel could hear that car again.

Pamela pointed a nail at the popcorn ceiling. "There's a shoe store in town now that sells Italian brands," she said conspiratorially. "Imported."

They all drank to progress as they traded rumors. Laughter lifted the atmosphere. It was the sound not of good cheer but of relief. In the warmth of wine and candle glow, Elias joined in the gossip long enough to claim that the best department store would soon carry lingerie, though it was a secret and a journalist never divulged his sources. He winked, eliciting sniggers. Even Rebecca shared in the indulgent chuckles.

"I've been here three days and find the ladies as exotic as the cuisine." Greenwood swept his hand over the silver-plattered food, finishing with a swirling motion. Turning to Peter, he added, "Am I right?"

The attempt at camaraderie failed. The professor studied him with pursed lips. Greenwood fiddled with his tie clip.

"Peter prefers California girls," Daniel said.

Greenwood smiled. "You can't blame the man."

Rebecca dropped her napkin on the table and rose. She vanished through the swinging kitchen door. She returned with an apology, explaining that she'd forgotten to check on dessert. She looked different somehow.

Ian tried to revive the gossip. A liquor store was to open downtown next to the shop with all the socks, he said to expressions of disbelief. It would pose as a candy store. He took his wife's hand and said he looked forward to champagne on their anniversary, which was three months away. Pamela turned to Rebecca and said, "Darling, I forgot to ask about your anniversary trip. Did he treat you as you should be treated?"

Rebecca nodded, staring at her food. "It was . . . unforgettable."

She could have told everyone that Daniel had given her custom-made jewelry, but she didn't. He now knew why she looked different since her retreat to the kitchen. She had taken the earrings off.

Greenwood raised his Sprite in the air. "Happy belated anniversary!" he said. He returned to the question of lingerie and probed Peter for details about the girls at UCLA, conceding that this was the single area where West Coast schools outranked Harvard.

Daniel and Peter glanced at each other and ignored the slight. Tie Clip didn't need to know that Daniel could have chosen any school he liked. That he'd headed to California because he'd grown up with sun-soaked deserts and dreamed of a place where desert and sea coexisted and you could leave things behind. Rebecca had wanted to flee her problems, too, which he guessed was the reason she had happily agreed to move here. She'd been born in California, a young place, and had longed for the weight of history. First, she'd lost herself in classical music, beginning with the Baroques before moving on to the Romantics of the nineteenth century. But not until she'd come here had she understood what ancient really meant.

"Speaking of trips," Ian said, "I noticed the Krautmobile isn't here." He spoke with his mouth full. "Is there something wrong with it?"

Daniel suddenly felt as if time had slowed and his guests had come only to hear him answer this question. He was grateful when Rebecca said, "A rock broke the windshield. You know how our street is."

"The streets are the least of our problems," Laila said. "What we really need here are things like better medicine. More X-ray machines. The Communists can bring that."

No, they can't, Daniel thought. When had they kept their promises to anyone? She ought to be embarrassed, spewing Russian propaganda that had all the depth of a Pine-Sol jingle. There was little to admire about the ogre to the east, with its five-year plans and blood-soaked imperialism. Communist Russia had done what every fascist regime had ever done. They had bastardized an idea to appeal to two kinds of people: those who felt downtrodden and those who felt superior. The downtrodden wanted a higher standard of living, and the superior liked to think they were on the side of the downtrodden. In his Santa Monica apartment in 1968, Daniel had sat and watched with his friends as the Russians crushed the anti-Communist rebellion in Czechoslovakia, the so-called Prague Spring. Twelve years before that, he'd listened on the shortwave radio with Sherzai as the Russians had violently quelled the same kind of rebellion in Hungary.

How odd to see Peter nodding at Laila's words. He had barely been able to stand the pro-Soviet slogans coming from the self-described enlightened left. The exuberance of McCarthyism and the Red Scare had been so sinister that some had jumped to the opposite side of the riverbank, stomping their feet in pro-Soviet indignation from the safety of their third-floor walk-ups, traded in by now for three-bedroom ranches. The rational center drowned, as it always did in times of crisis, when extremes ate up all the ground until there was no such thing as in-between.

Exhaling, Elias ran his hands through his mop of hair as if hoping Laila would notice Peter's was thinning. And yet, if she was looking for a fling, it was hard to compete with the casual inconsequentiality of a foreigner who was just passing through and who could do nothing to harm her local reputation. Elias knew too many people she would encounter at weddings, funerals, or the clinic.

"America could get you all the stethoscopes you need," Greenwood said, abandoning his efforts to discuss women.

Laila started to respond, but Elias was like a Mustang at a light. "America's help comes with strings attached."

"You ought to welcome American strings," Ambassador Sutherland said.

Tie Clip raised his glass and added, "They're made of gold."

"Except they're more like ropes than strings," Elias said. Sauce dribbled onto his shirt, adding a new hue to his tie-dye.

Daniel expected Laila to join in, but she was quiet, eyes on Peter. She took off her glasses and folded them beside her plate, smoothing her hair. For a moment, she seemed ready to loosen the scarf from her throat, but she changed her mind when Peter smiled her way. Rebecca was watching them both. She straightened, eyes darting about the room until they settled on a painting that suddenly fascinated her.

"America doesn't come like Santa Claus, sliding all groovy down the chimney and dropping off a free bag of gifts." Elias's voice grew louder with every sip. "It *always* wants something back."

Sutherland raised an authoritative hand. "Can the head of USADE please chime in here?" He spoke as if asking for a second serving of rice, modestly thankful and without guile. It was the tone of every diplomat Daniel had ever met, including Laila's late father, an Iranian who had been stationed here after the war. Ambassadors were all so similar, it was like they shared a private nationality, an irony no one ever remarked on.

Daniel gave an answer he thought Sutherland would like, one that had the advantage of being true. "The difference between America and Russia is that America wants something, but Russia wants everything. Moscow takes what it wants and puts up curtains and walls around it."

"True," Ian said, placing his knife on the tablecloth.

His wife nodded, her Cheryl Tiegs waves bouncing at the motion.

Elias disagreed. "America makes walls and curtains of its own, and they're worse because they're not visible. You can't protect yourself from what you can't see."

Greenwood shook his head, but his eyes never left Elias. "I don't get people like you. You—"

Daniel interrupted. "Bob—can I call you Bob? What Elias is trying to say is that sometimes, America conducts its foreign policy like a Greek drama. All the violence takes place offstage."

"Sorry, I didn't study much Greek drama in school. I was busy learning things that were actually applicable."

A server approached with a bottle of wine. Greenwood covered his glass and asked for another Sprite. "Besides, if the violence happens somewhere else, that sounds fine to me."

"Why don't I find that surprising?" Daniel said. The car was right outside the gate now, snarling like a predator.

Ambassador Sutherland locked eyes with Daniel. With a kind but studied smile, he said, "Remember who you work for, son."

"He works for the greatest democracy in the world," Greenwood said. "And democracy is what this place needs."

"Democracy." Elias spun a hand in the air. "Just because you've lived in one all your life, you think you know what it means. You think democracy will look the same way every-where. It doesn't."

A waiter struggled to open a soda can for Greenwood, who finally grabbed it and wrestled off the tab. The Sprite fizzed, overflowing. "And what would you know about it?" He wiped the spill with his napkin and drank straight from the can before pouring the rest into his glass.

Laila didn't care that the question wasn't aimed at her, nor did she acknowledge Sutherland's prolonged gaze. "I know that if you keep beating people over the head with democracy, they end up with a concussion. And you wonder why they can't hear you anymore."

"Maybe we should talk about something else," Rebecca said.

Daniel felt his heart harden. What did she want to talk about? How glad she was to see an old lover? Or maybe the flaws in her husband, who had given her a thoughtless anniversary gift.

To lighten the mood, Ian tried to coax Greenwood into drinking something more than Sprite. When he wiggled a bottle in his direction, Greenwood snatched his glass back and said alcohol was poison.

"I hear you're familiar with poison," Daniel said.

Greenwood said something he had likely wanted to say

all night. "Agent Ruby isn't poison. It's a state-of-the-art defoliant, meant to target certain kinds of noxious plants without harming the integrity of the soil." He sounded like he was reading from a brochure. "We've tested it, and it doesn't harm people. Unlike alcohol, which certainly kills." He looked pointedly at his host. "You would know about that. Didn't your father die of . . ." Greenwood searched for the precise term. "Alcohol poisoning? Terrible tragedy. I was sorry to hear it."

Daniel had no cause to be surprised. A brief study of local history might have mentioned Sayed the war hero and the rumors of his fatal habit, despite Sherzai's efforts to suppress the stories.

"I meant no offense," Greenwood went on. "Not every man has the courage to go to prison for what he believes." When the others turned puzzled eyes to him, he added, "Mr. Sherzai told me all about it. How Sayed Sajadi fought the English in the big war of 1919, when he wasn't even twenty years old. How he used his money to buy off British generals and German engineers and buy high-tech weapons from arms dealers in the States." Greenwood rubbed his thumb and fingers together. "For that, you've got to have some serious cash." He aimed a finger at Daniel. "And some serious balls. Not a bad combination."

He continued, reminding Daniel that Dannaco-Hastings was giving him Agent Ruby for free in this "trial run." Daniel thought of children sleeping on ruined fields long after the poppies were gone. "Free might end up costing us more in the long term," he said.

"It's a done deal, whether you approve or not. Again, no offense meant." Greenwood spoke casually, mildly distracted by the dessert preparations taking place nearby, waiters chopping pistachios at breakneck speed. Bringing his focus back to the table, he continued. "I'm sure you know, Daniel, but the people here really *do* want an end to the poppies. We had similar problems in Colombia, Peru . . ." He waved his hand to indicate the long roster of nations he'd singlehandedly lifted out of misery. "You've got to listen to the will of the people."

Peter watched him with contempt. When he spoke, he formed his words so slowly and sharply that his fellow diners stopped eating. "You don't mean that, Mr. Greenwood."

"Then what do I mean?"

"You mean nothing."

Daniel fought a smile. For that comment alone, he might have forgiven Peter all his sins. Greenwood seemed to try but fail to understand the professor's words. "I don't follow," he said. Rebecca struggled to control her mouth, which threatened to break into a smile, while Pamela laughed like someone who had missed the punch line. As Daniel listened to what Peter said next, he knew there would come a day when he'd remember it, although he could not say why.

"What I'm saying, Mr. Greenwood, is that the will of the people would likely frighten you half to death and would *definitely* be bad for business," Peter said. "One day, the people you're talking about will overthrow their governments and try to annihilate you in the name of their god, and when you finally understand that the end of the world will be brought about not by Communist dictators, but the will of the people, it will be too late."

The stillness that came over the party now was worse than the others. The music had stopped a while ago. As if on cue, the driver outside killed the engine.

Sutherland spoke. "Peter, no war is ever really about any god." A memory stirred in his aging blue eyes, maybe a prayer he'd whispered at Omaha Beach. "They're just there to help sell the fight."

The servants brought dessert, tea, and platters of fruit. Daniel had barely touched his dinner. He bit into an apple. It tasted sour, although he knew it wasn't. Ian cursed a pomegranate whose seeds wouldn't come out. "Screw this misshapen fruit." Giving up, he dropped his spoon on the tablecloth. Laila helped him coax out the seeds.

The night was dark, the open window like a white frame around a black canvas, a painting a modern artist might call *Space*. Or, since the nuclear arms race had the world on the brink of annihilation, *Future*. At some point, Peter mentioned that his hotel had no hot water, and might not for a few days. Rebecca avoided Daniel's gaze, even as he sought hers. The result of their impasse was that neither invited Peter to stay, and Pamela awkwardly returned to discussing shoe stores. When the meal was finished, the housekeeper told Rebecca the garden was ready.

"I had the croquet set up," she announced to applause. "We can play without rules."

Greenwood looked puzzled. "What does that mean?"

"It means nobody wins," Daniel said, leading his guests outside.

"Somebody always wins, whether you keep score or not."

As they walked toward the terrace, Peter asked Rebecca, "How's your sister? Or shouldn't I ask?"

Rebecca shook her head. "Nobody hears from Sandy unless she needs money."

The wickets were arranged on the lawn. Pamela asked to play first. She swung the mallet, spun, and nearly tripped. She caught her balance, but her spiky pink heels sank into the lawn, gathering tufts of grassy soil and tilting her backward. She let out a surprisingly bawdy laugh, then stepped aside, gazing out at the lush plants framing the yard.

When Pamela asked the hostess how she grew such roses,

Rebecca told her it was the work of the gardener. "I don't have a green thumb," she said. "I can't keep anything alive."

She had only ever tried to plant one thing, but Daniel knew she wouldn't tell the guests. She wouldn't tell them that she had brought home a sapling pomegranate tree after Laila gave her the happy news, that she insisted she would plant it without the gardener's help, that it had thrived for a month, and that she had never gone near it again after the morning that drained all her tears. Until Telaya came and showed her there were more.

It was her turn next. She struck the ball with such force that it veered off course and nearly hit a visiting cat, who popped up from the lawn and bolted. A car door opened loudly and creakily just over the wall. The guests turned to face the sound, save Peter and Laila, who were dangling their feet in the pool, and Elias, who pulled a packet of Kents from his pocket and shook a cigarette loose.

The car door slammed shut. The bruise on Daniel's brow twinged when Telaya began to whisper her pleas. Daniel tried not to think of what would happen if she never, ever stopped. Then he would be like the man without arms, living in symbiosis with a ruined child—except that she could never grow up and he would never know peace. It would be the everlasting purgatory of which Dante spoke.

Good night, Telaya whispered, padding away into dark desert sands.

The doorbell rang.

12

THE CROQUET PLAYERS TURNED TOWARD THE STRANGER'S VOICE, WHICH CAME FROM INSIDE the house. The newcomer was admiring the architecture and decor while the housekeeper agreed politely with each remark. Daniel would have recognized the man's voice anywhere.

"Someone's obviously lost," he said, urging the others to go on with their game. But half of them followed him into the parlor, as if hoping the new guest had brought a game of his own.

"Hello, my friend!" Taj was in the doorway. His voice rang of fond memories, inside jokes, and too much time gone by. Looking glossy and rich in his black silk suit, the khan held his arms out, but Daniel remained immobile. Taj laughed as if his paralysis were part of a long-running act. He held out his hand. He wore an onyx ring, and his nails were long but immaculate. The thought of shaking Taj's hand filled Daniel with revulsion. A handshake was more than a greeting. It was a bargain struck, an understanding.

Taj's reply was loud enough to broadcast to the whole party. "I know I said I couldn't attend, but I left my other engagement early so I could at least have the honor of calling on your most worthy wife and making the acquaintance of your esteemed friends."

Daniel glanced behind him. Rebecca wasn't there. She'd

stayed in the garden with Peter and Laila. Greenwood clapped Daniel on the back and introduced himself to Taj. The others fanned out in the room, their faces turned to their host, waiting for the introduction Daniel could not bring himself to make. Before he knew it, Greenwood had asked Taj his name, Ambassador Sutherland had asked a server for two cups of tea, and Elias was mixing drinks at the wet bar. Pamela dimmed the lights until the room felt like a nightclub. She danced over to the stereo and began flipping through a stack of records. She found one that made her clap.

"I left this here on the Fourth of July!" She placed the LP on the turntable and dropped the needle. ABBA blew into the room like a sweet, sticky wind. Arms in the air, she sashayed about the floor in her peasant skirt. Ian and Elias encouraged her with applause, but no one seemed as excited as Greenwood, who whistled as she twirled.

Daniel's ears throbbed. Night air rushed in through the French doors. His sole objective was to expel Taj from the house. He was relieved Rebecca wasn't in the room. The sour wetness of the apple rose from his gut.

Elias pulled a lighter and a plastic baggie from his pocket. Soon, a pungent sweetness floated in the air. Ian took part, holding the joint like a cigarette. He tried to blow a smoke ring and pounded his chest before passing the weed to Pamela. She coaxed Bob Greenwood until the young man relented, agreeing to try it. After negotiating the joint with practiced hands, Pamela tried to share it with Taj, too, but he retreated. "I have enough vices, madam."

Ian lit a Marlboro. "Doesn't everyone?"

"Some more than others," Daniel said as his guests fell into conversation with the opium khan, who now seemed disinterested in his host.

"This guy's cool," Greenwood said, throwing a convivial arm around Taj and asking him how he knew Daniel.

Standing in a loose circle, everyone listened as the newest guest wove a tale, the light catching the gleam of his Bryl-creemed hair. He said he had met Daniel when they were just boys, when Taj's father worked as a foreman at a gemstone factory in the 1950s. But oh, how the years had gone by! Wasn't it destiny that Daniel and Taj should run into each other last week and know each other instantly? That was the way of old friends, he said. Of kindred spirits.

He changed topics like a race car driver cutting between lanes, asking everyone about their lives. He talked to each guest in turn. Journalism was a calling on par with religious inspiration, he said. The Peace Corps was one of America's greatest inventions, though there were so many it was hard to choose. Ambassadors were the trustees of peace, behind-the-scenes heroes who took no credit for the friendships they forged between rivals. Turning to Pamela, who was still floundering around in her solo dance, Taj said that it was seldom a man found himself in the company of a beauty queen who was also such a gifted dancer. Pamela thanked him, but Taj had already moved on. Bob Greenwood's interest in Afghanistan showed vision and an admirable readiness for self-sacrifice, he explained, rare qualities in such a young man.

As Daniel listened, he understood that the Manticore was not primarily a landowner or a poppy grower but a salesman. Taj Maleki was the kind of man who could convince you not only that the emperor was clothed but that you were the emperor.

Greenwood spoke proudly of the Fortune 500 firm he worked for, of his success with coca fields in South America, and the brilliant defoliant that would replace Agent Orange.

"But Mr. Sajadi here doesn't agree," he said, prompting Taj to raise an eyebrow.

"Is that so?"

"Luckily, he doesn't get to decide," Greenwood said. He cleared his throat. "Wow, my mouth is dry." He grabbed a soda floating by on a tray. Taj asked him question after question until the others grew bored and fell away. The man was relentless, revealing his own knowledge of the poppy trade as he quizzed Greenwood, whose speech grew irregular and repetitive. He finished the soda and threw himself at a bowl of sugared almonds, then asked for his fourth soda of the night and nearly poured the Sprite down his throat. Daniel was tempted to let him keep talking about Dannaco-Hastings and the State Department, revealing to Taj the kind of organized power that lay behind the destruction of the Yassaman field. But men like Taj were best kept in the dark.

"Taj isn't interested in these details," he said.

"You've got that wrong," Greenwood said, peering around for more sweet things to eat. "Your friend wants to know what's going to be done about the poppies. He's a big fan of your agency."

Ambassador Sutherland had been reclining on a sofa, claiming an achy back. Now he was on his feet. "Bob!" He made the name sound like an order. "Daniel's right. Our new friend here has heard enough."

What happened next caught Daniel off guard. As ABBA sang about a lack of money they surely didn't suffer from, Pamela took him by the hand and drew him onto her impromptu dance floor. He resisted as she flittered her fingertips in the air.

The others were back to clapping and laughing, save for Taj, who was leaning against a wall with his arms folded.

"You're drunk," Daniel quietly told Pamela.

She told him to loosen up, grabbing the tip of his tie and twirling it around. She wrapped her arms around his waist. The audience played along. Unable to bear Taj's stare, Daniel asked her to stop, but because he was whispering in her ear as a lover might, the game escalated. She pretended to be scandalized, covering her mouth with her hand, making her eyes wide. Ian feigned jealousy, threatening a punch before grabbing a drink from a passing waiter. Daniel attempted to gently pry Pamela from his waist, trying not to embarrass her while ending the dance. She stepped on his foot with those obscene girl-woman shoes.

Looking bored, Taj unglued himself from the wall and explored the room. He paused at an armoire full of shiny things, a shelf displaying special-edition books, ornaments, and a portrait of Sayed. He held his hands behind his back like a gallery-goer. Daniel kept a constant watch on him from the corner of his eye. He finally pulled away from Pamela, harder than he meant to. Her lips formed not so much a smile as a rigid rectangle. When Ian approached, Daniel expected a reprimand, but instead, Ian staggered toward Taj and collapsed into him, spilling his gin and tonic on the Manticore's shirt.

"Woah! Sorry, buddy," he said. But to Daniel, he sent a look that said, *You're welcome.*

Taj smiled. "No apology needed, my fine friend. I was just leaving, anyway. I was only waiting to say goodbye to the hostess."

The guests followed Taj's gaze. Rebecca had come in from the garden. She stood by the French doors and looked from Taj to Daniel and back. Daniel went to her side and slipped a protective arm around her.

Taj bowed from afar. "It is time for me to go."

He thanked Rebecca for her hospitality, then followed Daniel down the hall to the front door. Despite his composure, the khan's complexion was sallow. Bags of skin swelled under his eyes, which were shot through with red. The smirk on his face looked strained. "I expected you at the Zoroaster last night," he said as Daniel led him into the night-washed courtyard. "Normally, I might give you a few more days, but my lookout boy told me you were having a party. I was polite enough to wait until you finished dinner, of course, but how could I miss the chance to meet your friends while reminding you that I await your answer?" He tilted his nose up and inhaled. "You served lamb." For a fleeting instant, he looked hungry. Taj pushed open the gates to Dollar Djinn Lane. Daniel followed.

"I look forward to your answer on Wednesday night at the same time at the Zoroaster," the Manticore said as he oozed out of his jacket and tossed it into the back of his car. "It really isn't my sort of thing, but the big show happens then, so perhaps it will be more entertaining for you." He left Daniel with a final thought before ducking into the Opel. "We are on the same team, Daniel Sajadi." There was no mockery in his voice.

The car receded from view, leaving behind a spray of dust. Inside, Daniel found his wife standing so still in the hall, it was as if she had always been rooted there and the house had simply come up around her. Her silence was almost worse than the tide of questions he had expected. She followed him to the parlor.

"I'm sorry," she told their guests, "but I'm not feeling well. In fact, I'm not sure I've ever felt like this before." When prompted, she said she had a migraine.

"If you don't like weed, I have pills that'll knock that headache right out," said Pamela, lying across the sofa with one foot dangling off the side.

But Rebecca had already gone, her heels striking the

staircase as quickly as if she were running an uphill race. Daniel saw that the last person she looked at wasn't him but Peter. In her eyes was a plea for something Daniel couldn't give her. The guests began gathering their car keys and handbags. Sutherland left, taking Greenwood with him. Peter dropped into an armchair and rubbed his eyes, glancing at the clock. A moth had found its way in, moving in nervous circles until it found a sconce, beating its wings against the glowing bulb.

"Do you know why a moth flies into a flame?" Peter asked the room. Pamela said she had always wondered.

"Because moths evolved to orient themselves by the moon. The arrival of humans and artificial light is recent. When a night flyer sees a lamp or a candle, it can't calibrate its path. It ends up flying toward its death."

"How Shakespearean," Laila said. "It moves toward its tragic fate because it can't help what it is."

BROTHERS AND SISTERS

They ask him how old he is, but he doesn't know. They laugh at him. The children standing around Boy are like the rich girls from the big house. They have better clothes than him, and they're holding books in their arms. One of them is sucking on a lollipop like he doesn't even care, like there are a thousand more lollipops in the world. His tongue is dark red, and the lollipop makes a sound every time it hits his teeth.

When he runs away, they call him a name. "Hazara!" they yell. But he is not a Hazara. The servants in the big house were Hazara. His mother told him they were there to serve the rich people, but he and his mother were guests. That night, the first night away from the garden and Mother, he walks on big streets full of lights and people. Boy is not afraid of the dark, but night isn't the same in the city. There are thin streets that disappear between buildings. He goes down an alley and sees children sitting together under the doorway of a shop that looks like it's closed forever. Maybe they'll offer him some of the naan one of the older boys is tearing into pieces. He's tearing it carefully, making sure all the pieces are the same size. But the children don't notice Boy. It's cold, and he crouches against a wall and buries his face, and he starts to cry because he misses the wool jacket his mother made for him. He will sleep with no blanket tonight, no jacket, no fire.

His feet hurt. They have never taken him this far before. A skinny cat glides past him, but when he reaches out to stroke its fur, it runs away.

"Why are you crying?" one of the children shouts at Boy. "We're in the same place as you, and we're not crying."

"Come sit here," says a girl.

He gets up and walks slowly.

"Can't you go faster?" she says.

When he is next to her, she gives him a piece of naan. "Eat." She is smaller than he is, and her voice is small, too.

After many more nights like this, Boy feels lucky. He has brothers and sisters. They go everywhere together. He isn't afraid of children with clean clothes laughing at him anymore. He's learned all kinds of things to say to them, bad things about their mothers and grandmothers. Every night, he thinks about his own mother and says a prayer for her. He has more food than before; he can steal, because he is so small and quick. He makes it a game, runs away from grown-ups who try to catch him.

He likes to steal from women who wear the chaderi because they can't chase after him very fast. He remembers Mother clutching his hand and running across the street, how he could feel her sweat seeping into his palm, how she would say, "Hurry, Mother can't see well."

Boy brings in more food than all the other children. Sometimes, he steals candy bars called Milky Way with white stars on their blue wrapper, and he looks up at the sky and dreams of a day he will have his own garden with its own stars. Most of all, he dreams of a place with walls. Sometimes he and the others play a game, pretending they are rich people who live inside houses, and they talk about how high the walls will be and take turns acting like they are the master or the lady of the house.

Late one night, when he is curled up in a cardboard box outside a bakery, one of the girls crawls in with him and whispers, "How come you're so good at getting food?" He shrugs and says, "Because I'm not afraid." That night, he does not say a prayer for his mother. For the first time in his life, he does not say any prayer at all. The girl snuggles against him, and they fall asleep under a stolen blanket. She is screaming when he wakes up. Three boys much older than Boy are staggering around and laughing, dangling the blanket over them, just out of Boy's reach. He yells at them to give it back, but they don't. They run away with the blanket. The little girl leaves Boy's side and curls up alone in another box. Boy realizes something for the first time: the entire world is like those rich little girls in the big house, coming to kill his bit of warmth.

13

DANIEL WOULDN'T WAIT UNTIL MONDAY TO ASK SMYTHE WHETHER GREENWOOD WAS REALLY right about Agent Ruby definitively being used, with no room left to negotiate. When everyone was gone, he called Smythe at home in Washington. The consultant hadn't been bluffing. When Daniel tried to convince Smythe not to proceed, Smythe reminded him that Kabul was still too close to Moscow.

"Daoud is letting the Communists have their way with him," the undersecretary barked. "When has that ever ended well? If you think it can, then I've got a bridge to sell you. And it's not in Brooklyn, it's in fucking Siberia." Smythe coughed. "We've got to get Daoud to see Uncle Sam as his buddy so he can wash off all that pink and put on his star-spangled boxers. You follow?"

"And if nothing ever grows on those fields again, then what?"

"Something's bound to."

Daniel tried to answer, but Smythe cut him off. His speech slower, he repeated, "*Something* is bound to."

"I'm telling you that if we poison all these—"

"Poison? Who said anything about any poison?"

Daniel tried a different tack, insisting that the Ministry of Planning wouldn't comply, but Smythe told him Sherzai's office had already signed off. "This is a great thing. A very great thing. And if I were you, I'd get on board, unless you want to be selling Chiclets in Yugoslavia."

"Chiclets?"

"What can I say, I hear they like gum out there. It's the sugar and the constant chewing, I guess. Ha!" The hacking sound reminded Daniel of that James Brown song.

He argued, but it was no use. Smythe had heard enough. "Son, most people don't even know where this goddamn country is. Let Dannaco do its thing with Agent Ruby. If it works, it could be big. Now, go to sleep or do whatever people do at whatever hour it is out there." He hung up.

Outside, leaves floated aimlessly on the surface of the swimming pool. Daniel stripped off his clothes and dove, and in the water he found much-needed solitude and silence. The pressure of the water against his temples provided him a kind of peace. He liked to imagine it was squeezing out what he didn't need, leaving behind only the essential truths.

He thought about the Yassaman poppies and wondered at the miracle of such flowers growing in the desert, eruptions of color and life rebelling against this fallow land. It was tragic that such beauty and resilience had to be destroyed. He swam laps beneath the surface until his arms ached. One. Two. Five. His chest grew tight. He pushed to the top and gasped as he swallowed air.

The blackmail churned in his mind. The answer came to him as he tried to catch his breath. Daniel was the one bluffing. Not Bob Greenwood or Leland Smythe. Not Taj Maleki. If they used Agent Ruby on Yassaman, Taj might slaughter dozens of people, their blood making the poison seem meaningless. He thought of his promises at USADE. Of his father's fight against the English, then the poppy growers. Of Telaya and the importance of being counted.

Daniel was no longer afraid. He knew what to do about

the blackmail. He had promised to reform the Yassaman field. And yet, a person's character was not determined by which promises they kept, but by which promises they broke. The Scale of Sages had yielded an answer. Some things simply weighed more than others.

Upstairs, the bedroom was chilly. He rarely thought about the revolver he kept locked in his nightstand. He was hardly alone in keeping one. But tonight he unlocked the drawer. He suspected Rebecca was awake, but when he whispered her name, she said nothing. Her breath was the rhythm he normally fell asleep to, although these past months that rhythm rarely came as she lay silently awake. Instead he listened to the rhythm of the nightstand clock, an antique his father had brought back from India. Even as a boy, Daniel had loved the clock because he'd noticed it was irregular, pausing between the tick and the tock longer than it should. His father insisted they were spaced perfectly evenly, but they weren't, and Daniel's solitary knowledge of the clock's flaw made him feel like he had a special relationship to time. He had brought it with him to college. The first time Rebecca spent the night, she asked Daniel if the ticking was supposed to be *off like that*. He knew then that he was in love. One day, he and this piano-playing girl would navigate time together with that synchronized understanding behind all great romances. They would form their own irregular rhythm, a cadence that belonged to no one but them.

He thought about what had happened at the end of the party. After Taj left, Laila had approached Daniel. "Rebecca doesn't get migraines," she'd said. "That's something I would know."

"She doesn't tell you everything."

"She doesn't tell *you* everything." Laila asked Daniel to fetch her medical bag from her car. When he found it in the trunk, it wasn't shut all the way. His eyes fell on a small mass of brown resin wrapped loosely in cloth. He took the bag upstairs and found Laila outside the bedroom waiting for him. The door was closed. She told him Rebecca was fine, just tired. He dropped the bag to the floor and held out the small brick. "So she won't need any of this?"

She took it from him and said, not without pride, "I buy it on the street sometimes. There are never enough pain pills for my patients. A piece like this goes a long way." She continued with her justifications, although he hadn't asked for any.

"It's against the law," he said.

She crossed her arms. "Sometimes you don't get a series of choices, but a lack of options. Speaking of which, Peter is here because he lost his job. He didn't get tenure. His stuff wasn't serious enough, apparently. Too journalistic."

Despite himself, Daniel felt a pang of sympathy for his old friend. "He didn't say anything."

Laila raised her eyebrows in a look that suggested he was stupid. It had never occurred to Daniel that Rebecca had told Laila about her affair, but now it was obvious she knew. "He's just traveling now, trying to think about what to do," she continued. "Visiting friends around the world."

Softly, she added, "Rebecca told me what happened." He thought she meant the affair, but then she said, "It's horrible, to have an accident like that." She took his hand and squeezed his fingers. "Don't feel too bad."

The tears came so abruptly it shocked Daniel as he fought them back. "I just didn't see her."

Laila said, "I mean, it's possible her parents didn't even care that much. You know how those people are about girls."

Yes, Daniel thought, *I know how they are*. He remembered Telaya's weeping father and crying mother. He was afraid Laila's words would provoke the girl, and that she would chastise him for the cruel company he kept. "What?" he said.

"They don't belong in the world we're trying to build."

Daniel wondered if he had heard her correctly. "Who's 'we'?" he asked. "The inspired crew I saw you with downtown?"

For a moment, she looked like she wanted to take up the fight, but then her shoulders slumped and she shook her head slowly. "It's the only way forward, Daniel."

"So it's either Russian puppets or a future of backward superstition? Are you sure you know what you're doing?"

"Daniel, no one knows what they're doing. We can't predict the future—we can only turn our backs to the past."

14

IN THE EARLY MORNING, BEFORE REBECCA WAS AWAKE, DANIEL WENT OUT TO HIS WOOD-working shed. He looked at the abandoned, half-finished crib. It was as he'd left it, his tools still on the floor like he'd just gone out for a break. He moved it to a corner. Today he would begin a new project, a table for Sherzai's *sandali*. He would try to make it with an overlay. He hoped he was good enough to make at least a simple geometric design. He gathered the pieces and lost track of time as he began to assemble and cut. He attached the joiners to the legs. He screwed in the side aprons. The rhythmic movements, and watching something form from nothing, still brought an element of calm but did not bring him the usual enjoyment. What was the point of creating things when they would eventually be ruined by time, if something else didn't ruin them first? He kept working perfunctorily as he thought about what to tell Rebecca about Taj's appearance. Hours passed. He almost expected her to come into the shed, but she never did. It was nearly ten o'clock when he went back inside. She had left.

"Where is Mrs. Sajadi?" he asked Firooz, who was tidying up from last night.

"Somebody picked her up, but I don't know who. Mrs. Sajadi wanted her tea brewed even stronger than usual this morning, sir. She drank three cups."

Rebecca went shopping some Sunday mornings. Perhaps she had needed time alone, and Daniel vowed to put her mind at ease when she came home. Daniel went to his study. From his briefcase, he retrieved the folder on the Yassaman field, which included reports on the neighboring Gulzar field. During his short tenure, Kauffman had created files on every plot of poppies in the valley, even the useless ones like the Gulzar field. Daniel's staff had added a few updates, but little had changed in this unremarkable patch of land.

He began to create a story on his Olivetti. It was a sweeping lie, but each piece of it felt small, and a collection of small lies was something he could do without feeling dishonest. In less than two hours, the new Gulzar file was complete. It was believable. He'd added graphs and notes by hand, made a diagram of the poppy pods' composition and growth patterns, expressed the anticipated yield with numbers and charts, and compared the potency of different breeds, complete with an analysis of the various shades that opium resin took, from translucent amber to opaque brown.

Daniel was surprised at the thoroughness of his own deceit. How had it come so easily? It was as Laila had said: sometimes you were faced not with a series of choices but with a lack of options. An iron curtain had descended over Daniel's life, the accident dividing it into a time he was free and a time he was not. He called Sherzai, who agreed to meet later in the day, apologizing for missing the party.

It was past noon. Where was Rebecca? As he waited, he thought of Peter. Lonely, jobless Peter, in his hotel without hot water. It had been petty not to offer him one of their two spare bedrooms. Daniel decided to call and issue an invitation, if not outright, in a way they would both understand. He dialed the hotel and requested Peter's room. The clerk connected him. The line rang twice, three times, four. At last, someone answered. It was not Peter.

"Hello, Dr. Whitbourn's room," Rebecca said with comically exaggerated formality. A beat passed.

"Hello?" she repeated.

Daniel hung up. He wasn't sure how long he stood there, but it was until a bruising ache in his hands forced him to look down. He had dug his palms into the corners of his desk. He began to tidy the study. He worked slowly and methodically, organizing documents into neat stacks, stowing pencils and pens in a leather case, gathering a mess of erasers, sharpeners, and paper clips.

When there was nothing left to tidy, he went to the parlor. He walked to the fireplace, picked up the snow globe from the mantel, and sailed it across the room. It shattered against the wall. Liquid seeped from the cracked Bakelite, spilling snowflakes onto the carpet, gold-foil particles settling into the silk. The skater's ankle had snapped, her foot still bonded to the base. She gaped at Daniel, her eyes eternally open, mouth frozen in a waxy smile.

Come with me, Telaya said from the skater's mouth. *I want to show you something.*

"You're a ghost."

Then look through me at my world. She swirled in the water that continued to drain from the snow globe.

Daniel thought about Rebecca in Peter's room. He wondered what to do. He wouldn't go and confront them like a presumptuous fool. It was likely harmless, although she could have told him she was going out. Maybe she had tried to find him, not thinking to look for him in the shed. He was scheduled to meet Sherzai in four hours at the Gardens of Babur, where the old man walked nearly every Sunday. Daniel looked at the broken snow globe and set off to buy Rebecca something new. Somewhere on Chicken Street, there had to be another, or something she'd like better than the earrings.

He walked to the main road and waited for a bus to pass. The driver stopped wherever someone needed him to, and soon Daniel wedged his way onto a step, where he joined others. It was packed, and some were holding on precariously, doors open. He jumped off when he was near Shahr-i-Nau.

Crowds choked the sidewalks in this new part of town. Along Chicken Street, Daniel passed tie-dyes looking for and finding cheap hashish; shops that sold rugs, lapis, trinkets, yarn, karakul skins, and the garlands of paper flowers people used to decorate cars for weddings. In front of a kebab shop, the sound of sizzling meat provided a background rhythm for a monkey wearing a gold vest and dancing while its owner played a small crank-powered organ. Daniel walked in and out of shops, ignoring the invitations to haggle over marble ashtrays and vases, impossibly fragile blue glassware from Herat, and carpets from every corner of the country. No snow globes.

"Sir! Carpets! The best carpets for you!"

He turned to the familiar voice.

"It's you!" the owner said, smiling and putting his hand on his heart and bowing. Daniel did the same. Humayun Carpets looked like a hole in the wall, but far in the back was a staircase that led to a room filled with stack upon stack of rugs. Daniel had bought his finest Bukhara carpet here, an intricate pattern of flowers and leaves, all in shades of red with fine accents in black. The place smelled of strong tea and rose incense. As Humayun asked him about Rebecca, about work, and about when he'd start having sons, Daniel's eyes fell on a tray set with two cups and a teapot. They were made of white jade, delicate green vines climbing up the sides. It looked almost exactly like his mother's favorite tea set, which had been lost or broken at some point. When he asked if he could buy it, Humayun said, "That isn't for sale. How about a small rug for the entrance hall?" Daniel couldn't take his eyes off the set. At last, Humayun said, "It isn't for sale, because it's a gift." He refused to take money, and his young son carefully wrapped the tea set in fabric and gave it to Daniel in a thick bag with handles.

"You're too kind," Daniel said, bowing his head. "My wife will love this." He left the shop. He thought about the carpets he'd just seen. Their makers understood humility. Because only God was perfect, every Afghan carpet contained a small but deliberate flaw. It might be hard to find, but the flaw was always there, known to its maker, and visible to the discerning eye.

Outside, Daniel stopped dead in his tracks. From amid the throngs, a little girl in tattered clothes had emerged, nearly slamming into him. She watched him with wide, focused eyes. There were no coins in Daniel's pocket, so he offered to buy her food, but she shook her head and ran across the road, darting past cars that almost grazed her. "Be careful!" he yelled. She stopped on the opposite sidewalk and turned. Standing still, she watched him. Except it wasn't her anymore. She had turned into a child covered in mirrors and shades of red. She hooked her thumb toward a side street, then took off.

Daniel ran after her. It was like chasing his friends down the nameless alleys of their childhood as they fled their governesses and cooks, ducking into shops where merchants hid them behind counters. He clutched the bag tightly and flew down a narrow street where cars weren't allowed. The girl vanished, and Daniel spun around, trying to find her. There she was again, not ten feet away, and he reached for her, but she fled like a cat. Her cheeks were wet with tears. "I promise I won't hurt you," he called out. "Please." The chase continued. Deeper into the labyrinth they ran, away from the boulevards and shops, into quieter streets.

The crowds thinned, and soon there was no one but Daniel and the girl, who came in and out of view as she darted between walls and parked cars and shot through one doorway only to emerge from another. Her mirrored red dress was like a shiny bouncing target. He picked up his pace. She swung to the right down a curving path, and he followed. The alley was a dead end. He stood still, looking around. Where was she?

"Hey!" he called out. "What do you want?"

Go back the way you came, Telaya said, and Daniel wanted to tell her that he wished he could, that he had dreamed every night that he'd turned the car around just before she ran into the road. He caught a flash of red in a doorway and ran toward it, but the door was boarded up. He looked in every direction. She had evaporated, absorbed into the air. Daniel heard the rhythmic sound of dripping water; a small puddle was forming on the ground. He looked up and saw that the drops were trickling from a *chaderi* drying on a balcony. A few doors down, a sign was nailed to a house advertising TEACHERS AND BOOKS of a nondescript kind. Farther along stood a shop the size of Sergeant Najib's station. Daniel asked the clerk if he'd seen the girl.

"No," the teenager said, gesturing to his goods. "But maybe you need a new watch!" Half his teeth were missing. Cigarettes, cassette tapes, toiletries, and food were on display alongside Timex watches. Next to a shelf of Lux soap and Nivea cream, artificial beards were stacked tidily in a bin, for men who wanted to look more pious when they attended mosque. Firooz owned one. They were on sale.

Daniel overpaid for a pack of Kents and retraced his steps,

walking back up the cul-de-sac toward the main road. The distant hum of traffic grew louder. He walked up the side street, which was deserted save for two men slipping into a low-slung dwelling on the corner. It was one of the city's few houses of ill repute, walls of cement and heavy drapes hiding its activities. President Daoud swore such places didn't exist, especially in the midst of the new buildings and good houses nearby.

He could hear a man and a woman arguing inside. The quarrel escalated as he came closer. Afraid for the woman, he pounded on the door and pushed in without waiting. He came upon an impossible scene. A girl was arguing with a gray-haired man who complained loudly about the bad service he had received. She shouted that she had done her best. She wore a *chaderi*, but she'd lifted it up to her neck, bundling it around her head like a billowy cloud. Faceless, she stood with her naked body exposed. The hair between her thighs was dyed henna-red and trimmed into a tidy triangle, like a traffic sign warning of risks up ahead. She was cursing.

A fat man with an earring stood behind her, ham-hock arms out to the side, ready to intervene on her behalf. Daniel asked if she was all right. She pulled off the *chaderi* entirely, threw it to the floor, and turned to look at him. Her face startled him. She was no more than sixteen. Daniel reflexively looked away as her shouts gave way to tears. The gray-haired man had told her she was too old, she said. Daniel felt sick. It was one thing to read about this in Communist propaganda and another to see it in real life. No, they were not wrong about everything. Maybe this was the place he'd read about six months ago, where a group of urchins had been found dead in an unspeakable suicide, their bodies arranged in a star shape on the floor beside empty jars of bleach.

The customer rushed past Daniel and out the door. The fat man with the earring said, "What do you want?"

Daniel couldn't answer. He wanted so many things. To turn back time. For his wife to come home. Right now, he wanted to take this teenager away from here, but she gestured sharply for him to leave. He gave her money, assuring her it was hers to keep, no service required. She threw him out. The stillness of the street rang in his ears. Sherzai had once told him, *When a cause is really lost, don't waste time looking for it.* He wondered how many causes in his life were lost. He kept walking, nearly in a daze, until he discovered he wasn't far from the Khushal. Had the girl led him here? Had she understood something he had not about the importance of going to see his friend and his wife? He quickened his steps. At the desk, the clerk greeted him warmly, asking if he had come to book a dinner reservation. Daniel only wanted the number to Peter's room. On the third floor, he heard Peter's voice before reaching the door. He was talking about currency exchange rates, surely not a topic to entice Rebecca.

Daniel knocked, his hand awkward and heavy, a chilly sweat forming over his skin. His body was rigid. What would he say? He didn't know, but if Rebecca was falling back in love with her old flame, he would fight for her. Losing Rebecca wouldn't be like losing a limb. It would be like losing his center.

"Daniel!" Peter said as the door flew open. "Come in."

Seated at a small dining table picking at pastries, Rebecca and Laila leaned out to see Daniel for themselves. They greeted him sweetly with similar expressions, their heads held to the side, eyes wide. They almost looked sad. Did exchange rates warrant such melancholy, or had his arrival brought this on? The fragrance of tea and coffee filled the room. A basket held muffins and bread, crumbs scattered on the three surrounding plates.

"We meant to call you," Laila said. "You look terrible."

"How long have you been here?" Daniel asked Rebecca.

She told him she'd woken up and found herself alone and had phoned Laila.

"I had plans for breakfast with Laila," Peter said. "She brought Rebecca with her."

Laila smiled almost too brightly. "I thought since Becca was by herself, why not join us?" More likely, Laila had made plans with Peter and then changed her mind about meeting a man alone. Daniel felt a great burden leave him.

When Rebecca excused herself to the bathroom, he followed, leaving Peter and Laila to a vigorous discussion about local bistros and bookshops.

"Why did you answer the phone in here?" he said.

"That was you? Why did you hang up?"

"You go first."

"Peter and Laila were looking cozy. I didn't want them to have to stop talking."

"I'm not sure I trust Peter with her. Why are you trying to push them together?"

"I don't have to, in case you can't tell. This is good for her. She needs this."

"And you're the judge of that?"

"No." Rebecca glanced toward the table. "She is." Peter was standing behind Laila, showing her something in a book as she nodded enthusiastically.

"All right," he said. He reached for her hand and laced his fingers with hers. "How are you feeling?"

"Can I ask you a question now?"

Daniel braced himself.

"That man from the desert. Why was he in our house?"

There it was. By way of reply, Daniel said, "Did you know the whole time that Peter wasn't going to a conference?"

"I forgot."

"I forgot Taj was coming."

"Don't do that. Don't bullshit me."

"It turns out Taj knows a lot of the farmers in Fever Valley. He was interested in helping us. I thought he should meet Greenwood. I should've told you, but I didn't think he'd come."

It astonished Daniel how easily the lie formed. It was as if those hours he had spent re-creating the Gulzar file had unearthed a side he hadn't known he had.

"Laila said he was odd," Rebecca said.

"Did she say anything else?"

"What else *should* she say?"

"You tell me. You know her better than I do these days."

"So you just met this man the other day and he knows all the farmers and is a swell guy who just wants to help you plant rice?"

"Wheat."

"All I'm saying is, that's not how he came across at the police station."

"Becca, the day of the accident, I think Taj was trying to help."

"Whatever you say." Rebecca seemed to shiver suddenly. She moved closer until there was no space between them and wrapped her arms around him. "You know I love you, right? I'm your family."

He held her close. "What's brought this on?"

She stroked his cheek, pulled away, and disappeared into the bathroom. When she came out, he told her he had a gift for her. He gave it to her in front of the others. She didn't smile. She held her breath and looked like she might weep. "I love this," she said.

As the morning ended, dust particles dancing in the sunlit room, the four drank tea, Rebecca and Laila from the new set. The women gossiped about last night's dinner guests. Peter bored Daniel, going on about those infamous exchange rates. Even discussing the last sultan of the Ottoman Empire or the tedium of Peter's work at the Treasury Department would have been more stimulating. Did Daniel know that the dollar had been on the gold standard from 1900 to 1971? Did he know that the afghani was even weaker at the turn of the century than now? Yes, Daniel knew. Peter looked surprised.

An hour later, Daniel found himself at the Gardens of Babur, an oasis of green that harbored a mosque, the resting place of the last Mongol emperor. It should have been counted as one of the Wonders of the World, if for no reason other than the improbability of such a place in this chaotic, windblown city. Sherzai was waiting for him by the entrance. They strolled onto the grounds, which were laid out as a sequence of rising terraces, a central watercourse running between them. The vice-minister leaned more heavily on his cane than usual, but did not complain. Daniel retrieved cigarettes from his pocket and lit two, handing him one. They walked past mulberry trees, pausing at the marble pavilion at the center of the gardens. Babur's mosque glimmered like an apparition, its pearly angles and domes silhouetted against the sky. Daniel rarely saw Sherzai outside, their exchanges confined to offices and dining rooms. The man's face was heavily lined. Like Sayed's, his features had changed, but not because of drink, only time.

"What is this about, my boy? First you rush me to your office on Thursday, and now this?"

Daniel flicked ashes on the graveled path and told him

about a turn of events that was about to flip everything on its head.

"Turn of events?" Sherzai watched him gravely. "What's happened?"

"I've been following up on information from an anonymous source, and I didn't want to say anything until I was sure it was true."

"What kind of information?"

"The kind that changes things."

"That's true of every piece of information that was ever of use to anyone." Sherzai tossed his cigarette to the ground.

Daniel helped him onto a bench that was shaded by an oak and hesitated briefly before giving him the file. There was no turning back after this. Watching *agha* leaf through the papers, he sat on his hands like a child hoping to get away with a lie. Each second was a small lifetime. Lying no longer felt easy.

He avoided Sherzai's eyes as he recited his tale, fighting the lump in his throat, explaining that the Gulzar field was more important than anyone thought, and that a new, richer poppy seed had been sown there last spring. The meager-looking flowers held a potent resin many times stronger than the ordinary *Papaver somniferum,* the outcome of an experimental hybrid, like the growers in Burma and Thailand bred. Worse, a second planting had taken place last month, and an additional crop of poppies was set to bloom in Gulzar in the spring, when the worldwide supply of opium was low.

Sherzai did little more than scan the file. "What is this?" he said. "This is impossible."

Daniel pointed to graphs that showed the anticipated rise in the Gulzar field's production and yield based on details of the new crossbred poppies. The specifics, such as weight, subspecies, and concentration of opiates, were itemized in a column. On Daniel's Olivetti, the typebar for the letter *n* did not strike the ribbon properly, so it hung a millimeter below the other letters. It was a visible flaw that revealed the file as Daniel's, and though no one would ever guess, he felt that tug of ownership, just like he once did about that nightstand clock.

"Why didn't you show me this last week?" Sherzai said.

"I had to wait for confirmation on this." Daniel looked into the horizon, because it was easier than meeting his old guardian's eyes. "We need to turn the soil over before the new flowers come in. We have to start now."

"With what equipment? What crews? You can't reform Gulzar and Yassaman at the same time."

"I think the Yassaman field will have to wait until next year."

The vice-minister pressed his cane into the gravel and rose. "Next year?" He stood pillar-of-salt still. "Is this a joke?"

"We can use the equipment Dannaco-Hastings built for Yassaman. Most of it can be modified for the Gulzar field. It won't be a perfect fit, but it'll work."

A pack of schoolchildren passed, the teacher walking backward, beseeching her bored students to pay attention.

"Have you told Mr. Smythe? Mr. Greenwood?"

"I thought I should talk to you first."

"What do you expect me to do, *batche'm*?" Sherzai had gone from moving too little to too much, and his voice was fluctuating, too, rising and falling as he cut the air with the file. "This could be a trick, somebody trying to protect the Yassaman field. Who are these sources of yours?"

When Daniel insisted that the information was correct but that he couldn't betray the source, Sherzai interrupted again and again, as if talking were a nervous tic he could not control. "I am a vice-minister in the Ministry of Planning.

Do you understand? You serve us, not the other way around. You're here to help, not decide." Sherzai breathed deeply, and it sounded not like frustration but like a summoning of untapped power, his lungs filling with something more than air. "Everyone is invested in the Reform, and everyone expects to see the Yassaman poppies destroyed. The army. Every minister that counts. President Daoud."

The schoolteacher shot them a look of reproach magnified by thick lenses. Daniel could read her thoughts like they were printed on a flash card: *The Gardens are a holy place, not a place where men come to fight.* But Daniel could think of no place more appropriate for quarreling than a religious site.

"I'm the director of USADE now," he said, "and the United States government serves nobody." He was reminding himself as much as Sherzai, telling himself he had a right, even a responsibility, to speak to Sherzai as a colleague.

"You know what else the United States government doesn't do? Change its mind because an upstart thinks he has a better idea. Mr. Smythe will never agree to this. Dannaco-Hastings will never agree. And what about your staff? Do you want them to think even less of you?" Sherzai immediately looked like he wanted to take back his words, but they were already there between them, spreading like a toxic spill.

"I can't worry about what they think of me. You were the one who reminded me of the Scale of Sages."

"You understand little about scales and wisdom. But let's hope you understand this. In Europe, politicians talk about saving the whales because it lets them pretend they're getting along and listening to what the people want."

"Whales?"

"We need something the country can agree on. And it has to provide a proper show."

"You agree with Smythe's decision to have it filmed?"

"And have it broadcast on TV?" Sherzai opened his arms as if television encompassed the whole world. "It was my idea!"

"Smythe thinks it was his."

"He thinks every idea is his. Daniel, the best thing you've done since arriving is convince Washington that Yassaman is the priority. Those poppies are relentless."

Sherzai snatched the file from Daniel's hands and riffled through the documents until he found the note that had allegedly been scribbled by Daniel's source. He read it again and again, like a man presented with an impossible fact. "Daniel, I've been thinking about something, and I want you to listen." He stood very close. "Are you sure this is the right place for you? Rebecca isn't happy here. Maybe you should return to California."

"What?"

"You're exhausted and half losing your mind, giving me things like this"—Sherzai tapped the folder—"and I think you'd be better off going home. If for nothing else, for the sake of your marriage."

"I came back to do a job I believe in."

"It's not going to matter anyway. You'll see. There will come a point where you won't want to stay. You're delaying the inevitable."

Though it hurt to think about, Daniel wondered if those neighbors and cousins had been right about Sherzai. Was it possible he was driven by envy? Was it possible he wanted to take over the project himself so Daniel would receive no credit, and he could outshine the Sajadis at last?

"*Agha*, you want to push me out?" he asked quietly.

"I want what's best for you." The vice-minister took Daniel in his arms, an old, familiar embrace that had given Daniel strength as a boy.

"I have to give the order to destroy the Gulzar field," Daniel said.

"I don't take orders from you. Agent Ruby will be used on Yassaman. The poppies will be destroyed in twenty-two days."

Daniel lit another cigarette, and when he shielded the match he hid his eyes as well. "You've seen the file. The information speaks for itself."

"The information never speaks for itself. It is those in power who speak for the information. And you, my boy, are not the one in power." The vice-minister tossed the file to the ground, papers fluttering in the gathering wind. He pressed toward the exit as Daniel scrambled to collect the documents before catching up. A gentle rain began. Daniel had never been so aware of entanglements of fate. His was entwined with those of his wife and his agency and Sherzai. And in this web of principles and obligations, those who were no longer there loomed largest of all: Sayed and Telaya and a teenage boy shot to death in Fever Valley. How had it come to this? The dead ruled over him like great emirs.

Daniel and Sherzai walked along the bustling road, leaving the gardens behind. Sherzai held out his hand for transportation. "I know one thing," he said as if stating a widely known fact. "This anonymous source of yours. He's dead."

"Are you threatening my source?" Daniel asked incredulously.

"Your father was like a brother to me." Sherzai's eyes were rivers of glinting light. "I remember how disappointed he was the day your headmaster came to the house and showed him the note you forged to avoid school. The one you wrote in your father's handwriting."

"I'm not sure what you mean."

"That's what you said then, too."

"Please," Daniel said. "*Agha*, you've known me all my life." He swallowed hard and continued with difficulty. "My father was like a brother to you, and you've been like a father to me. You know you can trust me."

"I'm an old man, and if there's one thing I've learned, it's that no one should blindly trust anyone. Your father taught me that." They stared at each other. "I don't know what sort of game you're playing or why you would do this. I always thought of you as an honest boy, Daniel. You are not your father's son." Sherzai's tone was gentle, without the contempt that should have accompanied such words.

A horse-drawn *gadi* carriage slowed at the edge of the road, the driver offering Sherzai a ride. He climbed in, his cane clunking against the seat, and lowered himself to the bench while the horse shook its mane and turned its face to Daniel. One of its eyes was covered with a patch, the other crusted with a thick excretion. Daniel stalked ahead, never turning around, the sound of hoofs behind him like a metronome. He rounded a corner and, moments later, stepped onto a bus. He stared at the raindrops that squiggled along the windshield. Some moved horizontally, some vertically, and others diagonally. No matter what path they took, they all reached a dead end at the edge.

CORONATION DAY

Today is the first day that Boy is helping with the poppy harvest. He does not know how long it has been since his mother died, but Nazook, who takes care of him, says it was years ago. He and Nazook are working alone in a mud hut near the field. He can hear the wind rustling through the red, purple, and white flowers and he likes to see them when he looks out the door. He has been living with Nazook for a long time now. Many New Year's Days have passed. He is proud, because at last Nazook trusts him enough to let him help in the field. Boy takes the poppy bulbs from a basket, and with a small knife he slices them and coaxes out the sticky sap inside. The blade has to be cleaned between bulbs or it will stick. Some people just lick the blade, but Nazook says not to do this because you can get addicted to the sap. They dip the knives in water.

Nazook says that at the end of today, if Boy has done well, he will help him choose a new name. A real name, one fit for a young man who does important work. Boy asks what happens to the resin after they are finished. Nazook tells him it will one day become "poder," a powder that is brown, although the best "poder" in the world is white. People smoke it or put it in their veins in England and America. People who hate themselves enjoy such horrors, and it is all right if the infidels want to poison themselves. Boy does not understand how a person can hate himself when there are so many other people to hate, like people who would chase and beat up a boy for stealing a single orange.

The mud shack is warm, and Boy wipes the heat from his forehead while he works. They don't stop until it is dark. Nazook hums a song through his teeth as Boy's stomach growls. There are blisters on his fingers, and he needed to go to the bathroom a hundred poppies ago. But he keeps working, never looks up. Slice the pod, get the resin out, put it in the basket. Slice the pod, get the resin out, put it in the basket.

When the day is over, the bosses come to inspect. They feel the sticky brown stuff with their fingers and smell it, look at the pods to make sure everything has been scraped out. They give Nazook one green bill after another. These are not afghanis; this is the currency of foreigners. "Real money," people call it.

"Don't worry," Nazook says, stuffing the cash in his pocket. "For now, you share in mine. Later, they'll pay you, too, when I tell them you are valuable." Nazook throws his arm over Boy's shoulder, and they walk to the Opel.

This is the car Nazook was driving when he and Boy met for the first time. Nazook had seen Boy stealing grapes from a cart. "Hey, thief!" he shouted. Boy ran. He could almost feel the heat of the car on his back. He ran as fast as the day his mother died, his bare feet pounding the sidewalk and the street. The city was a blur of colors flying past him as he twisted and turned. He dove into an alley too small for a car and crouched behind two donkeys tied to a post behind a teahouse. "Hey, kid," a man's voice said gently. He looked up and saw the man he'd soon call Nazook walking toward him. The Opel, engine still running, blocked off the other end of the alley. "I'm not going to get you in trouble," the man said. He squatted next to Boy. "You're very fast."

Boy nodded. "I know the streets."

"You shouldn't have to steal for food," said Nazook. "If you come with me, I'll buy you a good meal."

Boy was wary at first, but the man took him to a restaurant and bought him kebabs and rice and naan and cucumbers and talked to him about all kinds of things, laughing and asking questions. Nazook watched as he ate all of it, then bought him a big cookie.

From that day on, Boy lived in Nazook's house. He had never been inside one before and wondered if they were all like this. It looked like somewhere a king would live. Nazook said it cost a lot. Boy decided that day that he wanted to work with the poppies, too. He would never sleep in the alley again. He would live with walls. He would always, always live with walls. Sometimes he dreams that he lives in a garden with the children he used to run in the streets with as Boy. A wild, beautiful garden with tall walls around it.

Boy is almost a man now. He tries to rub the resin off his fingers as they drive away in the Opel. Nazook stops at a very fancy restaurant to celebrate Boy's first day in the fields. Before the meal comes, he says, "You did well. What shall we call you from now on?"

Boy shrugs because he can't think of any names. Nazook's name means thin, but thin like a thing, not a person. They teased him for being skinny when he was a little boy, and the name stuck. "It's too late for me," Nazook said, "but not for you. What do you want to be one day?"

Boy laughs and says, "I want to be king."

"Very well, then. Your name will be Taj Maleki. Your first name means crown, and your last name means king in Arabic."

"I could never be king! There's already a king, and when he dies, then his son or his brother or his cousin will be king."

"Taj, any man can be king. He needs only to find people who are looking for one."

15

On Monday morning, Daniel scheduled a staff meeting, bringing together Seth, Iggy, and a half dozen others. The conference table consisted of four plain desks pushed together. He asked questions and complimented his colleagues on their work. The men grew more relaxed and talked about the headway they had made—the workshops, training, and farmers who longed for new skills, equipment, and plans. Daniel nodded, thanking them. He loathed the story he was about to tell them, but it was the only one he could allow. He explained that the timeline for the Reform had changed. He showed them the same document he'd shown Sherzai. The air left the room.

After glancing at the Gulzar report, Seth skidded the papers back across the table. Slumping in his chair, he drummed his fingers, peering at Daniel over his heavy glasses. Iggy asked questions, rubbing his brow now and then. "I don't get it. Why can't it wait?"

Seth answered on Daniel's behalf. "Because Daniel here says it can't. Never mind that we've been working day after day, week after week, month after month on the Yassaman field. After he talked us into it."

"So you should be happy we're postponing that," Daniel said.

"Can't you tell that no one in here is happy right now?" Seth drew an imaginary circle around the room with his pen.

"Quit it," Iggy said, scribbling notes as he spoke. "Let's stay calm."

They asked questions. Daniel answered. "I know it's unexpected," he said. "But we have to get working on this."

The men traded glances, the local farming experts and hydro engineers seeking an explanation from their American counterparts. Iggy shook his head in a small movement Daniel pretended not to see. He also ignored Seth, who was humming a tune through gritted teeth.

"There's a lot of work to do and not much time," Daniel said.

"And whose fault is that?" Seth muttered, scraping his chair across the floor as he rose.

Daniel asked him to stay behind, wishing the others a productive day. "Do you have some kind of problem with me?" he said when they were alone.

"There were a couple of things you left out of that presentation, that's all."

"Like what?"

"Like what does Smythe think of all this? What does Sherzai say? How come he's not here backing you up on this?" Sweat seeped through Seth's shirt as his monologue gained pace. "And what about the money? I've been at this a long time, and this is going to cost a fortune. Redoing the equipment, digging channels and pipes bringing water from the river?"

"It's all been taken into account and worked out."

"What, over the weekend?" Seth snapped his fingers. "Just like that?"

"You don't need to worry about those kinds of decisions."

"No, that's apparently your job, and you must take it *very* seriously. Everything was working fine—"

"Everything was not working fine. I have reasons for switching gears."

"Is that what you call this? 'Switching gears'? See, that's not what I'd call it. I'm an engineer, so I understand how gears work, okay? Let me explain something. When you switch gears, you go from one to two to three. Or from forward to backward." Seth moved his hands like he was driving a stick shift. "It's a sequence. A closed linear system. This? What you're doing here?" He tossed a glance at the door as if about to let Daniel in on a secret. "What you're doing here is, you're jumping right off the train and grabbing an entirely new set of gears on a different train going in another direction nobody's ever heard of. We have a special term for that, but it's pretty technical. We call it 'fucking things up.'"

"Your concerns are noted," Daniel said.

Seth stood with his hands on his hips, his tie hanging crookedly over his short-sleeved shirt. For once, he had removed his jacket, which lay crumpled on the table. "Kauffman would never have done this."

"Kauffman meant well, but things went wrong under him. That's why I'm here, remember?"

"No. You're here because—"

"That's all, Seth." Daniel returned to his office, his staff falling silent as he passed.

Seth had asked what Smythe thought as if he'd known Daniel hadn't told the undersecretary. Evidently, though, someone else had, because the Teletype was stuttering out a message from the State Department, and all the buttons on Miss Soraya's phone blinked red as she shot from one line to the other, telling every caller that Daniel was unavailable.

He locked himself in his office and drank the strong black tea she'd brewed. It was bitter and hot enough to burn. He beat back the temptation to pour himself a drink from the liquor cart. Miss Soraya held his calls for several more minutes, until he told her he was ready. The conversation with Smythe could only be described as catastrophic. It wasn't Iggy who had alerted Smythe, nor any of the others at USADE. It was Sherzai. Daniel scarcely heard the words that poured forth from the undersecretary. Until this moment, he had imagined Sherzai might back him up, or at least wait until they had spoken again before doing this. But *agha* had not truly betrayed him: Smythe didn't seem to know the file was a forgery. He only knew that Sherzai was against the new proposal. Daniel set the receiver down on the desk and leaned his head in his hands as Smythe's voice thundered.

According to Smythe, the great obstacle to the Gulzar Reform was not the Ministry of Planning, whose influence he called "as limited as my first wife." Nor was it his own department or the committees in Congress. As long as the result was big, and could be filmed, a different field was not impossible. But Dannaco-Hastings's contract gave them the right to withdraw their equipment. The final say lay with them, just as Greenwood had said, and Dannaco wanted more than a spectacle. It wanted a test, numbers and statistics that showed Agent Ruby could lay waste to acre upon acre of the most resilient plants, a pesticide that could be used by farmers and soldiers alike.

"As for me," Smythe said, "I need footage of a whole lot of poppies coming out of the ground. It doesn't have to be the Yassaman poppies."

"There aren't that many growing in Gulzar, sir. There won't be enough for a show."

"There could be."

"How? We can't transplant thousands of poppies and then yank them out for the camera."

"Footage of poppies can't be that hard to find," Smythe

said. "Anyway, it's a moot point. If your evidence doesn't convince Dannaco, and it's not going to unless Greenwood says the same thing you did, sayonara to this new plan of yours. That's Japanese, by the way, and it doesn't just mean goodbye, it means you're deep fried. Do you follow?"

"Can't you put pressure on them? We're the client, and we're also the damn US government."

"Easy there. Sure, we can put pressure on them. But first of all, I don't want to. Second, it's a contract and it's their equipment. You still listening?"

Daniel was.

"Third, they just gave a barrel of dollars to the Democrats, and Carter's already gearing up for reelection. He's been in office seven whole months, for chrissake. Time to start planning his next campaign. Fourth, follow the goddamn plan. Fifth—and this is important—let's never talk about this again." His parting words were about Greenwood. Daniel was to "entertain the kid, do whatever tourists do in countries where fun is illegal."

Miss Soraya came in with the telex, which was a more polished version of Smythe's tirade, likely composed by one of his analysts. Shortly after, the intercom squawked, and Miss Soraya announced an urgent call from the Ministry of Planning. Daniel did not wish to speak to Sherzai. She told him it was someone else, a man whose name she wasn't familiar with. Maybe Sherzai could not bear to speak with Daniel any more than Daniel could bear the thought of speaking to him. He told Miss Soraya to put the caller through.

"My illustrious friend, what a pleasure to find you there. I so enjoyed your party."

"I don't think you did. Don't get me wrong. It was memorable, especially the part where I got to throw you out, but I think Mr. Greenwood scared you."

"He does cut a frightening figure, doesn't he?"

Daniel nearly laughed. But when Taj cleared his throat and emitted a chuckle, it sounded dry and strained. "I have faith in you."

"Like I said before, it's not just about me. Even if I wanted to delay your inevitable and highly desirable ruin, you would have to blackmail a corporation with more money than the Saudi king."

"If I was foolish enough to do such things, I would have done them long before meeting you. I won't be blackmailing anyone else."

"A wise decision."

"*You* will be."

Before Daniel could ponder what this meant, the khan added, "Again, I look forward to the privilege of your company on Wednesday at the Zoroaster." The khan's voice held a tremor, and he spoke more slowly than usual, as if every word was an effort. The more time passed, the more Daniel thought something had rattled him and that Greenwood may indeed have changed how Taj saw things. Daniel hung up. Sherzai called later in the afternoon, but Daniel could not speak with him. Sherzai left a message that Miss Soraya conveyed: he wanted Daniel to know that he had not discussed the anonymous source with Smythe.

He mentioned none of this to Rebecca when he came home after a day of silences and worried looks from his staff. She knew enough. All day at the embassy, she had heard Sutherland's side of a dozen telephone calls, which she mentioned to Daniel. The ambassador had spoken with people in Washington and here, and USADE was mentioned in every call, seeming to have disrupted the interests of an array of people on both sides of the world.

"Is your new friend being helpful?" Rebecca asked as they sat down to dinner.

"Not especially."

While Rebecca buttered her naan, Daniel told her that on Wednesday night, he would take Greenwood to the Zoroaster because Smythe insisted he be entertained, and visitors always loved the club, which featured drinks, dancing, and dervishes, a combination few had seen.

"Great! I'll ask Peter and Laila. I'm sure they'd love to come."

"I didn't think you'd want to go. Besides, it's business."

"I don't mind. We'll stay out of your way." Rebecca smiled weakly. "Are you worried we'll cramp your style?"

The thought of Taj in a room with Rebecca again made Daniel's stomach twist. "I just think you might be bored," he said.

She turned her attention back to her toast, running the knife over it in a rhythmic, deliberate motion. "That didn't stop you from bringing me here." Her words hit him like a sandstorm.

"I didn't bring you. You came with me."

"I followed. There's a difference." After a pause, she added, "You don't have to do any of this. Your father was just a person. A flawed, ordinary person, and you're working yourself to pieces doing something you don't know he would have wanted you to do."

Where was this coming from?

"It's what I want to do, darling."

"How do you do that? Make the word *darling* sound like an insult?" She looked sad, but then paused and seemed to change her mind. "I'm always on your side. No matter what."

These outbursts of affection, delivered at regular intervals these past few days, surprised him. She raised her glass and he did the same, but when they toasted the sound was muted and tentative, as if they both feared the crystal might break. They resumed dinner.

"I have an idea." Rebecca took his hands and pulled him to the parlor, leaving their food behind, and switched on the stereo. To the gentle cadence of a waltz, he drew her into a slow dance in the dimly lit room. They talked about ordinary things—her friend Rita's engagement, the things they wanted to buy, and letters they needed to write. Daniel asked why she hadn't played the Beethoven sonata in days, after rehearsing the piece for so many weeks.

She thought before answering. "It was too hard." She lay her head against his chest. "It just wasn't worth it anymore."

"Some things aren't," Daniel said, pulling her closer. He had forgotten how much he loved dancing with his wife. When they returned to the dining room, dinner was cold.

As it turned out, Rebecca was right about Peter and Laila, who were thrilled at the prospect of the Zoroaster's dervish show, which neither had seen. Greenwood seemed more excited than anyone. On Wednesday night, the hired chauffeur steered Rebecca's Ford from Dollar Djinn Lane at nine o'clock. The mood in the car was festive; Daniel squeezed into the back with Peter and Laila, who were drinking directly from a bottle of champagne that they handed to Rebecca in the passenger seat. She took a swig and let out a laugh.

"Do we have any music?" Laila said. Rebecca looked in the glove compartment. It contained nothing but paperwork, a flashlight, sunglasses, and a city map. Daniel looked away. Before him flashed the Neil Diamond tape he'd meant to play the day of the crash. The album was ten years old. *Just for You.*

As the chauffeur poked along through the densely packed evening roads, spinning the radio dial, Telaya began to whisper, quoting lyrics from the record, running down its titles, changing the words a little here and there.

Just for him, she said.

Peter made one joke after another. "A Soviet soldier was just sentenced to thirty-one years in prison for shouting in public, 'The premier is an idiot!' He got one year for insulting the premier and thirty for revealing a state secret." The women broke into laughter until the driver laughed, too, and Daniel forced himself to laugh until his laughter was no longer fake, forgetting for a moment the real reason he was going to the club.

"You're silly," Laila told Peter. He kissed her on the lips. From her reaction, it wasn't the first time.

They were almost at the club. The ladies drew combs and lipsticks from their handbags, and Peter put on the shoes he had taken off. As the merriment was replaced by a silence full of cheerful anticipation, Telaya went on with her ghostly songs. Daniel caught only snippets.

She eventually stopped singing, but as they drew to the nightclub, she said, *The man without arms can't help having no arms. You chose to be blind and deaf.*

The car slowly came to a stop. The Zoroaster was on the fringes of downtown, this side's Studio 54 for denizens of the night. Armored tanks were visible on the road perpendicular to the alley, but none of the clubgoers seemed to mind. The military often roamed the city since the coup four years ago, and the recent protests and army presence struck many as nothing more than a few extra snails in a garden. Ironically, the nightclub was a force for unity, because all quarreling factions agreed it should be closed. To the Communists, the place was an emblem of Western decadence with its thumping music, alcohol, and half-naked dancers. To Islamists, the place was an emblem of Western decadence with its thumping music, alcohol, and half-naked dancers.

The chauffeur let Daniel's group off at the mouth of

the alley. Greenwood was leaning against the wall near the entrance, which consisted of unmarked lead doors guarded by a man with a gun and an attitude. The consultant hurried toward Daniel but kept his eyes on the tanks until the bouncer beckoned the group through the door.

Plain and utilitarian, the facade of the building belied the Zoroaster's interior. Sequined cushions adorned low-slung sofas. Glittery scarves were hung in swooping patterns along a wall. Waiters with slick ponytails balanced bottles of Veuve Clicquot and Black Label on trays. Four men sat cross-legged on long pillows against a wall, testing their instruments, amplifiers magnifying the booming bass of *tabla* drums and the electronic strains of a keyboard. Daniel led his group toward the high tables that ringed the dance floor, the strobe lights reflected in their mirrored surfaces.

"This place is amazing," Greenwood said. "Check out those chicks." He pointed unsubtly to several girls in skintight dresses and heeled boots. They stood in a close circle, glancing at men over their shoulders, sharing opinions between sips of wine.

After seating the women, Daniel and Peter ordered cocktails at the bar, where a bottle blonde offered cigarettes and the bartender mixed cocktails with flamboyant skill. It was past ten o'clock. Walking back toward the table with overflowing glasses, Daniel searched for Taj in the sea of strobe-lit faces.

"Watch it," said a man, tripping out of Daniel's way.

Greenwood thanked him for the Coke and slapped him on the back. "You know it's not gonna work, right? My company can't go along with it."

"Let's not talk about it now."

"The Yassaman land is good soil, at least for these parts. We're excited about it. You will be, too. You'll see."

Maybe he meant it, or maybe he just wanted to make Daniel feel helpless. Either way, he reminded Daniel of the inexorable victory of forces he might never be able to control.

Daniel scanned the room. Still no sign of Taj. In the club, the crowd swayed in anticipation, bass pulsing against the walls. Just as the emcee announced the dervishes, the opium khan came into view in the entryway.

"Hey, there's your friend," Greenwood said.

Rebecca jerked anxious eyes toward Taj but lowered them before he could acknowledge her. Peter and Laila were too fascinated with each other to notice. Beckoning a waiter, Daniel asked for a bottle of whiskey, wishing Ian were here. But Ian loathed the Zoroaster, which he described as "kind of tawdry but not really, and basically a place that makes no sense."

Amid a riot of applause, three dervishes took their places on the floor: one in his early teens, one Daniel's age, and one an old man, all wearing cropped white jackets and matching skirts that grazed the floor.

It was a scandal for a traditional religious dance to be performed in a discotheque. From the bass drum rose a sluggish rhythm, a deep and echoing beat followed by two shorter ones. The dervishes began to twirl, heads tilted, arms hugging their shoulders.

Taj never cut his gaze from Daniel, standing on the steps near the coat and *chaderi* check. Rebecca pretended to be mesmerized by the show. Greenwood had drifted to some other world, staring at other patrons, including a group of young men accompanied by older gentlemen in gold chains and thick rings. Daniel used the break in conversation to think through his next move. He wouldn't easily be able to reach Taj, who was past the giant wall the crowd had formed.

The music grew louder and faster, and other instruments

joined in. People hooted to the beat. Heads bobbed and bodies swayed. The teenage dervish whirled vertiginously, faster than the others, his long hair like black water under the searching lights. Greenwood looked uncomfortable. He leaned toward Daniel and laughed. "They do like spinning tops, don't they?"

From across the room, Taj briefly flashed a yellow envelope. He threaded through the crowd, slipping toward the restrooms. Daniel waited a moment, then followed. The men's room was empty save for Taj and a man whose bladder could apparently hold several pints. Taj stood before the mirror, combing his hair, leaning against the sink with his other hand. His body swayed slightly. With a silent flick of his gaze, he indicated an empty stall. Daniel went inside and shut the door. The yellow envelope was wedged behind the toilet tank. He opened it and was soon holding the edges of a single Polaroid. The glossy paper felt both sticky and slick.

The clamor of the crowd and the music thumped at the bathroom door. Daniel turned the photo over, unable to look at it any longer. He considered bringing it to the office to shred it; returning it anonymously to its subject, who would certainly destroy it; or tossing it in his fireplace at home. He leafed through his options like pages of a book, already knowing what passage he was looking for. There was only one fate for this devastating photo.

He slipped the Polaroid back into the envelope and exited the stall. The bathroom's third occupant was finally gone, while Taj remained, leaning patiently against the wall.

"How did you get this?" Daniel asked.

"Surely you knew such places existed. And thus, they must be serving a clientele." Daniel heard his street-child accent break through his veneer. The smell of wine bloomed on the Manticore's breath.

"I thought you didn't drink," Daniel said.

"I didn't," Taj said, as if just realizing himself that this was true.

"Why did you start?" Daniel wasn't sure why he'd asked, but he sensed an opportunity to humble the khan.

Taj only shrugged. "Why did you?"

"It's just something people do."

"If a man must have a vice, he should at least know how it serves him."

Vice. Rarely had Daniel seen vice on display like in that photograph. Vice or maybe even disease—whatever it was, its entire incarnation was captured on that Polaroid. He knew what he had to do, but if he stayed here, he could delay the task by a few more minutes. "How does drinking serve *you*, exactly?" he asked.

"It's a matter of life or death."

"Nobody ever died from not drinking."

"As usual, you misunderstand me. I'm trying to save my own life by causing the death of another."

"You think that talking in riddles makes you sound deep? Anyone from here can tell you're a fraud, *saheb*." He invested all the irony he could into the word.

"Another thing we have in common." Taj bowed. "Good night, my friend." Before he slipped out of the restroom, he added, "And you're welcome."

Daniel was left alone, clutching the envelope almost tight enough to crumple it. The picture was etched into his mind like the poppies were on Taj's gun. It laid claim to all his senses. He could almost hear the music coming from the radio on the particleboard table in the photo, smell the stale cigarettes piled in the ashtray. He could hear the din of traffic, the cars and bikes visible through the frosted window, which was dirty and cracked.

Two men pushed into the restroom, apologizing when they

hit him with the door. He made his way back to the table, where Greenwood and Rebecca were talking and Peter was feeding peanuts to Laila.

"Do you have a moment to chat?" Daniel asked Greenwood.

"You want to talk shop?"

"Something like that."

Rebecca protested. "Can't you take a break?"

Daniel reminded her that tonight was about business. She nodded. Sometimes she was so lovely it took his breath away, and he vowed never again to forget, never to risk losing her to Peter or anyone else. He walked with Greenwood up a staircase to the second floor, where there was a restaurant that operated only during the day.

"Where are we going?" the consultant said as they crossed the darkened dining room.

"Outside."

The balcony door was closed but not locked. A gust of wind slammed into Daniel's chest as he stepped over the threshold. The alley below was empty except for a looming tank, which groaned nervously at the corner while a smattering of people argued amongst themselves.

"I told you," Greenwood said after glancing nervously at the alley. "It's a done deal. Yassaman is a go."

Daniel looked up at the sky. "Have you ever noticed that the moon looks like a lens?"

"A lens?"

"You know, a camera lens."

"Whatever you say," Greenwood replied. "Look, if you keep pushing this thing with the fields, I'll have to take steps."

"Steps? How concerning."

"I don't bluff. Learned not to a long time ago. My dad was a gambler."

"Mine wasn't. Tell your superiors at Dannaco-Hastings that the plan has changed, and that you're behind me on this. If you need to, you'll tell them that you've personally seen soil samples and talked to engineers. Even that you've talked to my source."

Greenwood searched Daniel's face. "What kind of game is this? Daniel, you don't write the rulebook here. You've got your orders, and if you don't carry them out, the State Department will replace you with someone who will." In his chiding was a note of genuine concern.

"You have to support the switch to the Gulzar field," Daniel said. "Or I have to do something I really don't want to."

"What, push me over the balcony? Is that your grand plan?"

"No." Daniel produced the photograph and averted his eyes as Greenwood looked at it. For a moment, he wished the breeze would sweep it away, and take with it the shame and pain. When Daniel looked at Greenwood again, the man had taken a step back, his face inscrutable.

"I thought this would be paperwork about the Gulzar field," he said. His companion in the picture was younger than the youngest dervish, years younger than the murdered teenager in the Yassaman field. The boy's chest was hairless, his ribs obvious, his arms long and disproportionate to his torso.

"I know what you must be thinking, but this isn't what it looks like."

"I didn't ask for an explanation."

"It's a fake. No one's going to believe this."

"And that's a chance you're willing to take?"

Greenwood let his shoulders sink. His next words were a sorrowful plea. "Why would you do this? Is it so important to destroy the Gulzar field instead of the Yassaman field?"

"Is it so important to destroy the Yassaman field instead of the Gulzar field?"

"If I tell my boss your data's good, that we need to change the plan, this goes away?" The young man's lips quivered as Daniel nodded.

Greenwood wrapped his fingers around the railing and lowered his gaze to the alley, and for a moment Daniel feared he would jump. A soldier glanced up. Daniel walked closer to the ledge, calculating how fast he could stop Greenwood if that was his intention. But the consultant retreated, studying the sky. Searching for the god who had done this to him.

As Daniel turned to leave, Greenwood said, "I was on the top floor of one of the Twin Towers once when I was a kid." He stared up at the moon. "Have you noticed that no matter how high you climb, the sky never seems to get any closer?"

"And yet it can fall at any time."

Greenwood turned to him. "Exactly."

For a fleeting moment, Daniel felt a camaraderie with the man. He left Greenwood on the terrace and returned to the club, the photo wedged in his jacket pocket. The club was rowdier than ever. Rebecca was ready to leave. Everyone agreed it was time. When their group reached the lead doors, the bouncer jangled into sight with a set of keys.

The entrance hadn't been locked earlier. Guarded, but not locked. The bouncer opened the door just enough for them to slip through, warning them to be careful. Outside, they were quickly caught in the crush. A tank was crawling up the alley like a panther, slow but relentless. Its barrel was aimed at the crowd. Standing in the hatch, a captain shouted into a megaphone.

"Disperse!" he bellowed.

A dozen people were waving flags—some red, some green. These represented not countries but ideas. Daoud had become a traitor and a joke, the Communists shouted, raising banners that read KALQ, the more radical of the two main factions. They demanded a revolution and called the Soviets their brothers in arms. Not to be outdone, the religious opposition waved their green flags and called for jihad against the Communist infidels.

Jihad. Daniel had never heard the word used like this before. It usually referred to an inner struggle. You waged jihad against yourself, against personal temptations and petty emotions. Not against other people.

Rioters threw stones and pumped fists as uniforms gave orders and people screamed. A man climbed onto the tank and seized the megaphone. Emblazoned on his red shirt was a gold star. "The land belongs to the people," said the man as the captain aimed a gun at him, "not the capitalists who want to take it!" He waved a finger in the air. "Down with Daoud! Down with America! They hire Kochis, those stateless savages, and leave us with nothing!" Cheers and boos rose in the air, tangling like smoke. The captain struck the man with the butt of his gun, shoving him off the tank and wrangling the megaphone back. Curses flew, but it wasn't clear if the men were cursing each other, the soldiers, the Zoroaster, or some other thing entirely. In the club, the show went on, hypnotized partygoers unaware of the chaos outside. Daniel led Rebecca and his friends along the wall to where the car waited, engine already running.

No one spoke on the drive home. Daniel could feel the photo against his chest. Possessing this image felt wrong, like holding the bloodied limb of your fallen enemy. Or maybe it reminded him of his car, which he still had not returned to. Like driving, photography was a modern, useful act, a way to discover places and make memories, but it could become a weapon, destroying a life in the blink of an eye.

16

AT HOME, FIROOZ WAS WAITING AT THE DOOR. REBECCA'S FATHER HAD CALLED TWICE, HE SAID.
She sped toward the study. Daniel's ears were ringing from
the nightclub, the crowd, and the echo of the photo, and he
was glad Peter and Laila hadn't come home with them. They'd
gone back to his hotel room or her apartment; Daniel scarcely
cared. He waited in the living room, wondering why Walter
had called twice in one night. When Rebecca was finished, she
went to the garden instead of joining him in the living room.
He thought he should leave her alone. When she returned,
her clothes and hands were covered with soil.

He got up. "What's wrong?"

Rebecca held her breath. "My sister is dead." Her voice
broke. "Sandy's dead."

Daniel rushed toward her and wrapped her in his arms.
She fell into him with a guttural sound, a single declaration of
pain. He led her to the sofa, where she held on to him tightly.

"She took too much. She fell asleep on her back. She threw
up, and . . ." Rebecca covered her mouth.

Daniel rocked her in his arms as the story poured forth.
Sandy had died in an apartment in a northern swath of the San
Fernando Valley, where all the buildings looked alike, the
only variation the color and message of the graffiti. It was one
of those places nobody knew, but everybody knew *of*. Her

mother was in the hospital, recovering from shock, sedated with something that ended in -*bital*. The funeral would take place in five days. Rebecca was shivering as she told the story. "Let's get you warmed up," he said softly.

He helped Rebecca upstairs. It seemed each time they'd climbed these steps since the accident, they were fleeing something. Usually each other, but not tonight. He drew her a bath and sat on the floor of the bathroom beside the tub. She said she didn't want to talk. Daniel held her hand in the bathwater until it was cold and thought about Sandy. Her death was a shock, but not a surprise. By the time he had met Rebecca, Sandy was already a painful subject. She'd been a flower child, belonging not to daisies and marigolds but to flowers that killed. The same flowers that filled Daniel's days. The most striking thing about Sandy, besides a beauty that had faded by twenty-five, had been her voice, an incongruous blend of apathy and overwrought emotion unique to addicts. Always looking for a cause, she had wanted to stand for everything, and so she'd fallen for anything put before her. Dubious groups solicited funds for nondescript causes, and she fell for their scams. Young men plotted revolutions and wrote novellas, and she fell for them, too. Sandy kept on falling until she'd crashed through the floorboards of her life and ended up squatting with her ill-weather friends in gray-block buildings and abandoned shops. She had died like the Stupid Man who used to loiter in front of Daniel's house when he was a boy. Despite her privilege and her wealth, she'd been just like him, the old wretch who would stare at Daniel's fancy house and shake his fist at its walls as he dragged his feet over the dust.

17

THE STUPID MAN GREW VIVID IN DANIEL'S MIND, AND HE THOUGHT HE MIGHT BE REMEMBERING him for the first time since he'd left Kabul. As a boy, Daniel had wondered why everybody called him stupid. How did they know? The man never said anything particularly stupid. Sayed warned him to stay away, and the Stupid Man would shout, "Have you no compassion? Look at me."

When Sayed went to prison, *agha* came to live at the house to take care of Daniel and would watch the Stupid Man with pity. He would also warn him to stay away from young Daniel, whose hand he held tightly when they walked past. Sometimes the Stupid Man went away for a few days, but he always came back.

Leaving for school one morning, Daniel saw him through the car window slumped against a wall, head hung low. He searched the man's face for a sign of this silent stupidity. The man's head jerked up, then fell limp again. But in those brief seconds the Stupid Man and Daniel made eye contact, and the man's eyes were full of a sharp-edged light. Daniel dipped out of sight, hiding beneath the car window glass.

"It's the flower." The chauffeur held Daniel's gaze in the mirror as he accelerated on the uneven road. "If you like the flower, you turn stupid like him." He gave a nod to underline the importance of what he had just said. Daniel did not understand. He fumbled around in his backpack, found his French grammar book, and pretended to be engrossed by the pluperfect. After a few minutes, he put the book down.

"What does the Stupid Man do with the flower?"

The driver straightened his back and said, "The first flower, he ate. The second flower, he smoked. He puts the third flower in his veins with a needle."

The next morning, Daniel awoke at dawn from a dream, and though he couldn't remember the details, he knew it had to do with the Stupid Man. He wanted to see him up close. He snuck outside.

"Good morning," said a hoarse voice.

Startled, Daniel took a step back. The Stupid Man was against the wall with his legs stretched out before him. The man was like the skeleton they used in class to show you what men were made of once everything was stripped away.

"Don't you have school today?"

"Later."

"School is important. Do you like stories?"

Daniel nodded.

"You can stand or sit, it doesn't make a difference to me." After a pause, the man added, "There's nothing to be afraid of."

"I'm not afraid."

"I was talking to myself."

"Oh."

"I like talking to myself. It's better that way, because I know what the answer will be. Wouldn't you like that in school? To know the answers ahead of time?"

To this, Daniel had no response.

"You came for a story, so I'll tell you one. I had a son once, but I don't now, so there's nobody to tell stories to anymore."

"Your son died?"

"No. I did."

For a half hour, Daniel sat beside the old man. They looked straight ahead together as he told his tale, pausing sometimes to cough or wipe his nose, smearing mucus on his pants, his arms, the ground.

The Stupid Man had grown up forty steps from a field of poppies, and when he was a young man, one of the farmers convinced him to help. The landowners were desperate for good men, not just to harvest but to help the growers keep track of numbers: amounts, weights, prices, profits. The Stupid Man had not been stupid back then—he had gone to school. They paid him well. One evening when he was working late, one of the harvesters whose teeth were all missing told him he would feel better if he smoked a little. "Don't you want to try?" He gave him some to take home. "Don't tell, or they'll cut our hands off." The man said this matter-of-factly and made a slicing gesture across his wrists.

Soon, Young Stupid Man was smoking a few days every week. The landowner was kind, and they became friends. One day, he asked if he could be paid in resin instead of money. The landowner agreed and started asking him to do more and more tasks. Tasks that were riskier or that made him very tired, like working longer than anyone else. He did everything he was asked because it was the only way to get the sweet smoke that he needed more of every day.

Then a girl he loved told him she was pregnant and told him to stop. She became his wife, and he turned away from the field and went far away from the poppies, vowing to never return. He tried working in a shop, but he missed the poppy and began to drink. It wasn't the same. He started to steal to make more money. His son was often sick, and one day the woman took him with her and disappeared. So Young Stupid Man, who was not so young anymore, lived alone with a three-legged dog he rescued from a gang of mean boys and slept in a box that he carried around, tying the dog to a hook in one of the boards when he went to work.

One day, the dog fell very ill, and Young Stupid Man needed money for a dog doctor, something only rich men could afford. He knew that dogs were just dogs, but he'd grown to love the miserable creature. So he went back to the fields. From then on, his life was both terrible and wonderful. He couldn't resist the resin's golden song. The old owner was still there and again agreed to pay him in opium—small amounts, enough to make him happy and keep him working. They weren't friends anymore. One day, somebody said the owner was caught and put in jail. The Stupid Man didn't believe it. Men like that were never really caught. The Stupid Man couldn't save his dog, whom he found dead one day, vultures already pecking at the animal's gangly frame.

Eventually, he became too weak to work. The fields didn't want him. He was poppy-sick and would remain so for the rest of his life.

"See, I am a wretch," the Stupid Man would say as he wandered through the country on feet so calloused they didn't bleed, begging for money or opium. "Please help me. Just a little."

When people saw the constellation of pinpricks on his arms and the rotten teeth in a face that was still young, they would shake their heads and say, "Stupid man, you gave in to the flower."

Nights were the worst. It felt like someone had pushed scrolls of ice down his throat, then dragged him into a spitting, mighty fire. It was all a terrible joke played by a wicked djinn. As he lay there, wondering if he was awake or asleep and hoping he was dead, the fire burned his skin, and he would sweat so much that he hoped it was the ice inside him melting and pouring out of his body. But the ice grew only colder and harder, and the sweat just kept coming like a boiling river. He shivered and shook, his legs kicking at imaginary enemies. He swore sometimes at God, sometimes at the devil. He blamed both for the chains that fettered him. He grew ill and sometimes coughed up blood. He had only one wish left in his life, and that was that he should die indoors, not in an alley like his dog.

The story ended. Daniel sat quietly beside the Stupid Man, and this was how Sherzai found them when he appeared from the house to greet a pickup truck that slowly rambled into view, depositing two construction workers on the street. When Sherzai saw Daniel, he grew angry and told him to go inside. Daniel gathered his books, and when he leaned out of his bedroom window, Sherzai was talking to the Stupid Man, who cried and said he was sorry and promised he had not hurt Daniel and would go away and never return. He got up and limped away, screaming nonsense. "This is what it looks like! This is what it looks like!"

Agha returned to the house, his face sad. He was a good man, kinder than Sayed, though no one ever said so out loud. His own wife had died a long time ago while giving birth to their daughter, who died, too, and Daniel thought this had made *agha* sad for the rest of his life. That afternoon, Daniel learned why the construction men had come. It was his thirteenth birthday, and Sherzai had hired them to build a fancy work shed for him. When he came home from school the shed was ready, though the paint was still wet.

Sherzai gave him a gleaming red box of new tools. After cake and a birthday song, he ran to his new shed. He pushed open the door, tripping over the threshold in his excitement.

Then he saw the Stupid Man slumped in the corner. The Stupid Man had wanted to spend the last moments of his life indoors; his wish had been granted. Daniel was sad, but also happy that his shed had provided the man with comfort on the last day of his life.

18

WHEN REBECCA EMERGED FROM THE BATH, SHE CURLED UP ON THE SHEETS AND REACHED FOR Daniel with tender despair. Her sister's death left her wanting to engage in the act that brought life. They lay awake afterward. She talked about Sandy as if recounting a story she'd heard long ago, not one she'd lived through. She'd forgotten about Taj, the club, everything. They held each other and whispered comforting things, and for a moment they were on the bluff in Santa Monica again, sitting side by side on a throne, the sea a glittering kingdom at their feet.

In the early morning, Daniel rose and peered through the drapes while Rebecca slept. On the dew-silvered lawn he saw a ruined flower bed. This was what she had done last night before telling him the news. She had turned over the soil, tearing up the new buds meant for next spring. Kneeling, the gardener, who had been there from Sayed's time, was picking at the earth with a small shovel as he repaired the flower garden. Daniel returned to bed and wrapped her in his arms.

While she slept, the awful truth dawned on him. He couldn't go with her to LA for the funeral. The destruction of the Gulzar field was coming, and the tale he'd spun to make it happen was so fragile.

Over the years, he'd thought about what would happen if Sandy died. He'd wondered if she'd be alone, how old she would be. In his sorrowful imaginings, the details changed, but one thing never did. He was always at his wife's side. He was holding her hand tightly during the service, and he would take care of everything, all the logistics that reduced tragic events to a collection of tedious moments—the paperwork and phone calls and schedules and dotted lines. He had never imagined that he wouldn't be there. How had it come to this?

When Rebecca woke up, he told her he loved her, and she said she loved him, too. They stared at each other, trying to remember what people said after that. When she told him to please find a flight for the next day, he told her he couldn't go. It just wasn't possible.

"I can't believe it, but it's the way it is," he said. It was true. "The way things are, there's no one else. There's so much hanging in the balance right now. If there was any way I could go, I would." He was falling over himself as she watched him quietly. He promised he would do everything he could from here. He asked her to please believe him. "I've been through this in my mind over and over. I just can't abandon this."

She pushed up on an elbow and continued to watch him, then she closed her eyes and breathed deeply. "What are you actually saying?"

"There are too many things happening here, Becca. Serious things."

"I'm sorry, *serious* things?"

"If I don't go, innocent people could get hurt. People could die." He tried to make it sound like this was a normal concern of his job.

"What are you talking about? Somebody's already dead. My sister."

"If I told you . . ." He let the sentence trail off.

Slowly, she said, "If you told me, then maybe I would understand."

He took her hand, but she pushed it away. It wasn't a forceful gesture, but it suggested exhaustion and resignation.

"Becca, please trust me. I wish things were different." He said what he found so difficult to say, and what he almost resented having to say because he thought it was obvious. "You're the most important thing in my life." A warm numbness came over him when he said it, a kind of relief painting over everything else he had felt. "You know that."

When she didn't respond, he added, "Please believe me."

She rolled away from him. "Don't worry. When I see my mom in the hospital, I'll explain that the day she's burying her daughter wasn't convenient for you." After a while, she cried. Not tears of grief for Sandy or that terrible night three months ago or the crash. These tears were for her and Daniel. She told him to leave.

"I just need to be alone."

Downstairs, he sat in the dimly lit living room. His eyes fell on an ornament, an intricately carved mahogany fox. In one of its flanks was a tiny dent, too small for most people to see. It grew in his vision until the ornament itself disappeared, and all that was left was the flaw in the shape of the fox.

19

THE NEXT MORNING, SHE TOSSED CLOTHES IN A SUITCASE LIKE COINS INTO A FOUNTAIN. HE tried to comfort her, but she pulled away. He felt helpless, like he had broken another thing in Rebecca. The Scale of Sages had been cruel. He said softly, "My being there won't bring Sandy back."

"No," Rebecca said. "But it might have saved something else."

She spent hours on the phone, and in the late afternoon, he brought her luggage downstairs. She strapped on her shoes. "I don't know if Laila told you, but Peter got a job at the university."

Surprised, he asked if Peter was returning to UCLA.

"No, the university here. He's going to teach English."

So it had come to that. He felt sorry for Peter. "We're going to be late if we don't leave soon," Daniel said.

He hadn't driven a car since they had come back from the trip. He felt his heart rate rise and his palms grow clammy as he thought about being at the wheel. In his head, he could hear the engine purring deceptively. He reached for his shoes by the entryway.

"Don't bother," Rebecca said. "I have a ride."

There was a knock before he could reply. Peter stood alone at the door, Laila's empty Volkswagen pulsing in the street.

Daniel pulled his wife aside. "What's going on? I'll take you to the airport."

"You're too busy," she said gently. She gave him a passionless kiss, then walked past Peter and waited in the car.

"How is she?" Peter asked Daniel.

"She's obviously been better."

Peter launched into a winding explanation of why he was here. Rebecca had called to ask for a ride. Laila was at the clinic and couldn't come. He was still talking when Daniel shut the door. He spent the rest of the evening in his study, poring over documents both authentic and false. He worked late into the night, trying not to think about poor Sandy dying in a no-name place with no friends, or about how much he wanted to be with Rebecca's family. Instead, he thought about Greenwood. Even the most transparent man could become opaque when his livelihood depended on it. What a swindle Greenwood had pulled, checking out girls every chance he got. Maybe he'd hoped the seed inside him would simply die. But it had sprouted and bloomed, no poison strong enough to destroy what was inside him. Daniel wished an Agent Ruby existed for men with twisted desires.

Daniel went upstairs and retrieved the photograph, which he had unimaginatively hidden under the mattress. He locked the envelope inside the safe in his study, spinning the lock again and again. The boy in the picture might have been Greenwood's first, but Daniel suspected he wasn't. He thought about the awful whorehouse he'd wandered into. Some youths were living under even worse conditions, used in back alleys and streets.

At first, Dannaco-Hastings balked at Greenwood's insistence that the Reform be changed. It would cost too much to reconfigure the pipes for the Gulzar field and re-dig the channel. Once he'd convinced them it would be worthwhile, they requested samples from the Gulzar poppies' resin.

"That's already been done," Daniel told Greenwood. The consultant tried to protest, but Daniel pushed the file across the desk. "It's all there. Everything was tested less than a year ago. If we test again, we'll be wasting resources, and you know both our employers hate that."

Seth, standing outside Daniel's office, let out a laugh of disbelief.

Eventually, Dannaco-Hastings accepted the report, taking Greenwood at his word. And so began the reshuffling of priorities in Smythe's office and elsewhere, committees signing off on the firm's request to destroy the Gulzar field. Daniel's made-up file circulated among senators and congressmen with limited interest in Afghan poppies. Smythe's office argued at first, but the information was undeniable, or so Greenwood told them. Dannaco changed its mind, and so did Smythe. Sherzai quietly went along but stopped taking part in meetings and calls, sending an assistant in his stead. Everyone moved fast. The smell of dark tea and Nescafé filled USADE night and day, and Seth and Iggy seemed to never leave at all. Neither spoke to Daniel. Iggy was too busy, Seth too angry.

If the office was too chaotic, the house was too quiet without Rebecca. There seemed to be no middle ground left in Daniel's life. Peter and Laila called and showed up at his door once, but he made excuses not to see them. Ian came by and asked for help on an old car. There was no time, Daniel said, when in truth, he no longer enjoyed working on cars. He couldn't avoid his friend much longer, though. Ian would be at the Gulzar field the day of its destruction. In Washington, a committee had decided that the Peace Corps should be on hand to "help farmers and their families adjust," whatever that meant.

The following Tuesday, Daniel received a message from Philip Kauffman, who now worked at a research desk in the

Department of Agriculture on fruit orchards in the Midwest. He told a cautionary tale. During his time at USADE, he had exhaustively studied the Gulzar land, as he'd studied every field in Fever Valley. There was no payout there, he explained, reminding Daniel that the directorship was an easy post to lose when poor decisions were made.

Though Seth had stopped talking to Daniel, he grew louder when he spoke with others, accentuating his selective silences. It worked. In Iggy's office, he audibly lamented the lack of good leadership, contempt for expertise, and futility of a program he compared to a "sniper with no aim." Daniel gave up trying to persuade him, and instead resorted to admonishing him for insubordination. Within days the veteran engineer was on probation, a decision Daniel explained only to Smythe.

"Do what you have to do," the undersecretary said.

"So you have my back on Seth?"

"Fuck Seth."

This sounded encouraging, so Daniel pressed on. "I want to revisit the question of using Agent Ruby. I'm asking again that we reconsider."

"Ain't gonna happen. I thought this was settled. You got wax in your ears?"

Daniel gave up. Even Greenwood didn't have the power to stop Dannaco from testing Agent Ruby. That was, after all, why they were here. They owned the product, and Daniel couldn't forge a file about its effects or its nonexistent history. He could only fight one battle at a time.

After Seth's probation was announced, the staff worked so silently it sounded like the typewriters were operating themselves. Farmers who had expected to soon be tilling food crops on Yassaman were given new guidelines. Daniel told Iggy to organize workshops and change the focus from wheat to corn, because he knew corn was easier to grow and the Gulzar soil was poor. Seed was ordered by the ton, hefty fees paid for swift delivery. Around the office, eyebrows rose and doors closed when Daniel passed. Elias called daily, insisting on an explanation for the change, which he'd learned about from the Ministry of Planning.

"I don't know anything Planning hasn't already told you," was all Daniel would say, and after a while he refused Elias's calls. The last thing the journalist said to him was a threat veiled as a quip: "Remember this, Daniel. A good journalist is like an octopus: he blinds his enemies with ink."

Greenwood came and went, endorsing Daniel's requests and justifying his conclusions. He clapped Iggy on the shoulder—never Daniel—and complimented secretaries on their dresses and their hair. One day he even flipped open his wallet and flashed a photo of a redhead he called his fiancée. After a while he came in with two-day stubble, a look at odds with his tidy hair. Within weeks, his class ring had loosened on his finger, and his watch no longer fit his wrist.

When the destruction of the Gulzar field was only three days away, Daniel spent the afternoon in Fever Valley with his crew. The poppy workers of Yassaman were there, picking at leaves and petals, pulling up weeds, and occasionally glancing at Daniel. One of the men smiled. By now, Taj and his workers guessed their land would be spared, since the machines had crawled away. Taj must have seen the newspapers too, including one where Elias had written about USADE's sudden change of plan and condemned the regime for its lack of control over American agencies. The most remarkable thing was that such a publication could exist at all. The last of the free newspapers had been shut down nearly ten years ago. Through Laila, Daniel heard that Elias had launched the paper with friends, hiding in different apartments, typing with the curtains closed, and printing as many copies as they could by bribing workers at another paper, then leaving them in stacks around the city.

Daniel got into the pickup truck with his colleagues, Iggy at the wheel, and they pulled away from the Gulzar field. On the highway, they crossed a column of tanks moving as calmly as the Manticore. One of them was flying the Soviet flag, its hammer and sickle gleaming like an illusionist's wink. It was what Daniel had seen the day Telaya died. While driving back to the camp with the nomads and Taj, he had passed a caravan of tanks, one of them flying the flag. That Russian advisers were present here was widely known, that they rolled along the highway in tanks less so. Long ago, Sayed Sajadi said: *Russia is a bear that doesn't hibernate. Never turn your back.*

The convoy was barreling toward the city. It was funny, really. The Russians didn't understand that when it came to opium and religion, Karl Marx had it backward. Religion wasn't the opium of the masses. Opium was the religion of the masses, making new converts every day of war vets and jazz stars and teens who mistook self-destruction for self-expression. Of so many of the workers who depended on it for their livelihood. Delivered through pills, pipes, and needles that the faithful shared, opium provided epiphanies that made its supply scarce against ubiquitous demand. Daniel wondered why he was here at all. He couldn't get rid of the poppies, not really. All he could hope for was to move them somewhere else. All over the world, governments were trying to kill the drug trade by passing tougher laws, driving it underground. But underground—didn't they know?—was precisely where roots took hold.

20

NO ONE WAS ANSWERING THE PHONE AT THE MENLOW HOUSE IN LOS ANGELES. REBECCA hadn't called since the day she'd left. Daniel missed her. More than that, he was worried. On the third day, Walter finally picked up. He didn't criticize Daniel for not coming; if he was angry, he was too consumed with grief to show it. He said they'd just let the phone ring for a few days because everyone was calling about Sandy and it had become too difficult, especially for his wife.

"It's fine work you're doing out there," Walter said. "Important work." He passed the receiver to Rebecca. Her greeting was brief.

"You're not angry with me anymore?" Daniel said.

"I don't have the strength for anything except this right now."

Sandy would be buried the day before the destruction of the Gulzar field. That future date had become Daniel's principal measure of time, the day all other days led to. Rebecca said she hadn't slept in forty-eight hours. She ended the call with a small good night. He held the receiver, wondering if she was really gone.

Late that night, a caravan of vehicles headed toward Fever Valley. Daniel decided he would drive. It was time. The destruction of Gulzar was his responsibility. It felt both right and inevitable that he should lead the caravan. When Ian wanted to hitch a ride with him, Daniel found an excuse to say no. He wanted to drive alone. The car felt unfamiliar at first, like a strangely formed cage. When he carefully depressed the accelerator, she was there.

Let's go, she said.

Daniel led, followed by Greenwood, USADE staff, and the Peace Corps contingent. Ian's Citroën puffed away in the rear. It was eleven o'clock when they nosed into the small compound a mile from the fields, a cluster of apartments rented by Washington. The space was utilitarian and drab, with drop ceilings and linoleum floors. There was no air-conditioning, no granite facade with Daniel's name etched in gold, but there was a stereo and a microwave in the kitchen. Iggy snapped an eight-track into the tape player. Buddy Holly filled the air. They found Budweiser in the fridge, clinking their bottles. Daniel sipped tea. Seth said nothing. Iggy talked nervously about the weather and everyone's Christmas plans. Greenwood was silent, with no strength left to play the requisite games. Ian moved from table to table, laughing at things that weren't funny and drinking with men whose names Daniel didn't know.

Shortly after midnight, he gathered his colleagues and led them through a rundown of tomorrow's plan. They rehashed details they had reviewed a dozen times: the protective suits, the crop dusters, the evacuations. The film crew that would arrive in the morning.

He wasn't tired when he settled into his bedroom. He fished out a bottle from his overnight bag and drank until he didn't know if he was asleep or awake. He spent the night on a narrow bed and rose before the alarm rang. Day hadn't broken when Greenwood, Iggy, and Seth loaded into his car, the others trailing as they made their way toward the fields.

The men tried not to spill their coffee as they bit into pastries so dry they crumbled. Daniel's mouth was parched, the whiskey still churning in his stomach. When Iggy made an effort at small talk, Seth grunted along. In the desert, a Kochi migration moved toward the road, men pulling animals and women carrying baskets while the children tried to keep up.

Daniel's group passed the Yassaman poppies glowing under the rising sun. Their petals had fallen. Next week, Taj's harvest would begin. His land was upstream from the river, so Agent Ruby would flow away from his precious flowers.

The poppy workers rose from the ground in the Gulzar field as Daniel's convoy arrived. Through the open window, he heard a boy say, "Mama, I'm thirsty." She told him the water in her bucket was for poppies, not people. They didn't know that trucks would soon arrive and drive them away—Dannaco-Hastings and the State Department had insisted that all people be removed and kept out until the week after the dusting was complete. Daniel wondered why this was necessary if Agent Ruby was as harmless as they claimed.

It seemed impossible that the Yassaman harvest would take place while Daniel cleared out the useless land nearby. This was not the Reform he had wanted when he'd come, but it was still a step forward, he hoped. Greenwood paced back and forth with his hands in his pockets, refusing to make eye contact with anyone. He checked his watch, likely impatient to fly home and never again be at the mercy of the man with that photograph. Daniel wondered if his own sins were as clearly etched on his face as Greenwood's were on his.

Then, in a single row, the trucks appeared. Soldiers jumped out, ordering the Gulzar poppy workers to get inside. The crowd huddled together in an attempt to resist.

Why? they said. *No.*

"Now!" the captain shouted.

Squinting against shafts of morning light, Daniel climbed on the hood of his car. It was warm, the engine asleep under the metal. From his podium, he told the wary crowd that a chemical was about to be used, and they could soon return to harvest the field in peace. He wondered what his father had said when he'd stood before their predecessors, rallying them to fight the English. He had convinced them to risk their lives for a war, while Daniel couldn't even convince them to save their own lives.

It was easier to give them no choice, as the captain understood: he fired a warning shot in the air. If it frightened them, they did not show it, other than a few children who screamed. The adults spoke amongst themselves and began moving toward the trucks, which stood puffing exhaust into the clean morning air. Daniel jumped down from the hood and walked with the poppy pickers. Soldiers divided them into groups. A woman shouted that her son was being taken to a different truck, begging the soldiers not to separate them. The captain consented, reuniting the two. A hundred men, women, and children crowded into the open-air trailers, pressing their backs against the rails and each other. Soldiers latched the tailgates shut.

Greenwood walked off to greet the van with the film crew. He told them they weren't to tape anything yet and made sure all the microphones and cameras were off. They were to capture only the crop dusters, aiming the lens high, away from "the six poppies growing there" in the Gulzar patch. Dannaco would edit in whatever else was needed. As Smythe had said, it couldn't be so hard to find footage of poppies. They would get their before-and-after shots—even if there was no real before and after. Donning their protective suits, everyone was silent as they waited for the crop dusters. The crew looked like astronauts with their white plasticky clothing and masks.

The low-lying aircraft appeared at eight o'clock, wobbling hunks of metal under a vast pale sky. Dipping toward the field, the pilots unlatched the release vents. The planes slowed and discharged their poison, a white vapor. Daniel thought of the little Cessnas he had learned to fly in California, where the view was a sliver of paradise, canyons and water gilded by sun. When it was over, the crew returned to its quarters less than a mile away. The contrast between last night and this afternoon could not have been sharper. There was no Buddy Holly, no beer, no jokes.

Refusing lunch, Daniel said goodbye to his colleagues and locked himself in his room. It was over. Maybe Agent Ruby would allow new crops to sprout the following spring, like Dannaco promised. They would do everything they could to fertilize the land just a few months from now. By late winter, planting could begin, and in the spring the corn would emerge. One day, maybe he would find a way to destroy the Yassaman field.

The days passed, blending into each other. He called Rebecca nearly every day. He worked with his staff in the mornings, ate dinner alone, and avoided Ian as best he could. When almost a week had passed, the crew returned to the field. Agent Ruby had vanished into the dry earth of Gulzar. The poppies were dead, their petals, pods, and leaves scattered across the discolored land. The men applauded, Greenwood leading the charge with enthusiasm.

Daniel went to bed at five o'clock in the afternoon, pulling the sheets high around his neck. It was done. He had struck a bargain, and the payoff had come. When he awoke, it was dark and the telephone was ringing. He ignored it, but moments later, it rang again. Eventually, he took the receiver off the hook. He didn't want to talk to anyone. There was nothing to say. Now that it was over, and he had done what he could to save the poppy pickers of Yassaman, something had drained away, leaving an empty space. He heard footsteps bounding up the stairs, followed by a loud knock.

"Daniel! Open up!"

Iggy stood on the landing, face glistening under the porchlight. He was breathing heavily. "The Yassaman workers. They . . ." He shook his head.

"They what?"

"You didn't answer your phone. Ian says you have to come right now." Iggy closed his eyes for a moment. "Seth's waiting in the car."

He stumbled through an explanation as they drove to the Yassaman field. When Daniel stood at its edge, he tried to understand what he was seeing. It was a completely different place than it had been before. Tonight, no one was sleeping at the edge of the field. The grandest harvest in Fever Valley was strewn with bodies. Stalks were flattened, flowers made red by blood. A donkey lay dead among the poppy pickers. Police cars lit the night with red and blue flashes. A handful of soldiers came and went with guns. Daniel saw Sergeant Najib from the police station. He stood motionless near the road, eyes fixed on the field. The wails of a child pierced the air.

Police and soldiers moved deeper into the field, painting the horizon with their flashlights. Their voices seemed obscenely loud in the Yassaman graveyard. Scattered among the bodies were hardened puddles of worthless sap. Journalists walked around the flowers, as did doctors from a nearby charity.

Daniel left the field behind. Faces blurred together until he saw the one he was looking for. Taj Maleki stood with his shoulders hunched and his back angled awkwardly. The khan was neither monster nor man, neither Manticore nor human, but a statue abandoned by its dissatisfied maker.

Ian appeared in the crowd. His jowls were stubbly, face

lined with shadows. "Jesus H. Christ. Most fucked-up thing I've ever seen. Makes the gangs in Queens look like Boy Scouts."

He kept going, but Daniel wanted to hear from someone else. Taj had to explain himself. Why had he massacred these innocent people, when Daniel had fulfilled his demands? He felt like not only a liar and a criminal but a fool. He should have sought advice from *agha* or reported everything to the authorities. He cursed himself for his hubris and mistrust.

Ian kept talking. He'd been woken by colleagues when police came by the compound, asking for the Americans. It was Ian who called the local Doctors Without Borders, a contingent that worked closely with the Corps. When they arrived, there was only one person left alive—a single child. That was something, at least. A survivor. Everyone knew who had done this, Ian said. He pointed to the horizon. "Take a look."

And then Daniel saw. Tied to a gangly bush, blowing in the night wind, was a red flag, a gold star sewn on the fabric. A poster was nailed to the trunk. It read, WE DEMAND LAND AND A LIVING WAGE. IF YOU DON'T LISTEN, MORE WILL DIE.

So this was why the police and army had come in such numbers. Not because the nomads were dead, but because the Communists had come to sabotage an American-led project of the Ministry of Planning. He looked toward Taj, whose gaze was inscrutable.

"Tell the soldiers whatever you can," Ian said. "They'll want to know if you've ever seen anybody here scoping the place out, or if your crew ever heard anything."

"There was nothing." But Daniel spoke with the soldiers anyway. He spoke to Sergeant Najib, too, who scribbled details in his yellow notebook, his arrogance gone.

21

AFTER AN HOUR, THE SCENE WAS WINDING DOWN. THE FEW CIVILIANS WHO'D COME TO SEE the carnage returned to their cars, mules, and wagons. Daniel rode in Ian's car, Iggy and Seth behind them. He and Ian sank into the sofa in his room. Its stuffing protruded like the sickly shrubs dotting Fever Valley. People sometimes described rage as white- or red-hot. But the rage inside Daniel was neither of these. It wasn't blinding, either. He had never seen more clearly. These men who, like the Russians, made both Communism and atheism into sinister caricatures, had done the unspeakable. It was one thing to be godless, but another to be soulless.

Ian filled two glasses with water. "Why was your weird buddy there?"

"Who?"

"The guy who wears too much cologne."

"I'm not sure." It wasn't entirely untrue. "Ian, you have no idea what I've just done."

"You did your best."

"You don't know that."

"But I do, my non-Celtic friend." Ian patted his arm. "Save the guilt for when it's yours to own." Roaming around the apartment, Ian found the whiskey. "I may need this tonight," he joked, stashing it in his satchel. He gave Daniel an awkward fist bump.

The door clicked shut, and Daniel waited until Ian was gone. He picked up a flashlight and left his room. He walked through the darkened compound, awed by its silence and stillness. He made his way up an unpaved walkway. Above him, the stars were a tangled necklace of gold. He didn't encounter a single car or truck, and there were no *gadi*s or other travelers at this hour.

The Yassaman field was filled with ghosts now. The only living thing was Taj, squatting at its edge, contemplating these shredded flowers and bodies. Daniel nearly grazed him when he stopped the Mercedes at the edge of the road. Taj rose in the beam of Daniel's flashlight. They stood close, face-to-face. Taj looked older. On the ground beside him was a flask, at his waist a cone-shaped pouch. Taj motioned to the poppies.

"Do you see them? The finest that have ever been grown." He wandered into the field. From his pocket, he drew a small blade. "Maybe I can salvage a few." He moved through the field, scoring the few poppy pods that had not been slashed or crushed. He worked fast, his hands gliding from one flower to the next. Daniel walked with him.

"Help me," Taj said. "Grab a blade. They dropped them when they were shot."

Sap oozed from the pods Taj could save, milky and white. By morning it would gleam like cloudy, amber-colored glass, crystallized by the sun. Suddenly he straightened, standing by a cluster of bending stalks. Voice breaking, he said, "I'm sorry for what was in the photograph." Then, in his usual tone, he added, "It's dangerous to have such a bad habit in the age of the Polaroid." He turned back to his massacred world, checking for any resin that hadn't hardened and any pod that hadn't been scored by a blade, torn open by a bullet, or crushed by a body. Daniel realized that he was lighting the man's way with his flashlight.

There was no reason for Daniel to be here, but he felt like he would come unmoored if he left. He looked up at the endless sable sky. The universe was expanding, even as his own world shrank. The opium trade always expanded, too, and would do so despite tonight, despite his life's work. Taj would plant again in the winter, and the Yassaman field would thrive. Blood was the greatest fertilizer of all.

DEAD WRONG

The doors to the banquet hall are closed. Taj can hear the sounds of a wedding party. Music is thrumming, and he can picture people dancing the atan, *moving in a circle, clapping their hands at intervals as the music picks up speed. They are all in their best clothes, and Taj imagines the sequins and hair spray and mix of perfumes, making the air a heavy syrup. Sometime before this, the young man's parents must have approached the girl's family, and everyone agreed they should get married. No one will reach out to a nice girl's family on behalf of Taj or present him as the suitor they have been looking for.*

He drives away from the hall and leaves the city far behind as he heads to Bala Hissar, where he feels more at home than anywhere except his gardens. The old citadel rises on a hill in curved and jagged lines, a fortress that once kept people safe. He has never seen walls like this anywhere else. Every time he is within them, calm washes over him.

Back when he was Boy, Socrates showed him pictures of Bala Hissar. Boy dreamed that he planted a vast garden inside those towering walls, a garden no one else could see, and there he lived with a girl who loved him and didn't care that he'd grown up in the streets. At night the old citadel is the largest, quietest place in the world, and it belongs only to him.

Tonight he is meeting a girl, but she isn't the one from his dreams. She is the first woman he was ever with. He leaves his car on the splotchy grass and climbs up the hill, as he has done a hundred times. She is there, crouching by one of the walls, shrouded in a chaderi. *She puts a hand on his arm when he sits down beside her. Her limbs are trembling and her pupils are huge, as they always are with someone who very badly needs opium. She cries and tells him her stomach hurts, that she is scared, her noises becoming small and clawing. He prepares the opium for her. She smokes, and when she is calm again, she curls up against him. They talk about nothing for a long time.*

When she pays him with her body, it doesn't feel like it used to. The first time, Taj felt something he'd felt only a few times before, when accompanying Nazook on an adventure to steal something important, like watches, jewelry, and cartons of cigarettes: that dizzying feeling that power meant owner-ship, and ownership, power. He had been all that mattered to this woman because he'd brought her opium. He'd owned her completely in those moments, and Nazook used to tell him that's what women were for. Owning. Tonight, for the first time, Taj feels pity for the woman huddled beside him, naked, using her chaderi *as a blanket. She is only here because he brings her opium, and now it feels like the very opposite of power. He helps her put on her clothes, and she insists on staying here alone when he leaves.*

Nazook was right about many things, but not this. Boy didn't realize Nazook could ever be wrong until the day his mentor made a fatal mistake. Once, when he was talking to young Taj about girls, Nazook told him that Taj's history wasn't beautiful at all. There was nothing beautiful about a man coming by with day-old vegetables and planting a seed in his mother inside a tent. Nazook laughed mockingly and told Taj his mother had sold her body for radishes and a bag of lettuce.

Taj walks through the old citadel and thinks of the other thing Nazook had gotten wrong. He'd believed he would one day reign supreme in Fever Valley. Nazook had been very wrong about that. He'd been the first to see Boy's potential—and the last to underestimate him.

22

IN THE DAYS FOLLOWING THE BLOODBATH, WHICH THE PRESS NAMED THE FEVERDROPS Slaughter, Daniel felt both overly tired and alert. The massacre woke him at night like someone pounding at the door. Thoughts raced through his mind or moved as slowly as the beggars downtown. The newspapers used the event to underscore the dangers of Communism.

Sherzai stopped by without notice. Daniel was glad to see him. They shook hands and embraced in a quick succession of stiff but earnest gestures. He appeared to be almost in shock.

"Which faction would do this?" he said. These aren't normal Communists." His voice was strained. "Where's the liquor cart?"

"I had it removed."

"I see." There was concern in *agha*'s voice. He squeezed into his usual chair, resting his cane across his legs and accepting a cigarette. "What will you do now? Rebecca won't want to live here after this."

"She's stronger than you think. But maybe you're right. I assume you know what Smythe said? You two seem to have a good rapport."

Sherzai sought his eyes, but Daniel would not look up from the stack of mail he was sorting. "I would never harm you, *batche'm*."

"You threatened to ruin me." Daniel tossed pointless letters into a wastepaper bin. "What would you call that?"

"What would *you* call lying to someone who took you in as a son?" Sherzai shook his head and changed the topic. "This is no place for your wife or for you."

"I don't see how I can leave."

"Please, listen, for once in your life. I'm trying to help you."

"I know. But sometimes I wonder if that's all there is to it. I'm not a child anymore, and I want to ask you something. Man to man."

Daniel asked Sherzai to forgive him for what he was about to say. Before, he would never have considered it. But *before* barely existed in the wake of the Feverdrops Slaughter. And so he said, "Maybe you want the Reform to be your legacy rather than mine. Maybe you're tired of it, being in Sayed Sajadi's shadow?"

As soon as he'd said it aloud, the idea sounded both absurd and cruel. Grief melted into tears in Sherzai's eyes.

"I'm sorry, *agha*," Daniel whispered. "I didn't mean for it to sound like that."

Sherzai dabbed at his cheeks with a handkerchief. He stood with difficulty and circled around the desk without his walking stick, then rested his hand on Daniel's shoulder. In that hand, Daniel felt the weight of a lifetime of promises and duties and love, along with pain.

Miss Soraya arrived with a steaming pot of tea. After cursing the Darjeeling for burning his tongue, Sherzai said, "Let's say you manage to turn a few fields into something better. So what? In the end, what will have changed? And what will it have cost you?"

"Everything worthwhile comes at a cost," Daniel said.

"Everything worthwhile has to be *worthwhile*."

"I have to believe it will be."

"Believe all you like. That won't make it so."

"I have to stay, Sherzai."

"All men are willing to make sacrifices before they understand what those sacrifices are," Sherzai said. "What if things get worse and USADE shuts down in a few months?"

"What if it does?"

"Won't you wish you had left earlier, instead of putting Rebecca through months of worrying, the two of you sitting an ocean apart, waiting for the inevitable?"

"USADE won't back down that easily, especially now. As Smythe likes to say, we can't let terrorists change us."

"He said that because he has to. Of course terrorists change us. They get us to change ourselves. How we act, how we think. And all the while, as we shout that they aren't changing us, they laugh and watch us become even worse than they hoped."

Daniel wished he hadn't asked Miss Soraya to remove the liquor from his office. Later that day, Rebecca called. She'd heard about the Feverdrops Slaughter from Peter and Laila, who had reached her hours ago. She wasn't calmed by Daniel's promises that he was safe. If anything, she grew more anxious when he described the steps taken by USADE and the regime. He tried to change the subject. They talked about Sandy. The gravestone had arrived. Rebecca's mother was better, but still finding relief in little blue pills.

Telaya had fallen utterly silent, though he found himself searching for her the morning after the tragedy. It was almost a betrayal, this silence when he expected her to join him in rage. At the State Department, everyone worked overtime, trying to formulate an explanation for how they hadn't seen this coming. Everyone wondered if USADE would continue its operations at all.

After a tense waiting period, the agency learned its fate. Secretary of State Cyrus Vance's decision was, as Smythe put it, unequivocal.

"Vance thinks Daoud looks weak if we pull anybody out, and if you ask me, he's right. Which isn't an everyday occurrence for Vance. Those Commies are terrorists, and we don't let terrorists win. The people who did this aren't regular red, they're big red." Smythe made a spitting sound. "That goddamn gum has too much cinnamon for me, but the grandkids like it."

Daoud's regime dispatched soldiers to guard every field slated for reform. It was an irony of sublime proportions, a military presence to help the opium harvest proceed undisturbed. The other great khans harvested quickly, their poppy workers looking over their shoulders. Everyone passing through Fever Valley was warned to bring an ID and an explanation, and no vehicle could bring in more than four men or six women.

Daniel wondered what Taj might be thinking. Washington and Kabul couldn't be the only ones talking; the Manticores would be deliberating their own fate.

At USADE, the focus shifted to smaller fields with farmers happy to hire local villagers. The office was now open only Monday through Wednesday. Guards patrolled the building. Telaya's commentary started again, but it wasn't the anger Daniel had expected after the massacre, just more pleas and provocations that he barely heard amid the deafening new silences in his head.

In the evenings, Daniel worked with Ian on projects in the shed. They barely spoke and never drank. Ian hosted poker nights, which Peter and Laila joined. An easy rhythm had returned to Daniel's friendships, as if the Feverdrops Slaughter had melted the fences around him. When they played cards, Pamela often sat with them, teasing them about their unimpressive skills, sometimes playing a hand. She made milkshakes and served homemade cakes and wore her hair in a ponytail. She asked if the men were okay, her voice different from before, now that of a woman who was done hiding both her fears and her strengths. Her nail polish was often chipped, but she seemed prettier without the layers of makeup. The stilettos were still present, especially the pink flowery ones, which she wore often. Where they had seemed creepy before with their too-girlish sexiness, they were now an emblem of a whimsical era quickly slipping away. Sometimes Daniel caught her studying her feet as if wondering whether that time had ever really existed.

"Royal flush," Peter said, displaying his hand.

Daniel pushed his tokens toward him. "You're better at this than I remember."

"I've been playing with Sherzai a lot."

"Really? He never mentioned it."

When Peter told him the vice-minister was helping him with research, Daniel was surprised. "I didn't realize you were writing."

"Why wouldn't I be? It's what I do."

"How much longer are you planning to stay?" Surely it couldn't be long. "Most foreigners are taking off, and here you are making yourself at home."

"A historian doesn't walk away from history when it's unfolding before him."

Ian reached into his pocket and scattered cigarillos across the card table. "You writing about the Commies, Mr. Prof?"

Peter shook his head. He said he wasn't writing about the massacre, either. "I write about the past, remember? I've had some ideas since arriving here."

Daniel offered to introduce him to other officials, but Peter declined. "Sherzai is enough. Most of what he's told me I'd already guessed, but it's good to have him as a source."

Afraid Peter would launch into a tedious lecture, Daniel changed the topic to baseball. "Who do you like for the Series?"

"Yankees," Ian said.

"Dodgers," Peter countered, handing him the deck.

Ian dealt while Daniel considered his old professor, who'd come here without much of a plan. He realized something else, too. If he and Rebecca were the best friends Peter had, the professor was a lonely man.

23

REBECCA RETURNED ON A WARM AFTERNOON IN EARLY OCTOBER. WHEN DANIEL SAW HER emerge from the gate, he was both relieved and apprehensive. Her smile made him happier than anything, and every time he saw her after a prolonged absence, his stomach did the same somersaults it had when they'd first met. He'd feared she would still be angry at his refusal to come to the funeral, but it seemed his absence was forgiven. He held her hand as he toted her luggage to the car.

"Wait," she said as he was about to start the car.

"How come?"

She squeezed his hand and climbed onto his lap. "I'm late."

He glanced at his watch. "Only by a few minutes."

She smiled, then stroked her belly and laid her forehead against his. "No, I'm later than that."

They had never loved each other more. Over the next few months, he saw the change in the curve of her belly. Her skin appeared illuminated from within. She slept deeply at night. He found that his love for his unborn child pushed back the colorless rage that swelled inside him when he thought of the Feverdrops Slaughter. He remembered clearly for the first time when he had been part of a family. He'd had a father— and a mother, at least for a time. But it had all been too big somehow. His father's name, his grand history and ambitions, the house, the gardens, Dorothy's sudden departure, the car that took his father to prison, Sayed's feud with kings. A happy home required smallness. Families were about indiscernible distances between people who claimed no greater ambition than each other's happiness. Daniel hoped he would never forget this.

Rebecca saw friends more frequently than usual, especially Laila, who came and went, often with Peter. Daniel eventually wondered why he had ever been uneasy about Peter's visit. Laila was the person whose presence grew more difficult with each minute. One day he asked her about the topic she never mentioned. "You're a doctor. You save lives. You can't honestly stay with a group that does such monstrous things."

"Daniel, this isn't who they are. It's just a lunatic fringe."

"You know this?"

"I know they believe in the equality of women."

"So do plenty of non-murderers."

She shook her head, not in dismissal but as if there was too much to explain.

"Daniel, do you remember the dog?" she said.

Yes, he remembered. Laila was breaking the promise they both had made never to speak of it again.

The dog had trotted into the Woodrow Wilson Academy one morning, ambling across the schoolyard. The children gathered around the animal, stroking its spiny back. But something was wrong with its gait, one leg shorter than the others. Daniel told the other kids to back away, because something else was wrong, too, and he saw it first. Saliva was foaming around the animal's slack jaw. It lowered its body to the ground, forelegs splayed, baring its teeth at the retreating children. Daniel helped a girl climb into an oak but failed to convince Laila to take refuge. He stayed with her on the ground, refusing to leave her alone. She moved calmly, never taking her eyes off the dog, as the groundskeepers came with jump ropes, bats, and a blanket.

Teachers corralled kids into the building, and over Laila's cries of protest, the groundskeepers threw a blanket over the dog while it barked and howled, twisting this way and that. They beat it until it collapsed. Then they dragged the dog to the road and tied it to a post some twenty yards from the school, where the injured creature spent two days winding the rope around the pole, snarling at passersby, some of whom threw stones. At home, Laila begged her father to send for the animal doctor, but it was no use. He was somewhere near Mazar-i-Sharif trying to save a rich man's goats. There was no one else.

Late that night, Daniel woke to the sound of pebbles on his window. Laila was alone. They ran hand in hand through the night-soaked city. Clutching her father's gun, she aimed the barrel at the snarling dog and pulled the trigger. Daniel wrapped his pinkie around hers, and they promised they would never tell. When they came to school the next day, they watched garbage collectors heave the dog onto a pile of trash.

"Should we say a prayer for the dog's soul?" Daniel said, before quickly correcting himself. "Sorry, that was dumb. I know dogs don't have souls."

Laila disagreed. "Why shouldn't they? People just want to pretend dogs don't have souls so they can treat them badly." She jutted her chin toward the other side of the street, where a trio of women walked together, hidden under their *chaderi*. "My father says it's the same with girls. Some men want to hide them. When they're hidden, you can pretend they're not real. But we *are* real."

Stunned at the simple truth of Laila's words, twelve-year-old

Daniel remembered that girls were wonderful, this one especially, and that he loved her. He wanted to tell her, but then Laila said, "The French have another name for rabies. They call it *la rage*. Rage. I think that's a better word for it." Something in her voice silenced him.

In the first months of her pregnancy, Rebecca was doing so well that she worked more instead of less, increasing her hours at the embassy. Laila wanted her to rest; it was hard not to think of her as breakable after the pain she had gone through last time. Almost six months had passed since that day. Maybe it no longer mattered, Rebecca's body like new now, her scars healed.

But by November, she seemed weak. She had grown pale. Her body ached. First it was just her back and hips, then her legs, her feet, her neck. She either slept too much or too little. Laila referred her to a specialist, a Frenchman who sounded very sure of everything he said. He told Rebecca things were normal and advised her to rest. Still, Rebecca and Daniel grew cautious in their excitement. Like the staff at USADE, they refrained from talking about the future. They scarcely referred to the child and stopped discussing names. Rebecca had said she liked Matthew because it meant *gift*.

Daniel wondered which guest room to convert to the nursery and when the remodeling should start. When should he return to the abandoned crib in the shed? Every time he tried, he found that he couldn't, and instead he worked on the table for Sherzai's *sandali*. All of this he kept to himself. He read books he had always told himself he should read. Texts that were assigned at the Woodrow Wilson Academy or in college, or that Rebecca had told him about. She had left a stack on his nightstand, editions of Steinbeck and Austen,

Nabokov, Fitzgerald, and, remarkably, Kafka. She wanted him to read an author who was haunted by wanting to get inside places that were forever closed to him.

She stopped working. She played the piano in the mornings, because her sickness came in the afternoons, and after she played she would linger on the bench, her eyes fixed on some unseen spot below the floor, and he wondered if she was having the same thoughts he was and keeping them to herself.

THE RAT

The man exhales a coil of smoke, his face to the sky, eyes closed. The only part of him that seems alive is his chest, rising and falling. Somehow his pipe stays rigid between his lips. Boy looks at him in the darkness, peering through bushes. Yes, this is the right man. His skin is gray and his clothes are gray and his hair is turning the color of ash. The Gray Man always sits there, crouched in a flower bed, his back against a tree.

Boy approaches him. His steps are the only sound except for the bell on a donkey's neck as it trots by. Everybody has gone home. There is not much to do near City Hall at night. The Gray Man sees him and hides his pipe behind his back. The smell of burning opium is like overripe fruit, and it always reminds Boy of the big garden and the mulberries in the summer before his mother died.

He raises a finger to his lips and tells the Gray Man that he means him no harm, that he has a proposition for him. He doesn't tell him he is the one who accompanies Nazook when the Gray Man buys opium every week. Boy always stands back like Nazook tells him to. It was years ago now that Nazook gave him the name Taj, but he still thinks of himself as Boy because he doesn't feel he has earned his new name. Not yet. There are many men who do not deserve the names they are given.

He looks closely at the Gray Man, who isn't as old as he thought even though his teeth are rotting and everything about him is skinny and long and ugly. Boy decides the Gray Man should be renamed the Rat.

"How much do you pay for the opium?" he asks, even though he already knows. The Rat looks around with darting eyes. He is still hiding the pipe behind his back, but the smoke is visible as it rises. At last he tells Boy what he pays.

Boy nods. "I will sell it to you for half the cost. Same quality."

"Why?" says the Rat.

Boy asks him if it's true he used to work for the government. The Rat points to the building behind him. "In there. I was a clerk. A very good position." This memory emboldens the Rat enough to bring the pipe out of hiding and inhale in front of Boy while knitting his eyebrows in a way that makes him look insane. Boy sits down beside him in the flower bed, taking care not to crush the daisies. All flowers are related to poppies, which Boy has learned to respect. "I'll give you the best deal in the city," he says, "if you teach me how to read and write."

He takes a resin bead from his bag, slowly, like a jeweler producing a rare stone, and shows it to the Rat, who tries to claw it out of his hand. Boy pulls it back swiftly and says, "I'll give you this for free if we can start now."

The Rat bites his dirty nails. Boy is disgusted; he makes sure his own nails are always clean. From his bag, he retrieves a nail file and a book. "Use this, please," he tells the Rat, who gently snuffs out his pipe and complies.

Boy shows him the book, which he stole a few weeks ago and has been hiding from Nazook. It's for children, he can tell, full of colors and faces that don't look like real people, because grown-ups think children can't understand real faces. Boy tells the Rat they should find a place with more light. On the steps of City Hall, the Rat finishes filing and cleaning his nails. Before beginning the session, Boy tells his new teacher his name is Taj. The Rat's name is Zalmay. Two hours later, their first lesson ends, and as Boy prepares to leave, he notices the Rat looking at City Hall with tears rolling down his sunken cheeks. Boy slips the resin into the Rat's hand, and the man's fingers tighten around the clump. They agree to meet again tomorrow at the same time. Boy hands him a watch he brought with him because he thought the Rat would not have one, and as his teacher straps on the cheap plastic wristband, Boy changes his mind about something. This man isn't really the Rat, nor is he the Gray Man. But he cannot be Zalmay, because the rich man who owned the house and the garden Boy lived in when he was small was also named Zalmay. Boy chooses a name he has heard from Nazook's father, a teacher at the university. "Good night, Socrates," Boy says. But Socrates is already asleep against the wide trunk of a hundred-year-old tree, his sweet poison glowing in his pipe.

Boy comes every night and learns things that seem impossible to him. The earth spins, according to Socrates. At first, Boy thinks he's lying, but it's right there in a book that Boy can read as long as Socrates helps him. There's more—stories of the stars and the sky, the past, faraway places. Socrates is a demanding teacher. He makes Boy recite poetry verses, slaps him on the head if he pronounces words the wrong way, and tells him about famous men who were wise and other famous men who were stupid. One day, Boy turns in his math homework and gets upset when Socrates wants him to show how he came up with the answer.

"Why does it matter, if the answer is right?"

"It matters," Socrates says. "Otherwise, I don't know if you understand."

"I know how I got there," Boy says. "I just can't explain it."

24

FROM THEIR FIRST-CLASS SEATS ON PAN AM FLIGHT 673, DANIEL AND REBECCA WATCHED LOS Angeles resolve in the smog. Lanky palm trees reached for the sky, their fronds swaying in the December breeze. In this city of perennial summer, everything grew. Orange trees grew in ordinary yards. The city grew, sprawling to the valleys and beyond. Gang membership grew with the drug trade, and boys grew up on street corners fighting turf wars while just ten miles away, rich men's investments grew beyond their wildest dreams, and so did their egos, along with the piles of money they spent on hopeful actresses whose breasts grew overnight thanks to surgeons and silicone. It was a city where red was the color of carpets and gang emblems, where red could get you shot if you wore it on the wrong street just as easily as it could get you photographed if you made it to the premiere in your designer shoes.

Despite a flight full of Americans, the Buicks and El Caminos that circled LAX, and the smog that greeted him upon landing, Daniel wasn't truly back in LA until he slipped into Walter Menlow's wood-paneled station wagon. As they drove toward the Palisades, Daniel was unbothered when traffic came to a standstill on the 405. There were too many people on the freeway, that was all. There was no camel blocking the road, no rabid dog foaming its way around the cars. None of the drivers leaned on their horn, and all of them stayed in their lanes. Rays of sun glanced off a thousand metallic hoods.

At the Menlow house, a stucco ranch with plush carpeting and parking for two cars and an RV, they ate barbecue ribs on the patio and retired early, exhausted. In the days before Christmas, Daniel and Rebecca saw friends and visited favorite restaurants. She seemed to find a second wind. He accompanied her to expensive maternity stores, telling her she looked good in everything. It was true. One morning, he did what he'd longed to do since arriving. At the Santa Monica airport, he reserved a small plane. He had never been confident enough to have a passenger with him, and Rebecca had never asked to go. Alone, he raised the Cessna into the sky, and as he rose the world sank softly into the sea. Sometimes, it was easy to forget that the ocean was neither blue nor green. The sparkle ran no more than forty feet deep. Below that, it was darkness. The sky was deceptive, too, with its illusory thin blue veneer.

Christmas Eve was a subdued affair. Friends and neighbors gathered in the living room around the lightless tree, which graced the room like a somber but beloved relative. Everyone talked to Rebecca's belly in a high-pitched voice, as if the baby had already said something cute. They all told Daniel he would make a great father. People said all sorts of things they had not the slightest basis for believing. He eventually fled to the garden with his cigarettes, taking refuge on a bench by the orange tree.

Well past midnight, when everyone else was asleep, he rose out of bed to watch television, as he had every night since arriving. Twenty channels broadcasting day and night was a diversion he had missed. He flipped through the channels, spending no more than two minutes on any one show. Hours later, he was nearly asleep on the couch when he was jarred by the sound of Farsi being spoken alongside English. The screen displayed a map, showing the audience where Afghanistan was. An invisible voice rattled off a list of American agencies and organizations that were there.

A few miles from downtown Kabul, the broadcaster said, three men on horseback had laid siege to a Russian auto parts factory. They'd ridden into the compound, drawn their swords, and killed eight men who were unlucky enough to be standing outside, beheading two of them. The foreman managed to slam the gates shut before they could do any more damage, locking himself and the others inside. Cursing the infidels, the horsemen displayed the heads on spears and rode downtown as cars and people stopped, incredulous.

Witnesses spoke of crying men, fainting women, and screaming children. Cars stopped and beggars watched, paralyzed. Wild dogs appeared from the alleys, drawn by the smell of flesh. Soldiers arrived. As if made crazy by shock, one of them cocked his weapon and shot the first horse, which collapsed on the boulevard. The horsemen shouted, calling the soldiers atheists and Communists, and the soldiers fired more shots, killing all three horsemen.

Religious militants reacted. The clothing shop that secretly sold liquor, which Ian had mentioned at the party, was ransacked. Clothes were dumped on the sidewalk, doused with alcohol, and burned, every bottle smashed. Places Communists gathered were sprayed with graffiti, their windows broken. Clerics decried the mayhem committed in the name of their religion, but the vandalism continued into the evening.

One incident was unlike any of the others. The whorehouse Daniel had wandered into, where he'd tried to help the teenage girl, had been brought down with a very different tactic. A masked assailant had killed the owners and two customers inside, setting the women and children free before fleeing as silently as a cat. In Los Angeles, the anchorman read off a list of names. Among the bodies was an American identified as Robert Jeffrey Greenwood.

25

DANIEL RETURNED ALONE TO KABUL IN EARLY JANUARY, ALONG WITH THIRTY PASSENGERS ON A plane made for many more. He would rejoin Rebecca in California at the end of April, a few weeks before the baby was due. She'd wanted to stay, and he was grateful for it. He had never thought of his homeland as a dangerous place before. Not even the coup of 1973 had brought fear to ordinary people. Something was changing. If he was meant to play a role in it, so be it. But he couldn't bear bringing Rebecca and their unborn child to a place where no one knew who was in power from day to day.

In the arrival hall, President Daoud's portrait loomed larger than ever. Footsteps echoed. Armed personnel vehicles monopolized the space reserved for cars at the curb, the sour smell of urban slush and snow in the air. Shivering in his jacket, Daniel looked for his driver. Instead he found Ian, who wore a heavy coat and a scowl.

"Ian? Didn't expect to see you here."

"I ain't interested in staying, either. Let's go."

As the Citroën sputtered away from Arrivals, the Departures hall came into view. It was full. Downtown, the bustle of ordinary life went on. The army was more visible than ever, its presence twisting through the city like a vine.

"There's been talk at the Corps," Ian said. "I heard some

stuff. Thought I should tell you so you don't get a shock on Monday, in case you don't already know."

Daniel said he'd spoken to Smythe two days after the horsemen attack, and USADE was going to stay open, at least for the time being. Washington had already sent private security to bolster the soldiers guarding USADE's staff.

"It's not that. There's some rumors about Greenwood. Not to speak ill of the dead, but that guy was a sick son of a bitch."

It was inevitable that the Corps should hear about Greenwood's predilections after his very public death. Every American in the city must know. According to Ian, Greenwood's files were sent back to Dannaco-Hastings a week after the murder. Among them were notes found in his home, scribbled sheets of personal brainstorming sessions.

"I never bought Greenwood's Casanova act. Shouldn't be a surprise he was a closet disco queen, and I got no problem with that. Ain't my business. But this shit he was into? Kids? Fucked up."

A stone moved through Daniel's heart. There was no use dancing around the question. "What was in Greenwood's notes?"

"That's the thing. He thought the Gulzar field was no good. He wrote a bunch of stuff about the soil, info he got from your staff and some locals. He was dead-set against the change. Couldn't make sense of it."

Daniel agreed that it was strange and changed the topic. "What are people saying about the horsemen and everything else?"

"I never thought of the religious guys as violent. Commies are like that everywhere, but if this is the opposition, what side are people supposed to pick? Anywho, I guess most people don't care enough to bother with sides."

"These aren't the religious guys," Daniel said. "It's a lunatic fringe."

"Yeah. Maybe there's no real difference between radical Communist and radical religious. Fanatics are fanatics, kind of like M&M's. Red or green, they're the same inside."

As Daniel reflected on this, Ian added, "Pammy thought about buying a *chaderi*. Said it could be interesting and a good story someday. But they're saying it might be banned soon." When he asked Daniel about Christmas, they fell easily into talk of California, which Ian found endless ways to make fun of. He and Pamela had gone home to New York for two weeks, and Pamela had stayed. The men talked superficially about their wives, Christmas gifts, and the weather, and more fervently about what might happen in baseball when spring training started. Dollar Djinn Lane drew near. The broken traffic light flashed. Ian downshifted, the car protesting.

"So it looks like it's just you and me now. A couple of bachelors with jobs that don't make sense no more, if they ever did." Ian laughed. "The Peace Corps can't bring peace to a place that won't admit it's at war."

At home, Daniel brought his suitcase in, and Firooz greeted him and told him Laila had called and invited him to come for dinner and a game of cards with friends the next evening. He had no desire to go. Within minutes, there was a knock on the front door. Keshmesh was there, shivering in short sleeves and faded jeans, a dusting of snow on his hair. He said he'd been waiting for Daniel's return. In his arms was a shoebox full of cassettes that he wanted to listen to together.

"I have a better idea," Daniel said. "Let's go sledding."

Keshmesh widened his eyes. "You mean like in movies? I've never been on a sled."

"Then it's time."

Daniel asked Firooz to fetch the sled from the attic, and

soon he was pulling the boy up a hill near the house. He placed Keshmesh in the front, then wedged himself behind him, wrapping a protective arm around his waist before pushing off. Keshmesh laughed every kind of laugh: nervous, happy, grateful, alive. The sled spun, gaining speed. Daniel laughed, too.

"One more time!"

Daniel obliged. They rode for an hour or more, watching the day end in a silvery haze as they pulled the sled back to the house. Their fingers were wrinkled, their hair and clothes wet.

"Thanks, *saheb*," said Keshmesh. Daniel sent the boy home with a thermos of cocoa Firooz prepared. Sledding had been exhilarating. One day, maybe he would share evenings like this with his own son, and he would never grow tired of listening to his cassettes or his laughter while sliding down a snowy hill.

What will you do if you have a girl? Telaya asked, angrier than he'd ever heard her. *Would she count?*

At work, things were worse than Ian had inferred. Elias's newspaper detailed the Gulzar fiasco, excoriating Greenwood for his weaknesses, including his surrender to Daniel's bad judgment and his much worse surrender to urges that should have led him to die by his own hand. But most of the reporter's ire was reserved for Daniel, whom he attacked in paragraph after paragraph. Telex messages were piled high in Daniel's mail tray, where the whole sorry affair was cataloged in a series of notes from Smythe.

> *January 1. Dannaco furious. Ruby wasted on Gulzar. Talked to Sherzai, says he warned you, agrees with Dannaco you need a different position in project.*

Most important thing is Reform. Will discuss with Sec. Vance, committees, etc. L.S.

January 3. Followed up with various. Consensus: USADE needs new leadership. Vance and Carter say massacre in Kabul potential game-changer. L.S.

January 6. Happy New Year. Sherzai wants you off desk and off Reform. Seth reinstated, probation finished. Dannaco likes him. Seth been working over Christmas. Available because he's Jewish. Has smart plans for 1978. We'll discuss when you're back. L.S.

The fourth note was dated January 8, just two days ago. It said: *Sherzai requested that State Dept. replace you. Sec. Vance says you can stay for now, but on basic admin duty. Has some desk jobs in DC that may work for you later.*

Seth was standing outside Daniel's office, holding a cup of coffee in one hand and a stapler in the other. "Hello," he said. He ambled away, calling over his shoulder, "I'm glad you're back. I'll help you move your stuff." His gait was different. His shoulders were straighter, his stride longer. Soon he was back with a few aides in tow and a box in his arms.

Daniel found the alcohol cart in the supply closet, took a bottle of whiskey, and locked himself in the bathroom with it. He left the building moments later, and for the first time he felt complete ownership of it. It was *his* building, his name on the facade. His project. His goddamn Reform. They had achieved almost nothing before him. And if it weren't for Taj—he cut short the thought. Laila called the office and told him again to come by. "Elias and Peter are coming. And Sherzai. We haven't seen you in ages," she said softly. He thanked her but said he had too much to catch up on.

He didn't return to the office that day, wondering if he ever would. He went inside a hotel that catered to foreigners and ordered a drink, then another. He wandered on foot until the city was dark. A pair of soldiers told him to go home and sober up. What did they know? What did it mean anyway, to be sober, and why was it better? Where was home? It was where you were needed. Rebecca needed him. He should be in LA with her. No. He should be here, as he was, making a dent, no matter how small, in the scourge of the opium trade. He should be stopping people like Taj, and making up for his own cowardice in the face of blackmail. Why *had* he given in? The man had probably been bluffing. Daniel dismissed the idiocy that kept asserting itself: that maybe he'd capitulated because he'd wanted to save not only the people but the poppies. No. Daniel had wanted to save lives, and he'd done the only thing he could. He had lied and become a blackmailer, too. A criminal. And yet.

Laila's apartment was close. The world was gently spinning, and he decided he'd go after all. Maybe seeing friends would do him good. When he appeared on her steps, Peter opened the door and embraced him without a word, pulling him inside with urgency. The apartment smelled of onions and freshly baked naan. A card game was in progress. Reams of paper were scattered across the coffee table, a typewriter on the sofa.

The floral curtains seemed oddly out of place. They clashed not with the other decor but with Laila herself. She was all business in her trousers and high-collar blouse, her sensible watch and small gold studs. She held her cards with unvarnished fingers, nails trimmed all the way to the fingertips. To her left sat Elias, to her right, Sherzai, both with cards in their hands. Sherzai rose when Daniel walked in. Peter apologized for the mess and began tidying up, shoving papers into a satchel and lugging the Smith Corona to the bedroom. "We thought you weren't coming," he said.

"*Agha*, how's the *sandali*?" Daniel asked Sherzai. He'd given him the table for Christmas, and Sherzai had been moved nearly to tears. "Is it keeping you warm?"

"What's the matter with you, *batche'm*," Sherzai whispered. "I've told you so many times. Only medicinal, and never more than one."

"Is everybody having a good time?" Daniel asked. The floor undulated, rising and falling like the road after the crash. He had longed for the company of friends, but they felt like strangers to him. Elias watched him, unflinching.

"Sit down and have some soup," Laila replied. "You're going to catch a cold." She spoke rigidly as she buttered a wedge of naan.

He shut his eyes and steadied himself with a hand against the wall, which was bare except for a framed image of Marie Curie and her husband standing side by side in a lab. Laila brought him a tray and led him to the coffee table, where he ate slowly. He drank the hot cider that Peter had made, while Laila returned to her cards with Elias and Sherzai. Peter veered from one mundane subject to another. He was glad for his new post at the university, though he launched into detailed descriptions of his students' mediocrity, as he always had done. The faculty were worse, of course. Daniel saw Laila raise her eyes to the ceiling and shake her head, but she was smiling. He asked Peter about his book.

"It's coming along. Sherzai is very helpful."

"You've mentioned that."

The five of them fell silent, the only sound that of cards being plucked and moved between fingers. Then Daniel said, "Sherzai is always helpful." He heard the liquor-flavored chill in his own voice and felt *agha*'s gaze, and couldn't bring himself to look back at him. Instead, he aimed his next words at Elias. "And you. You're so helpful, so principled. Always doing the right thing."

Elias dropped his hand. "I gave you a thousand chances to talk. You could have given me your side of the story."

Sherzai got to his feet. His cane clattered to the floor as he laid a gentle palm on Daniel's cheek. "Sometimes other people know better, *bache'm*." He bore a hardened expression belying his sorrow, the same look he had worn the day Dorothy left. And the day the royal police took Sayed away.

"How can you still call me that? Like I'm a son to you?" Daniel was surprised by the emotion in his own voice. "My father would never have tried to get me fired."

"You can't know what your father would have done."

"He's right," Laila said.

"I don't understand," Daniel said. The room swayed as he stumbled to the couch and lay down.

When did you ever? said Telaya, and he could swear he felt her patting his hand.

DREAMSCAPE

Once Boy learns words and numbers and time, his mind becomes as quick as his feet. When he'd fled from his mother's body, he'd run without stopping. Now he can think without stopping. He can read the signs that say, JALALABAD THIS WAY, PAKISTAN THAT WAY. *He pores through magazines that talk about Fever Valley, where he used to cut poppy bulbs with Nazook, and where there's still land for the taking, if a man has courage and imagination. The magazines don't put it that way, but Boy understands.*

Soon, Taj feels he has earned his name. He walks into the field, enchanted by the rustling of the stalks, the warmth of the life-giving sun, and the vastness of the sky. These are the finest poppies in the valley. More important, they are his. The Kochis roam with their knives and containers, working, scarcely looking up, doing what he says.

It took eight years. For so long, he did what he was told, still thinking of himself as Boy. With a small blade that fit in his palm, he scored poppy pods, kept his head down, followed orders. In each field, he wrapped a brightly colored scarf around the best poppies, like the farmers told him to do. After every harvest, Boy helped round up the good poppies, the ones with brightly colored scarves, because the farmers saved their seeds for next year so they could plant only the best—the ones whose sap flowed like a river, hardening into copper-colored resin.

In a field of a thousand flowers, maybe one hundred were good, and half of those were extraordinary. He wandered from field to field like this, working harder than the others. He became known for his skills. A poppy pod would continue to give resin for a few days, and could be tapped four or five times. Taj was the best at getting every drop, tapping a pod six or even seven times.

For every hundred exceptional poppies Boy bundled for the farmer, he set aside ten or twelve for himself. The farmers never saw, because Boy had always been the best thief. He cut the poppy at the stalk, keeping only the pod where the seeds were.

He hid the pods in his turban. Nobody would dare ask him to take it off. At home, he meticulously extracted the seeds and dried them over a flame, adding them to his collection. At first, he kept them in a jeweled box he'd stolen from a shop, but soon he had far too many seeds. When he still lived with Nazook, he sometimes hid the seeds in plastic bags for oranges or pomegranates, shoving the bags under his mattress. But now Nazook is dead because he tried to hold Taj back, telling him he should know his place, and that he wouldn't be anything without his mentor. Taj knew by then that his place was to be king, and kings got rid of people who stood in their way. No one will ever find Nazook's body because only Taj knows the Valley so well, and there is no better burial ground than an endless garden.

He stored more and more seeds, and one day he piled the boxes and bags into crates he found in an alley. Temperature mattered, so in the summer Boy buried the containers in the earth, just behind the kitchen, and in the winter he stacked them in a hole behind the fireplace. After eight years, he had *thousands of seeds. The older ones wouldn't yield much, but they would help fill the fields he dreamed of, and one day he would have the grandest flowers and the finest resin.*

Today, he is more than a king. He is a Manticore. The flowers whisper hello when Taj comes around, and sometimes he drives to the field late at night and sleeps between the stalks. There is an American agency that has been very helpful. A few years ago, it came to Fever Valley and gave land to farmers to grow corn and whatever else Americans liked to eat. First, they nourished and tilled land that belonged to nobody. Then they struck at a field full of poppies, but the poppies came back, laughing at them along with the Manticores. The Americans were very angry, not because the poppies were still growing, but because people were laughing at them.

Sometimes Taj still had dinner with Nazook's parents, who thought him a nice boy like their late son. It was there that he heard the American agency was struggling with money. A few years ago, he wouldn't have believed it. He'd heard about Americans and their money since before he could read. Surely money in America was as plentiful as sand in the desert. But now that he can read the newspaper, Taj thinks that in America, some people have too much money, but the government doesn't have enough. There is a new group from Washington coming to the agency this year to convert everybody's poppy fields to wheat and corn. Nazook's father says, "They think they're magicians, these Americans, that they can just instantly turn one thing into another."

26

IN THE FOLLOWING WEEKS, DANIEL FELT A CALM SETTLE OVER HIM THAT MATCHED THE STIFF quiet of the army-strewn streets: a forced order rather than peace. He spoke with Rebecca every week, at least when the phones worked. Living at her parents' house was hard because of the constant reminders of Sandy. But she talked about LA as if reading from a brochure. The air was soft, the climate soul-renewing. Sun had a direct effect on mood, she recited. Scientists said so.

He didn't want to tell her about his demotion, but it wasn't something he could hide. She was angry on his behalf, insisting that he'd done wonderful work and concluding that his colleagues and superiors were either jealous or stupid and likely some combination of both. She told him he didn't have to work for Washington at all. He could do anything he wanted, she said.

At USADE, Daniel moved into Seth's old office, a small space with a small window and a permanent smell of tea and sweat. He kept to himself, crunching numbers for the budget, writing reports when Seth asked him to, telling himself the work was still worthwhile. But with every day that passed, it became harder. Nothing more had been mentioned about the desk job in DC.

The State Department's fears that the horsemen had

signaled a game change faded. The turmoil was over, Smythe said, nothing but a moment of drama, unsurprising in the restless third world. Sometimes the Teletype spilled over with nervous thoughts from the State Department or the desk of an especially interested congressman. But the program continued, the USADE staff growing calmer as time passed. Locally, President Daoud held occasional radio chats. His voice grew tired even as his message grew more forceful.

Daniel met with Ian every week, sometimes more. They spent hours in the shed building things they'd tried to convince themselves were useful. A rocking chair. A new drawer for Ian's desk. One afternoon in the middle of April, they completed a bread box they agreed was "rustic" when it turned out less elegant than the picture. When a project went south—the shape of the item wrong, the wood splintering, or the hardware going in crooked and refusing to come out—Ian insisted that these projects were just quick-and-dirty skill-honing sessions anyway. "Tools like these, you gotta use them or they go bad," he said, making muscular gestures around the shed.

Daniel nodded, though he knew that tools didn't go bad just as he knew these afternoons weren't about honing skills. They were, like so many events during those strange and sour months, an effort to force a sense of normalcy on life when things were turned upside down. Spending his days in an office run by Seth, coming home to a house without Rebecca, being on a side opposite Laila . . . it was like tuning in to a baseball game and finding out your favorite players had all been traded.

Seth had completely commandeered the office, calling meetings at all times of the day. To say he was unkind would be an exaggeration. He mostly ignored Daniel. To say that Daniel plotted against Seth would be an exaggeration, too, but he began to think about ways to regain his position, spending hours laboring over new strategies for the Reform. He pored over maps and talked with local engineers, some of the more successful and cooperative farmers, and officials from the Ministry of Planning, although he never called Sherzai, who had officially requested that Daniel be sent back to America. Sometimes he appeared in Daniel's mind the way Telaya did, staring at him with deep, glassy eyes and whispering the truths he couldn't bear to hear.

Sherzai had spent much of his life working for the government, first hired by an official who admired Sayed and agreed to do him a favor by hiring his friend. He had risen because he was wiser and smarter than anyone had guessed, even if he was from the wrong tribe. *Agha* knew about Daniel's forgery and had said nothing, so he hadn't betrayed him, not really. He had protected him. This was how Daniel decided to look at it from now on.

Days later, looking at a map, Daniel drew a small *X* in a southeastern section of Helmand Province, which lay hundreds of miles southwest of Fever Valley. Somewhere near that *X*, a field of poppies had once grown. Washington had a project there with a much bigger budget than Daniel's fledgling office, but it had little to do with poppy fields. They built dams, reservoirs, highways, and canals and supported farmers who were working to become more efficient, all with the help of the river basin and reservoir. There was even a place called Little America, a place some eight blocks deep and two blocks wide, where Americans and Afghan officials lived, working with a big corporation that made Dannaco-Hastings look like a corner store. The scattered poppy fields that were coming up were designated as "out-of-project areas."

Many years ago, that *X* had contained an explosion of red blossoms. Not like Fever Valley, but still a respectable

sweep of delirium. It was abandoned now. The 1953 Sugar
Fire, thus named because opium resin smelled like overripe
fruit when it burned, had driven the growers out. The winds
had carried the cloying scent for miles on that September
morning. Daniel remembered. He had been eight then, old
enough to form lifelong memories. His father had started
that fire. And not by accident. Sherzai had told Daniel and
insisted he stay in the car, but Daniel had secretly followed the
men, who walked into a mountain and vanished. He sneaked
through the same crevices they did, climbing down the ragged
paths made by nature, and then he saw it. A massive valley
ringed by mountains and bursting with poppies. It was like
a mythical kingdom, perfectly hidden and impossibly rich.

There was even a small river, albeit a shy and pale one.
Sayed and the others poured gasoline on rags and tossed them
on the flowers, which coiled and twisted in the flames. Daniel
slipped from behind a boulder, and Sherzai caught sight of
him, taking him back to the car. His face smeared with soot
and his clothes smelling of smoke, *agha* told Daniel his father
was a brave man who did what needed to be done. At home,
the Sugar Fire went undiscussed, Sayed refusing to answer
Daniel's questions. As always, the task fell to Sherzai. Daniel
sometimes wondered what he would think of his father if
Sherzai hadn't been there to make sense of the man. After the
fire, fear drove some of the poppy growers out. The poppy
operations still in progress in Helmand were not on the best
plots, nor were they run by men with Taj Maleki's skill.

The highlight of February was Ian's purchase of a car made
for royalty: the former king's limousine. Daoud's regime had
confiscated the monarchy's fleet of cars the day of the coup
four years ago, and their long-promised auction finally took
place. Standing at Daniel's front door on Valentine's Day,
Ian's whole face was a wide-open smile, his cheeks pink. He

wore blue jeans and an old T-shirt, his standard uniform now that Pamela had gone back to America in the rising tide of violence. No more pistachio shirts with arrow collars; the bolo ties were gone, too.

"Did you get me chocolates?" Daniel said.

"Heart-shaped ones, and a dozen fucking roses." Ian grinned. "They're in the limo." He crooked his thumb over his shoulder. "But if you want them, you'll have to come along. You haven't worked on a car with me for ages. Let's go."

The royal limo was in good shape, but it was old, its coat dented and dull and the radio dead. While Ian tidied up the body with a dent-puller, Daniel repaired the radio. He felt himself sweating through his oil-stained shirt, although the weather was cool. He also felt happy, as if making the car whole again made him whole again, too.

"She's ready," Ian said, tossing his tools to the ground. "All she needs now is a new coat of paint and she'll be fit for a king. Again." He leaned in, screwing up the volume on the radio.

"Pretty staticky," Daniel said.

Ian shrugged. "Some antenna somewhere not working, I guess."

"It's a beautiful car," Daniel said.

Ian slung an arm around his shoulder. "How come you call a beauty like this an 'it'?"

"Because it's a thing."

"Whoa. It is *not* just a thing."

"Whatever you say." There was a time when Daniel would have agreed with him.

Ian pointed to the tiny fridge pushed up against the back of the driver's seat. He wiggled his bushy eyebrows. "Open it."

Arranged neatly on the only rack, which was marred by patches of rust, was a heart-shaped box of Belgian chocolates. Ian was laughing silently, chest heaving.

"Where are the roses?" Daniel said, laughing too. He felt giddy from hours of work, hunger, beer, and the smell of gasoline. They leaned back in the car's luxurious seats, eating chocolates and wondering why girls liked the stuff so much. Daniel had talked to Rebecca just hours ago. She was happy. She was healthy. The baby was growing. She missed him. Everything was normal. Except that nothing was, and a seed of dread was growing inside him. He sensed that when everything exploded, he would be going with it. He fought this feeling night and day, finding solace in the thought of reuniting with Rebecca and making a new home somewhere in a tidy little house with a tidy little fence. Every time he thought of this, his stomach tightened.

27

BY THE END OF THE MONTH, WINTER RETREATED AND THE RAINS CAME, ANNOUNCING SPRING. ON the city's sidewalks, last year's trash surfaced on the pavement as the snow melted: old candy wrappers, disintegrating cigarette boxes. Daniel both dreaded and anticipated the day the agency would visit Fever Valley to see whether Agent Ruby had destroyed the Gulzar soil or crops were growing normally. When that morning came, it was humid and cold, the sky a slate of steely gray. Daniel arrived at the USADE office just as the others were gathering by the door, ready to go.

Seth led the USADE delegation, which he packed into two vans. Lukewarm tea spilled from Daniel's glass as he twisted himself into the last row of seats between Iggy and a local expert whose name he forgot. At first, everyone was quiet, even Seth. After a short while, the choppy, awkward sounds of small talk began. As they approached Fever Valley, the chatter slowed and eventually stopped. Seth's knuckles were pale, his fingers wrapped tightly around the wheel. The nameless expert took long drags off his cigarette. Iggy tapped his foot and kept his eyes on the landscape.

They passed the last village. The turnoff appeared, and Seth took his foot off the gas. It was clear he was unsure where to stop. In winter, the land lay buried under a blanket of snow that blurred the boundaries between the fields, though villagers and nomads always knew where one ended and another began. In spring, the snow thawed a little at a time, creating a beige-and-white quilt that stretched toward the mountains. Daniel recognized the curve of the Yassaman field. When they arrived at Gulzar, he called out a good stopping point for Seth, who edged the van to the side of the highway, the second van following suit.

Engines fell silent; car doors slammed loudly. They crossed the highway. Iggy had forgotten to wear fieldwork shoes, and he tiptoed across the road in his loafers, avoiding patches of crushed, dirty snow. Standing at the edge of the Gulzar field, none of the men spoke. Even before they had stopped the van, anyone looking outside knew what they would find. Seth stood with his hands on his hips, Iggy's tie flapped in the rising breeze while sweat trickled down his face.

"It's normal for plants to come in slowly after a strong herbicide is used," the local expert said. He spoke too loud and too fast. He walked away, stroking his mustache. Iggy waded into the cracked snow and bent low to examine the growth. But there wasn't much to look at. The corn was unrecognizable, just a spill of limp leaves clinging to stalks that struggled to grow. The stream, filled by recent rain, flowed amply, and its waters tumbled into the Gulzar field through the channels that had been built last year.

Seth rubbed his chin. "The Gulzar soil was never good."

"The way we fertilized this place?" Iggy said. "All the water that's flowing in? All the work we put in? It should still be coming in better than this."

"Agent Ruby," Daniel said.

"No one asked you," Seth replied, but his voice betrayed disappointment.

"Can't you see what's going on?"

None are so blind as those who will not see, Telaya said, quoting from a Bible she couldn't have read.

Daniel walked over to Taj's land. It was like the Yassaman and Gulzar fields were experiencing entirely different seasons, springtime coming to only one of them. Planted in January, the green poppy stalks of Yassaman were coming in dense, crowding each other like belles in line for a dance. Kochis wearing heavy scarves used scythes to thin the sprouting plants. They worked as if the Feverdrops Slaughter had never happened.

USADE had several weeks to prepare a report on the Gulzar field. The staff couldn't disagree about what they had observed, but continued to disagree on its causes. The conclusion reflected Seth's views. None of it was surprising, and Daniel had stopped arguing. At the office, Miss Soraya was Seth's secretary now, but she didn't seem to know it, and if she did, she didn't care. She would stop by Daniel's office with tea and offers of assistance. She even continued helping him with personal matters. One afternoon in the middle of April, she delivered the quarterly reports for Daniel's gemstone firm. Sherzai had dropped them off.

"This is January through March," she said. Daniel scribbled his signature on the report. That same day, a Communist whose name he'd heard before was assassinated outside his own home. Elias called Daniel and told him what everybody was saying: the government had killed him. Two days later, thousands of sympathizers marched in the streets. President Daoud warned of a crackdown. The streets fell quiet.

On the morning of Thursday, April 27, Seth opened the USADE office to hold a special meeting about the Gulzar field and Agent Ruby. The call included Smythe and John

Marquette, the vice president of Dannaco-Hastings, who apologized for making everyone come in when the office was closed. His schedule alone had dictated the time. Miss Soraya came in for a few hours to provide assistance. She offered her help to Daniel, not Seth. When Daniel entered the conference room, he felt a certain satisfaction in seeing Seth's tired face. Hadn't he wanted to run the office? By all means, let him report what Agent Ruby had done. After brief pleasantries, Seth began to describe the state of the Gulzar field. Marquette dissipated the tension with a single phrase. From his office in Arlington, five thousand miles away, he explained that nothing was growing in that field because the soil had always been bad. It had nothing to do with Ruby.

Seth pointed to the speakerphone, the color returning to his face. "That's exactly what I said." He slapped the table.

In the measured, reasonable voice of executives everywhere, Marquette said he had expected this outcome. "Ever since we got Greenwood's files, we knew," he said. "The field just isn't usable and never was, no matter how much water and other good stuff you throw on it."

Smythe, who was breathing heavily into the phone and apologizing regularly as he complained of a cold, gave a vigorous endorsement of what was emerging as the official position: Agent Ruby had not failed as much as been wasted on the Gulzar field.

"With all due respect, nothing like Agent Ruby has ever left the land unharmed," Daniel said. "I'd suggest dumping it into the sewer, but who knows what that'll do to it."

From Arlington, Marquette's voice replied, "Mr. Sajadi, I think we all know the value of your contributions. This is your mess. That whole batch was wasted. We'll move the rest of it down to Little America in Helmand, where good Americans are doing real work." Before Daniel could reply, he continued. "Frankly, I'm not sure what you're doing in this meeting. You've personally cost my firm a lot of money."

"If you specify a dollar amount, I'll reimburse you with interest." Daniel excused himself, grateful for Iggy's half-hidden smile. As he passed Miss Soraya outside, she told him Ian had called to say the limo's radio was broken again. It was completely dead. She laughed and added, "My radio isn't working either, and it was made in Japan."

He was glad for her laugh, but it brought little solace. He was now counting not just the days but the hours until he could fly back to California, to Rebecca. He asked Miss Soraya to bring him the bottle of whiskey from the liquor cart, which was now in a guest office. Once he was alone with Johnnie Walker, he locked the door to his tiny office and drank from a glass she'd filled with ice. When the glass was empty, he poured the cubes onto the floor and watched them melt. Time passed quickly, and he could hear the others leave the office, silence filling the suites before the clock struck noon. Alone, he drank until the bottle was empty.

When he lay down on the sofa, he felt as if he were falling a great distance, only to land on cushions that were hard and punishing. He closed his eyes because the sky was spinning and the ground was spinning and he was spinning, too. Spinning like a dervish. Like the earth. Straight into an abyss. The room began to fade.

28

WHEN DANIEL AWOKE, HIS BODY WAS SHAKING. BENEATH HIM, THE FLOOR WAS SHAKING, TOO. How could he still be so drunk? Or was this an especially horrific hangover?

The windows began to tremble. The wedding photo on his desk tipped over, its glass cracking. It wasn't him, then. The world was shuddering. Daniel struggled to rise. His stomach tightened, and he spewed hot bitter liquid everywhere. Outside, men were shouting. These were not the chaotic shouts of the mad but the precise, self-assured shouts of people who worked for the law.

"More to the left! Stop there. You! Do you hear me? There!"

What was happening? Crawling on his hands and knees, Daniel went to the window and peered over the ledge. He tried to make sense of the scene below. The traffic circle and the road were overrun with uniforms. There had to be thirty men out there. This was no ordinary parade of military might. What had happened while he'd slept? Jeeps were parked along the circle, their engines running. He could hear the eager voices of obedient young men asking questions, ready for a fight. Excited. Daniel knew now why the earth was shaking. A column of tanks was moving toward the circle. He reflexively put a hand on his chest as if feeling his heartbeat would prove this was real.

He saw men and women stalking and running away from the scene, disappearing into nearby streets. But others simply stood on the sidelines, staring. Two soldiers were arranging the installation of signs and barricades around the area as the tanks came closer. Others brandished machine guns, which they aimed at the Ministry of Finance. Their medals and stripes shone in the sun. So did the emblem on their chests. They were close enough that Daniel could read the word at the center of the red logo: KALQ. The more radical of the two main Communist factions was now shouting orders outside his building, no longer marching in the street or waving flags in front of a nightclub. They were here. Armed, organized, and with intent. Above the name was the gold star. He pictured *agha* with his cane, alone at home, unable to flee. They wouldn't harm an old man with a bad leg—surely they wouldn't. His stomach twisted, squeezing out more liquid. Fighting to catch his breath, he backed away from the window. When the room stopped trembling, his terror deepened. It meant the tanks had come to a stop. There were more shouts, more loyal men obeying orders.

Hugging his knees, Daniel lowered his head, willing his mind to work. He crawled to his desk and pulled the phone to the floor. He lifted the receiver. Nothing. They had cut the lines. He switched on the radio. Nothing. That was when he realized that they had taken control of the radio signal yesterday afternoon, shutting it off throughout the city. He got to his feet and left his office, but it was as empty as he'd thought. Everyone had gone home.

He didn't have to hunker here alone. There were civilians in the street whom the Kalq seemed to be ignoring. And Daniel had diplomatic immunity. He tore off his soiled shirt and took a clean one from his desk drawer. He rummaged for his wallet and took out his diplomat's ID. He found a satchel in Iggy's office, dumped its contents, and stuffed it with every document he could find about Fever Valley. He left everything else behind, wondering if he would see any of it again. His broken wedding photo remained facedown on the desk. His intoxication was rapidly turning into a hangover, stabbing at his eyes and the back of his head. In the bathroom, he washed his face. The cold water stung. He walked slowly down the stairs and exited the building into an alley, where his car was parked.

It was a beautiful day. The springtime air was soft and cool, and the sky was the color people meant when they said "sky blue." Not far, a shepherd coaxed his fluffy flock away from the men with the guns and tanks. The world of pastels made the garish red and gold of the Kalq uniforms uglier, the jagged violence of men tearing apart the contours of the gentle day nature had made. A few of the soldiers were smoking, leaning against their trucks, but others were now watching a huddle of urchins who had emerged from the alleys. A boy walked boldly toward one of the tanks and clambered aboard. A soldier nonchalantly lifted him off and told him to scram, but other children came now. "Coins?" said a little girl, her hand outstretched. The soldier slapped her fingers, sending her running.

Daniel's eyes were on Imran. The street sweeper had just come into view from behind the Ministry of Finance. He held his broom tightly to his chest as he made his way toward the circle. He tried to talk with a soldier who was visibly bald under his cap. The man in uniform grew angry, shouting, "Go sweep somewhere else."

"No," Imran said, tapping the ground with his broom handle. "Please, *saheb*. I count a certain number of strokes for each block, and I have to start here or I lose count."

When the soldier shot Imran in the leg, he crumpled like a

cartoon character, falling to the ground in a sequence of sharp movements that made his killer laugh. A short, redheaded soldier threw open the doors of an unmarked van, dragging one of the urchins inside. His comrades helped, herding the kids into the van, lifting the smaller ones and manhandling the taller teens, who protested loudly. He promised the children they wouldn't be harmed, that he was taking them somewhere better. He didn't know that the innate wisdom of children about the untrustworthiness of adults was magnified a thousandfold in those who'd grown up in alleys. Fighting with all they had, the urchins called the man a liar and pounded their abductors with their fists. Daniel got into his car, put it in reverse, and drove backward, aiming directly for the circle. The soldiers dispersed. Guns were raised and safeties released.

Are you going to run them over? Telaya asked as gunmetal flashed in the mirrors of her dress.

"Stop!" the soldiers shouted as Daniel drove toward them.

He stopped. The bald soldier who'd shot Imran tapped on the car door with his gun and ordered him out. Daniel tried to look surprised as he stepped into the road with his hands up, diplomatic ID clutched between his fingers. The man examined his credentials and jabbed him in the stomach with his rifle.

"What do you think you're doing, Mr. Abdullah Sajadi?"

Soldiers corralled more children into the van. A boy biting his captor's wrist earned a slap across the face. He didn't cry, nor did he stop fighting.

"I was just leaving work, listening to a tape with headphones on. I didn't realize what was happening here."

"Headphones?" The redheaded soldier, who had ambled over, sounded more jealous than skeptical.

His bald colleague spoke. "Let me explain something to you, Mr. Abdullah Sajadi." He wagged a finger inches from Daniel's eyes. "If you do not go directly home—though you must stop at every checkpoint—and if you make any detours or disobey my orders, your immunity will be revoked."

Daniel promised to comply. He desperately wanted to gather some of the kids who were fleeing down the alley and get them into his car before they were caught. As he spoke, the earth shook again, a sudden, terrible tremor, and billows of smoke rose in the distance.

"Go home now," the man said. "And be careful. I cannot promise my comrades will take the same magnanimous view of you." Before he walked off, he said one last thing. "You know how children play that game where you look at something with your left eye closed, then you switch, and it seems like the thing you're looking at has moved? It's an optical illusion. The object doesn't actually move." He tapped Daniel's chest with his gun. "You are that object." He closed his right eye, then his left. "If I look at you through my left eye, you are the worst of the old regime, the smug and complacent who deserve to die. But when I look at you through my right eye, I see a member of the American government, protected by diplomatic immunity, and maybe a man who deserves to live. I choose my right eye for now." He walked away backward. "We are not savages, after all."

Daniel nosed the car down the street and pushed open the back door, calling to a knot of urchins who had taken refuge in a stairwell. There was nowhere else to go. Soldiers' footsteps rang in the background, boots coming closer.

"Get in," Daniel said. "I'm a friend."

Most of the children scattered, but two jumped into the moving car, a girl and a boy who tried to pull the door shut. A soldier was upon them in seconds, and the boy tumbled to the pavement. It was too late for him. Daniel picked up speed and told the girl to duck. She curled herself into a ball on the floor behind the driver's seat.

"I'm sorry about your friend," he said.

"Just drive faster," she replied.

Daniel wanted to switch on the radio, wondering what the insurgents were broadcasting, but he didn't want to frighten the girl. As he drove through the city, soldiers were everywhere, barricading roads, setting up checkpoints, ordering civilians to go this way or that. They pushed some into military jeeps.

"Stay down low," Daniel said. "Do you understand?"

She made a face. "Just because I don't have nice clothes doesn't mean I'm stupid." She wore a ragged ensemble of a mismatched top and bottom. The pants were too short, leaving her ankles bare.

A whistling sound made him look up. Fighter jets were in formation. At a manned intersection, a soldier signaled for him to stop, leaned into the window, glanced at his ID, and waved him through. Laila's apartment was close, and just now he wanted more than anything to see her. He parked out front. Like most houses, hers had no street-facing windows. He knocked quietly first, then louder. No one answered. As he came back to the car, he saw the little girl running away, vanishing into a maze of alleys no car could enter.

He drove slowly. Soldiers were telling beggars to move. He passed the man without arms. A soldier barely out of his teens struck him with the butt of his rifle and told him to find another place to sit, but the old man cowered and shouted, "I am full of broken glass, I cannot move! I will cut you if you break me!" The soldier left him alone.

Daniel made it home. His hands were hot, the wheel wet with his sweat. Footsteps rushed toward him in the foyer.

He expected to see Firooz or Ahmad. It was Peter. His eyes looked like they hadn't been shut in days. He was holding up a transistor radio. He'd found Voice of America on shortwave, a reporter breaking through the static. Daniel had never been so glad to see him. They embraced.

"Where's Laila?" Daniel said. "Are the phones working yet?"

"I don't know." Peter fixed a bloodshot gaze on him. "And no, the phones aren't working."

29

"THEY KNOCKED ON LAILA'S DOOR AROUND EIGHT O'CLOCK THIS MORNING," PETER SAID AS Firooz entered with tea. "Maybe a bit later."

"Who knocked on the door?"

"Two soldiers. Laila had the same membership card as them. They called her 'our sister' and told her to move fast because the Party was going to need doctors today."

"And she went with them? Willingly?"

"They promised she would be safe," Peter said into his coffee cup. "That she would become a hero."

"She was already a hero. But maybe not anymore."

Just as Peter told him he was being too hard on her, Daniel noticed he had brought his typewriter, which was in its case on top of the Steinway. Daniel asked how long he had been at the house, and Peter told him he'd come right after Laila had left. That had been hours ago.

"It didn't seem like a good time for either of us to be on our own," he said.

Daniel went up to the bedroom and retrieved his gun from the nightstand, wondering if it would do any good. Downstairs, Firooz had finished pouring tea and turned to leave. Daniel told him to stay. He didn't want the man to be alone in the kitchen or his quarters while things fell apart. "Tell Ahmad to come in as well," he said.

Firooz stared at the floor.

"What's wrong?"

"I think Ahmad was tired of being a servant, *saheb*."

"I see. And you?"

"I am no servant to anyone but God. Here, I clean things and cook a little. I do this because I am skilled." Firooz gave a tight nod. "When I go into my house at night, I pray. It is only then that I am truly a servant." He left the room.

Daniel sat with the gun on his lap. On the radio, news trickled in. Several ministers had been killed. Daoud and those loyal to him were in a firefight with the insurgents at the presidential palace.

"You'll be fine," Peter said. "You've got immunity, but I'd still keep my head down. US agencies have arranged the first planes home for their people in three days. Any of their employees who want to leave can just show up at the airport."

"I can't just leave now, Peter."

"You should. The world is about to change, especially for you."

"Why me?"

"You're about to be a father," said Peter, sounding incredulous.

Daniel looked at his old professor, whose intelligent eyes held a shadow of contempt. Voice of America played a recording from the insurgency that was clearly a piece of propaganda. The Communist president's name was Taraki, and he talked about a grand future, the patriotic Left, the nobility of his trusted Russian friends. All lies, thought Daniel. Truth had no place in the minds of men who wanted to reshape the world to their liking. The broadcast went on. Taraki quoted Lenin and used the words *brotherhood*, *equality*, and *rights* like exclamation points.

"Does a revolution really count as a revolution if there's

nothing new in it?" Daniel said. With their tired slogans and borrowed logos, these insurgents were the opposite of revolutionaries. They were the kinds of people Peter used to warn against at the start of every class: plagiarists. They were the worst kind, too, because they were repeating things that had already been proven wrong. Taraki said he'd soon announce the cabinet members of the new regime. As they waited, Peter said, "I'm sorry, Daniel."

Before Daniel could ask why, the announcements began. It started with a list of officials who had lost their lives. Daniel waited. *Agha* was not on the list. Thank God, he thought. Thank God.

Fighter jets flew over the house; the walls shuddered as the new government was introduced. Many were from the old order, while others were names Daniel had never heard. Then came a name he had known his whole life. At first, he thought it was a mistake. But then the appointees came forward one by one to share a few enthusiastic progressive words. As the new Minister of Planning, Sherzai made promises to many people, including those who had long been sidelined. Daniel thought of *agha*'s eyes. True power had been kept away from men with those eyes. Maybe that was changing, which would be a good thing. But was this really the only way? Daniel felt like he did when he stayed underwater for too long, wondering how much more pain his lungs could take. Eventually, he had to come back up. Everybody did.

"As I said, I'm sorry." Peter's voice was gentle.

Daniel felt the urge to shoot something, but instead, he wiped his forehead with his sleeve, fragments of his past flashing through his mind in no particular order. The Sajadis' old driver telling Daniel funny stories about his wife's family, including her three brothers, who he said were three different kinds of crazy: Scrambled Egg, Fried Egg, and Soft-Boiled.

The first time he'd rolled around in a tub full of raw gem-stones in his father's warehouse, wondering what the ugly brown ones were called and how they could become glossy and fine. The day he'd reached for Laila's fingers after school, so they could hold hands like they always did, and she pulled away and told him he didn't believe in the same things she did. It was her fourteenth birthday. The time he called Sherzai *baba*, father, by mistake, months after Sayed's arrest. The first time he saw Rebecca. The day USADE told him he'd gotten the job because Peter and Sherzai had assured them not only that he could do it but that his surname would mean people trusted him. The crash. The gunshot in the shack. He didn't want these memories now, when there was no room for the past, only the corroded, impossible present.

"I know things aren't going your way right now," Peter said.

"Not going my way?" Peter must have misspoken, his mind made clumsy by the unfolding drama. "It's a bit worse than that." Daniel leaned toward the coffee table and shoved the radio. It shifted a few inches, balancing precariously near the corner. "Are you not hearing what I am?"

"I doubt I ever do. I'm not sure how well you listen in general."

From the kitchen came the warming fragrance of freshly baked naan and the sound of Firooz moving frantically about.

"I listen just fine," Daniel said. "And I see just fine, too. You just showed up here last year—"

"You want to talk about that now? Really?"

"Yes. You showed up using some pretext—"

"What pretext? And maybe you should put the gun away, Daniel."

"You made up some nonsense about a conference. You wrote letters to my wife, arranging everything behind my back." This should have been unimportant now, but the words pushed forth as if they were the most urgent concern in Daniel's world, as if his mind was trying to make small issues big again, just to give the world back its ordinary dimensions.

"Isn't that normally how one arranges a visit? By letter or phone?" Peter was leaning back into the sofa, but his voice was more controlled than calm, his words frosted with ice. "Yes, I mentioned my plans in a letter."

"Not your actual plans."

"Becca flung me at Laila from the moment I got here. That was how I knew."

"Knew what?"

"The same thing that you should know without my having to tell you. If you can't see it, your marriage is in trouble."

Daniel rested his head on his knees. The kitchen door creaked, and he looked up to see Firooz entering with naan, butter, honey, and more tea.

"For having been a bright student, you're pretty slow on the uptake," Peter said. "Being smart isn't worth anything if you only use it to understand what you want to understand. Get your priorities straight. Go home."

Firooz quietly returned to the kitchen. Somewhere in the reaches of Daniel's mind, he knew what Peter meant, and he had that feeling again, the one that had come and gone since the day of the accident. That something wanted in and another thing wanted out.

The sound of approaching engines filled his ears. Men's voices rang out in the street, and a woman screamed. Daniel tucked the gun in his back waistband and went outside despite Peter's protests. On Dollar Djinn Lane, Communists were taking away the Yusafzai and Nesbar families. Maybe selling carpets was illegal now. Certainly, a family could no longer own a bank. The Kherzadas were in France, but that had not stopped the Kalq from entering their home. A half dozen men came out with documents, boxes, and bags.

"Move!" a uniform shouted as he shoved his rifle into Mrs. Yusafzai's ribs. Her husband yelled for him to stop.

"I'm moving," she said through tears.

Their six-year-old twin boys clinging to them, the Yusafzais walked to the van. They were saying soothing things to their children, but in their eyes was a terror Daniel had only seen in the Kochis' eyes the day he'd killed Telaya. "No, no!" Daniel shouted. "You can't do this."

A colonel emerged from a Jeep. Telling his men to stand still, he stalked toward Daniel and ordered him back into the house.

"Have you lost your minds?" Daniel said. "Stop this."

"Go inside, *saheb*."

"I'm an official with the United States government."

"We know." Coming closer, the colonel added, "That's why you're allowed to go back in the house. Do it."

Daniel watched his helpless neighbors, who avoided looking at him. The boys trembled like small statues about to crumble. Above, the blue spring sky was marred by heavy swirls of smoke rising from the city, the color of endings and ruins and history being rewritten by people with tanks. The sound of cannon fire filled the air and rattled the earth.

"Daniel," Peter said. "Come inside. There's nothing we can do."

But Daniel didn't want to go inside. "Who ordered this?" he asked the colonel.

"We have work to do, and it doesn't involve you. Why are you still standing here?"

"I have the same question for you."

"Smart-mouth. Get inside."

"Do you know who I am?" Daniel gave him his full name.

The colonel shoved him, nearly sending him to the ground. He narrowed his eyes as two soldiers joined him, prepared to help their superior deliver his message more decisively. "You tell me your name, which I already know, and you think what, exactly? That I'll change my mind and let your friends go so you can all have breakfast?"

"This is a crime."

The colonel came closer. "Under whose laws?" He waved over one of his young helpers. The blow was sudden. As Peter shouted his protests, Daniel fell. The young soldier produced a switchblade, and with a single movement raked the knife along Daniel's right cheek. He flinched and let out a sound of pain, reflexively pressing his hand against the wound. The blood seeped through his fingers. The Yusafzais and Nesbars held each other.

The soldiers surrounded him, knocking him back down. They took the gun from his waistband. He curled up reflexively, protecting his skull from a barrage of arms and legs. As someone kicked him in the ribs, Daniel thought, *I will die here*, and he was overcome by the futility of everything he'd ever done. How he had hurt his wife and shamed his father's name, and it had all come to a close with him lying on the street he'd grown up on, being kicked to death by foolish men whose lives would be just as futile. He felt tears gather in his eyes. Firooz was at the courtyard gates, pleading with them to stop. With Peter, he tried to pull the men off Daniel, but the soldiers barely noticed. A second fleet of fighter jets came, lean metal hissing through the sky. Peter's voice boomed as he threatened to report all this to the American embassy.

"Sounds good," the colonel said as if agreeing to a date. He ordered the soldiers to stop. "Until then, you'd better stay inside, Mr. Sajadi. You never know what might happen."

He was holding Daniel's gun in his hand. He raised it

slowly and aimed it at Peter, who did not flinch. When Daniel heard the gun go off, the wheezing of the fighter jets merged with a sharp ringing in his ears and he could hear Peter and Firooz yell, and Daniel heard that he was yelling, too. And then it was over. The colonel had fired into the air. The smoke lingered as Daniel struggled to his feet. The colonel sent his men to search the house to take away any weapons, since Daniel had what he called "a bad attitude." They rummaged through the home that his father had built, turning drawers upside down, pushing their hands into closets and cupboards. When the men were gone, silence fell on Dollar Djinn Lane. Only Keshmesh's home had been left alone, and Daniel was grateful the boy was safe, even if it was because his father was one of them. Inside, Firooz and Peter cleaned and dressed his wounds and bandaged his face.

"*Saheb*?" Firooz stood by the sofa, his hands and clothes covered with flour and scraps of dough. He wanted to apologize, he explained. The naan was going to be too salty.

"It's never too salty," Daniel said.

"Today it will be too salty." Firooz's voice broke. "My tears, they fell in the dough." Daniel struggled to his feet, and employer and servant embraced like the brothers the Communists wanted them to be.

30

THAT NIGHT, THE SOUNDS OF BATTLE RAN LIKE A SOUNDTRACK. THE BOOMING BASS OF cannons, the wheezing of fighter jets slicing through the air—a crescendo, followed by the cratering echo of rocket fire—the staccato clip of helicopters rising in the sky, noses dipping toward a target illuminated by a bright half-moon. Now and then there was a lull, and the house would fall silent, only to be rattled again by a battery of attacks.

Daniel's body hurt more than he'd ever imagined it could. Aspirin did nothing to soothe the pain. When Firooz changed the bandage around his ribs, he said, "*Saheb*, you need something more for the pain." He disappeared and came back within minutes with a tiny smudge of brown resin. "This will work." Daniel refused at first, but as the pain wore on, Peter urging him to take the illicit medication, he relented. The relief was near immediate and profound. The pain still existed but seemed to have drifted far away, something he was considering from a distance rather than feeling. There was nothing he would have described as a high. Only relief. He wondered how much people had to take to feel what they longed for, whether that was bliss or nothing at all.

The three men never went to sleep. They sat around the radio, where announcements came and went through whistling static. In the morning, the phones were still dead.

President Daoud was dead now, too, along with his wife and children.

By now, Rebecca would be sick with worry, and Daniel wondered how to reach her. The exiled clerics in Pakistan and Iran were broadcasting on shortwave, moving from frequency to frequency as the Communists jammed them. In calm, rhythmic paragraphs, a stark contrast to the Castro-esque agitprop of the Kalq, the clerics cursed the takeover, telling their countrymen to rise, to find the strength against the godless tyrants who'd seized power. Daniel and Peter spun the dial throughout the day, switching between the clerics, Radio Afghanistan, which was now owned by the Kalq, Voice of America, and Radio Free Europe. Everyone called it a revolution, and it seemed this was all the world was talking about. The Kalq rattled off all of their planned next steps: Distribute land. Get the poor off the streets. Crack down on the drug trade. They didn't explain how they would do these things.

"You know you can stay here as long as you like," Daniel said to Peter.

"Thanks, Daniel. I'll take you up on that. I think it's better for Laila if she doesn't have some American in her house right now."

It was almost nighttime when someone was inside the courtyard, ringing the doorbell. Few people had the key to the main gate. Through the window, Daniel saw Sherzai silhouetted by the rising moon. He went downstairs, and they stood before each other in the courtyard. Daniel couldn't find the right words, because he couldn't find the right thoughts. He only said: "*Agha*, you had no choice, right?"

Sherzai's eyes were tunnels of glinting light. "I don't believe there was a real choice, no, but I don't think that's what you're asking me." His town car was idling in the courtyard, the youthful voice of his driver drifting in from the road along with tobacco smoke. He was talking with a handful of guards who had evidently been sent to patrol the street. Sherzai told them to take a walk, and their voices faded slowly into the night.

Daniel asked him how long he had known, whether he had been part of the planning. All Sherzai would say was that this day had been inevitable.

"I have something to give you, and I'm very sorry to have to do it," Sherzai said, producing an envelope from his coat. "But first, I've brought somebody with me." He indicated the trunk of his town car.

Daniel quietly pulled the latch. Elias was coiled inside, fists clenched and eyes pleading. Down the street, the men were laughing at a joke.

"I thought he would be safe here. Elias is a good boy."

Climbing out, Elias soft-shoed his way to the house. Once Daniel was alone with Sherzai, the old man searched his face, his formidable brow furrowed. "They hurt you." He gently reached up to touch Daniel's bandaged cheek. "I wish you had listened to me. I told you to go." He waited for Daniel to respond, but nothing came. "Take that flight to Los Angeles and don't come back." He held out the envelope. Arthritis twisted his aging hands, but his eyes were lit by a vigor Daniel had never seen before.

From the envelope, Daniel withdrew a stack of papers bound by string. The top report was familiar. He had seen it just weeks ago. He tore off the string and leafed through the pages. When he understood, he let them fall from his hands. "This is impossible." They studied each other as the papers fluttered in the wind. "You had me cede my father's company over to the government? My company? I signed it away?"

"I asked you to read these reports—"

"You did this to punish me for not paying attention?"

"Watch your tone with me," Sherzai said, voice rising. "I asked you to read these reports over and over."

"So it's my fault that I trusted you."

"That's what you call it, never bothering at all with the gemstone firm your father built? That's not trust. It's privilege!" Sherzai was angry now. "You really believe it was better for that company to just keep enriching you? You, who couldn't be bothered to so much as look at a report, instead of turning it over to a government that actually wants to help the people of this country?"

Daniel's throat had gone so dry he was struggling to swallow and speak. "I never thought I would say this, but I'm glad my father's dead."

Sherzai grew calmer. "Listen to me, *batche'm*. For the past six months, I've made sure you would be as comfortable as possible." He explained that he had altered the numbers in his reports to the government, downplaying profits, steering cash into American accounts he had opened in Daniel's name. "It was all I could do to make this easier on you."

"This company was who my father was. It was his life's work."

"The company was never who your father was." Sherzai articulated every word as if revealing a great secret. "And you are in no position to talk to me about betrayal. You got your way with that ridiculous file. You lied to my face. I have protected you all your life, more than you know."

"I ran over a little girl," Daniel said.

"What?"

The words tumbled out on their own. "I had to forge that file. Someone blackmailed me. He was going to murder people. Completely innocent people."

"What is it that you're saying?"

Daniel finally told him. After all this time keeping it secret, he was astonished at how simple and short a story it was. A horrible accident. A dead child. Blackmail by an opium khan. Capitulating because he'd thought it was the right thing to do.

Sherzai listened quietly, holding his breath. "Why didn't you come to me for help?"

"I didn't want to burden you. What was the point? There were only two choices."

Sherzai exhaled. "The Scale of Sages doesn't leave any of us much choice, *batche'm*. This is how things are."

The guards ambled back into the courtyard and asked Sherzai, "*Saheb*, how many people live here besides Mr. Sajadi? How many servants are in this house?"

"Three." Daniel turned at the sound of Peter's voice. He was standing at the front door. "There are three servants in this house," Peter repeated. "Their names are Firooz, Elias, and Abdullah."

Sherzai eyed him with a hint of understanding on his face. "That's correct." He vouched for Peter as well, and then left without saying anything more. Daniel stood in the courtyard for a long while before collecting the papers on the ground. When he returned to the house, Peter was waiting in the hall. Daniel told him what Sherzai had done; over the past year, Daniel had been signing over his father's gemstone firm to the government piece by piece. It belonged to the new Communist regime now. Daniel felt as if he had lost a family member he'd taken for granted, never thinking they would die. He looked down at the papers. What had once been Sajadi Gemstones and Mines was part of the newly minted National Corporation of Precious Stones and Metals, which also owned the nation's principal foundry.

"I'm sorry," Peter said for the third time that day. "Come, let's go see Elias. He's in the servants' quarters."

Elias had already changed into Ahmad's abandoned

clothes. Gone were the peace sign and swagger. His thick hair was flattened under a skullcap, though he was still wearing his Birkenstocks. His face was pale and his eyes wet, and something in his countenance was more genuine than when he wore his tie-dyes.

"Did you know?" Daniel said.

Elias stared at the floor. He had counted the hours, but when the time came, he hadn't gotten his revolution, only a prewritten story and a set of orders.

"They came to my place yesterday and told me what I'd be writing tonight. They said that on Saturday, I was to write that any reports that they'd killed ordinary people were lies. They hugged me." Elias told Daniel they'd seemed sincere, which was the strangest part. "I almost believed they really did know the future, and things I'd seen happen personally were lies." They had told Elias to proclaim that they would never shoot anyone who didn't shoot first. "Sherzai's a good man," Elias said. He raised his arms, looking at the loose cotton sleeves. "Wearing this feels like theft. Like I'm making fun of someone. But I suppose they're just clothes."

"They're not just clothes," Daniel said.

"Next time you leave the house, you'll have to dress like that, too, and make yourself unrecognizable," Peter told Daniel. "You go by your middle name now. You're Abdullah, the third servant. I hope you're not too proud—pride can get a man killed in times like this."

SLAUGHTER

Tonight is an important night, because Ashura is coming. Taj is in his house, watching the maid polish the floor. When the house was built, he had men lay lapis lazuli tiles because it made the floor look like the evening sky, and he liked the thought of walking on the sky at night. This is his home. These are the first walls that belong completely to him.

The maid is working hard, beads of sweat glowing on her forehead. The house smells of scouring powder and ammonia. She says to bring cut flowers that smell good, but Taj won't do this because flowers are not to be cut and thrown in vases where they die a pointless death.

There is a knock, and he sends the maid away. Taj and Ashura play cards while she drinks cognac, and it makes her giggle and move her limbs in a languid way that he likes. She was one of Nazook's girlfriends, and long ago she looked at Taj like he was a child. She called him Boy, because that was what he was. Ashura is the daughter of a bookseller, and she is prettier than girls who take their clothes off in foreign magazines. There was a time those pictures excited him, but now they do not because girls who are paid are not worthy of a king. He is tired of them. He has not paid a girl in four months. He has been saving himself for Ashura, crossing off each day on the calendar. He read in a wise man's book that he who has power over his body has power over his mind. And Taj knows the happiest kings are those who exercise absolute power.

Ashura looks into his eyes and runs her hand through her hair, letting her fingers glide down her neck as she returns to the cards. Taj takes something from his pocket and leans across the table to give it to her. She gasps when she opens the box and discovers the emerald earrings. He tells her they sparkle like her eyes, and she laughs when she puts them on, slapping his hand away when he tries to help. She tosses her head so the earrings dangle, and she asks: "How do I look?"

She undoes a button and smiles when she slips out of the blouse. He pulls her close, but something is wrong. Taj does not feel what he should feel. Nothing stirs except a dark, churning thought in his brain: that all she wants are the jewels, that he is nothing, nothing without the poppies, that he is a man made of brown sticky resin inside.

He bundles the blouse into her arms and tells her to get dressed and go. Before slamming the door, she tells him he has no class, even though he pretends to. When she is gone, Taj slips into Nazook's old Opel, which is his now. He could drive something fancy, but if everyone knows you are a king, many will want your crown. Outside, his house is modest, too, a plain place without a garden, and no one knows that he walks on a lapis lazuli sky-floor.

His heart is pounding fast. He goes where he often goes when he feels like this. Soon he pulls up in front of the big house with the big garden. The girls no longer live there, and the lady with the henna hair and the tiny waist has grown large, while her husband has turned gray. Tonight Taj scales the wall while the people sleep. The flowers and the grass are not asleep. They rustle quietly, welcoming him home. There is no tent anymore. No one living in the yard. But his mother

is still there: he thinks they buried her in the tiny plot surrounded by white stones, and he has come here many times
late at night.

He lies down on the grass and gets lost in the dark sky,
and soon it starts to rain. He lets the rain soak him as he
falls half-asleep for hours. When it is almost light, he looks
around and sees that the garden isn't the same as it used to
be. They've made new flower beds, and the hedges aren't
cut the same. It isn't his garden anymore. Taj decides he will
never come back.

Lying awake on his toshak pillow at home, he thinks
of Ashura. He will always remember how pretty she was,
and how much he had wanted her once. Most of all, he will
remember that the last thing she did before slamming the
door was touch her ears to make sure the earrings were still
there.

When he falls asleep, he dreams that he is wandering in
the old garden with the high walls, and that he knows that
outside them he will never be safe.

31

DANIEL CRADLED THE RADIO IN BED, LISTENING TO A STATICKY BROADCAST. CURFEW WAS IN effect. People would be allowed to go outside in the morning to buy groceries and run errands, but the new authorities gave a small window. Daniel made plans. He knew whom he wanted to see, and a few hours was enough, as long as he could leave the house without being hassled by the guards. Maybe it was a bad idea, but he had nowhere else to be. Voice of America had announced that US agencies were to remain closed for two weeks, and that personnel who were staying should remain inside and listen for updates. Kalq officials confirmed this on their own broadcasts. Telephones were being switched on at haphazard times, leaving desperate people checking the lines day and night.

Elias and Peter were in the guest rooms. Their lights were on when Daniel walked by at midnight, and he could hear Peter banging away on his typewriter. He tried to call Rebecca again from the study, but there was no dial tone. His remorse was tinged with relief, because he wasn't sure what to say to her. She would be glad that he was safe and coming home in two days. He longed to hear her voice and to join her in California. At least, a part of him did, though the thought of Los Angeles, with its easy warmth and lively seas, felt more like a mirage than something real, seducing you if you allowed it and dissolving fast on arrival. Reality moved slowly, though never more slowly than now.

When he told Peter over breakfast that he wanted to go out for a few hours, Peter said, "Then let's make you someone else."

Twenty minutes later, Daniel stood in the servants' quarters dressed in a *piran tomban* and brown cotton vest. Elias made a feeble joke. Peter used the makeup that Rebecca had left behind, dabbing thick foundation over Daniel's bruises with clumsy movements. It helped, as long as you didn't look too closely. They asked Firooz for his artificial beard, which he turned over without a word of protest. Daniel looked at himself in the mirror. Watching himself, he remembered a fantasy story he'd read as a boy in which there were a thousand parallel universes. It hurt to move. He took a tiny dose of opium.

"I feel useless," Elias said, picking up Firooz's copy of the Koran, which the cook kept on his nightstand but admitted he could not read. "It's like I've lost a limb."

"This isn't about you," Daniel replied, the words harsher than he'd meant. Elias wasn't the first man to be taken by an idea that looked better on paper.

By the time Daniel was ready to leave, Elias was engrossed in the text, reading as intently as he'd once read Marx. Some men were attracted to anything that demanded devotion and sacrifice, the nature of the idea mattering less than its potential to turn things on their head.

"Come with me," Daniel said. He asked Firooz to fetch the bicycles, which hadn't been used in years.

"Where are we going?" Elias said.

"I want you to meet someone."

Because victory had come quickly in the twenty-four-hour battle, the city seemed peaceful. There was no silence as loud as the one that followed war. Daniel and Elias cycled past the guards, who asked where they were going but didn't ask for ID because most people had none, especially servants. They let them pass, reminding them of curfew. The day was damp and gray, the threat of rain heavy in the air. The new clothes felt cool, the breeze floating through the fabric, but they did little to relieve Daniel's pain. His bruises throbbed, limbs protesting with every stroke.

He angled the bike onto the sidewalk, which was thick with crowds making the most of the remaining hours. No one so much as glanced at Daniel. He had joined the ranks of the invisible. Billboards shouted clever slogans at passersby about the value of all men. *You can always count on a murderer for a fancy prose style*, Telaya whispered, quoting from the Nabokov book on Daniel's nightstand.

The smell of smoke and gunpowder lingered; the blood on the sidewalks hadn't yet dried. The facade of Sajadi Enterprises came into view, its granite flat and drab against the April sky. It was completely unscathed. The same could not be said of the ministry. A gaping hole exposed several ground-floor suites. Red flags rose from the roofs of both buildings. This was more than vandalism and violence, wrecked windows and walls. A kind of blasphemy had taken place.

A hundred customers were waiting outside the bank. Flags and bombed-out walls mattered less than the fate of their investments and accounts. A large sign was affixed to its glass doors, warning everyone they would not be giving out more than small sums because most of the accounts were frozen. The sun pushed through the clouds, casting a gentle light on the city. Daniel and Elias rolled down an alley where a tea shop was the only sign of life. It should have been spilling over with customers sitting at tables on the sidewalk, but was nearly deserted. As they stopped to let a shepherd by with his flock, Elias said, "I'm not afraid of them, you know. That's not why I changed my mind. I'm not a coward."

"I know. It's the bravest thing you've ever done."

"Are you making fun of me?"

"No, Elias," Daniel said. "I'm not making fun of you."

It was true, and yet Daniel thought Elias didn't understand that courage and cowardice weren't fixed values. If you resisted a revolution that resulted in a better society, you were a narrow-minded bigot. If you resisted a revolution that resulted in a worse society, you were brave and enlightened. So much was in the eye of the beholder, and those who would judge Daniel and Elias in the future benefited from twenty-twenty hindsight. He thought of *agha*. Had it been hard for him to betray Sayed and Daniel? He tried to reconcile what had happened with the loyal guardian he'd known all his life, returning to one particular memory again and again.

In the months before Sayed was taken to prison, Sherzai started coming to the house more often to help Daniel with his homework or play chess with him. One night, after they thought Daniel had gone to bed, Daniel snuck over and listened to them in the living room. He heard ice cubes tumbling and liquid splashing into a glass. Someone set a bottle down on the table.

Sherzai asked Sayed, "What do you think of the new man next door?"

"Do you mean the new naan shop or Mr. Khrushchev?"

"I'm surprised you can still make jokes, knowing what awaits you."

"Prison's the biggest joke of all when a jester is your jailer. I have no respect for this fool king of ours."

"Your son probably doesn't think it's funny. But I don't suppose you have given that much thought."

"I'm not a young man and I have a finite number of

thoughts left, so I must allot them carefully." More ice was dropped into tumblers, more liquid poured. "To answer your question about Khrushchev," Sayed continued, "I would prefer the Russians not invade while I'm in jail. It would be a shame to have prepared for so many wars only to have this happen when I can't be of use."

"And if they do? It won't be like the English decades ago. This enemy has fighter jets."

"And I have you." Sayed chuckled wistfully. "I wish I'd had you back in 1919, but you were only nine."

"You shouldn't be so sure you have me now, either."

"What does that mean?"

"Which part confused you?"

There was a long silence.

"How's your leg?" Sayed asked. He spoke slowly, and only later did Daniel understand that his father's relationship with Sherzai was summed up in that simple question.

"I'm glad I have it," Sherzai said. "But in some ways, it is getting worse."

"How so?"

"The older I get, the worse it seems that the only reason I am alive is that your father thought I deserved to be. The virus struck thousands. Every time I pick up my cane, I am reminded."

"You would prefer to be dead just because thousands of others are? That's a teenager's notion of justice."

"Your interpretation of right and wrong is more questionable than mine."

"That isn't fair," Sayed said.

"What isn't fair? That I should challenge you? Who else is going to do it? Look at the mess you've made."

"You call it a mess, I call it destiny. This is inevitable."

The men's voices were growing louder. Daniel heard Sayed

rise. He could tell it was Sayed because when Sherzai walked, his walking stick struck the floor.

"Every decision I've made is the right one, because it was the only one I could make," Sayed said. His footsteps stopped. "Choosing between two things is easy as long as you can compare like with like: hate with hate, and love with love. If someone asks me, 'Whom do you hate more, the English or the Russians,' I would say the English, because they attacked us so relentlessly. But if you ask me to compare two different feelings, how much I love something compared to how much I hate something else, that's a conundrum. Apples against oranges. So if I ask myself, what weighs more, my hatred of the invaders or my love for my country? How to answer this when the two categories are distinct?"

"Not every decision is easy even when you compare like with like, Sayed. Are you proud?"

"Of what?"

"When you think about going to prison. Is it worth it? Leaving your son like this?"

"I weighed the options before me. The Scale of Sages is unambiguous."

Sherzai's cane struck the floor with great force. "Don't blame your imaginary scale. You made the decisions. You. The boy is paying the price."

"I have you to take care of the child. Or what was it you said earlier? That I couldn't be sure I had you?"

Sherzai sighed. "I will be there for the boy, always."

Sayed changed the subject. They argued about politics like they always did, and the debate was about power—who should have it, and how much. Sherzai insisted that the way forward was with a strong ruler.

"You mean like our king?" It was not mainly kings who had fought back the Russians and the English, Sayed reminded him, but ordinary people from every desert, village, and field, and they had fought not for the king but for their kin. The tribes had gotten the job done. And now poppy growers were farming right under His Majesty's nose. Only a few arrests had been made. Sayed laughed contemptuously when he said, "I've destroyed more poppy fields than the whole damned government. I'm tired."

"Then stop. Make a new life when you get out of prison."

"There's no such thing as a new life. Everybody's life is just a recycled version of something from the past. We are not a creative species. How do you like your job at the Ministry of Planning?" Sayed said in the tone he'd used when he'd asked about Sherzai's leg.

"I'm content."

"Nothing more than that? I worked hard for you to get it."

"Goodbye, Sayed." Sherzai's awkward gait grew louder. Daniel retreated to the living room. When the housekeeper came walking by, Daniel asked him, "What is a tribe, exactly?"

"I don't really know."

"Am I part of one?"

The housekeeper looked at the armoire at the end of the hall, its shelves ablaze with crystal and gold and diamonds, malachite, silver, and gems, and at the walls adorned with antique weapons and paintings.

"Yes," he said. "I think you are."

32

THE BUILDING DANIEL WAS LOOKING FOR WASN'T FAR FROM THE ZOROASTER, WEDGED BETWEEN a beauty salon and a grocery. Both were closed. Paint was peeling from the walls, and a geranium struggled bravely on a balcony. Daniel carefully removed the fake beard. The glass pane in the door was cracked and covered by black fabric. He knocked, wondering if the person he'd come to see still lived here. He heard someone shambling down the stairs.

The fabric parted. A stranger in dark glasses peered out at Daniel. Expecting to be turned away, Daniel quietly gave his name and Elias's through the crack. The man didn't have a chance to reply. A second figure was already coming down the staircase, his laughter filling the air. It was a sound that Daniel had never forgotten, because when mullahs laughed, they usually did not sound like boisterous uncles.

Khaiyam opened the door and bowed with his hand on his heart. "Come in, my brother, come in." He kissed Daniel on both cheeks, adjusted his glasses, and tightened his skullcap, which had shifted during their embrace. He was as thin as ever.

"Who is this?" he asked before letting Elias in. Daniel promised that Elias posed no danger. They exchanged a warm, polite greeting.

"We haven't talked in so long," Khaiyam said to Daniel. "Fifteen years?"

"More. I was a child the last time."

"You were never a child."

After Khaiyam brewed tea, he gestured to cushions on the floor. To Daniel's aching body, the journey down to his seat seemed endless, but Khaiyam would not sit before his guests did.

Khaiyam wanted to know everything about Daniel's life and work. Each time Daniel answered a question, he clapped or opened his arms in a display of grand approval. It was as if nothing had happened, yesterday a day like any other. When he quietly asked about the Feverdrops Slaughter, Daniel disclosed nothing about his role in Yassaman.

"An evil weed, the poppy," Khaiyam said.

Daniel refrained from saying the poppy wasn't a weed—weeds were plants no one wanted. After talking about family, friends, and work, they paused, sipping in silence. Elias hadn't said a word, looking around the apartment with suspicion.

After his third cigarette, Daniel finally said, "So, Khaiyam. What do you think?"

"I think they're monsters," the mullah said without hesitation.

"They'll come for you. They're already going after the imams. It's on the foreign news."

"I'm lucky to have good friends who insist on protecting me."

"It won't be enough. Everyone knows who you are."

"No one knows who anyone is. Judging by your clothes, you're hardly immutable yourself."

"You know what I mean."

"Perhaps. But what do they really know? They know I oppose injustice. They know the last president did not like me.

The king before him also didn't like me." Khaiyam smiled, a wisp of pride blushing his face.

"I thought you'd find these new men much worse," Daniel said. "They're godless."

"And what about you?"

"What about me?"

"Are you not godless? You told me you didn't believe in the divine when you were twelve years old. As I said, you were never a child."

"I'm not godless. I'm an atheist."

"I'll ponder the difference later." Khaiyam lay a gentle hand on Daniel's leg. "Are you going to tell me what happened? Are they the ones who hurt you?"

Daniel told Khaiyam everything. That he'd been in his office when the coup began. How the uniforms had taken his neighbors and beaten him when he'd tried to stop them. About the one girl he'd managed to save, though he wondered how many had been hauled away. How he'd crossed the city looking for Laila, whom Khaiyam remembered as one of the brightest children he had ever met. Elias smiled.

When Daniel finished, a silence settled over the apartment, which was unchanged from many years ago, with its stone floors and crooked stairs.

"I have to do something, Khaiyam. I can't sit here and watch them win."

"You have some idea of how to fight this?" Khaiyam said.

"I want to know what your people are planning."

"My people?"

"There's no one else who can confront them. You are the only ones with enough strength in numbers."

"There were always many of us. But we don't have much money, and what you're talking about takes a lot of it. Dollars or diamonds or gold."

Daniel knew all about idealistic organizations with small budgets. "What if I could arrange for the money to come through?" he said.

Elias stared at Daniel, excitement building in his eyes.

The mullah set down his glass. "I would be most grateful, of course. But Daniel, may I trouble you with something that has burdened me for some time?"

"Of course. I'm surprised you're asking for permission."

"I fear your father found me a great disappointment for failing to instill in you any reverence for the divine."

Perplexed at this change in topic, Daniel said, "My father didn't believe in a god. The way he insisted that I learn about religion was hypocrisy."

"It's easy to mistake love for hypocrisy. All fathers want their children to have the things they didn't. Sayed did not have the gift of faith."

"My father had faith in some things. Like power."

"He failed to understand that there is great power in faith. There are none so powerful as those who believe. When the world ends, the radically faithful may well be the ones who end it." After a pause, he added, "Why exactly are you here?"

"To help you. I loathe these men and what they've done. I want to give you money for everything that fuels a good resistance. Bribes, weapons."

Khaiyam shifted on his pillow, repositioning himself tailor-style. "Yes, but what are you fighting *for*? What do you love? If you don't know that, your devotion will fade. Hate makes you a good killer; love makes you a good fighter."

"Do you trust me?" Daniel said.

"My father trusted yours."

Daniel tried to answer, but Khaiyam said, "Unfortunately, you've made yourself useless."

"What?"

The mullah turned his eyes to the kitchen table. Newspapers were spread across the surface. "I assume they threatened you, but how can you come here and tell me you want to fight when you've capitulated at the first sign of peril?"

Daniel asked himself what was worse: that Khaiyam should think him a coward who had caved to threats, or an arrogant scion who had signed on the dotted line without looking. He told him the truth. Khaiyam watched him inscrutably. As Daniel explained why he had never glanced at the quarterly reports, the mullah went completely still. It was like talking not so much to a wall as a shadow. Elias, however, had surprise painted plainly on his face.

"What does it matter now?" Daniel said. "The company's gone."

"It's not the only one." Khaiyam fetched the newspaper and dropped it at Daniel's feet.

The front page chronicled the seizure of fifty businesses, his neighbors' companies among them. The worst was a paragraph describing Daniel's voluntary forfeiture of his firm. After thanking him for his cooperation, the article took a different path. It described Daniel Abdullah Sajadi as a counterrevolutionary by nature, a scion of the old elite, with an estate and servants and a cache of treasures stolen from the people. Though he had given Sajadi Enterprises to the regime, he would not be able to stand living without its riches. He would soon plot for the return of his undeserved wealth. Daniel looked at his own face staring out from the page.

"As I said," Khaiyam began, "you aren't of much use to us. Any accounts you have here are already frozen. If you try to send anything from America, they'll seize it."

Daniel might have guessed this, given his feature in the paper. He thought of an old saying: *Anything that isn't in the hands of God is in the hands of the English*. Now it was all in the hands of the Communists—even the man who had cared for Daniel as a son. "I have some money hidden away," he said.

"In afghanis? What good will that do? Real war takes real money."

It was nine o'clock when a motorcycle rumbled to a stop. A man pounded on the door. Khaiyam quickly uncoiled his body and pulled back a rug to reveal a trapdoor. He slid it aside and dropped into a crawl space, pulling his guests with him as his bouncer made his way down the stairs. The visitor had evidently brought a photo, because the guard denied recognizing someone. He insisted that he had lived here for four years alone, but the man stomped into the apartment, his boots passing over their heads. Before he left, he warned he would be back.

As he lumbered up the stairs, Khaiyam's watchman said, "It's only a matter of time, my brother."

When the men had pulled themselves up from their hiding place, Daniel said to Khaiyam, "You have to move."

Khaiyam's eyes were twin pieces of coal. "As with every skill, dissent takes practice. I've been doing this a long time, though I appreciate your concern."

The meeting had come to a close. He wrapped Daniel's hands in his own and held them tightly. "Thank you," he said. "I wish upon you every blessing, Daniel Sajadi."

His words were not unkind, but Daniel was cut to the bone by the mullah's real message: without money, Daniel had nothing to give. Their host embraced Daniel and Elias and walked both his guests to the door.

They cycled toward home, and in the heart of the city found themselves caught behind a clash of bicycles and cars waiting at a checkpoint. He tried to navigate around them, but the uniform guarding the booth held up a hand. Daniel waited. When his turn came, the guard asked questions about where he lived and worked, and Daniel answered easily. When he said he worked for Daniel Sajadi, an American diplomat, the guard raised a quizzical brow. "I know the name," he said. He lifted a thick book and began thumbing through pages, taking his time. The guard flipped the book toward him and jabbed his finger at one of two photos of Daniel.

"This man?" he said. "This is who you work for?"

Daniel nodded, hoping Elias would stay quiet. The makeup on his bruises grew warm and soft, and he began to pull away, hoping the guard was finished with him, but he wasn't.

"How long have you worked for him?" the man said.

"I'm not good with telling time."

"Why are you working for a man like this? Do you like being in servitude?" The guard pointed to the bandage on his cheek. "Did he do that to you?"

Daniel said no, that he'd fallen on a sharp stone. The uniform let them both go. As he cycled away, Daniel's legs were heavy. In the second photo the guard had shown him, Daniel had been standing outside his house on a sunny day, leaning into the passenger seat of his car. His hand was on the door, bearing the star-sapphire ring Rebecca had given him. The ring he was still wearing. He took it off as he rode, tucking it in his pocket, feeling that it was, at that moment, the most precious thing he owned.

A pitiful scene was unfolding just outside the record store. A woman in a *chaderi* was standing so still that she seemed to be posing with the cardboard cutout of Elvis, who watched from behind glass doors. A soldier held a bayonet to her chest. "Don't move," he said. He raised her entire *chaderi* with the blade of his weapon and made a great show of dropping the garment on the ground, where the blue fabric spread like an ink stain. People gathered, but no one dared move close.

The woman held her eyes half-shut, gazing far away. She was hugging herself, trying to hide what was now exposed: a long skirt and a high-collared blouse embroidered with flowers. Elvis glittered in white sequins, offering up his microphone. Daniel felt anger rise inside him at how the woman was being treated and his own impotence in the face of it.

As soon as he was home, he went to the bedroom. He found the whiskey he kept in the wardrobe and filled his toothbrush glass twice. Then he attached his ring to a chain that he hung around his neck, out of sight underneath his shirt.

What about me? Telaya said. Daniel took her mirror from its black velvet box and slipped it into the pocket of his pants. Light and thin, the mirror carried an unexpected weight.

Laila came to the house that night. Her doctor's coat was bloodstained, but her Communist Party ID was glossy and clean, and the guard let her in without question. Daniel found her in the living room. He had little to say to her. She wanted to check his body for breaks and sprains, but he refused. When he asked if she'd known about Sherzai's plan, she shook her head. He told her he was going to bed and asked her to see herself out. As a doctor and party member, she had no curfew.

"Be careful," she said before she left.

"I will."

"I don't mean with what's happening outside."

WALLED IN

They trek across the desert, pulling their children, camels, and mules, their carpets and tents from place to place as they go. When Boy was very small, he felt sorry for these people who had lost their homes. Then one day Nazook exploded into laughter and told him, "You are an idiot who would be lost without me. Those people are homeless because it is how they have always lived. They're nomads." He stretches out the word as if Boy might be too stupid to understand. How can there be such a thing, Boy wonders. Wall-less by choice?

He asks Socrates. Some nomads hate living inside, the teacher explains. The government tried to force them into high-rises, which the English and the Germans and Russians came with cameras to film. But everything inside the high-rises was wrong. How unnatural to live up so high, so dangerously close to where the spirits lived, with loved ones separated by walls, doors, locks. Within four weeks, three had already taken their own lives because they could not live this way. A woman and her twelve-year-old twin girls killed themselves days later because strange men could watch them from a building across the way, and the shame became unbearable. Soon, the Kochis all packed their belongings and moved back out. When Socrates said this, Boy felt sick. To be human was to want walls—wasn't that what separated humans from animals?

Taj walks among the Kochis now; they are the best poppy workers around. But their very existence is an affront to him. They mock everything he has ever wanted, satisfied without possessions or dreams of a bigger life. When Taj built his house, he treasured his walls so much that he refused to hang carpets or photos or scarves on them. The walls had to be blank. It wasn't fancy art that reminded him of his success. It was the walls.

33

THE BEDROOM BALCONY WAS LIKE AN ISLAND, DESERTED AND WARM DESPITE THE FALLING temperatures of the post-storm night. Daniel tried to lose himself in a book, to no avail. He had to think about what he had said to Khaiyam. He had to decide if the seed in his mind was worth watering or a poisoned kernel to be destroyed. Over the wall to the east, the lights were bright in Keshmesh's house.

Daniel watched the boy's father come home, draping his car with a tarp as meticulously as a mother tucking in her child. More remarkable was the flag that hung from Keshmesh's balcony. Its black, gold, and green stripes were already blocks of memory, and Daniel wished he could chase away the red that now flew over the city.

Keshmesh emerged onto his balcony. Daniel raised his hand in salute, but the boy didn't respond. They'd met countless times like this, the boy putting on goofy shows. There were no antics tonight, because Keshmesh's father walked onto the balcony and began quarreling with his son. It ended with a loud admonition: "You have no idea how lucky you are, you ungrateful child." He pulled the old flag up and bundled it in his hands, storming back inside while his son sulked. Over the other wall, in the road, Daniel could see a guard asleep in his Jeep, already bored with his revolution.

Daniel went back inside, wondering if he would be able to sleep. He laid his pajamas on the bed and sat in front of the dresser, watching himself in the dimly lit mirror. The beard made him look older. His eyes were as they had always been, his pupils like two brown stones from his father's mines.

His father's mines. He had never felt they were his own, and fate had agreed. His flight was scheduled for tomorrow afternoon. Rebecca expected him. But he expected something else of himself now. He went downstairs to call her. He thought he would find Peter and Elias playing cards in the living room, lamenting their bad hands and applauding at trivial victories. Instead, he found Elias sitting there in the dark.

"Don't," Elias said when Daniel reached for the light switch.

They spoke for a while, the journalist rambling like a drunk man even though he was sober. He would not apologize for what he had believed in, he said, but he'd made one big mistake: assuming that men who had the same ideologies believed in the same things. But there was more to belief than ideology, wasn't there, he wondered.

As Elias spoke, Daniel decided that tomorrow he would find Taj. It was the only thing that made sense.

Then, after Elias had gone to bed, he saw what Laila had done. She'd lined up empty bottles at the wet bar, with a handwritten note: *We love you.*

He picked up the receiver, relieved to finally hear a dial tone. Elizabeth Menlow answered on the first ring. She sounded strained, her voice thin and small, and once he had convinced her that he was all right and in no danger, she began to weep. "We're all counting the hours until you arrive, dear," she said.

He was going to tell her that he had to stay just one more

week, but her next words weren't what he expected. Rebecca was at St. Luke's. Daniel jerked out of his chair. Elizabeth described the ambulance and the medics in detail. She talked about their accents and clothes, as if these things mattered. She said Walter was with Rebecca now, and that Elizabeth had come home only to pack some clothes and books for her. At least that was something, Daniel thought. Books. That meant Rebecca was alert and awake.

"Did she go into labor?" he asked. Laila had said three or four weeks ahead would be early but not catastrophic.

"No. At first they thought it was. Wait. There was something about early labor. But that's not why she's there."

"Elizabeth, is Becca in labor or not?"

"Oh no, she's not in labor, dear. They just need to keep her because of the complication."

"What complication?"

"The one she had to go to the hospital for. She's fine. I mean, there are no contractions, so don't worry about that. That's what the doctor said. He said don't worry. About that . . ." She trailed off.

Daniel rubbed his eyes and began to pace, stretching the phone cord as far as it would allow. He asked for the number to St. Luke's and Rebecca's room. The phone rang twenty times. He tried the front desk and they connected him from there, but again, it only rang. He slammed down the receiver, then raised it back to his ear. Silence. The connection was down. He tried again and again to no avail.

He finally reached Rebecca at five the next morning after another fitful night. She sounded weak. She asked anxious questions, telling him how glad she was that he would be on a plane in a few hours. The revolution was on the news every night. CBS had interviewed Smythe, who assured everyone that things could proceed as usual for the time being. The new regime might not be impossible to work with, he said. Daniel had no interest in what Smythe thought. He wanted to know what was happening to Rebecca. When he thought about her, it made the regime change seem smaller.

"Remind me what time you're landing," she said.

There it was. "It's actually going to be another week until I can come home. Just administrative things." This was different from all the other things he'd kept from her. Everyone was careful with what they said over the phone now. But when he returned, he would tell her everything.

"It's out of my hands," he continued. It was true. He had two lives now, although he lived in a space in between them, a gray area that wasn't gray at all, its spectrum made up instead of shades of red and green. "Becca, are you still there?"

"Yes," she said. "It's just that I don't believe you."

"What do you mean?"

She hung up. When he tried to call back, the line was dead. Daniel tried again several times before lying down on the couch. For the next hour and a half, Elias silently read the Koran, absorbed like a student who had at last found a philosophy with the answers he'd been seeking, while Peter barricaded himself upstairs with his typewriter. Daniel was sure he would always associate these days with that clicking sound. Every time he thought about Khaiyam, he wanted to go back up the stairs of that crooked building and correct the mullah on one point. Daniel wasn't worthless without his inherited wealth; he could still offer something.

As he waited for the clock to strike seven, he tried to distract himself with small pleasures and tasks. He ate an orange. He rearranged his LPs alphabetically. He picked up random books, thumbing through a few pages of *Death in Venice*, which he found boring and a little twisted. He drank, but only a little. It helped with the pain, especially when he mixed it with tiny bits of opium. Finally, he looked at his watch. It was time to go. He checked his beard, makeup, and turban, still unused to working its layers and folds, which only looked right with Firooz's help. He hoped he would be able to find Taj. He wondered what the khan would say when he saw Daniel in his disguise. Walking through the living room, he was taken aback by his father's glare. He seldom noticed the portrait. Today, the bespectacled eyes followed him even after he left the room. He slipped out of the house and mounted one of the bikes. He felt Telaya's mirror shift in his pocket.

Daniel reached the Silk Road at eight thirty. Tucked away on the outskirts of town, it was a place he never thought he would visit. Like the Zoroaster, it could only be found by those who knew where to go. It stood alone on a concrete slab, surrounded by a patch of desert on a dusty road. He hesitated. If he was slipping into some kind of madness, so be it. He pushed open a ragged screen that led into a hallway without a ceiling. At the end was a heavy door. He tapped several times and waited for what seemed like an eternity before a gleaming eye appeared in the peephole. A sleepy voice asked what he wanted.

"I'm looking for a friend."

More questions. The portal unlocked and the hinges creaked open. A young man led him inside. Organized in a tidy row were loafers, oxfords, sandals, and heels. Even a pair of cowboy boots. Two armed men searched him. They asked if he had come to smoke. No, he said. He just wanted to talk to a friend who might be here. He followed them through a restaurant, crossing the kitchen, and was ushered through another creaking metal door at the end of a hallway. They gave him five minutes.

The smell of bitter sweetness rushed toward him. The opium den looked nothing like the image painted on its ceiling, a gilded fresco depicting a harem where women drank from goblets, turbaned men enveloped in twirling smoke and lustful girls. The space was dimly lit by sconces, the flames making shadows jump on the walls. Plush cushions lined the edges of the room. Scattered around were ottomans and low tables. There was no music, only hushed whispers and peaceful breathing.

No one seemed to notice Daniel as he moved about the room, not even those who looked straight at him. The fevered ones were lost to warm dreams and each other. One of the paradoxes of opium was that people could feel deeply connected to others while enjoying a sense of sublime solitude. Or so he'd heard when he was a boy eavesdropping on his father's servants. It wasn't the kind of information you found in USADE handbooks. He felt like an intruder.

Taj Maleki was known to many in the room. Most had heard his name, and some had even seen him, but they all described him in different ways. Sometimes he was tall, other times short. So he had sent decoys. Ingenious. When Daniel asked where he lived or how often he came here, the Fevered Ones looked at him as if his questions had no answers. He approached a couple playing chess with marble pieces that were as green as the smoke, and they smiled like Daniel was the person they'd been waiting for. The woman told him no one saw Taj Maleki anywhere outside the Silk Road.

"Doesn't he sometimes meet people at the Zoroaster?" Daniel said.

The couple smiled. "Nobody here goes to a place like that." They went on to explain that other Manticores sometimes came here, too, but there was no agreement on the names of these men or their appearance. They came now and then to ask their customers if they liked the latest sample and wished to arrange a regular purchase. "There's no predictability to their visits." Manticores came and went in rhythms known only to them.

"How often do you come here?" Daniel said.

"How often . . ."

He scribbled his name and number on napkins, handing them to everyone. "If you see him," he said, "tell him it's important."

The guards searched him again before he left. He was glad to walk out into the sunlight and leave the addicts to their fever dream where opium was the beginning, middle, and end. It was a place without time, a place without place. Daniel envied them.

STARS

Socrates is dead. He overdosed on the flower he loved, as Taj knew he would. Socrates made Taj into an educated man, and he'd been proud of his pupil. They had traveled together to the Gardens of Babur, to the Blue Mosque in Herat, to the Buddha statues in Bamyan, and the home of the great poet Rumi in Balkh, where the Mosque of Nine Cupolas stood. Before he died, Socrates taught Taj about great men. There were kings and poets and warriors like Mir Masjidi, who fought the English in the early 1800s. And Sayed Sajadi, beloved by the people for his fierce fight against the invaders when he was not yet twenty, using the wealth he received as the sole heir of a gemstone company to help build a resistance army unlike anything the English were prepared for. Once the English were expelled, the Russians were so scared they made peace two years later, and after that Sayed Sajadi rose to challenge the monarchy, criticizing it in public, becoming more popular than the king ever was. Socrates admired this man very much, and one day he told Taj a story.

When Socrates was a small boy, he lived with his family in Herat. One spring day, when the cherry blossoms filled the air with perfume, his parents dressed in fine clothes and young Socrates wore a silk outfit purchased for his grandmother's funeral the year before. With their neighbors, they lined the main boulevard in the city, It was the most exciting day of Socrates's life. Sayed Sajadi arrived by car but stepped out so he could walk and greet the hundreds of people who had come. When Sayed Sajadi saw Socrates, he picked him up in his arms, and looking into his eyes, the hero said, "You will grow up to do great things, won't you?"

Years later, Socrates was proud of his government job as a clerk. He never thought much about what Sayed Sajadi had said, until one day he noticed that his portrait was on one of the walls. How silly, he thought—Mr. Sajadi disliked the government, and everybody had heard he was locked up in prison for the things he'd said about the king. But when Socrates saw the photo, he felt a little ashamed of his job. Surely this was not what Mr. Sajadi had meant by "do great things."

Socrates had grown up and done nothing great, and never would. It was opium that saved him from the shame, he said to Taj. Opium took away everything that caused him pain. God lived inside that sweet green smoke, and Socrates knew this because when he smoked, forgiveness came, too. To be with God all day, all night, to inhale the essence of the divine, this was a gift discovered by few men, and Socrates died grateful, so grateful that he was one of the chosen.

But Taj does not believe in God. Under the stars of a lonely night, he wipes his tears and gently closes his teacher's eyes.

34

THE NEXT FOUR MORNINGS, DANIEL RETURNED TO THE SILK ROAD. STILL NO SIGN OF TAJ. ON the radio, propaganda dominated the airwaves during the day, and at night the announcer read off the dreaded arrest report. Daniel stopped listening after it seemed like half the people he'd grown up with had been taken. Voice of America gave updates at random times, never announcing the next broadcast, forcing the Communists—and everyone else—to search for the right frequency. Daniel stopped listening to them, too. He had reached Rebecca twice since she'd hung up on him, and though she was still at St. Luke's, she said she was fine. It was only a precaution, she said. She didn't sound angry now, but there was fear and sadness when they spoke, which wasn't as often as he wanted because the phones still worked sporadically.

He saw nothing of Ian, who was unhappily holed up at the US embassy with most of the Peace Corps staff. Daniel washed his clothes by hand, hanging them to dry on the balcony. He read and stayed inside, while Firooz ventured out for groceries and cooked elaborate meals that made for copious leftovers. Stuck in the house together, Peter, Elias, and Daniel spoke little, and he wondered if they had seen Laila's note and the bottles she'd lined up at the wet bar. Daniel had removed them and stowed them in the kitchen. The next day, they were gone. He was grateful for the discretion of men like Firooz. The faithful housekeeper was like the servants he'd grown up with, a multitude of men who rushed silently from room to room, talked in code, and gave cryptic answers to Daniel's little-boy questions. If he asked when the crates of Coca-Cola were coming, they would nod knowingly and say things like "When the mule is gone, a wise man puts away the saddle and stocks up on onions."

Every day, Firooz changed the bandages on Daniel's face, ribs, arms, and legs, chastising him when he split open a wound by doing too much, whether it was trying to work in the woodshed, fixing a leaky faucet, or tending to a flower bed after he heard the gardener had died the day of the revolution. His heart had stopped, Firooz said. Together, they grieved the gardener who had been with the Sajadis since Sayed's time.

The days passed. Daniel had told Rebecca he only needed a week, but his hopes dwindled. Maybe it was time to leave and forget what he wanted to do.

Then it happened. On the fifth morning, one of the patrons at the Silk Road gave him a note with the details for a meeting in Paghman, one of the loveliest places Daniel knew. He took a few essentials with him, hiding them in a pouch under his *piran tomban*.

He arrived late, but Taj was nowhere in sight. He sat at the edge of a stream and plunged his blistered feet into the chilly water, surrounded by weeping willows and poplars silhouetted against the fragile sky. It wasn't a wonder that Paghman was known as the country's garden capital. Across the rustling brook, a smaller replica of the Arc de Triomphe was edged with manicured hedges and flower beds.

"I suppose you've seen the real one," said a voice behind him. The opium khan joined Daniel on the leaf-strewn ground, leaning back against a trunk. Picking through a mound of pumpkin seeds he held in his palm, he considered Daniel's disguise with amusement. "Although I hear France doesn't let in people who are dressed like that."

"Why did you choose to meet here?" Daniel said. It was an hour from the city, and surely there were back rooms in teahouses that could have served just as well.

"I'm not so at ease in the city just now, you might understand," Taj said. "And I've always liked gardens."

Daniel nodded. The Arc was beautiful, but it still paled compared to its surroundings. He loved this oasis of lush and fertile green where he had spent childhood summers with his father, Sherzai, and friends from school.

"You look well, Daniel Sajadi. Truly."

"I wish I could return the compliment," Daniel said. In the swelling morning light, Taj looked even worse than that night at the Zoroaster. "I'm afraid your criminal life is catching up with you."

Taj bowed his head. "Your new clothing is excellent. That shade of nonwhite flatters you, by the way. Perfectly colorless."

"Better than transparent. If you're going to pick a fake name, you could come up with something less obvious than Taj Maleki."

"Judging by your costume, I'm not the only one pretending. Has it saved you?"

"So far."

"I am delighted." Taj laughed. "I would hate for you to come to any harm. You add a certain vigor and glory to my unremarkable life." After a pause, he asked, "So, what is it that you want? It's not every day that one is summoned by a Sajadi."

"I assume you've seen what the new people in power are capable of."

"I have," Taj said.

"They're going to destroy you and everyone like you," Daniel said.

"You planned to destroy me, too."

"But I didn't."

"Only because you didn't have the chance," Taj said.

"This isn't the same thing. They're going to take everyone's land and redistribute it to whomever they want, which means mostly their own friends. They're already killing people who haven't done anything wrong. Imagine what they'll do to you."

Taj flashed a forced smile. "I'm touched that you're so concerned about my fate that you galloped to the nearest opium den to warn me."

Daniel couldn't hold back a laugh. "Well, I am concerned about fate, although maybe not yours in particular."

"You believe in fate, Daniel Sajadi? That surprises me."

"So many surprises lately. They took my father's company." A fish flipped over above the water, landing with a splash.

"I know. You've made front-page news, and not because of your ridiculous agency this time."

Daniel told Taj about Khaiyam and the opposition rising in the cities and countryside. He told him they needed money. As much as possible, and soon. Then there would be a way to combat the Communists before they truly took hold and people forgot there'd been a time without them.

Taj shrugged. "So give them money. You have so much of it, Daniel Sajadi, as the son of a great family."

"I don't, Taj. The firm is gone, and anything I have is far away in America. I can't just bring it over." As Taj considered this, Daniel said, "How much influence do you have with the other khans?"

Taj watched him silently, waiting for more.

"You'll all either have to find somewhere else to grow your poppies or start growing something that isn't against the law."

The Manticore threw his head back and laughed before fixing Daniel with a frank and candid smile. "*This* is why you wished to meet with me so urgently? To tell me I must finally start growing wheat or corn, just like you've always said?" He shook his head. "By the way, I've noticed that your people like to describe those crops as golden. 'Fields of golden wheat.'" His smile vanished. "If you have to pretend it sparkles, it isn't gold."

"If I were you, I would choose the first option," Daniel continued, ignoring the jab. "Find somewhere else to grow your poppies. Much farther from Kabul."

Taj reached for a branch and plucked a blossom. "How long *did* you spend at the Silk Road?" he said. "Or have these musings been brought on by alcohol?"

"There's a way for you to keep growing your poppies, but if I help you, you have to help me do something to weaken these men." Daniel tried not to think of what his father would say at hearing him propose a deal to an opium khan.

"Men? Is that what you call them?" Taj tossed the blossom into the stream. "I call them pigeons, strutting around with their chests puffed out. Taking people's crumbs."

Encouraged, Daniel continued trying to convince him of the harm the new regime would do. He described the wrecked farms in Communist Russia, the seizures of land, and the concrete blocks where they forced the undesirables, street children, and anyone they labeled a criminal.

"Your people already made sure our trade would die," Taj replied. "The new government is not a problem. The world is full of people chasing after other people's crumbs."

"If you and the others make a single new land purchase,

that money could be put to good use. Toward something that can help you," Daniel said.

It took a moment for Taj to respond. He was watching the fleeing stream. "It's warmer than I expected," he said. He loosened and removed his turban, long hair falling down his back. A flicker of sun fell on the glass-cut onyx. He polished the stone, which glittered in the sun.

"Where else would I grow my poppies?"

Daniel spoke as the minutes ticked away. The frogs and the birds chimed in, seeming to debate the merits of his plan. There was nothing remarkable about the land in Fever Valley, Daniel said. It wasn't like the lush fields of the northeast, where acres of poppies had grown until the government banned them. Fever Valley had come up spontaneously, reaching its status by chance, word of mouth, and tribal clusters who knew little of the rest of the country. It had never possessed great advantages, and now had none at all.

"It's close to the Pakistani border," Taj countered.

"So is the land I have in mind."

The opium khan picked up a beetle and studied it carefully before releasing it. He turned his attention to his nails, which he cleaned with a twig he sharpened into a pick with his knife. "I am not interested in politics," he said, "but if the pigeons are the future, we can deal with them. By sharing what we grow with them, for instance."

"You're going to give them half your poppies?"

Taj threw the pick into the water. "They won't ask for half. Just a little. That will be enough."

"Like it was for me and my agency when your people came to bribe us?"

"It used to work, before any of you came. We've had an unusual run of shortsighted people recently."

"Shortsighted or just honorable?"

"So the plan you're suggesting is honorable? Or did they beat that honor out of you?" Taj pointed to the bruises Daniel had done his best to cover. "I must say, you are splendidly accident-prone. Every time I see you, you've been injured somehow. In any case, honor fatigues, Daniel Sajadi. One cannot blame it for falling asleep and not waking up."

Daniel told Taj that he and his fellow khans might be able to bribe some of the new leaders, but they couldn't bribe all of them, and certainly not enough to subdue the most fervent of the ideologues.

"Yes, they can be quite dangerous," Taj said. "Luckily, it turned out you weren't quite as fervent as we might have feared." He went on, and it became clear to Daniel that for all his talk, Taj only understood the old, local way of doing things. He didn't know what the people who had just seized power were capable of.

The water seemed to rush faster as the day wore on, and the imitation Arc de Triomphe loomed larger. Daniel felt something land on his foot and gently kicked off a frog. "I have a proposal. How much opium do you have in reserve?" he said.

"Perhaps you didn't hear, but my last harvest was unexpectedly poor. My crew and my poppies were massacred, you see."

Daniel asked again, and if Taj was telling the truth, he had more in reserve than USADE had thought. He explained that he and the other khans kept a supply in case they needed to flood the market and drive prices down to punish foreign competitors.

"Like OPEC," Daniel said.

"Who's that?"

"Never mind, it's not important. Are you paid in dollars or diamonds?"

Taj confirmed what Daniel had long suspected: that the ISI, the Pakistani intelligence agency, paid in diamonds, while organized crime in Iran paid in dollars. When Daniel finished his proposition, Taj shook his head.

"I find it hard to believe that you know of some secret land you'll simply hand over to us."

"It's not a secret. Just difficult to get to."

When Taj reminded Daniel that he had no reason to trust him, Daniel told him that he'd been there as a child and offered to take him there himself.

"As I explained, my concern is you, not the location of this place," Taj replied.

"I'm here because I have no choice," Daniel said. "Some enemies are worse than others. I can't sit here and do nothing while these traitors massacre people and offer my country to the Russians."

You're the traitor, Telaya hissed. Daniel kept his eyes on Taj, refusing to blink.

Taj retrieved a chocolate bar from his pocket and peeled off the wrapper. "Things may have changed since you were a child. Maybe the path you knew doesn't exist anymore."

"If not, I'll find another way in."

"Even if you do obtain the resources you need, how does one bring down an enemy of this scale?"

Daniel told him what he'd learned from Sayed about war. That the way to weaken an enemy was not to pour everything into a single attack that determined everything, but to draw him into a long struggle where he spent all his energy trying to hold on and control you, never knowing where you might be hiding or when you might appear.

"Does it make life easier or harder?" Taj asked. "To imagine that you can simply remove whoever displeases you."

"It's not about removal, not yet. The land I'm talking

about is far south. You know how the governors are down there."

"Why would I?"

Daniel explained they did not like state interference, and that the new regime would be reluctant to face off with them.

"This plan sounds like a trick," Taj said.

"If I wanted to destroy you, I would stand back and let the new government do it."

"You might deceive me for the sake of revenge."

There was indeed something of a trick in Daniel's plan. It seemed right that he should still be fighting to stop the poppy trade, even in the small way he pictured now. "That's your sort of thing, not mine," he said.

"And on top of everything, you insult me. You're a terrible salesman."

"And you're a terrible businessman, or you would see an opportunity here. No one else is using that land—barely anyone knows about it." With that, Daniel pulled a small silk pouch from underneath his shirt.

Taj's eyes widened. The contents of the bag looked like ordinary poppy seeds, something you might see on a bagel in America. But they were seed samples Daniel had kept in a box in his home office. Taj put his chocolate down.

"They're a gift," Daniel said. "I have a larger bag for you, if you want it."

Taj examined the seeds. "These are high quality."

"Confiscated from local harvests. These were the highest grade. Some people might give cigarettes or figs, but I thought you might prefer this."

"Thank you," said the opium khan, bowing his head. "This doesn't make me trust you, but I'll call the khans for a meeting. You may show us the land."

"I can arrange for it today."

"Are you out of your noble mind? It will take more time than that to convince them."

But Daniel was out of time. He proposed a meeting in three days at a place that was easy to find, a landmark near the northern edge of Helmand Province. Taj promised to be there.

"This insurrection you speak of," he said. "Do you believe they can win?"

"They only need a few victories." Daniel reminded him of how the Communists had come to power. It was a three-part formula: they'd had greater numbers than people realized, a store of weapons, and the element of surprise. He told Taj that Khaiyam and other men of his position had thousands of followers, and those numbers were swelling. Given weapons and a plan of attack, they could be a formidable force.

"These clerics, you think they have better ideas than the Communists?"

"They won't be lackeys to the Russians. And anything is better than a puppet government." Daniel thought of Khaiyam, whose compassion and peaceful aura were shared by every cleric Daniel had ever encountered. Of the exiled mullahs, in hiding but bravely cutting into radio frequencies. Of Keshmesh, who was at the age where a single event could change who you became. And of Elias, who saw opposition to power as romantic just because he needed a fight to win. Daniel tried not to think of Sayed, and what he would have said at this moment. He took his feet out of the water. They were blissfully numb.

35

AT HOME, SAYED'S EYES AGAIN FOLLOWED DANIEL THROUGH THE HOUSE, HIS PORTRAIT LOOMING
larger than ever. Peter, Firooz, and Daniel talked, played, and
drank tea, and Daniel found himself laughing at their jokes,
everything growing lighter for a while. The night came quickly,
painting the windows black, the feeble lamps a poor match for
the encroaching darkness. Daniel wondered when he would fly
home, and whether Sutherland could arrange a ticket or if
he would have to find a way to Pakistan to catch a plane there. He
turned on the radio at eleven. A nasal voice rattled off the arrest
report. The list was long. Daniel listened for friends, acquain-
tances, and old classmates and heard one: "Laila Sharifi."

Peter rose, his cup dropping to the floor. Dr. Sharifi had
been caught buying a large quantity of illicit opium, the voice
said, and unlike the king or Daoud, the Party made no exceptions for its own. The rule of law was absolute, principles
unbendable to personal favor. The voice went on to read more
names. Daniel wondered how many nameless people had been
killed, too. He kept Peter as calm as he could, hiding his own
distress, but the professor was inconsolably shaken.

"I'll go see Sherzai in the morning," Daniel said. "He might
be able to get her out."

"Maybe I should come." Peter wrung his hands like an
old woman.

"I think I have a better chance."

Waiting for daylight, Daniel felt no pain, his wounds soothed by the bitter rain of what he had to do. He felt strangely empty, as if he'd been reduced to some essential element, a single atom, with a great force threatening to split him in two. In the morning, Peter set off for Laila's apartment, insisting he would wait for her there. It was closer to downtown, and Daniel was to get her out and bring her straight there.

When Daniel appeared at the Ministry of Planning an hour later, he introduced himself to the clerk as Abdullah, one of Mr. Sherzai's servants. She scanned him head to toe. "You're here to see the minister?" She leaned her chin in her hand. "Maybe you can wait until he returns home."

He told her it was urgent. She slowly dialed Sherzai's extension. He was in a meeting. Daniel waited on an uncomfortable couch, flipping through a magazine about architecture. He asked her to try again after twenty minutes. Sherzai sent down his secretary, a pretty woman in high heels and a formfitting suit. She wore a crystal brooch, a butterfly that caught the light as she led Daniel upstairs. Sherzai did not ask Daniel about his disguise.

In a large but utilitarian office, they stood appraising each other before Sherzai quietly left to fetch tea. Daniel was grateful for the moment alone. The newly minted Minister of Planning brought a pot from his secretary's desk and poured two glasses. He closed the door. He wanted to know about Rebecca's health, but Daniel wasn't here to talk about that. He pilfered a cigarette and lit it with unsteady hands. Without preamble, because he could think of none that wasn't absurd, he said, "They took Laila. Laila's in prison."

Sherzai was about to say something but stopped himself. He leaned back in his leather chair. "Laila is a fine girl," he said. "An excellent doctor."

"If you ever cared about me at all, and if you care about the things you say you do, you'll get her out."

"I'll do everything in my power." Sherzai walked to the door, his limp worse than ever. "You shouldn't be here. It isn't safe."

His hand was on the knob when Daniel said, "I've planted a fistful of opium seeds somewhere in this office." He heard the indignation in his own voice and hoped he didn't sound like an angry teenager. He was far from that. The filter through which Daniel had seen his old guardian had been shredded by the revolution and the ugly stories it had already made, betrayals more terrible because they were inevitable. War and revolutions were like X-ray photographs: they revealed fractures and decay, and what people were made of deep inside. What gnawed at Daniel besides the pain of feeling like he didn't really know the old man was a sense that Sherzai had been right. The gemstone firm had been useless in Daniel's hands. It had given him so much, and he'd never given it anything at all. He should have gifted it to *agha*. He would have, if he'd thought of it at all. What he couldn't bear was seeing his father's life's work in the hands of killers who would certainly do no better with it than he had.

"You did what? Impossible," said Sherzai. "I was only outside for a few seconds."

"A lot can happen in a few seconds."

"What's the meaning of this? I told you I would do everything I could."

"I don't know who you are anymore."

"You ingrate. They search these offices whenever they like. They search everyone. They don't trust us."

Daniel's former guardian haphazardly shuffled through books on shelves, ran his hands under cushions, opened and shut drawers. In his frantic search, he tripped on the carpet, which had shifted under him, and fell to his knees. Daniel rushed to his side and helped him up. He wondered if Sherzai really believed in the ideas of this regime. Perhaps he had borrowed them to get ahead. Plagiarized the plagiarists.

Daniel lifted the receiver. "Please make the call and tell them to let Laila go."

Sherzai returned to the desk and dropped heavily in his seat. He dialed. He spoke to five individuals in four agencies, and at last told Daniel that Laila would be free within the hour.

"Thank you," Daniel said. He could not leave without saying the next thing: "I never thought there would come a day when we wouldn't be on the same side."

"It's not really sides." Sherzai had raised his voice.

"Yes, it is. My father never forgot which side he was on." Daniel admired Sayed now more than ever. He reminded Sherzai that he had never compromised and had still built an army and gone to war against an empire. "What would he say if he could see you now? He thought of you as his brother."

"Not everything is about your father, and not everything is about you."

"Exactly, this is *not* about me!" Both of them were nearly shouting now. "I'm not upset about the company, *agha*. I don't really care." Daniel pointed to the window. "You see what these men are like. The Russians are behind this. Do you want them here?"

"Enough!" Sherzai tossed his hands up as if throwing something high into the air.

"I don't know how to fight an empire, Sherzai. I'm not my father."

"No, you're not. I've said so before."

Daniel put his head in his hands. "I don't know how he did it."

Sherzai's features grew heavy and he let his hands fall in exasperation. "Don't you, *batche'm*?"

Daniel looked up. He felt his breath slow down. "What do you mean?"

"I think you know. Somewhere deep down, I think you've always known." He dropped heavily into his chair, as if carrying the weight of a thousand years.

Something Khaiyam had said came back to Daniel. Real war required real money. Then he remembered something Peter had said in his hotel room the morning after the party, when Laila and Rebecca were there. Something about currencies that Daniel had found odd.

Sherzai's skin looked clammy in the sunlight that streamed mercilessly through the windows. "Do you remember the Stupid Man?" he asked. He leaned forward and his normally grave voice was a forceful whisper. "Of the five houses on the street, didn't you ever wonder why he sat only in front of yours?"

Daniel nodded. Yes, he had wondered this as a child. It was as if the answer had always been there, but written in a language he could not read.

"The Stupid Man wanted Sayed to see what addiction did to a man," Sherzai said.

"My father saw many addicts in his time."

The chair creaked under Sherzai's body. "Not men who had once been his friends."

Daniel's thoughts began to siphon through a tunnel. With reluctance, he asked, "What did my father do?"

"The best he could, *batche'm*. Now fly home and be there when your child is born."

"What do you mean, the best he could? *Agha*, tell me."

"Daniel, do you know what it costs to bribe English businessmen and Russian generals?" Sherzai shook his head as he spoke to the floor. "They don't take just any currency. Neither do arms dealers who sell the most modern guns made in America and Germany. You cannot pay them in afghanis." Sherzai leaned forward. "Corruption is paid for in dollars and pounds."

There it was again: something that wanted in and another thing that wanted out. Daniel didn't blink. "You told me a thousand times that Sayed was arrested because he challenged a king who couldn't bear that Sayed was more loved than he was."

"That's part of the truth. Your father and the king struck a bargain. If Sayed promised never to challenge him again, he would only serve one year in jail, and the real reason for his arrest would not be made public. It was a good trade for both of them."

Daniel shook his head. It had to be a lie. He searched for holes in the story. "He burned down a field of poppies. I saw it."

"Did Sayed burn down the field of a criminal, or the field of a rival?" Creases of sorrow lined *agha*'s face.

"God." Daniel slumped back into his chair, giving in to the truth. "Why didn't you tell me?"

"You had no mother. I couldn't take your father from you, too." Sherzai loosened his tie. "He wanted you to remember him as the man he wanted to be, not the man he was. It's what most fathers want."

"All these stories about my father being a great man—"

"Sayed *was* a great man. That was never a lie. At first, he used opium only to fight the English. He bought poppy fields and consolidated them. His father had made him swear to never sell gemstones for anything but the local currency, but opium was another story. That was Sayed's own business. He sold opium for dollars and pounds and deutsche marks and francs."

"I was in gemstone mines and warehouses all of my childhood. They were real."

"Oh yes, the gemstone business was real. And what a gift it was!" Sherzai told Daniel that Sayed hired men by the hundreds to score the poppies, collect the resin, and fracture it into small, irregular pieces that looked like any other freshly mined stone.

Daniel hacked out a laugh. Those tubs full of ugly little brown stones, the ones he couldn't imagine becoming beautiful. The pain from his wounds returned. Another memory shattered.

Sherzai brought his thumb and index finger together. "They were this small. Painstaking work." He shook his head in awe. "Rolled out by the truckloads into India and Iran with the real stones. When Sayed and I were preparing to resist the English in World War Two, he told me." He rubbed his face as if trying to wash something off it.

"The field of a rival . . ." Daniel pressed his palms over his eyes. "That wasn't during the war. I was eight, maybe nine. What need was there to be dealing with opium then?"

"Opium is addictive, whatever side of the business you're on. Sayed always said that as long as opium was the easiest way, it would remain the primary way. He knew better than anyone how true this was."

"And after he died? All these years, my company has been—"

"No. You remember the years that the company faltered? I knew you resented me for that. I could see it in your eyes whenever it came up. It was because I divested the company of opium. Profits fell, obviously. I eventually made up for it by selling for foreign currency, as Sayed had refused to do. But that part you already know."

With shaky hands, Sherzai picked up his tea and slurped.

"Luckily, lapis lazuli started soaring in price a few years ago." He chuckled. "The hippies like it."

"The Stupid Man was a customer of my father's?" Daniel asked.

"Not a customer. An employee. Later, a friend. He was a brilliant poppy scorer. He made the finest cuts into the pods."

"Did my mother know about all this?"

"I'm not sure what she knew. But Dorothy understood much more than she said, unlike Sayed's second wife. In the end, I think she left because of the new woman. It was a question for the Scale of Sages: her humiliation by Sayed weighed even more than her love for you. And her love for you was very, very great."

Snippets of the past rearranged themselves, changing colors. It was like Daniel was looking at his childhood through a kaleidoscope held the wrong way. He met Sherzai's eyes and realized he was truly seeing him for the first time. "My father always said that opium was the only enemy he couldn't defeat."

"And it was," Sherzai said. "It has haunted me for so long, this story. I dreaded the idea that you were going to find out through a book."

So that was what Peter had been writing. He asked Sherzai, who confirmed. "Peter figured it out a long time ago. The great man who wouldn't take payment in hard currency but somehow bribed expensive men and waged war against England itself? The story didn't fit. The book will not be unkind, Daniel. Peter likes to write about men who do what is necessary." After a time, he added softly, "Did you really hide poppy seeds in here?"

"No."

"Laila will be out soon." Both men stood, and Sherzai put his arms around Daniel, who let himself be embraced but could not move. "I know this hurts, *batche'm*. But sometimes, the past demands to make itself known, or it will drive you mad without you ever really knowing why."

Tears threatened to flood from Daniel's eyes. How familiar and yet how foreign the feeling was, a bruising pain behind the eyes, a sharpness in the nose. The dam broke. Daniel wept in *agha*'s arms.

36

LAILA HAD BEEN TAKEN TO A PRISON NOT FAR FROM DOWNTOWN. DANIEL FOUND HER SITTING rigidly among the slumping girls broken by either the injustice of life or the injustice of the law. She didn't look at him as he led her away, the guard pulling the iron gate shut behind them. From a cell, a young inmate shouted accusations, telling everyone who could hear that her guard had raped her, although she was a good Muslim. An elderly woman replied, "They rape bad Muslims, too."

Twisting her hands like she was lathering soap, Laila watched the road as Daniel drove her Golf, agreeing to pose as her servant if they were stopped. She conveyed nothing with her eyes, nor did she speak, other than to tell him he looked ridiculous. Every time he shifted gears, the jerking motion punctuated stretches of silence. At last she said, "Thank you."

"Did you know about my father?"

"Yes," she said without hesitation. "Peter told me that morning at the hotel. He was asking if I knew, but I didn't."

Daniel wanted to explain how this made him feel but had no words for this emotion, no precedent. He cursed the limitations of language.

"I'm finished as a doctor."

"Without an investigation or a trial? You'll be cleared. You're one of them, after all."

"But I did it. Their accusations are true."

Telaya piped up. *What is accurate isn't always true.*

"You'll still work for them?"

"It's not about them. It's just time for real change, Daniel."

Daniel dropped her off at her house. Peter was already there. None of the guards matched Daniel's bearded, turbaned profile to the photos of him in the book. He was beginning to feel inordinately lucky, just as he had when he was a small boy living in a big house before his mother went away and his father went to jail. Once he was home, he waited until it was nighttime and took every bottle of alcohol that was left and poured the contents into the pool. Daniel fetched Sayed's portrait from inside and went into the shed and smashed the frame with a hammer until it was nothing but splinters. He tore at the canvas but couldn't destroy it, so he stalked to the pool and dropped it in the water and watched the oil begin to smear, his father's features becoming indistinguishable. Sayed Sajadi had died not once but twice. Once in his bed, when his body collapsed after decades of drinking. And again in a swimming pool, fifteen years later, when his son drowned him along with the alcohol he swore to never touch again.

RED SCARE

They strut like pigeons on the sidewalk, puffing their chests out. They call themselves Communist but care nothing about the communal. Like Taj, they are salesmen, but they are the lowest kind, peddling things made by other people. They make nothing themselves. They grow nothing. Socrates taught Taj a little about their ideas, which are well known and sold in many countries, but seemed to be made in Russia and, like their cars, not built to last.

The difference between a good and bad salesman is how well he sells the commodity that all salesmen carry: lies. One might think lies are easy to sell, because people pay dearly to hear the ones they like. But in fact, they are the hardest to sell because there is so much competition.

The urchins are glued together these days like they're a single organism. Taj watches from an abandoned bakery whose owner disappeared last week, the day the red pigeons came. The bakery isn't far from that terrible place that used to exist, where urchins were sold, although everyone pretends it was never there. At least it is gone now, its owners and customers dead. They died like the cowards they were, trying to escape, begging for their lives.

The children squat against buildings, and without seeing their hands Taj knows how dirty their nails are, how blistered

their hands are from helping people scrub floors or clean win-
dows with chemicals too harsh for their skin. For their efforts,
they will get a little food. He looks at one of them, a boy with
mischief in his eyes and a smile that says, "I know something."
Taj can tell he is the thief of the group, which means he can run.
He has a chance to escape this wretchedness, because the trick
in life is to be someone other people cannot catch.

The Communist soldiers are patrolling the sidewalks. A
sergeant struts over to a man who sells fruit and jabs him in
the stomach with his rifle. "You're in the way," the sergeant
shouts.

The old man picks up his wheelbarrow and teeters off
to another corner, but the sergeant keeps shouting. His
comrades laugh, and the old man wheels his apples and
pomegranates farther away until he is out of sight. Taj real-
izes these men will do the same thing to him: they will chase
him from Fever Valley, force him to move his fields farther
and farther until it is like they never existed—unless he finds
a way to stop them. Taj recognizes the sergeant. He is a
client, as are some of the others who weren't revolutionaries
before but are now.

The children are holding hands, forming a chain, when the
soldiers come toward them. Taj walks out of the bakery. It
happens fast, a camouflage van leaving the curb and chasing
after the children. The soldiers round them up and promise
a better life awaits them. But Taj knows that once they get in
that van, they might end up with no life at all. The children
know, too. A few of them are crying, and a few look like they
have never cried. Ordinary men and women pass by, one or
two trying to interfere, but these are only street children, and
the soldiers are dangerous. A mother in slacks rushes past the
scene, squeezing through the crowd with her two children,
afraid the soldiers will take them, too. But they will not

take her daughter and son. They target the weak ones—the unwanted, the invisible. Pigeons only go after crumbs.

Taj pushes the sergeant in the chest. The man looks at him like he's a dog who gotten into his house and aims the gun at him.

Taj doesn't move. "Leave them alone."

"You'd best go back to where you came from."

This is where I came from, Taj thinks but doesn't say. He pushes the gun away and shoves the sergeant again. Here they come, the rest of the pigeons. Some of the urchins flee. Some are held in iron grips and look pleadingly at him. Taj hits the sergeant in the face, and suddenly there is some whistling and even laughter in the gathering crowd. But everyone disperses when the soldiers fire into the air. Two soldiers take Taj by the arms as others beat him, landing blow after blow. Taj tells the children to run. A little boy tries to save him, pulling the soldiers by their legs, but they kick him away and Taj says, "Run, child."

When it's all over, Taj is alone, facedown in the street. The soldiers disperse, telling everybody to remember what happens to people who don't know their place. Passersby either stare at him or pretend he doesn't exist. One woman asks if he needs help. No. Boy has never needed help. He will never be caught, not only because of his speed. The trick is to let those who are chasing you believe they have caught you. Sometimes, to survive, you have to act like you're already beaten.

That night, he dreams he's standing alone in an orchard, walking among mulberries and cherries and figs, and he plucks the fruit and hands them to urchins and all of them say thank you. All except one. The girl in the red dress with mirrors. She only curses him. He shouts in the dark that she doesn't belong here. She grows louder, and he begs her to be quiet. He says he is sorry, and he thinks he has gone mad.

Trapped inside him, she rattles him like a prisoner rattling her cage, but Taj is the one who is imprisoned. When it first started, he tried to drown her voice in wine, the vile red liquid Nazook used to drink. What a revelation alcohol was. Boy had always been afraid to drown, ever since his mother washed clothes in the river and warned him that nobody could swim so he couldn't be saved if he drifted too far. But water couldn't drown you unless you were in it, while alcohol worked the other way around: you drowned when it was in you. It was upside down, just like having someone stuck inside of you and being the one who is trapped.

Taj wakes up. He reaches for the bottle. It brings warmth, and he falls back on the bed. For a moment he is Boy again, running away from the tent and the garden. Again he begs the girl inside him to be quiet, and he calls her by her name, Telaya. He holds his head and squeezes his temples to crush her, but Telaya's voice only becomes louder. She begins to run, sparkling in the sunlight, running like he used to run when he was Boy. A car glimmers on the horizon, speeding closer. Telaya says, He doesn't see me. I can do it. And then she is dead.

Every night, Taj dreams that he turns and runs after Telaya, faster and faster but still unable to catch her, and then the car is there. Now, in the darkness, he clutches his sweat-drenched sheets. "Please leave me alone," he cries. But the girl in the red dress never leaves him alone. It is as if she slammed into him the moment the car slammed into her.

37

JACK SUTHERLAND BEGAN HIS CAREER IN THE FOREIGN SERVICE AT THE AGE OF TWENTY-SIX, A year after graduating from the Fletcher School of Diplomacy. Fighting on the beaches of France, he'd earned a Purple Heart and a Bronze Star. Daniel had learned this from Leland Smythe. Sutherland always deflected questions about his service, preferring to highlight the bravery of the men he had fought with.

He was murdered in Kabul shortly before two o'clock on a Thursday afternoon, six hours after he was abducted while entering the embassy to start his day. Elias ran downstairs and told Daniel after the news broke on the radio. Some blamed the murder on the regime, while the Communists swore a splinter group was behind it. Whoever had killed Sutherland, Washington's wrath echoed around the world, and one by one nations closed their embassies and called back officials, civilians, and aid agencies. It wasn't long before the Peace Corps was gone, USADE shuttered indefinitely. The UN closed several programs, recalling its staff. Even the Russians decried the attack, though they didn't withdraw their ambassador.

Daniel couldn't listen to the reports, not only because he wanted no details of his friend's brutal death but because no greater gift had ever been given the new regime. The assassination was grounds for an intensified crackdown, stringent martial law, the consolidation of power into an even smaller group. Everywhere, paranoia rose and tolerance fell. Borders were tightened, strangling those inside. Foreigners had thirty-six hours to leave.

Evacuations began by nightfall. The UN landed three planes in quick succession. The nearest American plane, a Pan Am flight, was diverted from its layover in Istanbul to rescue personnel. On Voice of America and Radio Free Europe updates ran without break, directing people to terminals and runways, identifying pickup spots where hired cars and private shuttles would collect them. Anyone who stayed behind would be viewed as having abandoned their post and could not expect US support. Once the embassy was closed, there would be no more diplomatic immunity for Daniel. He was to meet with Taj tomorrow. Daniel was struck by the absurdity of his dilemma. It was like the gods were experimenting with different fates for him and his country, coming up with one scenario after another, casting people in roles they did not want.

The guard who patrolled Dollar Djinn Lane was gone, called away on more important duties. When Daniel heard a car idling outside, he looked out to see Sherzai coming toward the house. It seemed impossible. He'd been sure he would never see him again at all. Despite everything, the sight of the old man comforted him, and part of him wanted Sherzai to stay with him until he awoke from this bad dream.

"Change into your regular clothes and I'll escort you to the airport," Sherzai said. He told Daniel that Peter was leaving, as well as Ian and everyone else.

"What about Laila?" Daniel asked.

"She stays, of course. She would never want to leave, *batche'm*."

As Daniel watched the flames crackle in the fireplace

Firooz had set up for the cool spring night, Sherzai described the danger. "They have no reason not to come after you now," he said. "Their government has nothing to lose—Washington is already as angry as they're going to get."

"What would they want with me?"

Elias appeared in the living room. "To make an example of you."

But Daniel was preoccupied only with tomorrow and his meeting with Taj. He had come to believe that this was the moment he had been waiting for, not merely for days or weeks but his entire life. This is what it came down to. Not being kicked in the street by Kalq soldiers or reforming poppy fields. It was down to this—a deal with Taj Maleki, and if he left now, Daniel was sure a part of him would die. Tomorrow night, after the last plane left and the borders became prison fences, the Communists would check boarding lists to make sure foreign personnel were gone and discover that he hadn't left. They might be glad Daniel was still here, preferring to have him in their own hands.

But he would find a way to escape. He was the son of Sayed Sajadi, no matter what Sherzai thought. He asked Sherzai to drive him hundreds of miles south, to Helmand. The request was received as a joke.

"If you want to do something for me, that's all I ask."

"It's much too far," Sherzai said.

"Then we need to leave now." Daniel wrapped the old man's hands in his. "I'm begging you. This is the last thing I will ever ask you for. The last thing. Do you understand, *agha*?"

Sherzai gave him a silent nod. Daniel packed a bag with water, food, a small shortwave radio, and essentials. Inside the town car, Sherzai said nothing, sighing heavily every few moments. On the open road, the driver accelerated. They fled the chaos of the capital, the desert still untouched by the turmoil made by men. They cruised through roadblocks under a sapphire sky.

"I keep meaning to tell you, the *sandali* is wonderful," Sherzai said. "I warm myself with it every night. The table you made is perfect. Beautiful."

For hours and hours they drove, either sitting in silence or talking about small things. The cherries were coming in, Sherzai's garden fragrant with flowers. Los Angeles was nice this time of year, wasn't it? Yes. Before the summer heat. Kabul and LA weren't so different. They laughed a little. Daniel knew he would never see his old guardian again. After Sayed's death, he had lain awake at night, terrified that Sherzai would disappear, too. He had never imagined it would happen like this.

The driver was going too fast, but the speed was exhilarating, and Daniel breathed deeply through the open window, the stars fleeing above. Telaya laughed and said, *Drive faster.* At first, his limbs tightened upon her return, and pain twisted through his still-recovering body, but then he thought, *All right.* If speed was what she wanted, he could oblige. Over Sherzai's protests, the driver did as Daniel asked, and Telaya laughed as the car went faster. When they arrived, it was dawn. At the foot of a tall plateau that shielded the largest, bluest reservoir in Helmand Province.

"Take this," Sherzai said, reaching forward to the glove compartment and giving Daniel a revolver. They got out of the car together and Daniel said farewell to his old guardian. By the water, they shared the final embrace of two people who had never known a world without each other. Sherzai wiped his eyes with a handkerchief.

Daniel slipped the gun into his bag. "Thank you." He forced a tight smile. "Goodbye, *agha.*" They stood there as if with more to say, but there would never be enough time, so Sherzai turned away, and Daniel looked at the sloping outline of *agha*'s back until he was back inside the car. Daniel saw his shoulders rise and fall, his face buried in his hands.

Daniel entered the fading darkness alone. It was a long while before he heard the car leave. He climbed down an embankment, the water before him like an extension of the desert, here meandering and there wide, grazing the distant sky. He took his clothes off and washed, the contusions on his skin softened by the pearly light of the rising day, the rush of water the only noise. Daniel took a fresh *piran tomban* from his bag, wondering if his now-former housekeeper Ahmad had taken any clothes with him at all or assumed his new Communist brothers would give him what he needed. He walked barefoot across the tickling sand, climbing a low hill, letting the breeze stroke his skin and feeling like he was part of the nothingness. The length of his turban floated behind him as he went, and the longer he walked the more of the nothing there was, until it was everything and he was completely at peace.

Finding shelter in a cavern in one of the hills beyond, he covered himself with a blanket. He found a weak radio signal that came through intermittently. They were talking about Sutherland and the exodus of foreigners. Everyone had gone to the airport. Daniel had gone much farther. The signal vanished. He switched off the radio and read by the halo of a flashlight. If he made it out of this alive, he would tell Rebecca he'd finally finished *The Grapes of Wrath*. He would also tell her Steinbeck had no idea what a dust bowl really looked like.

Daniel slept like he hadn't in many months. He spent the hours after that hidden in his nook, buried in his novel, or tearing off pieces of naan that had never tasted so good, rationing his water, and slipping in and out of sleep as he waited for twilight, when he was to meet Taj and the other

Manticores near the crest of the dam. They weren't there when he arrived. He waited.

When Daniel finally heard footsteps, Taj was alone. He had been hurt. On his face was a bruise. His right cheek was swollen and he moved stiffly.

"You look great," Daniel said.

"I can only hope I look as good as you." Taj told Daniel to walk with him.

When they skirted the bend of a hill Taj pulled him into a cave. A small lantern was on the floor. Daniel took a step back when he saw them, six pairs of eyes gleaming in the near-darkness. They wore rigid expressions, *chapans* across their shoulders and guns across their laps. Before Daniel could speak, one of the men rose and struck him across the head with the butt of his gun. The world went dark.

Daniel woke with his hands and feet bound. He laid his chin on his chest, too weak to raise his head.

"Why?" he said.

Taj sat cross-legged beside him. "I do apologize, Daniel Sajadi. As I said, there is nothing about you that inspires trust. I, for one, overcame my misgivings, given your noble blood and name and, shall we say, business acumen. But my friends are less easily impressed."

In pickup trucks they flew down the highway, Daniel in the back between two of the khans, one of whom was almost too tall for the cab and who handled his gun like it was just another thing he carried. They watched Daniel with neither fear nor hate. There were no roadblocks this far south, at least not yet, but Taj told him the Communists had gone to Fever Valley and set a fire that swept over the entire Yassaman field. Daniel pictured it engulfing Taj's flowers, burning the mud shack where he had seen Taj shoot a boy.

They untied Daniel when he signaled that they'd arrived at

the destination. The men trekked against the whistling wind. His belongings were in the second truck, and he wondered if they had taken the money he had brought, that he'd hoped would be enough to take him to Pakistan. The Manticores had already taken the gun Sherzai had given him.

They walked in a straight line, Daniel in front. He felt the muzzle of a gun against his back as he trudged through the sand, hoping his memory was correct. His feet found the trail easily. He moved northeast, heading toward a crevice in the mountain. It was too small for a heavyset man to get through, but there were no heavyset people among them. The Manticores told him to stop as he prepared to squeeze through. Taj raised his gun and released the safety.

"What game are you playing, Daniel Sajadi? I must warn you that these men have no sense of humor."

"It's through here."

Taj proposed going in alone with Daniel and returning if all was safe. Together the two pierced through the mountain and found themselves on a craggy downhill path, a makeshift walkway of sharp boulders and rocks, moguls of sand, and steep drop-offs. Nothing had changed here in decades, maybe even since the beginning of time. Taj went back and fetched the others, who followed.

Daniel led them down the path, catching himself when he almost fell. The Manticores never slipped, their vision as honed as their balance. One of them shouted "Water!" before Daniel saw it. It was only a thin trickle fed by the distant Helmand River, but it was indeed water. After forty minutes of twisting and winding down between the mountains, they took the final turn, and Daniel was stunned by the beauty before him. This was the valley he remembered, acres of land shielded by a ring of mountains that rose like great kings. The khans did not smile, but Taj opened his arms and closed his eyes, inhaling deeply.

Patches of grass grew here and there, and a few bushes and thin trees protruded from the earth. Weeds were everywhere, no one here to stop them. Daniel wondered if one day the southern edge of Helmand would be a sea of red, violet, and white, the poppies like dissidents standing up proudly to the many regimes that tried to crush them. He couldn't help but smile at the sight of rampant weeds, because they were testaments to the fertility of the valley and the tenacity of life. He remembered his gardener's valiant efforts against the weeds in their garden. So often, the thing you did not want growing was the one thing that did.

More than twenty years ago, Daniel had watched his father burn down a poppy field here. Today, he struck a deal on that same land. Of the seven Manticores, five accepted Daniel's bargain—Taj and four of the six who had come. The other two refused, eyeing him with suspicion. They preferred to face the Communists, who were already destroying their land, but their fields would be destroyed here, too, they were sure, and the land was too remote. Daniel couldn't convince them. It didn't matter. The other khans had enough opium to sell. They would be paid in diamonds, they told him.

So Khaiyam and his religious opposition would receive diamonds. More wealth than he had ever seen. It would go a long way in recruiting men, bribing less-than-scrupulous officials, procuring weapons. Daniel felt a twinge of regret that he wouldn't be here to see the result of what he was helping to create.

38

DANIEL ASKED HOW LONG IT WOULD TAKE FOR THE KHANS TO MAKE THE SALE AND RECEIVE the diamonds. A few days, Taj said. The transaction would not be difficult. The Manticores used nomads and villagers, who passed the bricks of resin to other men like them until someone took the product to the edge of Pakistan. They did not use the formal crossings but crossed anywhere along hundreds of miles, some empty and unguarded, some part of a no-man's-land, a disputed zone few dared approach. The Manticores were allowed to cross, thanking the local warlords with cash, opium, gemstones, and gold, and sometimes medicine, food, and blankets in winter. There was an understanding between them and the Manticores, who also refused to be part of any government.

"Where will you go afterward?" Taj said.

"I'll find a way home."

"And where is home, Daniel Sajadi?"

"I'll know when I'm there," Daniel replied, but he suspected he already knew. All he could see now when he thought of home was Rebecca.

The khans gave Daniel's belongings back to him, even the gun. Taj left with the others to seek out their carefully hidden stores of resin. When they were gone and cooler nighttime temperatures came, Daniel walked toward Little America. It was eight miles away, and he stopped twice to rest. He arrived at dawn. It was framed by three sides of desert and a bluff overlooking the Helmand River. Water looked almost out of place here. He passed the project's abandoned apartments and the shuttered café that served burgers with Thousand Island dressing. No one was there except a local shopkeeper who was asleep behind a counter in a cigarette and soda shop. When Daniel knocked, he rushed out the glass doors and said, "Sir, buy something, please. I have many things for you, many things!" and Daniel bought cigarettes and water before asking the puzzled man for a crowbar, anything he could use to open the gate to the shuttered compound. The man rummaged around under the counter. He found an ax. It would do.

Daniel struck at the lock until it yielded. Then he found the warehouse and broke its lock, too. Rolling up the corrugated door, he dropped the ax and wiped his hands. The Americans had left everything behind: bins of Agent Ruby and two crop dusters parked side by side, already covered in a layer of dirt. He tore off his turban and wiped the windshield with it. He thought he could fly it but struggled to load the spraying systems, which were attached to the edges of its wings. He turned the warehouse inside out looking for instructions and finally found them in a cupboard that held dozens of manuals along with Styrofoam cups and a radio. He felt the old thrill of lifting a little plane into the air. He flew toward the distant mountains, trying to maintain control, the wings tilting more than they should. He hoped he hadn't miscalculated. Crop dusters weren't made to fly so high. Theirs was an intimate relationship to the soil. Soon he crested the mountain, gliding over the field he had admired as a child and again as a man.

He lowered the aircraft until he was twenty feet above the hidden valley with its tall weeds, and just as he moved to pull the lever and release Agent Ruby, something caught his eye. It was a cluster of flowers. Not poppies but yellow wildflowers that had no name, pretty and alone like wild princesses. They trembled in the winds caused by the plane, bending until their petals were level with the flat, patchy grass, rising again when he pulled higher.

His hand on the controls, he turned and sailed above them once more. Again he pulled away. He tried a third time. His knuckles were white like the hills of Middle-earth in winter and his fingers disobedient and stiff. Perhaps it was stupid to do this before knowing if Taj had sold the opium, but the line between stupidity and courage had dissolved, leaving only necessity. It was all that was left when time was running out. Daniel flew the length of the tranquil valley, circled back, then dove toward the earth until he almost grazed the shrubs. The plane teetered. He struggled to keep it steady.

The flowers were under him. They bowed in the wind, then straightened. They had found a way to push through the earth, to come alive without the help of people and little help from nature, and they had survived. They were everything that was good about life, strong and free and determined to thrive. The flowers had a right to be. Their home was here. Daniel wondered how he had ever thought he would or could do this. Their presence was so self-evident that he felt as if he'd just plotted a crime against nature. The valley untouched, Daniel flew the plane back to his hideaway.

He spent two days waiting for the khans and their diamonds, the crop duster still on the sand. He explored other caves, finding the bones of small animals in some. An eagle stood alone on a peak, watching the world below. On the third evening, a pickup truck arrived on the highway, a glimpse of metal reflecting the sun. Anxious, Daniel scurried down the mountain. When he asked Taj how it had gone, the man said, "How should it go? It always goes the same." Taj glanced at the grounded plane. "I see you've upgraded your form of transportation, but I suggest we take my truck if it isn't beneath you."

There was no way to explain a crop duster at the foot of a mountain. Daniel had expected to hitch rides on *gadi*s and trucks to Kandahar and, once there, use one of the diamonds brought by Taj to procure a car and flee to Pakistan.

"I know what you did," Taj said.

"I'm not sure what you mean."

Taj told Daniel he had followed him through the night, stopping when he did, wondering where he was going. "For the last time, I'm telling you that you don't inspire trust, which my colleagues knew immediately when they met you."

"I didn't do anything to harm you or your friends."

"They are not my friends. I don't mix business and friendship. Except, apparently, with you. Get in the truck."

"Did you get the diamonds? How much?"

"Get in the truck." The elegant accent and causticity were gone. His gun was with him, as always. Daniel saw a street boy who had grown up to become a killer. "Do as I say," Taj said. "Your life depends on it."

The Toyota shuddered when Daniel engaged the gears. It smelled of diesel and stale cologne. Taj laid the gun across his lap. "This is in case you get any ideas," he said. "I can't allow you to stop me from saving your admittedly questionable life."

"We have to stop in Kandahar."

"Yes. And then I will take you to Pakistan." Taj's face was damp with sweat, and his eyes red.

"Why are you helping me?"

"What a stupid thing to ask. Explain the airplane."

"I told you, I didn't do anything. Your land is intact."

"I know. I would have smelled it. When you sprayed Gulzar, anyone could smell it for a week. But the others won't believe you, so let us be on our way."

"Where's the payment?" Daniel asked. There would be no point to his having stayed if the Manticores hadn't made the sale. He couldn't bear the thought of having shown that land to them for nothing, not because the land had value to him but because the khans were among the few who could raise enough money to fight. They were part of this, even if they liked to think they were in a separate world.

Taj switched the radio on. A singer struggled against the weak signal. He and Taj drove in near-silence for hours, stopping twice, refueling with the gasoline cans in the back. After dusk chased away the day, night came quickly, their headlights barely piercing the viscous darkness. That night's warrant report was the longest yet. The evacuations were over. When the announcers said Daniel's name, he felt like he did when Sandy had died, receiving long-awaited news that still struck like a small bomb. He was a fugitive, they said. They had seized his home, which they'd found abandoned—Daniel was grateful for this, as it meant Firooz and Elias had left in time—and had found many expensive things they claimed didn't rightfully belong to him.

In a few terse sentences, the Kalq mouthpiece claimed that the people had taken back items of value that would help the great cause. They had also found a Mercedes that would be put into service of the state. Daniel couldn't help but chuckle. Those preaching equality apparently needed luxury cars to drive around, liberating in style. He tried not to think about Rebecca's things still at the house, or the few pictures he had of his mother. He had left those behind.

He steered the truck into Kandahar. Military shadows hovered everywhere. The Communists were infiltrating like an invasive species. The place Khaiyam had written on a piece of paper was hard to find. Finally, Daniel saw the unnamed road, smaller than an alley. He inched his way forward and pulled up at a low mud house. He'd been told to look for a cherry blossom on the wall. This was it. He glanced around. No one. No Kalq, no shepherds or beggars, no ordinary men, and no women at all since it was night.

Taj pulled two canvas sacks from under the seat and gave him one. At the bottom were thousands of glistening teardrops, maybe a million dollars' worth of diamonds—of opposition. The drop-off was quick. Daniel used the code word Khaiyam had given him, *blossom*, and the cloaked woman who cracked open the door gave her word in return. She snatched the bag and thanked him, locking herself inside.

When he was back in the driver's seat, she slipped out of the house and ran to the car. She lifted the *chaderi* from her young face, her eyes wet with joy.

"Thank you," she said. "I don't know how you did this, *saheb*, but thank you. It's more money than our jihad has ever seen."

Daniel sat quietly until Taj finally said, "How long is your profound contemplation going to go on for? I'm starting to get bored."

"Only boring people get bored," said Daniel, quoting one of his mother's old sayings as he brought the engine to life.

Hours outside the city limits, the truck twitched as Daniel rolled over something sharp. For four miles, they traveled with a flat left tire before finding a cluster of shops the same color as the desert. They served kebabs and tea and sold onions, candy, rice, and tins of margarine along with clothes, jewels, and shoes. An upbeat instrumental blared from a cassette player, an old melody set to a modern rhythm. Daniel knew they would have tools and gasoline here for the cargo truckers who drove this road into Pakistan. They gave him what he asked for, and Taj watched from the window as Daniel patched the tire, a boy illuminating the spot with a flashlight. The clerks seemed uninterested in helping and showed him little courtesy. Normally, places like this were run by hospitable men who offered a free Coke or a cigarette.

As Daniel pulled away, he saw a cluster of military trucks half-hidden behind the shop, soldiers craning their heads to watch him. The store window glided past. Among the shoes on display in the dimly lit window was a pair of hot-pink slippers with silk flowers, like Pamela's fuchsia pumps, though with a lower heel. Something a girl Telaya's age might have worn. Or something Lolita might have worn. Daniel had never finished that book, although everyone knew the story. Nabokov was still in the pile that for years he had promised himself he would read.

"Those men at the gas station, they were behaving quite normally," Taj said. "You only found it surprising because you're used to special treatment, Daniel Sajadi."

That dissonance between memory and truth returned, each breath becoming sharp and painful.

Lolita.

Look at me, Telaya said. *Look.*

She was framed in the windshield, a sheer and pale mirage hovering over the road, but instead of pushing her away, this time Daniel looked. She drifted away, growing smaller. Farther and farther, until he could see not only her but everything around her. Her family, the camp, the tents, the wide blue sky. They floated in the distance, faint but unmistakable, like a natural part of the road.

Telaya was wearing Pamela's pink shoes, which were far

too big for her little feet, and she said, *I am only ten years old. Maybe nine. It's not fair.*

And then Daniel saw it.

Taj was still talking. "You are not special today. Today you are an ordinary man from the village. Today is reality, Daniel Sajadi."

Today is reality. Daniel would never forget those words. *Traitor*, Telaya had called him when he'd struck the deal with Taj. He would never forget that either. His breath was like barbed wire scraping his lungs, his heart, his chest. It wasn't over, that struggle between old details and new epiphanies. Chips of mica sparkled in the asphalt, and it was like the whole road was winking at him, daring him to keep coming.

The scene from August seventeenth continued to unfold, the story becoming whole. He saw the elders sweeping into view as Telaya's parents wept. *Go find Taj*, they said.

Telaya's father appeared. *She was the only thing of value in my life.*

Daniel saw Taj take the money at the police station, count it—and never give it to the Kochis. That morning downtown that Daniel had chased the girl, a mirage. She hadn't led him to the hotel where Rebecca was with Peter. She had led him to the brothel where children were being used by men.

There was so much more. The truth crashed toward him, gaining strength and speed.

I am faster than you are. I can make it.

Telaya had shown him a thousand times. He wanted to reach across and wrap his hands around Taj's neck, squeezing the life from him. Instead, he tightened his grip on the wheel.

"You didn't save my life," he said to Taj.

"If we make it to Pakistan, I believe I should be given some credit for your survival."

"The day of the crash," Daniel said.

Taj paused before answering. "I never said I did. Only that I got you away from them. You seemed to think I'd saved you, and who was I to argue with a man of your birth and standing?"

"God help you. You're a monster."

On the highway behind them, two Jeeps rushed up in the darkness, passing them abruptly before coming to a stop diagonally across the road. Daniel slammed on the brakes, which screeched in protest. Four uniforms charged toward the driver's-side window and told Daniel and Taj to step out. They were looking for fugitives, they said. One of the men had that terrible book with him, the collection of photos of wanted men. When he flipped through it, Daniel noticed a red X drawn across many of the faces. There were few left, and he was among them.

Taj was unflustered. He told them his name was Ahdam and deftly lied about driving to work in a soap factory near the border, a new job his cousin had found for him and his friend Abdullah. His poor-man dialect was back. The soldiers stood close to Daniel, almost nose to nose, and asked him the same questions again and again. What was his name? Abdullah, he said. Where was he from? They kept coming, as if trying to catch him in a lie. What did he think of the new government? He knew nothing about it, he insisted, but he was sure it would be good.

Telaya hid in the ditch and waited. If the driver in the big car saw her, he would stop. Did he see her? She prayed he did not. *I am faster than him*, she thought. *I am faster than you*. The man wasn't looking. Even if he tried to avoid her now, he couldn't. She would win. And they would be sorry, her parents and that awful man Taj. They would be sorry, and she would be free.

One of the officers wanted to separate Ahdam and

Abdullah to ask questions, but the captain refused, reminding him that they had more important things to do in Kandahar. The cities had to be brought under control. They reluctantly let the men go. One of them seemed especially unhappy, watching Daniel, checking the photos in the book twice, three times. Daniel drove away, fighting the urge to gas the engine.

As he rolled toward the border zone, which was maybe ten miles away, Daniel noticed that his star-sapphire ring, which he still wore around his neck, was dangling freely outside his *piran*. In the right light, the star inside the sapphire was plain to see, but from other angles, it wasn't there at all. For the last nine months, his life had been like that stone, the twinkle of truth always there for him to see, but he had been looking from the wrong angle. *He's been bluffing from the start*, Telaya had said, and Daniel had thought she meant blackmail. When she had said *Look at me*, he'd believed her to be cruel.

"I didn't do what you think I did," Taj said.

"Let's not talk."

"I considered it, I admit. You compensated me well. Five hundred dollars was three times what I paid for her. The government imposes larger fines than the elders would have."

They were mere minutes from the border zone. Headlights approached from behind, slashing at the rear window.

Taj turned his head. "It's them," he said. "Drive faster!" Taj pushed the gun into Daniel's temple, nearly crying when he said, "Go. I cannot save myself if I don't save you."

Behind them a soldier was standing up in the Jeep, waving the photo book and shouting Daniel's name, but they called him Abdullah, just like they did when they thought he was a poor man hoping to work in a soap factory. The youngest soldier had seen the star sapphire around his neck and connected it to the ring in the picture. It was the only explanation. Daniel slammed the truck into a higher gear. The man raised his gun and fired, Daniel zigzagging on the road, the car jerking forward when it took a bullet in the back. Another gunshot blew out the sideview mirror. Taj turned around and shot back. The rear windshield exploded. The Jeep lost a headlight, swerving before the driver righted course and sped up. Taj pointed to the empty desert off the road and told Daniel to swerve onto the sand.

"Are you crazy?" Daniel said.

"It will save our lives. Do try to drive faster."

Daniel drove off-road into the desert. It seemed endless and flat, embedded with baked-in stones that barely slowed him down. Everything looked the same. It wasn't possible to know if he was heading toward an empty, unmanned stretch of the Pakistani border or a zone settled by unfriendly tribes. To Taj, it didn't all look the same, because he told Daniel they were heading close to a tribal zone. The locals would know him, he said. On the antenna was a green and white ribbon they would recognize as his, and when they aimed their weapons at the car, as they would, they would wait and see before they shot.

"They're not unreasonable," he said. "You are not the first man I've had to help out of the country, Daniel Abdullah Sajadi. My business is a delicate one."

I am faster than you, Telaya had said.

Thirty yards away, poles rose from the earth, displaying gray flags. A formal, printed board explained that the government couldn't help you past this point and advised drivers to turn around and head a few miles north to a border checkpoint. Daniel pushed past the signs, the new army on his heels.

Crouched in the seat beside him, Taj lamented the new military's insensitivity to borderlands. "They're not supposed to come in here," he said. "They must have a death wish."

A fluttering shape appeared on the horizon. It was a wall of men on horseback, riding as if they spent their lives like this, never dismounting. Taj told him to flick the lights in a special sequence, a sort of Morse code shared by border-zone warlords and Manticores, who most of the world did not know existed. The riders aimed flashlights as they rode by, and when Taj leaned from the window they raised a hand in salute, riding on toward the soldiers. One of the Jeeps slowed down. Uniforms jumped out with assault rifles and opened fire, the horsemen shooting back with long guns, and the screams of horses and men rang out as Daniel drove, drove, drove, watching the line of horses dissolve. There was still no border in sight, no Pakistan, only darkness without end.

"Now!" Taj said. "Jump."

Daniel seized his gun and jumped, and bullets tore the sand at his feet as Taj jumped from the truck, too. A small light bounced in the night, and Taj gave a strange whistle: long, then short, then long and very high, and someone was running toward them with a light in his hands. A towering man wearing a Pakistani uniform resolved in the darkness.

"Help this man cross," Taj told him. "Fast. He is a friend. I will pay you later."

The man seized Daniel by the arm and said, "Come."

Behind them, a soldier was dead. The second Jeep kept coming, swerving through the hail of bullets, taking fire from warlords who disliked any man they didn't know. Especially ones sent by the state. They had never heard of the revolution or the Communists, but they had heard of soldiers and governments, and they wanted no part in either. Taj turned his back to the border and walked back the way they had come, toward his nation, the Jeeps, the violence and death.

"Wait," Daniel said, clutching the gun tightly in his hand.

But Taj did not stop, nor did he turn around. He moved quickly, crouching to avoid the guns, and Daniel lurched toward him and took his arm, pulling him toward the border as bullets pierced the night, the warlords barely keeping the red soldiers at bay.

"They'll kill you!" Daniel shouted. "Come with me."

"I belong here," Taj said, breaking free from his grip. "Until next time, Daniel Sajadi." He extended his hand as if they were meeting for the first time, and in the blood-soaked night, under a thousand gaping stars, Daniel shook Taj Maleki's hand.

"Come!" cried the Pakistani gatekeeper. "There's no time!"

"Go," said Taj, and Daniel watched him turn around and head into a shower of bullets. It happened suddenly. Taj's body jerked and he fell to his knees, blood spilling from his chest, which he clutched with his hand. Daniel raised his arm, and it was like he had no choice at all when he fired into the night at the man who had shot Taj Maleki, and the Pakistani pulled Daniel back and dragged him away. Soon Daniel was across the border, slumped in the back of a pickup, speeding away from Afghanistan, wondering what would happen to Taj, the country, *agha*, Laila, Elias, and an old way of life. His fingers were tight around the gun like they had been around the steering wheel the day of the crash, and it felt as if they would never come loose. He thought about Rebecca. He would call her from Quetta and tell her he was ready to come home, and it would finally be true. He loosened his grip and put the gun down. As the truck lurched deeper into Pakistan and the sound of gunfire became an echo, Daniel thought of Telaya's last moments on that road and saw his own face in a hundred small round mirrors, and in his reflection he saw his tears as they melted with hers.

Do you see me?

He closed his eyes, and in the darkness everything became light. "I see you." He crushed the pain rising in his throat. "I see you now."

Goodbye, Abdullah, Telaya said. And she went out like a candle.

TELAYA

The day before he sells the last of his opium and helps Daniel Sajadi raise money to fight the Communists, Taj looks into the sun in hopes it will blind him, because he no longer wants to see the dead girl in the mirrored dress. She is everywhere. He wishes his ears would fail him, too, because she is never silent. It's all because of that whorehouse, that place that everybody knows about but nobody mentions. The place that made Taj do something he never, ever should have.

Taj hates the disgusting place and its disgusting owner, a man with sausage arms who wears an earring, and yet the place is useful. Taj gave one of the urchins a camera and told him to take pictures of the customers, because important men come to the forbidden house and Taj wants power over these men who have no power over themselves. Taj gives the children chocolates and blankets, and to one who likes music he gives a guitar.

In the city one night, a rich man who buys opium from Taj tells him about something else he wants to buy. Something that sells for an even better price than drugs. He asks Taj if he can find a special girl, one not yet used up by the men in that whorehouse near Shor Bazaar. He will pay more money than Taj can imagine. But Taj recoils. He is a businessman, but he cannot sell those desperate urchins.

It comes to him late one night. There is a way to sell the man what he wants: a child of those who don't live like people should. The kind that aren't really human, preferring to live without walls, trekking around deserts and towns, never settling. Even in a whorehouse, at least these creatures would have walls. But they wouldn't care, because they aren't really people. Not to Taj.

As he drives to the desert, the sun peers at him like a glass eye, and he is glad he does not believe in God, or it would seem like God was watching him. He walks among the Kochis, giving them jewels, medicine, rifles, and business advice, helping them with their affairs.

Then he sees the girl in the mirrored red dress playing with her doll. She is twirling, carefree and wild, singing a song she has made up, and her brothers laugh at her until she chases them away. The sun catches on her dress, the little mirrors like spinning rainbows. Taj laughs, too, because she amuses him. He finds out her name is Telaya. The transaction is easy. Her father, Baseer, agrees without much discussion, when Taj says it will be a better life for her and he will pay well. The mother tries to protest, but she is only a woman and she loses.

Telaya smiles when she sees Taj and wraps her arms around him and calls him Uncle. He has brought her a necklace today, the first truly nice gift in his haul. Incredibly, she shrugs and says, "Give it to my parents so they can sell it." Most girls like jewelry, Taj tells her. "I like my mirrors," she says, pointing to her dress and giving him a theatrical bow. "I don't need anything else."

Something in his heart stops. He never thought a girl would say such a thing. When Telaya hugs him, the empty place in him is replaced by a voice that says, this one is special. She is not like her kind. She is not like the urchins, either. And most importantly, she is not like Ashura or the girl who exchanged herself for opium. Maybe she dreams of walls, and if she doesn't, she will discover their beauty. If Taj shows her what they mean. If, within walls, she finds peace and the wonders of keeping the good things in and the bad things out.

He decides there and then. He will not give Telaya to the rich man in the city. And he will not touch her, not in that way, not until she is older. He would never do such a thing. It is as if destiny has brought her to him, because Tela means gold, so together their names could form the phrase Golden Crown of the King. She is nine or ten, her parents think. Taj does not know how old he is either. He likes that they have this in common. His heart swells when he realizes that he can teach her to read, just as Socrates taught him.

As Taj and Baseer finalize the details, Telaya hears them. She makes a sound of terrible shock before backing away, shaking her head, clutching at her doll. She starts to cry, hiccupping through sobs. Her parents promise life will be better for her and also for them, although the mother weeps. Her father says this is a chance at something other girls have when they grow up, better clothes and better shoes, and he says this is how things are and that he loves her enough to give her away. But he didn't give her away. He sold her. Telaya knows this, and she hates her father for it and she shouts at him as she runs away. "You can't make me," she screams. They try to catch her, telling her she will go with Taj, and to stop making a scene. But they cannot catch her. "Let her go for now," says Baseer. "She'll come back." He goes into his tent to polish silver and asks his wife to return to her tasks.

The mirrors on Telaya's dress sparkle as she runs through the desert. Taj watches her as she shouts, "No! I would rather die." She runs faster. He does not chase her. Her father is right. She will return soon, and one day she will be grateful and she will care for him.

In the distance, a big beige car is coming closer. Suddenly, Telaya turns to Taj with a strange and terrible grin he never thought he would see on a child. She dips down into the ditch, sliding on her heels. He turns away and walks back into the sea of nomads and tents, leaving her for now to play. Alone, she cannot go far. He tries to erase that hideous smile from his memory.

Then, carried on the wind like the cry of a thousand birds, comes a terrible screeching sound. Something slams into Taj, nearly knocking him off his feet, and he hears her voice as if she were standing inches away. I win, she whispers. She is inside him now.

At the beginning, Telaya says very little, hissing small cruelties to him at night. Then she awakens, terrible and strong. It happens as Taj is walking away from a bistro one night, after Taj tells Daniel Sajadi that he will kill Telaya's kin if Daniel destroys his poppies. After that, Telaya never goes back to sleep, haunting him even though Taj never believed in ghosts.

Sometimes she whispers and other times she screams, but she always tells him she knows what he is, and at night Taj lies awake, tortured by her voice. One night, he steals a bottle of wine and drinks until her voice grows dim. But eventually the wine wears off. She comes back louder. He drinks again. She tells him she hates him for making it so she had to die, had to had to had to.

Then she proposes a bargain, late one night when Taj is walking in Paghman Gardens after meeting with Daniel Sajadi, who has decided to become an opium prince now that the red pigeons have taken Kabul. As Taj begs the girl to leave him in peace, Telaya makes him an offer. She will leave him alone if he saves Daniel Sajadi.

"You must do this," she says, and she sounds like she did on the day the horsemen cut the heads off foreigners at *a Russian factory in the city and ended up shot by soldiers. Religious men went smashing windows and bottles that night, and Telaya told Taj to avenge the children used by evil men. He went to that disgusting house and killed its owners and customers, including that American named Greenwood, whose picture he already had, and whose hand he'd unknowingly shaken at the Sajadi house.*

Driving toward the border zone with Daniel Sajadi, Taj knows that at last he will be free, because he will do what Telaya wants. He will save the man. Beside him Daniel is quiet, and in his silences he is more frightening than in his furors, with eyes ablaze and jaw set tightly. But Taj knows the man will not kill him. There was a time when Taj wasn't sure of this, and he believes Daniel wasn't sure either.

Close to the border, he counts the moments until he is free of Telaya. The bullets fly between the pigeons and the horsemen as Taj leads Daniel to the border, and as he shakes his hand, Taj says, "Until next time, Daniel Sajadi." And the man is saved, vanishing into the sands of Pakistan. He will fly to America, and Taj is sure the man will forget all about him and become someone who was never on the same side as Taj. Not even during the days when bombs blew holes in buildings and people, and flags were replaced, and blood fell like rain.

As the pickup truck carrying Daniel Sajadi rolls out of sight, a great force crashes into Taj, tearing open his chest, and suddenly he feels lighter than ever, as if something has finally escaped through the wound. Before Telaya dissolves in a shimmer of splintering mirrors and crimson mist, she whispers, I forgive you, Boy.

Taj cannot walk. The sudden weightlessness leaves him so dizzy he drops to his knees, and men take him by the arms and lay him down in a tent. Someone dabs his forehead with water while a man tries to pick something out of Taj's chest, and a boy squats beside him, fanning him with peacock feathers. Taj feels blood drain from him as he falls asleep, and in the darkness he sees his new garden in Helmand, acre upon acre of flowers that will be shielded by proud mountains all around. His new garden has tall, towering walls. Like the garden he was born in. Like the garden he has dreamed of since he was Boy.

EPILOGUE

ON THE ROAD BEFORE ME, I SEE A BLUR OF SHIMMERING WATER. I KNOW IT IS A MIRAGE. I AM almost alone on this length of desert highway. I pass a sign that tells me I can dine, refuel, and sleep at the next exit. If I stop, I can eat fast food and exchange friendly nods with other travelers. Families heading to the Grand Canyon. New Agers on their way to Sedona. Bachelorettes driving to Vegas. I don't take the exit.

The drive to Scottsdale is more than six hours, and desert drives put me in a somber mood. The whispering engine is the only sound. Sometimes I listen to music in the car, but not on desert roads.

Thoughts of my past, present, and shrinking future float into my head uninvited. I am nearly seventy now, the age when people look back at their lives and tell others they have no regrets, even though they do. Some things don't matter so much. Like the veins on my hands that look like purple worms, or the brown connect-the-dots on my thinning skin. Why don't they call them freckles when you're old?

But there are some things that time has forced me to reckon with. I'm not at death's door, but watching your wife die forces a conversation not only with her but with yourself. Sending your son to war does the same.

When I arrived in Pakistan that night, the men drove me

to Quetta. One of the guards' cousins took me in. They fed me and let me shower and sleep, and never have those things meant so much. From there, I was able to call Rebecca. I learned I had a son. The labor nearly killed them both. I hitched a succession of rides to Islamabad, where the American embassy helped me get home. During that trip, I had hours on end to think. I was proud of having started something with meaning, something that would last. Not the destruction of the poppy fields, as I'd once hoped, but the religious resistance to the Soviet-backed Kalq.

I now know what I helped create when I gave that *chaderi*-clad woman a bag of diamonds. Would I go back and undo it? Sometimes I think, *If only I could*. But *if only* is a reflex that helps us build myths of what else could have been. I understand now that really, there are no alternate endings, only different paths leading to the same end.

I could never have gone back to that red flag, oozing like a wound in the Afghan sky. I could never have chosen that picture over the one I helped draw. Like war, love, and addiction, regret is a labyrinth with blind turns. I couldn't have predicted the horrors that were eventually born of that movement, nor my son's involvement in trying to free my homeland from what I helped build.

I never thought I would say this, but I miss the Cold War, when the enemy didn't want to die any more than we did. How easy and predictable the Soviets seem now. How quaintly conventional to face soldiers who represent countries instead of the rogue battalions that roam the earth today, blowing people up from London to Baghdad. I remember when men wore uniforms instead of bombs.

Matthew returned from Afghanistan years ago, after his third tour of duty. He was stationed in Kandahar. The first time he was in Jalalabad, the second in Kunduz. His third tour was what killed Rebecca. I lost her to cancer ten months ago. They said it started in her liver and spread to her lungs, but I know it began and ended in her heart. My son was awarded a Purple Heart. No mother wants her child to earn a Purple Heart. Shrapnel tore through Matthew's leg after an explosion that blew his Humvee off the highway. I know that road well. I once had an accident there, too.

Matthew will survive if he can end his dependence on the pills they gave him for his pain. Some of the soldiers smoked weed—do they still call it that?—and some drank, but more and more discovered the elegance of tablets and the tidy narcotic high. As Matthew says, one war ended for him and another began. My grandson is nine years old, living with his mother, who left Matthew last year. The place in Scottsdale is supposed to be one of the best. He's been there thirty days, and it was his decision to go. I'm prouder of Matthew than of anything else in my life, and yet he has broken my heart.

Six months after he was born, I told Rebecca what I did in those last days before I fled. Having a child dissolved the divisions between us, and I was never able to hide anything from her again. When I confessed, she took my hand and made a confession of her own: she'd known about my father. Peter had told her that morning after the dinner party, when I found her and Laila in his hotel room. Still today, I watch the shadow play between my memory of my father and who he was.

Maybe one day my son will know the truth about his father and think of me with the same ambivalence. Rebecca added to the family myth with a story about me. She told Matthew that long ago, when Daddy's people needed him, when terrible men hurt his country and his friends, he fought back. Daddy did what needed to be done. So little of this sounds true to me, but when everything is plunged into darkness, as it was in that red-versus-green world, truth ceases to exist. It is, to borrow a phrase I have checked off on countless medical forms, not applicable.

Scientists say the universe expands at an accelerating rate as more and more space is taken up by dark matter. But not all things that are infinite are dark. Rebecca's love was infinite, and I have been blessed with glimmering color and light, the jewels that were my marriage, my family, my career. USADE feels far away now. After I came home, I spent the next thirty years fixing cars with Ian. In the sun and the surf, our children grew up together in the waves. I loved running that shop in Venice Beach.

I sent letters to Laila the first few years but never got a response. Rebecca sometimes said, "Leave her be. She's part of a different world now." I kept telling myself that one day, I would write to Sherzai. But there was too much to say, and so much less time than I thought. *Agha* was killed after the Russians invaded at the end of 1979, plunging my homeland into a war that never ends.

When I think back to that time, much of it is blurry. Maybe it's better that way; there are things I do not wish to revisit. Now and then, when I read about the men and women who came back injured from fighting the movement I helped create, and the ones who didn't come back at all, I feel as if I've just come from my own funeral and didn't like the eulogy.

Peter never finished the book about my father. After I told him what I'd done, he quietly put it all away, and we never spoke of it again. He wrote a book about the opium economy instead, warning of its rise, and twenty years later was praised as prescient, appearing in newspapers and on TV.

When I was at USADE, Afghanistan produced one-third of the world's opium. Now it produces eighty percent, maybe more. Almost all of that is grown in Helmand, with heroin labs stretched across the province. The pills my son is addicted to are derived from poppies grown legally in Turkey, while my father's people struggle for food, water, and life. And there is an onslaught of new ways to feed those addicted to pills, with cheap, synthetic powder in tiny envelopes killing people like never before. Did it need to be this way? They fade in and out of the headlines, but they are always there. The addictions. The terror. The radicals. The war.

Years ago, I affixed Telaya's mirror to a ribbon. It hangs from the rearview mirror of my car, which is the perfect place for it. It helps me see things that are behind me, reminding me that they are closer than they appear. Sometimes, I still hear Telaya's voice in my dreams and awaken in the dark to her whispers, and it is as if the past itself is whispering to all of humanity: *I am faster than you.*

Tomorrow I drive my son home to Los Angeles, where he will live with me. Ian and Pamela are down the street. Their son, Sean, fought alongside Matthew in the war. All of us will do what we can to make my boy whole again. It is spring, and we have plans to go see the California wildflowers, Matthew, Sean, and I. Few things are as unforgettable as a sea of poppies pushing toward the horizon, striving for infinity.

ACKNOWLEDGMENTS

THIS NOVEL WAS YEARS IN THE MAKING. IT WOULD NEVER HAVE HAPPENED WITHOUT THE extraordinary support, friendship, and expertise of dozens of people along the way.

I am deeply indebted to my agent, Jacques de Spoelberch, who fell in love with this book and worked tirelessly to find the right editor. That editor turned out to be Amara Hoshijo at Soho Press. She believed in this story and invested so much of herself to make it the best it could be. I can never thank her enough. To the whole team at Soho—Bronwen, Juliet, Mark, Rachel, Paul, Rudy, Steven, Janine, and Alexa—my lifelong gratitude for taking a chance on me. David Litman, thank you for the stunning cover.

To research this novel, I read countless books and spoke with scholars, government officials, and others who shared their expertise or their personal memories. I'll name a few here, knowing the list is too long to capture. This novel's strengths are thanks to all of them and others I have neglected to mention, but any mistakes are my own.

Dick Scott, formerly of USAID, was an invaluable source of information about US projects in Afghanistan in the 1970s. His knowledge is encyclopedic and he was always willing to talk and to help. A big thanks to Dr. Nazif Mohib Shahrani for answering my many questions and sharing his expertise about nomadic groups and more. Dr. Shah Mahmoud Hanifi was supportive from the start. Despite being retired, Dr. Sieten Chieng took the time to patiently answer my very basic questions about seeding and soil.

Many people read early drafts of this book, gave critique and encouragement, or shared their memories of Afghanistan to supplement my own. Thank you, Mahmud Shah Aimaq, Jamila Niazi, and Eleesa Aimaq, for the details about Kabul life, streets, shops, and neighborhoods. Graham Fuller, thanks for being an early champion of this book and for your incisive critique and unwavering support. Betty Keller was among the first to guide me through this story, with her sharp eye, blunt commentary, and passionate encouragement. To Ali Blythe, Justin E. A. Busch, Caroline Cederström, Chaya Deitsch, Susan Finsen, Laura Grunberger, Alyson Knop, Erica Otto, Susanne Otto, Karen Simring, Jessamyn Smyth, Karen Sperry, and Marjorie Wonham—your feedback and your friendship meant the world. To my mother, thank you for encouraging me to do what made me happy, instilling in me a love of books, and celebrating every victory with me.

Finally, all of this was possible because of my husband, Darcy Otto. Writing a novel is a journey of dramatic valleys and peaks for authors and their partners alike. Darcy willingly got on the roller coaster with me and never asked to get off. I hope he hangs on for the next ride.

Other Titles in the Soho Crime Series